WITCH SHIFTER CLAN

C.D. GORRI

WITCH SHIFTER CLAN

The Hybrid Assassin
Fire Wolf
Snow Fox
River Dragon

by C.D. Gorri

Edited by BookNookNuts
Copyright 2024 C.D. Gorri

Before you begin sign up for my newsletter here:
SUBSCRIBE HERE

DEDICATION

To the leaders,
It's not easy being the one everyone looks to, but know this:
you are seen, and you are important. The ones who follow
know you and love you. Even when you're a hard ass. So
don't doubt yourself and don't ever let up.

To the smart asses,
You know who you are. Keep going with your bad self, you
know we love it. And when you need someone to bounce ideas
off, we are so ready for that. Never doubt yourself for a
minute.
Nerdy is the new sexy.

To the troublemakers,
You are what makes everything interesting. The perfect

combination of rough and soft. The bits we need that make the world worth it. Keep sharing your gifts, even if we seem ungrateful. We know who you are, and we need you. All of you.

del mare alla stella,
C.D. Gorri

USA TODAY BESTSELLING AUTHOR
C.D. GORRI
THE HYBRID
ASSASSIN
LEAGUE OF SUPERNATURAL ASSASSINS

THE HYBRID ASSASSIN
LEAGUE OF SUPERNATURAL ASSASSINS

By C.D. Gorri
A Witch Shifter Clan Prequel

To the outcasts and the misfits,

You over there, doggy-paddling alone on the fringes of the pool of life...
Come on over here, the water's great. It might shock at first, but you'll find your mellow. At the very least, you will have us to hold on to.

xoxo,
all your peeps

THE HYBRID ASSASSIN

LEAGUE OF SUPERNATURAL ASSASSINS

A Witch Shifter Clan Prequel

Hybrid Shifter. Assassin. Outcast
This assignment might change her future...

LIKE OTHERS IN THE LEAGUE, I was designed to be a hollow killing machine. Taught to have no feelings, no desires, no dreams of my own.

That part was easy when you were a loner. I did not need friends. I just wanted to survive.

Unlike the rest, I was classified as a mistake.

Created in the Lab by a foolish scientist who'd been killed for his failure on the day I first Shifted into the hybrid monster he'd given me, I was a living, breathing error. The director and Avalonia never failed to remind me of my shortcomings, as did everyone else in the Assassin compound in the realm of Icarus.

ERR394N was my designation. I had no name. Nothing personal to humanize me to my handlers. I was a weapon, and I was good at my job, obeying orders, and taking lives.

I learned early to hone my skills. Hacking difficult systems, burning through firewalls, and uncovering secrets were only parts of my talents. I was an expert marksman, too. What could I say?

For a Shifter, I liked guns.

But even my prowess could not save me from drawing the jobs no one else wanted. My latest assignment was supposed to be easy.

Go to Earth. End the target.

Only everything went sideways the moment I saw him. He was the one person who was not supposed to exist—*my fated mate.*

Both our lives were now in danger.

Unless I could stop it.

A NOTE FROM THE AUTHOR

Hello Readers,

Thank you so much for grabbing The Hybrid Assassin, my story in the League of Supernatural Assassins shared world.

I am so excited for you to meet Erryn and Davian.

Please note parts of this tale occur on the realm of Icarus, but most are in good old Maccon City, NJ, my fictional werewolf run town, circa 2005.

This is the origin story for a brand new series published in 2024, the Witch Shifter Clan, read on to find out what the heck I am talking about.

I also wanted to give a huge SHOUT OUT and special thanks to the multi-talented Sheri-Lynn Marean for inviting me to write in her vast and amazing world with so many other talented authors and for this amazing cover. I only hope I do it justice.

To read more stories set in the League of Supernatural Assassins World, go here:
    https://www.sheri-lynnmarean.com/league-of-super natural-assassins-shared-world/

Happy reading!
  del mare alla stella,
  C.D. Gorri

CHAPTER ONE
ERR394N

ASSASSIN COMPOUND, **Realm of Icarus**

STEALTH. *Cunning. Precision. Resourcefulness. Skill. Fearlessness. And lack of conscience.*

These are attributes every assassin needs to survive. But in order to thrive in the compound, there is something else you need.

Favor.

Unfortunately, that is something I don't have. Never did and never would if the creatures here had anything to say about it.

"Get up, you sniveling hybrid cur!" RJ453, my training partner of the day, sneered as I spat a mouthful of blood onto the mat.

Everyone went through the same rigorous indoctrination. Physically, our skills were hard taught, the lessons demanding, and the instructors without pity or compassion. Hell, we hardly knew the word, except to say it did not exist in the compound.

"I think you broke her!" One of the others heckled from the periphery of the training ring.

I wheezed, trying to catch my breath. That blow to my chest did a number on me and I felt dizzy from the lack of oxygen. Oddly enough, despite there being multiple realms and countless creatures inhabiting them, oxygen seemed to be a common denominator.

"We gonna finish this, hybrid puke?"

The bastard I was fighting grinned at me, flashing sharpened teeth that looked like little knives behind his blackened lips. I growled as I struggled to my feet. Hand to hand was not exactly my forte. I preferred guns to fists.

Another reason Shifters here loathed me. What kind of monster brought guns to fight where tooth and claw reigned supreme? The answer was me.

RJ453 kicked me twice in the ribs while I was down. A real winner, that one. RJ453 was a Wolf Shifter assassin. The motherfucker was always giving me a hard time. His mind was broken long ago. But after the kind of shit we were forced to do, who could blame him?

"That's what happens when they send a mutt to do a man's job," he growled.

The sack of shit grabbed my face, hurting my cheeks as he squeezed before he leaned over to swipe his tongue over my chin, across my nose and cheek, marking me with his disgustingly foul breath. My inner beast growled in fury, and it was all I could do to rein her in.

Feigning a worse injury than I had, I waited till he shoved my face back down to the mat. The preening imbecile hovered directly over my prone form, arm raised as if the handlers would offer praise for his supposed victory.

Fucking dick still didn't get it. The trainers did not give a shit about us. He was nothing more than a pet to them, begging at their feet for a treat like a good boy.

But that wasn't RJ453's only miscalculation. The fucker had no idea who he was dealing with when he agreed to spar with me on the mats today. I almost felt bad for him, but I still smelled his foul spit on my face, so no, he got no sympathy from me.

I allowed my anger to rise. I could feel it, like a living thing, slithering around me, winding tight like a boa constrictor. I liked to read in my spare time, and one of the books I'd smuggled back to my dorms was about animals from the Earth realm. Fascinating creatures, really. So I waited for the right moment, like a snake in the grass, then I attacked.

I moved fast as lightning, going right for his balls, I growled as I punched, gripped, and twisted his nards till the mouthy fucker was on the ground. I pulled myself off the floor, using his ball sack for leverage, as I climbed the big bastard, finally releasing my grip on his puny nethers to grab him by the neck.

Next, I head-butted him, avoiding the blood spurting from his now broken nose. Then I leaned forward and closed my teeth over his earlobe. Biting down hard enough to break the skin, I snarled at the whining pup and shoved him away, delivering one hard kick to his gut before he dropped to his knees.

"Point for the hybrid. Do better next time, RJ453," the handler said in a bored tone.

The damaged Wolf remained on the floor for over a minute. I backed up slowly, moving to my corner, never turning around while my opponent was still on the mat. I had learned that lesson the hard way a long time ago.

Never give your back to the enemy. And *everyone* here was my enemy.

I was a mistake. A blight on the face of the otherwise perfect reputation of the director and his consort, Avalonia. They were responsible for this entire thing. The

League of Supernatural Assassins was their creation, as were I and countless others.

I did not choose this life. Heck, I did not choose life at all. But I was here now, and I would do whatever I needed to survive.

"Where do you think you are going, ERR394N?" the handler asked.

"Shower," I mumbled, hating his eyes on me.

There was something off about the guy. I was not one of those assassins with their own handler. No one wanted to work with me on a permanent basis. Not the reject. Not the mistake. Handlers and trainers all had their parts to play, and every single one of them vied for a better spot in the director's line of sight.

All of them plotted to attain glory via the assassins they brutalized. I don't know what it was they wanted. Currency? Power? Fame? A better room at the compound? All of that, maybe more.

Those who worked for the director were unscrupulous at best, and if I were religious, I might even call them wicked. But I wasn't that. I did not believe in the gods. Why would I, when it was so blatantly obvious, they did not believe in me?

No. Religion was a drug meant to sedate the masses. I did not do drugs. That was a rabbit hole I would not go down. Some of the assassins here could not live without them. I didn't judge them. To each their own.

With all the gory ghosts of their past deeds haunting them, who could even blame them for using anything they could to numb themselves? The creators had designed us to have no moral compass, but some of us did.

We hid those flaws from them, and from each other. Weakness was not a good thing here. This was a life we had to live.

Those of us who survived knew we were never safe. So, *no*, we never dropped our guard. Some were lucky to have friends on the inside. Not me, of course. Solitary. Alone. That was my path. I watched from the fringes.

I was passed around to those trainers and handlers who had even fewer scruples than the director himself. Vile, loathsome, heartless ingrates the whole lot of them. Most were nightwalkers and they had the balls to call us animals.

When I'd been assigned to H67, I knew it was not good. His beady eyes raked over my body, and despite wearing a long-sleeved training jumpsuit, I felt violated. The sleazy male made my skin crawl.

"The director has need of you," he said.

I nodded, not meeting his gaze. I hated looking at him, and he knew it. Anger at my rejection rolled off him in waves. Emotions, especially negative ones, were easy for me to pick up on. Just another in the list of oddball quirks of mine.

But what did you expect from a mistake?

I grabbed my water bottle from the floor and took a long pull as I walked out of the training complex. Stealing myself against what was coming was akin to pulling a mask over my face. There was no sense delaying the inevitable. If the director wanted me, it could only mean one thing.

I had a new assignment and somewhere out there, someone's time was running out.

CHAPTER TWO

DAVIAN

"DAVI! You are the worst big brother ever!" Martina screeched.

Her eyes glowed purple, and I frowned. Her magic was starting to show. That could be problematic. Martina was a Wolf Shifter, but the local Pack had an asshole Alpha name of Zev Maccon who kinda sorta hated witches.

"Martina, all of you have to eat your vegetables before ice cream. It's like the one rule I have for you," I said, ignoring her glare.

Mom, I am trying. I swear.

Gods, I missed her. Mom was diagnosed three years

ago with an aggressive form of lung cancer. Damned cigarettes. They were her one vice. Everything else about the woman was damn near perfect. For a Witch, she was a saint. I don't know how she did all this.

As I stared at the three little faces around the old scuffed up oak table, I felt like ten thousand pounds of pressure just got dumped on top of my fat head. I heaved a sigh and went back to serving dinner.

Scooping veggies onto Nova and Sybil's plates, as well as Martina's, who looked mutinous as all get out. I was no Parisian chef, but the food was edible. Even better than that.

It was a one pan meal. Heck yeah, I freaking loved making those. The day I found the thirty-minute meals group for busy parents on social media was one of the best days of my life.

Take one cookie sheet, line with parchment paper, add six boneless chicken breasts on one side, broccoli spears, carrots, and thinly sliced potatoes on the other, spray with cooking oil, add seasoning and bake at 400 degrees for about thirty minutes.

Boom baby. Dinner was served.

It was about the only thing I had time for anymore. Of course, I could have lived off of chips and snack cakes, but my three ten-year old sisters needed good nutrition. I loved the little cuties, even if they defied my rules. I couldn't help but worry about them. Their anger and resentment were growing, but that was to be expected.

I couldn't replace our adoptive mother. But I couldn't let them go either. No. It was too dangerous out there for what they were. The world was never kind to those who were different. Harbor House was known as a home for supernatural runaways and delinquents. Of course, after Mom passed on, I had to close the doors. But I would never turn Martina, Nova, and Sybil over to foster care.

How could I? No one would be able to handle what they were. Each of my adoptive siblings had mixed Witch and Shifter blood. Neither side would accept them fully, which was why they'd been orphaned to begin with.

Left alone in the cold with no one to care for them, only Andrea Harbor, our mother, had found them, just like she'd found me. She gave us a home and kept us fed, educated, and safe from harm.

I was way older than this lot, but Mama Anne had had sent for me the moment she got her diagnosis. I closed up my penthouse in New York, moved back to Jersey. I started working from home, making a living, and helping out as much as I could. That was the beauty of science. I could do my research anywhere.

"One rule? What about the brushing your teeth

rule?" Nova asked, her blue eyes practically glowing out of her face.

"Yeah. And what about your laundry rule?" Sybil added, rather unhelpfully.

"Okay, okay. Look, I have to stay up late if I want to finish this project for Mr. Graves. Think you three can just give me a little break?" I pleaded, knowing full well the three little heathens were going to make me pay. They were lucky I loved them.

"I will eat one more bite of my vegetables, and you will give me ice cream, but I will also fold the towels after dinner," Martina compromised.

"Deal, but only if you also help clear the table and load the dishwasher."

"Done."

Nova and Sybil grinned at Martina, lifting their cute button noses in the air when they glanced my way. I only wanted the tiny she-Wolf to eat one more bite, so technically, I won the negotiation. But they did not need to know that.

I scooped out three bowls of double fudge chocolate chunk, leaving it up to the girls to top them off with canned whipped cream and sprinkles or not. A couple of fist bumps later and I was off to my office, which was just off the living room, to the left of the small eat in the kitchen.

It wasn't much, but it was home. Mama Anne had

busted her butt, making this place a home for us kids, and I was eternally grateful. If I had to work for the rest of my life to make sure my three sisters were taken care of, I would and gladly, too.

"Hey Davi?"

"What's up, Nova?" I asked, turning around.

"She would have eaten three bites," the young Snow Fox Shifter grinned.

"I was only looking for one," I confessed, winking at the blue-eyed beauty.

Nova was going to be a knockout someday. All three girls were pretty, for sure. But there was something about her coloring that I just knew was going to draw the boys like moths to a flame. Good thing I had enough control over my own magic to give any hooligans sniffing around my sisters a run for their money.

"Hope work is easy tonight," Nova said before rejoining the girls, who were now camped out in the living room.

They were seriously into this reality show about ordinary people competing for a spot on a talent show. I would never understand their obsession with stuff like that, but maybe it was because those people entering were looking for acceptance. Just like us.

It wasn't safe for Witches in Maccon City, and my sisters were something else. They were half-Witch, half-Shifter. Their very existence was supposed to be impossible, and yet, here they were. I promised Mama Anne on her deathbed that I would keep them hidden, safe.

What better place to do it than right under the nose of the very Alpha who swore to wipe Witches off the face of the planet? Zev Maccon was a vile man, but he was the Alpha of the largest Wolf Pack in the world.

The Macconwood Pack was powerful, and their reach was far. Rumors had spread all over town about the sudden disappearance of the Alpha's mate, Lilly Maccon. They said she'd cheated on her husband and mate. They said he killed her.

I shivered in revulsion just thinking about it. How could anyone do such a thing? I had no idea. Hiding my magic from the Wolf Pack was easy enough. Hell, I even worked for one of its members. Randall Graves was a computer genius, and my own personal guru. He knew what I was, but he kept my secret, and for that he had my loyalty.

The man even allowed me to work from home, which made watching the girls easier. I had security cameras set up all over the place. Mama Anne set up this place on the edge of town and as far away from the Pack as possible.

We did nothing to draw attention to ourselves and kept our outings to a minimum. Public places were fine, as keeping the Shifter secret was the key to the Pack's survival. Besides, Werewolves had their own limitations. The Curse of Natalis kept them bound to the full moon. They could not access their supernaturally enhanced senses till then, nor could they change into their beasts.

I worried about Martina for this very reason. She was the only half-Wolf among us, and as she drew closer to puberty, I feared that the separation from her Wolf might drive her mad. It was something all Werewolves struggled with, but maybe her Witch side could help. I was not sure, but I hoped.

Only time would tell.

Nova and Sybil did not have those drawbacks. Those two could already shift into their animals, though they knew to be careful. Nova's Snow Fox was a thing of pure beauty. White-furred and cunning, her animal's coloring was in direct contrast to her black hair.

Sybil was something else, though. A female River Dragon with a magical connection to waterways neither Mama Anne nor I had ever even heard of. They were a handful. Smart, strong, beautiful, clever, and so innocent, I worried about them constantly.

When my friends all left for college, I stayed local. I completed my degree online and found a good job at Graves Enterprises. Did I want more? I mean, who didn't?

I was speeding towards thirty, single with three young girls to raise, but so what? I loved my sisters and there was nothing I would not do for them. They needed me. If I accomplished anything good with my life, it was getting them to adulthood unscathed.

The only thing I was ever really certain of was that I would do everything in my power to keep the girls' secret safe. Even give my life for them.

CHAPTER THREE
ERR394N

ASSASSIN COMPOUND, **Realm of Icarus**

"COME IN," the director said.

His lips made a thin line across his face, and I wondered not for the first time how that part of his anatomy could be responsible for so much pain. Sure, he was a Nightwalker, another word for Vampire. But that was not what I meant.

From those thin, cold lips, the director gave orders and his orders meant someone had to die. I did not like my job. But I was good at it.

We all were. Assassins killed. That was why we were created.

It was not a good idea to make the director wait, so I

entered his office at his request. He did not bother to look up. Why should he? I was the lowest of the low. A mistake. A blight on his otherwise perfect reputation for creating only the best in the business.

But I got the job done. So, there I stood. Waiting until he was ready to speak. Twiddling my thumbs behind my back to hide my impatience.

"ERR394N, your talents have been requested for an assignment on Earth," he said, his voice nasal and grating on my sensitive ears.

The hybrid creature inside of me had particularly strong auditory senses that carried over when I was in my human form, but that was not the talent he was talking about.

"Here," he said, holding out a file, and I stepped forward to take it, careful not to touch his skin.

The director did not like contact of any kind, and I was one hundred percent with him there. Physical contact was not something I had much experience with outside the fighting arena. Pain and touch were one and the same to me, so I avoided it as much as possible.

"Our client has assessed a threat on Earth. Your job is twofold. First, neutralize the threat."

By *neutralize* I knew he meant *kill*. I nodded my understanding. It was my job, after all. The reason I had been created. You got numb to it after a while.

"Second, you are to clone the target's computer onto

one of our portable drives. Destroy everything he was working on there. Erase it completely, ERR394N. Then, bring the drive directly to me upon completion."

I nodded once more, my face passive. But inside, my mind was turning. Earth was behind most realms with technology, medicine, and any number of things. In fact, the planet was so overrun by humans, supernaturals barely eked out a living.

The paranormal world was secret there. Supes blended in with humans just to survive. What could my target have uncovered that would pose a threat to any of the director's clients?

Interesting.

"You will find all the information we have on your target there. Go now. Do not come back until it is done."

"Yes, sir."

My fingers itched, and I had to admit my curiosity was piqued. It was not often I got to play with technology. Secretly, I thought the director might have been holding a grudge over the last time I breached his private server.

Of course, the Compound had superior tech, but that did not stop me. For some reason unbeknownst to me, technology was a language I was fluent in. Hacking into systems, getting past firewalls, decoding security keys were as natural as breathing.

It was nothing I could really explain. Just some weird, secret part of my chemical makeup. Like my innate magical abilities. My affinity for guns. My vicious fighting skills. My standoffish attitude.

I don't know why my creator chose the unique combination of DNA that I was comprised. But I was what he made me, what they trained me to be.

Badger. Mountain Lion. Witch. It all amounted to one word, Hybrid, and that was my death sentence. The director would use me until I was useless. Then he would have me killed.

I knew it. He knew it. And he knew I knew it, which made the utter calm with which he dealt with me even worse. He dismissed me with a mere flick of his finger, his eyes going back to whatever he had been reading before I'd entered.

I was nothing to him. Less than nothing.

"Well?" H67 asked. He'd been waiting in the hallway.

The stink of his sweat made me want to wrinkle my nose, but I did not flinch. Not even when he stepped into my personal space. The creature inside me snarled, hating his unwanted invasion. But I learned long ago if I showed my distaste, it would only encourage him.

The sick fuck liked that I loathed him.

"I have an assignment," I replied, steeling myself against what I knew was coming.

His beady eyes lit with excitement as he reached out

with gloved hands and touched my hair. He always did that. Something about the white and black locks seemed to fascinate him. My hair reflected my inner beast's unique coloring. The thick black tresses were wavy, sometimes curly, with wide streaks of white coursing through them.

His touch made me want to shave my head. But I had tried that once, only got so far as to cut the length with scissors before he found out. Some rat saw me in the locker room and told. I was punished for my efforts and bore the scars on my back from the lashing I had received.

Now I just left it alone. His fascination repulsed me, but he never crossed the line. H67 was a piece of shit, but he was very aware of the fact I would kill him, dooming myself, if he ever tried to force himself on me.

It was nothing less than the truth. I'd seen it happen to the others, and I never understood. We were trained to kill. Sure, I would be put to death, but it was a death I would choose any day of the week over his unwanted attentions. And I would choose it gladly, too.

"I see. Show me the file," H67 said.

"If the director wanted you in the meeting, he would have asked for you."

"I said show me, filth," he hissed, his rank breath making my eyes water.

Footfalls drew closer, and my handler stepped back.

I would not give him the file unless the director ordered it, and he knew it. Surely, it was odd he'd not been in the office with me. But that sort of thing was above my paygrade.

The incoming guards glanced at us, and I took H67's momentary distraction as my cue to leave. My backpack was already packed, and I just had to grab it before heading to the nearest Earth bound portal.

I glanced at the file, committing the prominent details to memory in just a moment's time, and hustled to my dorm.

My target's name was Davian Harbor. There was a small photo beneath his name, but it was grainy, and the colors seemed muted. Still, he was young and handsome. Not that I cared about that. He appeared human for all intents and purposes, but the word Witch caught my attention. The man had magic, which meant I needed to be ready for anything.

Be careful, my inner predator whispered. As if I needed the reminder.

"Davian Harbor," I whispered his name, as was my ritual before a job.

Killing was never easy, but I was used to it. I was usually given assignments others deemed beneath them, going after low lives who owed debts to the wrong creatures. Beings who'd sold their souls to demons, gambled away their lives, or messed with the wrong mate. That sort of job I could handle, but something about this was off.

My gut tightened as I pictured Davian Harbor's photo in my mind. He did not look like the average cretin or cheat. He looked good. Not handsome, though he was that, but honest, loyal, worthy.

I shook off those unnatural for me feelings and headed out. I had already checked my guns. They were clean and full of ammo. Others scoffed at my choice of weaponry, but I liked guns.

I was no Dragon or Wolf Shifter. My physique was hardly impressive. At five foot five, I was short for an assassin. My legs were thick, my hips round, and my bust too big for most sword harnesses, so guns it was.

The hip holster I wore was comfortable. It allowed me to move freely, and I could cover it easily enough with a sweater, cloak, or jacket. My weapons were custom forged using alloys from multiple realms by expert craftsmen. I spent almost an entire year's earnings on them.

After I got the pair, I took them apart, cleaning them of tracking charms and any other tomfoolery those who would seek to spy on me might have used. With magic and technological savvy, I put the pair of guns back together again, and they never left my side when I was on a mission.

They called me the Hybrid as if it was a curse.

Sometimes it was she-Beast, or simply the freak who prefers bullets to brawn. But what did I care what anyone else said? I did not fit in there.

Never had. Never would.

That's why I had a plan to get away from the Compound and the director's heinous hold on me. First, I had to kill the earthling Witch. Then I could put my escape plan into action. Should be a piece of cake.

CHAPTER FOUR

DAVIAN

MACCON CITY, **New Jersey**

"GIRLS? Hurry or you'll miss the bus!" I shouted down the hall, hoping my sisters heard me.

The schedule for the school bus seemed completely irrelevant to Mrs. Lapinsky, the bus driver. She'd been doing that job since before I was a student at the Maccon City Public School. She never minded the times, just showed up when it suited her and right then, that meant she was seven minutes early.

"Nova, get out of there!" Sybil screeched, pounding on the bathroom door.

We had two, but apparently that was not enough when there were pre-teens afoot. I rolled my eyes as they harassed each other and gathered their backpacks. It was chilly in the mornings, but for some reason they never wore jackets. Just put on hooded sweatshirts, like all the other kids.

I could have made it a big deal, insisted they wear a jacket, but why would I? They were part Shifter, and as such, the girls ran hotter than I did. Besides, all the other kids wore sweatshirts, too.

It made them feel normal, and I was all for that. Life was difficult when you were different. I should know. A male Witch was hardly a common thing, but there I was. Using magic, I wrapped up the lunches in half the time and handed them out as the three of them zoomed past me.

"They are getting big, Mama Anne," I whispered, knowing the older Witch's ghost was likely watching them scurry off towards Mrs. Lapinsky's bus.

The old woman honked the horn just as they stepped into the vehicle and gave me the stink eye. I just waved and smiled. She would probably never change, but what would life be like without an ornery school bus driver? I shook my head and walked back inside.

Three hours later, I was making good headway on the latest sprint I'd been assigned by my project manager over at Graves Enterprises. With all the progress in software development and applications, there has been an increased need for better security.

Everything had vulnerabilities, and since I had started as a hacker, it was kind of my job now to find them so the other developers could patch holes, build walls, and keep the clients happy. I was a big fan of that.

Happy clients meant more projects, and that meant happy project managers, which in turn could lead to a possible promotion. If I got promoted, I'd make more money. Some said it was the root of all evil, but when you had three sisters, it meant an easier life.

I worked hard so I could be a better provider for the girls. More money was a good thing. With those heavy thoughts weighing on my mind, as well as what to make for dinner—the absolute bane of my adult life, by the way—my perimeter alarm sounded.

I was elbows deep in my work and ignored it at first. It had happened on occasion that a small animal, a cat, a bird, or even a squirrel, had messed with my cameras. I'd placed them all over, surrounding the entire property in my efforts to keep the girls safe.

I waited a beat, checked the monitors, but there was nothing there. Shrugging it off, I went back to work, surprised when the girls came filing in what seemed like minutes later.

"Davi, what's for dinner?" Martina asked.

Shit. I forgot dinner. Giving her a wicked grin, my

sister rolled her eyes and turned back to the other two preteens watching the byplay.

"He forgot to cook! Now he's going to pretend it's some lame *build your own sammy* night again!" she shouted, but there was no heat in her voice.

The girls giggled, taking off for the bedroom they shared to dump their stuff. I heard them giggling over the sound of the bathroom sink as they washed up before joining me in the kitchen.

"Hey, that's not sandwich stuff," Nova observed.

"That's right," I said, popping four enormous Idaho potatoes in the microwave. "We are having loaded potatoes. Martina, grab the block of cheddar and start grating, please. Nova, you get the broccoli florets in the steamer. Sybil, you are on chive duty. And I am frying the bacon," I told them.

Carnivores needed meat, and I knew better than to try to deny them. So, with three pounds of the fatty good stuff in my hand, I sliced the raw bacon into thin strips and started frying while the girls got to work. Twenty minutes later, dinner was served, and we sat around the old table, eating, and talking about our day.

"So, anything interesting happen today?" I asked casually, knowing someone would spill the beans sooner or later.

"Timmy sat next to Martina today. I think she likes him," Nova said.

"Oh, really?"

"OMG! Nova, you rat," Martina growled at her sister, which was par for the course as her first change was getting closer.

I was used to the growling. The tiny stream of fire that burst from her fingertips and onto Nova's potato, burning her cheese? Not so much.

"I like it burned!" The Snow Fox replied, sticking her tongue out.

"Whoa, time out, girls," I said, catching Martina's angry stare. "What did Mama Anne say about our tempers getting the best of us?"

"The way to fix a short temper is to take a long walk," she mumbled.

"Right. So go on, walk around the yard a bit, then come back when you are ready to apologize," I said in a gentle voice.

"But I'm eating," she argued.

"It will keep, Martina. Go on."

It was important for each of my sisters to maintain control. Not only did supes in general have to stay hidden, but we were hiding from our own kind. It was difficult, but our lives depended on it. If I wasn't, who knew when a sudden burst of hormonal preteen rage might attract the wrong person?

It might seem unnecessary, but really, it was. This was serious. Martina, Sybil, and Nova had to practice hiding what they were from the outside world. Using their magic in a controlled atmosphere was part of their training, and outbursts like this were not allowed. It demanded constant attention.

They might not like me for it, but I would be damned if my soft heart was the reason any of them got hurt. I frowned as I walked her to the back door, checking the yard to make sure it was safe.

It was empty, my alarms were quiet, and the sun was still out. She would be fine. Martina growled and stomped away, and I returned to my seat. The other two girls had dropped their forks. Nova was close to tears, and Sybil had reached out to pat her shoulder.

"I was only teasing," Nova whispered.

"I know, but maybe next time ask if she wanted to share information like that first, okay?" I said and gave her a weak smile.

"I think I want to go outside too," Sybil said, biting her lower lip.

"Me too," Nova added.

"It's not a punishment, guys. You know that, right?" I asked them, slightly embarrassed by my own weak need for reassurance.

"We know, but she's our sister."

"Alright. Let's go—" but that was all I got out when the first scream sounded. Both girls looked at me, eyes wide with fright. My heart damn near stopped in my chest.

"Martina!" Nova yelled, making for the door.

Thank goodness I got there first. I pulled her back, nodding at Sybil to take her hand. The River Dragon was young, but strong, she held our sister back.

"Stay inside and lock the doors!"

I reached for the shotgun I kept in the locked cabinet by the door. A wave of my hand undid the lock with a metallic click, but depending on what waited outside, I could not depend on my magic to help.

I ran in the direction I'd heard my sister scream, the sounds of shuffling and voices caught my attention.

"You really pack a punch, kid." I heard someone say in a husky, feminine voice.

The tone of that voice made the hair on my neck stand up and tendrils of magic snaked around my body. My powers were awake now, and they wanted more of that sound. I shook my head, trying to clear it from errant thoughts as I rounded the corner of the house and came face to face with a woman pinning my sister's arms to her sides.

"Let go of my sister or I swear I will shoot," I commanded.

I wasn't a killer, but for my sisters, I could be. The female was strange looking, foreign or something. She had jet black hair with thick streaks of white running through it. A shapely figure decked out in tight, black pants and a long-sleeved shirt with a thin strip of skin at her waist peeking through.

Holy fuck.

The trespasser was gorgeous.

Her purple eyes blazed ferociously as night fell around. The way she canted her head like a strange animal at me only aroused my own curiosity. I sucked in air, almost forgetting to breathe, and caught the scent of blood.

"Stay behind me," she told Martina, moving in front of my sister in a protective stance.

She was limping, obviously injured, but super fucking brave as she faced my shotgun. Her grin surprised me and that was when I saw them, two nasty looking pistols, one in each hand, pointed right at me.

Fuck, she moved fast. A Shifter, for sure. I strengthened my hold on my weapon for one moment before pointing it away.

"Look, that's my sister, and this is my land. Who are you? What do you want?"

"Davian Harbor? I'm here for you."

CHAPTER FIVE

ERR394N

PORTAL TO PORTAL

THE TRIP from the Compound to Tartaria was uneventful, which was fantastic. I'd done it a thousand times or more, hunting down targets for whatever job I was assigned.

From Tartaria, I traveled to Earth through the portal, which was like wading through a thick, viscous mess and made me feel nauseated and lightheaded for several moments after. Moving between realms took its toll on you physically, but it was something all assassins were trained to deal with.

I emerged from the portal at the Poulnabrone dolmen in the Burren, County Clare, Ireland. The first time I came through, I'd been lost, and it took me a full day to find civilization. Since then, I'd adjusted my comm unit, and I now had a contact who would fetch me within minutes. A few clicks and my message was sent.

I tapped my foot while I waited for Ezekiel to show up. The Sleep Demon had been one of my assignments a few years back, but after discovering he was relatively harmless, I brought him here to hide. Sleep Demons fed on nightmares and by doing that, they relieved the sleeper of those bad dreams.

Nothing wrong with that in my book. But his nature was not why I'd been sent to kill Zeke. He'd fallen victim to his own carnal lusts and got caught with the wrong man's mate.

An understatement if ever there was one. Truth was, poor Zeke had the bad luck to pick a female belonging to one of the underground pit bosses in Joustal. A newer realm, it was more like the old West on Earth than any place I had ever seen.

I liked to read in my spare time. In fact, Earth was one of the subjects I found most intriguing. It was perhaps one of the most complicated places I had ever visited.

I found it fascinating the very beings who claimed they were top of the evolutionary chain were the same who were destroying the very resources they needed to live. Humans were a mess. But so were supernaturals. Just look at me.

I was a paid killer. A gun for hire. Even worse, I answered to a being with fewer scruples than those I was sent to kill.

The file on my most recent assignment was thin. Davian Harbor, whoever he was, had caught the attention of the wrong people. It didn't matter. Or rather, it couldn't matter to me.

This was one more step in my plan to escape the director's clutches and after I killed the male, I would send word to Treya, a former Dragon Assassin for the director, for information on how to remove my tracker. She was living on Corsica Di'osa with her mate, not bothering to hide the fact from the director or his minions. Why should she?

Treya was the original motherfucking badass, and I'd always looked up to the Dragon Shifter with something akin to awe. She seemed to know I was plotting my escape the second I had decided to go through with it.

That was before she'd left the fold, of course. Treya's offer to help was unexpected and very much appreciated. I'd even developed a way to communicate with her and anyone else wanting to slip free from under the director's thumb.

It was all about the comms. My talent for hacking

was perhaps my greatest asset. Or at least, it was in this case. I found a mistake, a bug if you will, in our comm units. Getting through the firewall undetected to the real code was easy enough. Finally, I'd found a way to get around their corrupt system.

Zeke was bringing me the last piece I'd need to finish my multiversal transponder. This unit was going to save me and anyone else who wanted out. After I finished this last job, I would disappear from the director's purview.

If there was any benefit to being an outcast, it was that he wouldn't waste resources on finding me. I was no one, unimportant, and after all these years of self-loathing, I was actually grateful for that.

I was getting hungry, and there was nothing around those parts for miles. Walking would do me no favors, so I crouched down and closed my eyes, listening for movement. My inner beast was silent as the dawn. The hybrid creature knew the importance of patience.

Where the fuck was Zeke? I was an assassin, not a saint. Yes, I'd learned to wait, but I was so close now, I could almost taste it. Freedom was elusive for people like me. But I would take mine. No matter the cost.

Speak of the devil.

A rumbling sound to my left reached my ears a millisecond before the Sleep Demon apparated. I was always startled by how normal Zeke looked to me. He was my height, which meant short as fuck, had dark brown skin with darker, super curly hair, and bright, amber-colored eyes.

"Wassup, girl?" he asked, his mouth split open in a wide smile.

It was like he was glad to see me, though I could not imagine why. I'd once hung him over the side of a building, my gun pressing hard against his throat. That was a minute before I'd decided not to kill him. It was a decision I had never regretted.

"You expect me to ride that thing with you driving?" I asked as he appeared out of thin air atop a baby blue Vespa.

"I don't know why you gotta hate on my ride, Err," he mumbled, using the nickname I'd never authorized him to use.

"It's a bike for a baby, Zeke," I pointed out, in case he missed my scathing glare.

"Complaints! That is all I ever get from you. You comin' or what?"

"Yeah, yeah," I said, shaking my head as I got on behind the Demon.

"Where to, buttercup?" he asked, and I told him, noticing his tension when I said the address.

"Maccon City? You do know that town is run by some psycho, fucked up Alpha Wolf who hates everyone? As in, all supes and normals alike, right?"

"You talkin' about Zev Maccon?"

"Yeah, him," Zeke said, stinking of fear.

I crinkled my nose, and a growl rumbled deep in my chest. I had no love for Werewolves. Especially not ones rumored to be as bad as the Macconwood Pack Alpha. Guy was a total psycho. Power hungry and mad with it.

"I am not here for him," I told Zeke.

"Oh, well, that's too bad."

I glared at the Demon before he shrugged and took off on the ridiculous machine. I didn't even know how it held the both of us, but it did. He whispered some words in demonspeak, using his magic to propel us and the Vespa through the air, faster than the speed of light.

"Dammit, Zeke, you broke every law of physics getting us here," I muttered less than an hour later as we fell off the Vespa onto a rocky dirt path seconds before we would have plowed right into a sturdy-looking oak tree.

"I break records crossing the globe for you, and you don't even say *thank you?*"

"Shut up," I grumbled, wincing as I stood.

"Um, Err. I don't think your leg is supposed to look like that," Zeke winced as he whispered, pointing at me with shaky fingers.

"Fuck," I growled, lifting my head up and looking at my body.

I'd landed in a twisted heap, and he was right, I definitely broke something. Pain radiated from my left leg, and I looked down to see blood and a bit of bone sticking out of my pants.

"Shit, Err. Should I do something? Can I call someone?"

"No," I growled, and fuck, I was really pissed.

Injuries were not supposed to happen on jobs unless it involved some sort of combat. Not like I could phone my handler, that swine, and tell him I fell off a baby bike and broke my leg.

"Come here," I growled at the trembling Demon, tearing the bottom of my shirt.

"You gonna hit me?" he asked.

"Not yet," I said honestly. "Tie this around the protruding bone," I instructed.

"Like that?"

"Yeah. Good, now get that stick over there, and bring it back. Okay, use it like a tourniquet—"

"No way, Err. I do that, and it will hurt. Then you really will hit me," he said, shaking his head.

"Zeke, get the fucking stick. I have to pop the bone back in place before it starts to heal all wrong."

"Shit," he mumbled. But he did what I asked, so I couldn't complain.

I growled through the pain, hardly even feeling it as I twisted the stick until I could feel my bone go back where it belonged. Shifter healing notwithstanding, my creator had tried to give me an extra boost by using Badger Shifter DNA.

Unfortunately, Badgers did not heal any faster than other Shifter animals. What it did, however, was give me an even higher tolerance for pain, and an insane survival instinct, making the first attempts on my life at the compound unsuccessful. Obviously.

Thank fuck for small favors.

I was still alive and kicking, and I planned to be for a very long time. No thanks to the director and his mate. Those two barely tolerated me, but a buck was a buck. They used me, and I was finally going to get away from them. Just one small job away from it all. But how the fuck was I going to succeed if I had a bone sticking out of my leg?

Ugh.

"Did I mention I have a queasy stomach?" Zeke said, moaning as he helped me tighten the makeshift bandage.

"You're a fucking Demon, Zeke? Grow a pair," I muttered, slapping his hands away from the bloodied up fabric and tying it myself.

"So? Don't I have feelings? A soul, even?" he asked, and I shook my head.

"No, Zeke. You don't. Like I said, you're a fucking Demon."

"That is a misconception! Demons have souls, they're just tainted. And I do to have feelings!"

Great. Now, the fucker was all butthurt. I sighed and counted to three, growling with the effort it took to stand up.

"Um, seriously Err. Do you need help?"

The question slowed me up for a sec, but I shook my head. I hobbled over to his baby bike and grabbed my shit, then I waved him away before he got all mushy.

Demons might have feelings, but I sure as fuck didn't.

"Alright then. Lemme know if you need me," Zeke muttered, waving me away while he hopped back onto his magical Vespa.

It was unsettling to know I had a friend in the short Demon, but he'd offered help and that was not part of the debt he owed me for saving his life.

"Fuck this. You have a job to do," I muttered, uncomfortable with the turn of my thoughts.

Inside my bag I found the transponder and told myself later as I tucked it back inside its compartment and pulled out my target's file.

"Davian Harbor. Where can I find you?" I whispered, plugging the coordinates into my custom-built locator.

Sure, map apps were all the rage, but those things left

a trail. Any assassin worth her salt knew better than to do that. I'd bought mine from a hole in the wall gadget place in the realm of Icarus but added my own custom bells and whistles. Not to mention, I'd removed the tracking software the asshole who sold it to me had added without my consent or knowledge at the time of purchase.

After a few minutes, my locator showed me where to go, and I set off.

Slowly...very slowly.

CHAPTER SIX

ERR394N

AFTER WATCHING my target for a few hours, I developed a cramp in my slowly healing leg. It was still oozing blood, and that was worrisome. But I had no time for that crap.

Inside the dwelling, my target was sitting at a desk that was loaded with monitors, a backlit keyboard, and some other Earth tech I'd have given my left boob to check out. Sparks buzzed along my fingertips, and I worked to control that part of me I rarely tapped into.

This Hybrid mutt had more than Badger and Mountain Lion DNA, I had magic, too. The witchy kind though it was possible it was Druidic in nature, or maybe even some Mage. Since my creator was murdered for making an abomination like me, it wasn't like there was anyone to ask.

It didn't matter. I only used magic when I was hacking or trying to glean information from computers or visualize any techy gadgets I was building. That was the only circumstance I trusted my magic to not misbehave.

Davian Harbor was tall, but not too tall. Almost six feet, if my guess was correct. He had straight, chestnut-colored hair that was short on the sides and back and long on top. His skin was a nice, healthy shade of pale, spotted with freckles on his nose as if he enjoyed being outdoors, though it was Autumn on Earth.

He had a singular focus for his work, but now and then, he would check his monitors. Yes, I'd noticed the cameras along the perimeter of his land and reluctantly approved. He was smart—for a male.

The equipment was pretty foolproof too, and I hated to admit I was impressed. But I was. There was just something about him that drew my eye, and I wondered if it was feasible to keep him out of the line of fire.

Probably not.

The director knew where he lived. If I failed to perform my duty and just disappeared as I planned to after the job, he would simply send someone else to eliminate Davian Harbor. Someone with fewer scruples than I was currently in possession of, and that was something I did not want in the slightest.

"Who did you piss off, Davian Harbor? Why do they want you dead so badly?" I whispered to myself.

I was not one to rush into a job. So, I sat hidden on a sturdy branch of an enormous oak tree on the border of his property. Surveillance was often the most boring part of what I did. Oddly enough, I was not bored watching him.

He worked diligently, only stopping when three young girls came to visit. No—not a visit. They were coming home from somewhere. School, perhaps? Huh. I did not know he was a father. That changed things for me.

I did not like to kill parents. Especially not ones who seemed to be doing the job alone. I could spy nothing that suggested Davian was mated or had a spouse to share the burden of raising three girls.

Good, growled my inner beast, and I frowned.

Shaking my head, I attempted to crawl down from the tree, but fell instead. Thank goodness I landed on my rump. That soft part of me could take the brunt of any fall, with all the resilience of my Badger DNA. I might be graceless, but I was strong.

Unfortunately, my injured leg protested when I tried to stand, and I broke out in a cold sweat. Something was seriously wrong with me. My inner animal was clawing at my insides, and my heart was pounding like a drum. Night was falling, offering more coverage, but with it, I was reminded time was slipping away.

My Comm unit beeped, and I looked down to see my message to Treya had finally been received. Setting up the transponder had eaten up some of my time that afternoon, but I knew it would take hours before my message would get through to the realm where Treya lived with her mate.

Multiversal messaging was new and, in its infancy, but I had cracked the code and was determined to use it to get myself free. Who could tell? Maybe others would find some use for the tech I had created.

It was a waiting game now to see if Treya would read and respond to my message. She was the first assassin to break free of the chains the director had on us, and an inspiration to those who wanted the same chance at having a real life. Those like me, who had nothing to lose and everything to gain.

I didn't know how much time passed while I lay there on the forest floor, but I'd been daydreaming and blinked back to reality to find a pair of deep brown eyes staring at me.

Shit.

One of the girls had found me. Not good for an assassin whose spying skills and ability to blend into the background were all but imperative for a successful career.

"Who are you?" she asked.

I sat up slowly, eyebrows raised, when she startled and backed up.

"Easy," I whispered, eyeing her hands, which were now ringed in fiery flames.

The girl had magic, but she smelled of Wolf. She gasped, lifting one hand, and forming a ball with her fire magic. I growled. I did not like being threatened. She tossed the ball in reaction to my aggressive behavior, and I rolled with it, dousing the flames. I had to admit I was impressed. Even as she fell over her own feet and landed on her ass.

Hybrid, like us, my beast whispered. But I ignored the animal in me.

"Easy, I am not here to hurt you," I growled, dusting myself off as I tried and failed to stand.

"You're hurt!" she exclaimed, rushing forward to come to my aid.

Shit. I was there to kill her father, and yet, here she was helping me up. I wanted to shake her, to scream at the man raising her. Didn't she know she was in danger? That I was the danger? Could she not tell?

"Here, lean on me," she instructed, and I was both shocked and in too much pain to do more than grunt my reply. "There's a tree stump a few feet to the left. You can sit there."

"Thank you," I replied gingerly as I settled on the

stump. "You shouldn't help me. I am not a good person, little girl."

"Yeah, well, neither am I," she replied stubbornly, and I bit back my grin.

She had grit and spunk. I admired both character traits.

"Okay. But you should be more careful," I drawled.

"Why? Are you here to hurt me?"

"You? Why would I want to hurt a child?" I asked.

"I know you're a Shifter, like me. And I can sense something else inside you. I think you have magic. You already saw what I could do with my fire. So, you know then, that Witches are banned in this town. Did he hire you to kill us?"

"Slow down. I am not following," I said, frowning. "This is the Maccon City limits, correct?"

She nodded her reply, and I wracked my brain to try to think of what she could be talking about.

"Zev Maccon is the Alpha of the local Wolf Pack. He hates Witches. Hates all magic. That's why we stay here. Out of sight, out of mind," she told me, and I felt a wave of sadness roll off her.

What was going on in this town? I wondered.

"So, did he send you to kill us?" she asked, eyeing my guns.

"No. Zev Maccon is not my employer," I replied carefully.

Her eyes narrowed as she considered my words. She stayed like that for a long moment before nodding.

"I believe you. But then, why are you hiding out here, injured and smelling of magic and strange fur?" she asked, wrinkling her nose.

"Strange fur? I think I should be insulted," I said, and tried a tight smile.

"Well, you aren't a Wolf or a Fox. What are you?"

"I'm a—"

I paused as the sound of footfalls reached my ears a moment before she heard them, too. Fuck the pain, I thought and got to my feet. I did not want to hurt her, and I gasped as a strong protective instinct welled inside me. And I sure as fuck would not let anyone else hurt her, either.

"Stay behind me," I told the child, moving in front of her,

I was limping, it simply could not be helped. I turned to the male holding the shotgun pointed right at me and I grinned, lifting my pistols faster than he could blink. He strengthened his hold on his weapon before surprising me by pointing the nozzle away from me and the child.

"Look, that's my sister, and this is my land. Who are you? What do you want?"

Sister? Not daughter? Hmm.

I was surprised by the confession. Didn't he know

he should give nothing away when facing an assassin? Then again, he did not know me or that he was being hunted. So, like him, I dropped my pistols, but held them tight, ready to bring them back up at the slightest hint he would try anything funny.

"Davian Harbor," I said, though it came out more question than statement.

My heart was pounding inside my chest. My inner beast watched him like a hawk. Something was different about this male. I had thousands of jobs, but I never faced a target who made me feel quite like this.

My body seemed to swell, my core warming at the strange but delicious scent wafting off him. He smelled like nectar infused berry shots—the kind I'd sampled once or twice when on assignment just to see if I could feel anything. Nectar was added to alcohol so supes like me could feel the effects without our enhanced metabolism burning through it.

I never liked the feeling it gave me, of being out of control. But that was how I was starting to feel in his presence. Davian Harbor loomed before me, his head canted and eyes curious as he stared, and I knew then what this was, just as I knew it was impossible.

Mate, my beast hissed inside my mind's eye.

But no. It could not be. The Hybrid Assassin was a loner. An outcast. A cold-blooded assassin.

I had no mate. Shaking off nerves I was not even

aware existed, I looked him dead in the eye and said as calmly as I could before a wave of dizziness washed over me.

"I'm here for you," I growled right before I crumpled into a heap at his feet.

CHAPTER SEVEN

DAVIAN

"DAVIAN! HELP HER," Martina shouted, tears welling up in her eyes.

I looked from her to the beautifully fierce creature unconscious on the floor and made my mind up swiftly. This might be the dumbest thing I'd ever done, but I could not just leave her there.

"Put this back, carefully," I told my sister, handing her the shotgun after putting the safety back on.

She nodded and took it from me, having had lessons the last two years by my side, I knew she could do it. I took the strange-looking pistols from the woman's limp hands and tucked them into my waistband before lifting her into my arms.

She was solid and warm, and she smelled amazing.

Like pine forest and chilly November mornings, the kind where you lazed around and indulged in warm cinnamon buns and hot coffee before getting to it. Yeah, I imagined it. Being with her on a morning just like that after a long bout of lovemaking. The vivid image startled me so, I almost dropped her.

Fuuucckk.

I shook my head. Clearing it so I could see what needed to be done.

"Put her here," Nova yelled, clearing the cushions off the couch as Sybil placed a sheet over it.

I nodded and placed the limp female on it, careful not to jostle her. I wiped the hair from her face, struck by how very pretty she was. No make up. No glitter or gilt. She was simply her, and the result was stunning.

"She said she was a bad person, but I don't think so," Martina was telling our sisters, and I listened briefly even as I assessed her injuries.

"It's her leg," Sybil said and stepped closer to look.

Her River Dragon was sensitive to injuries, which made sense since her powers seemed attuned to healing. I'd been working on her with smaller things like injured insects and birds. I found the bandage immediately and winced as I unraveled it.

Shit. She was bleeding.

"This is too much for you, Sybil. Look, the three of

you need to go to your rooms. She is a stranger and a dangerous one. I won't have you harmed," I said, and ignored the growls, sighs, and eye rolls.

It sucked sometimes, but I was in charge. I had to make sure they were safe, even though everything in me said I had to help this woman.

"Look, Davi, I found her. She is my responsibility. Nova, go get some clean water, washcloths, and antiseptic. Sybil, get scissors, tape, and fresh bandages," she told the girls with the natural leadership skills I knew she had.

Before I could protest, the stranger moaned and shook her head. Startled purple eyes met mine, but before she could do anything, like hurt me as I sensed she would have, recognition flared to life.

"What is going on? Where am I?" she asked, closing her eyes.

I knew she was hurting, and I hated it. I did not want her to be in pain. That was weird and unexpected, but there it was. For some reason, she felt big to me. Important.

"Why did you come here?" I asked, needing to know.

"What does it matter? She's my friend!" Martina stated, and the stranger looked at my sister and smiled.

Holy shit.

The smile did it. I suspected she did not smile often, and I really enjoyed seeing it on her face.

"Didn't I tell you I was dangerous?" she asked Martina, but I felt no threat in her question, so I did not step in.

"It's okay, you're my friend. This is my brother, Davi. You said his name," Martina replied.

"He is your brother, not your father?" the woman asked Martina.

"Yuck, no! Do you even know how old he is?" Martina asked, and both females acted like I was not even there. I frowned and listened, waiting for an opening.

"Yes. He's 32," the stranger stated, and I raised an eyebrow.

"Yeah, and I'm like ten. He'd still be in college! Gross!"

The stranger huffed a laugh, eyes wincing as I touched her wound gingerly. Shit. I could tell it was starting to heal wrong.

"Sorry," I muttered. "Look, you know this is in the wrong place, right?" I whispered my question. Purple eyes met mine, and she blinked hard. Yes, she knew.

"It's okay, Davian Harbor, aged 32, brother of these three special young women. You will have to put pressure to reset the bone. I am ready," she said blandly.

Warrior, I thought, nodding my head once as I placed my hands on her leg, tending to her with as much care as possible. I needed to gauge where to apply my strength before I went all in.

"You know a lot about me, which is kinda worrisome, since I know nothing about you," I stated casually, as I took the scissors from a quiet Sybil and cut open the pants covering her wounded leg.

Those pesky little shivers of awareness that had begun the second I saw her continued to assault me, and I was no closer to finding out why.

Everything about her screamed danger, but for some reason, that drew me in. My magic was pretty good at letting me know when someone meant to harm us, and though she'd been armed to the teeth and looked capable of killing someone with her bare hands, I did not feel as though I was in danger.

Quite the opposite, in fact. I felt safe around her, and that was totally fucking bizarre.

"Girls, wait in the other room," I said, but they remained where they were.

"It's alright," the stranger said, touching me once on the hand before bracing herself. "Do it."

I looked her in the eye, readying myself for what was about to happen. Mama Anne had many friends in and out of the house while I'd been growing up. Many were Shifters and had required bone resetting and tending to other wounds and injuries. Her talents were many, and she taught me the ways of healing.

I was not gifted as Sybil would one day be, but I was good in a pinch. She needed my help. Friend or foe, I had no choice. My magic bade me help her, and I listened.

"Aghhhh!" she screamed a short loud yelp as I snapped her bone and put it back in place, cleaning the wound once more as bright red blood gushed from it.

"Why?" she asked. "Why are you helping me?"

I was amazed at the strength she showed, her sweating and breathing was back to what it was before I had to re-break her bone to set it properly. Amazing. Fierce. And terrifyingly beautiful, I thought as I stared at her, helpless to look away.

"Martina says you are her friend," I replied.

"She is my friend," my little sister insisted.

"Okay. So, what's her name if she's your friend?"

"Oh, I don't know," she said, and bent down closer to the strange female's ear.

"What's your name?" Martina asked.

I noticed Nova and Sybil were not as trusting. They stayed farther away, but with their supernatural senses, they could hear what we said just fine.

"I have no name," the woman replied, and frowned. "I am known as Err394n."

"What does that mean?" Martina asked.

My kid sister scrunched her nose as she tried to

process what the female was saying. I could not blame her. I was having a similar problem myself.

"I have a designation. No name. Just Err394n," she repeated, and her purple eyes seemed sad as she spoke.

"But that's not a name," Martina said, and the stranger winced.

I knew it was not from anything I was doing, and my heart squeezed inside my chest. I pretended to have all my attention on cleaning out the wicked wound on her thigh, but I was listening to everything she said, every breath she took, and the way her heartbeat slowed and sped up as Martina continued to question her.

"It's not? Oh, well, I have a frie—or someone I know, and he calls me Err. Is that a name?" she asked.

"Hmm. Err? Oh, like short for Erryn? Cool. I like it.," Martina enthused, and the woman—no, it was *Erryn* now—smiled.

"Will Erryn do?" she asked me, and I bit my tongue to stop from agreeing too quickly.

"Erryn is a fine name," I answered, my voice a little huskier than I would have liked.

What was wrong with me? I was completely turned on by this woman who, for all intents and purposes, could have come here to kill me or hurt my sisters.

"Thank you. Martina, it is nice to meet you. My name is Erryn."

She said it with a little more confidence and not too little happiness, I thought as I listened. Pride filled me, and I could not explain why. I had no right to the feeling, but there it was.

"Ouch," she grunted, and I loosened the fresh bandage I was applying to her wound.

"Sorry. I need to wrap it tight, so it doesn't get infected. Did you break the bone?" I asked.

Her eyes flicked to the three girls who were now standing together and whispering about our new guest, most likely. I nodded my head, getting their attention.

"Ladies, Erryn here needs a place to heal. I vote to allow her to stay here. What about you?"

"I don't know," Sybil began reluctantly. "She is a stranger. What if the Pack hired her to hurt us?"

"Sybil," Martina hissed. "That is not nice to say!"

"Marty, let her say how she feels," I said, not wanting Martina to bully our sisters.

She had a habit of doing that, and I, for one, was hoping she would grow out of it. Being a leader did not mean being a tyrant.

"Sorry," the Fire Wolf mumbled.

"I think she seems nice. I like her purple eyes. But why does she have guns? And why was she in our yard?" Nova asked.

"I don't know," I answered, frowning at the fact I

was ready to put us all in danger, all because of a pretty woman.

What kind of brother did that? I closed my eyes and shook my head, trying to rein in my almost out of control magic. It was like she had a magnetic pull on my powers, and they craved being near her.

"I do not work for Zev Maccon," Erryn whispered.

She didn't seem insulted at all by our frank speech. I mean, we were talking about her, and the results of our talk could very well mean putting her out on the street.

"I apologize, Erryn. But me and my sisters all have to have an equal say in what goes on in our home. I hope you are not insulted—"

"Not at all, Davian Harbor," she said my full name, and there was that knockout smile again.

Sweat beaded on her brow and I knew she was hurting, but careful not to show it.

"I will tell you my truth, if you care to hear it?" she asked, her gaze meeting all four of ours before she sat up without struggling.

I admired her grit and perseverance despite the fact I knew she was in pain. Her wound looked bad, and for some reason, her Shifter healing was not kicking in.

"Do not worry about it. I never heal right on traveling day," she explained, but it was hardly an explanation.

What the fuck was traveling day? I did not know,

but if she was going to tell us anything about herself, I was all ears.

"What I am about to tell you is going to sound strange. I will answer questions, but after I am through, okay?"

When we nodded, Erryn, the beautiful, purple-eyed stranger, started telling us an unbelievable story.

CHAPTER EIGHT

ERRYN

ERRYN. *E-R-R-Y-N. Not ERR394N. My name is Erryn.*

I repeated the name the Fire Wolf child had given me in my head, and though it felt strange on my meta-physical tongue, I had to admit I liked it. The other two young females had reservations about me, and deep inside, I was glad for it.

They were neither stupid nor gullible, and I respected that. Still, I could hardly think with how my inner animal was behaving. The beast was growling and scratching at my insides, desperate to be free, and it was all because of him.

"I come from another realm that co-exists with this one and over fifty others. You see, you have been taught there is one universe with intelligent life, but that is wrong. There are many, and in this multiverse, we all live and do what we can to survive," I said, gearing up for my confession.

"I was created in a lab for one purpose and one purpose only. To kill. Without conscience. Without question. I am part of a group known as the League of Supernatural Assassins located in the realm of Icarus. The director is in charge, and he has many clients who hire us to take out specific targets across the realms."

"What do you mean you were created in a lab?" Martina whispered.

"I have no parents. My creator was a madman, killed after he'd gone rogue. His genetic experiments on me were discovered after my first shift and, suffice it to say, the director was not pleased. I was ostracized, kicked to the lowest possible ranking, but I suppose it was good I was not killed. Though, I suspect some of my assignments were doled out to me in hopes of that very thing."

"So, why didn't you run away?" Nova asked.

Bright girl.

"Running away was not an option. It still isn't. You see, they've embedded each of us with a tracker."

"Okay, even if we believe all that, why are you here?" Sybil asked, joining her sisters.

I did my best to answer their questions, wondering

all the while why he was ignoring me. The male I had come to eliminate merely watched me, his stare direct and trained on me. For the first time in my life, I wondered if my appearance was unattractive to a male.

I must have looked a complete mess, dirty and bloodied with my clothes torn to shreds. My stomach growled, and I could have groaned aloud. Of course, I was hungry and now embarrassed.

"Here," Sybil said, having run from the room, she came back with a heaping plate of food. "You are using up a lot of energy trying to heal. This will help. It's a baked potato with broccoli, cheese, and bacon," she explained.

"Thank you," I said, and tucked in.

I was starving, and that trumped worrying about my looks any day.

"Okay, ladies, I think that is enough for tonight. Are we letting Erryn stay or not?" Davian asked while I ate, watching the byplay.

"Staying."

"She stays."

"For a while."

"Okay, now you three are off to bed," Davian instructed.

I knew he was doing so for their protection, and I tried not to let it hurt me, but it did. They told me goodnight, and I smiled, waving them off to sleep.

How wonderful to be so young and well taken care of, I mused.

"They are lucky to have you," I began, placing my fork on my empty plate.

"Hmm. Remind them of that when it's time to clean their room," he replied, running a hand over his face.

"Look, I am trying to have an open mind, but I need to know why you are here?"

"I am here for you," I replied as I had before.

"To hurt me? Am I your target?"

"Yes," I told him, watching him tense and hating myself for a moment. "I was sent here to kill you, but I don't think I can," I confessed.

"Why not?" he asked, eyes narrowed.

"Because there is something about you that I had not expected at all. I don't know what I am going to do about it, but you don't need to worry. I swear, I will not hurt you or any of your sisters."

It was the only promise I was certain I could keep. Davian's stare never wavered as he took my plate and handed me a bottle of cold water.

"Alright. There is a spare bedroom next to mine. We will get you settled in there for the night."

I nodded my thanks, exhaling as he left the room. All I wanted to do was rub my skin along his, mark him with my scent. Crap. What was happening to me?

Mate, my beast whispered, and I froze.

This should not be happening. It was not possible. And yet, as the word repeated in my brain, I knew in my soul it was right.

Mate. Mate. MATE.

I had come to Earth to end a life and run away to gain my freedom. Instead, I found my mate. Why did life have to be so complicated? I couldn't bring the four of them into the fucked up world I was a part of, but I could not trust the director to leave them alone.

I could move them, maybe. But I doubted that plan would work. Davian and the girls had ties here. They would not want to go. Shit. What could I do?

Something. Anything. I tried to stand on my own and was greeted with a rough curse and a surprisingly strong arm around my waist.

"Can't leave you alone for a second, can I?" Davian murmured, his breath so close and warm it tickled my cheek.

"Sorry, I just, I mean—"

"Come on. Let's put you to bed," he said, and was it my imagination or had his voice dropped half an octave?

He helped me to a room at the end of the hall, next to his, as he'd said it would be. Once inside, Davian found her some clean clothes that smelled like him, and my inner beast purred at the thought of being surrounded by his scent.

"Do you need help?" he asked, and I could smell his embarrassment and his interest.

The first was interesting, the second flattering, but I shook my head. Plenty of time to figure that out later. My leg was throbbing, and I frowned as he placed a small vial of something in my hand.

"It's a healing potion Mama Anne used to make us whenever we were sick. I gather you know what I am, so there is no danger in my telling you," he said.

"Witch," I murmured, sniffing the vial before upending it into my mouth.

I gasped and coughed, ignoring his chuckle as he handed me a cup of something sweet.

"You didn't give me a chance to warn you about the taste. This is grape juice. It will help."

"Fuck, that was bitter," I mumbled and drank the whole glass of juice in one gulp.

"Yeah, well, like I said it will help, Erryn."

I tensed at the sound of my new name on his lips and felt a wave of vulnerability wash over me. That was new. The sensation was foreign, and I shivered involuntarily.

"Are you cold?" he asked, a frown marring his otherwise serene façade.

"I suppose I should change first," I muttered, wondering how to achieve that without hurting myself.

Davian stood and walked to a closet, taking out a

soft-looking blanket. His frown deepened as he realized my predicament, but he turned around, offering me some privacy.

"If you need help, um, just let me know," he murmured.

I grunted my reply, removing my torn top, holsters, and belt. I slid the giant shirt over my head, quietly reveling in the scent that enveloped me. It was his, and I wondered why I should be so affected by something as simple as his berry sweet smell.

Perhaps it was because being near him made me feel drunk as if I'd imbibed the nectar infused shot his scent reminded me. Was that what lust felt like? I could only wonder. It wasn't like there was a lot of opportunity for this sort of thing where I came from.

"Um, I might need help to remove my pants," I whispered, slightly embarrassed.

Living in the Compound had taught me never to show weakness. Doing that could cost me my life, but here, with him, I felt safe enough. Besides, I would never heal right if I kept re-injuring my wound, and standing on it now would only mean having to break it again later.

Davian turned to face me, chestnut hair gleaming in the yellowish light coming off the wall sconce. My, he was handsome. He leaned forward, his berry scent surrounding me as his fingers gently reached under the borrowed shirt, finding my waistband.

He cleared his throat, as aware as I was of the tingling sensations sizzling all over my body, starting from the place he touched me.

"Put your arms around my neck," he whispered.

I obeyed, knowing where this was going. I was quite strong, and I pulled myself up as he tugged my pants carefully over my hips and ass. I lowered my body when they were under my thighs, wincing slightly as he gently lifted them and continued to undress me.

We were both breathing like marathon runners by the time he freed my feet from what was left of the material. I felt woozy and tired, but that was likely the potion he'd given me.

"Were you telling me the truth before?" he asked as sleep started to take me.

"Yes. I was sent for you, Davian Harbor, but there is more to it than either of us knows," I mumbled.

"I think you're more dangerous than you're letting on, Erryn. But we can talk more in the morning."

"The morning," I repeated, nodding slowly. I was almost out now.

Whatever brew he'd concocted I trusted would not kill me in the night. Already I could feel my supernaturally enhanced system start the process that had been delayed after traveling through the portal.

It was always touch and go when moving between the realms for a bit. I should have known better than to rush into this, but there was something about Davian I could not resist. And now I knew what it was.

Mate.

CHAPTER NINE

DAVIAN

I SPENT most of the night watching the monitors and looking through every journal, grimoire, and annal I could find in Mama Anne's small but valuable library. She kept her magical books hidden behind a regular-looking shelf in the living room.

Three hours later, the words were blurring, and I closed the heavy leather-bound volume in my hand with an angry thud. Stupid. I was wasting time. I should simply go to bed and call it a night. Erryn would be here in the morning, and I could question her then. Whimpers from down the hall drew my attention, and I stood up quickly.

"Not tonight," I murmured, frowning as I hurried to the girls' room.

"Davi, I'm scared," whispered Nova, and the little girl's bright blue gaze found mine in the darkness.

"She's dreaming of the Wolf again," Sybil murmured sagely.

The young River Dragon was keenly aware of our sister's struggle with her beast. Martina's Wolf was bound by the Curse of Natalis, which held all Wolves in thrall to the phases of the moon, separating human from beast by a magical spell which meant a separation that was keenly felt.

It was cruel and terrible, and many Werewolves did not survive after their first Change. No wonder the local Pack, though powerful, was an angry thing governed by a madman. I sat down next to her, checking her pupils to see if I could wake her before things spiraled out of control.

"Last time this happened, we had to take her outside and turn the hose on her. It was horrible," Nova whispered, and I heard the tears in her voice.

"I know, sweetheart, but we can't just let her burn the house down. She would be so upset if we did," I told them, and hated myself for the cold comfort it offered.

Martina was years too young for her first Change, but she was no ordinary Werewolf. She had one foot in that world, and another deeply imbedded in the kind of magic even Witches shied from.

"What is going on?" a husky voice asked from the doorway of the girls' room.

I turned my head. My gaze locked with hers and my whole body tensed. Erryn stood, cheeks flushed with sleep, still groggy from the healing potion I'd given her, but well enough to show no signs of limping and only a hint of sleep in her softly glowing purple eyes.

She'd somehow managed to find her pistols and had one in each hand and her holster tight around her waist. She looked fierce and, if I had the time to admit it, sexy too, considering she had no pants on. Just my t-shirt and something primal inside me was very happy about that.

"Martina is having a bad dream," Sybil explained, and I shook my head, bringing my attention back to the present.

"Why don't you wake her up?" Erryn asked, and I found I liked her name very much.

Wherever it was she came from had sounded barbaric to me, and I hated that kind of existence she must have suffered through. What kind of people gave someone a designation instead of a name? Monsters, that was who. And if monsters had sent Erryn to hunt me down, then I must have pissed someone off.

Whatever. They could all hang for all I cared. Right then, I was concerned with one thing, and that was safely waking my sister up.

"We can't," Nova said, beating me to the punch.

"Nova, don't tell," whispered Sybil.

"It's alright, she knows," I said.

"I know and I will keep your secret, little ones."

"So, you know Martina is a Fire Witch?"

"Yeah. She tried to hit me with a fire ball earlier tonight," Erryn replied without heat, but perhaps a hint of a grin.

Interesting woman. I wonder if I would have a chance to get to know her. Something about her sparked my interest, my magic, and that secret place inside that allowed me to see the supernatural side of others. Erryn was a mystery. An enigma. But she was so much more than that.

"She did?" Nova asked, a little awestruck.

My sisters were not easily impressed, and they rarely let outsiders into our circle. No wonder. We've been hiding what we are for so long, keeping folks on the outside was second nature. But here was Erryn, breaking down barriers without even trying. I wondered if she knew how important that was and how rare.

"Anyway," I interrupted. "Martina's powers are volatile. You see, Erryn, we live on the outskirts of town as a precaution. To keep us safe. You were sent here to hunt me, but you're not the first and you won't be the last. My sisters are special. Each of them is the offspring of a Shifter and a Witch."

"Go on," she said, holstering her weapons.

"Do you know about the Curse of St. Natalis?"

"I have heard it, yes. Wolf Shifters on this plane are bound to its rules. Only able to change into their Wolves on the full moon, correct?"

"That's correct. The first shift usually occurs somewhere around puberty, but Witch magic is different. A Witch can have powers right off the bat, or they can get them as they grow older. Martina here is on the brink of puberty, and she's had her powers the last two years. Right now, her body and magic are at war with each other."

"Always happens when she has nightmares. It's scary," Nova whispered.

"Dangerous," Sybil added, and shivered.

Nova wrapped her arm around Sybil and pulled the smaller girl back as sparks sizzled up and down Martina's small body.

"Shit. I don't know if I can hold it," I grunted.

I'd started weaving a spell the second I saw what was happening to Martina. I used my magic to form a sort of shield around my sister's body, protecting her and us from her fire powers.

"I know someone who can help with nightmares," Erryn said. "But I need your permission to invite him here."

"Him? Who is he?"

"His name is Ezekiel, and he's a Sleep Demon. He feeds on dreams, well, nightmares now, after the deal I made with him."

Martina's back arched, and her whimpers grew louder. Shit. I was running out of time. As she struggled with her nightmare, her magic would try to stop it the only way it knew how. It would burn and I would have to choose between saving her and my other sisters. It was an impossible choice.

I needed help, and here was this strange woman who'd come from another realm to hunt me down, offering exactly what I needed. Erryn waited as I decided, her purple eyes clear and steady.

"Can I trust you?" I asked as the tension in the room spiraled higher.

"I don't know if you have a choice, Davian. Her magic is growing more volatile, and your shield is about to fail," she said, her frown deepening.

She was right. Fuck. I grunted, pushing more of my powers into the shield.

"Girls, go into the kitchen for now," I grunted.

"Davian, let me call Zeke. I swear to you, I will allow no harm to come to anyone in this household."

I looked up, sweat dripping from my brow as my sister's whole body became encased in flame. My shield was weakening, but I could not give up. Not while there was still breath in my body.

"Davian, please," Erryn begged.

She crouched next to me and grabbed my hand. Shock and amazement flowed through me as Erryn pushed her own magic towards me, like a backup battery powering my spell. It was good, but neither of us could match Martina's powers, and my sister was unreachable, lost in her nightmare.

"Call him," I said without further hesitation.

Erryn nodded, lifting her wrist, and tapping something out on the strange watch she wore. Seconds later, the engine of what I thought might be a motorcycle sounded outside the window.

"Yo Err, twice in one day?" a high-pitched masculine voice asked.

"Shut up, Zeke, get in here," she growled.

"Oh snap. Hey man, I'm Ezekiel. What's going on?" the stranger asked.

"Erryn says you are a Sleep Demon?" I asked.

"That's right. Um, she's having one helluva nightmare," the Demon growled, amber eyes glowing gold as he licked his lips.

"Help the girl, Zeke, and keep control of yourself, or I will make you eat this gun. Do you understand?" Erryn asked, raising her pistol.

"Shit, Err. How long have you known me? I don't take the good no more, just the bad," Zeke said, but

Erryn only pressed her pistol harder against his cheek.

"Don't hurt my sister," I echoed Erryn's sentiment.

I was equal parts grateful and impressed. She was not backing down from her promise to protect, and my esteem for her grew insanely in that moment.

"You got it, boss. Yes, ease up on the pistol, Err, would ya? I will take her nightmare only. We good to go?" Zeke asked.

"Yes," Erryn replied.

"Nah, I need you to say it, bro. My contract is with you, not Err for this, since I assume you are her guardian?" Zeke asked, talking directly to me.

I had never dealt with a Demon before, and this was a little out of my realm of expertise. But one look at my sister writhing in pain and I knew something had to be done.

"I am her guardian," I told the shortish Demon.

"Then shake my hand and let's make a deal," Zeke said, eyes glowing.

"I give you permission to take this nightmare from my sister, but nothing else. You hear me? You will do no harm, or I swear on my very soul that there is not a hole deep enough for you to hide in where I won't find you. I will hunt you down and make you wish you were never born if you betray us," I said, my voice deep with the promise of my threat.

"Damn man, you need a chill pill. Hell, I guess you

would be a hardass with Err looking at you all goo goo eyed. That female is the grumpiest, toughest supe I ever met," Zeke mumbled, moving to kneel beside Martina.

My eyebrows raised at his description of Erryn, and I wondered if that wasn't a blush creeping across her cheeks. Hard to tell with the glow from the fire in the otherwise dark room.

"Ahem. Will you stop batting your lashes at her, Mr. Man, and take down the shield, please?" Zeke requested.

I spared one look at Erryn, who was thankfully ignoring Zeke's embarrassing statement. She stood behind the Demon with her pistol raised directly at his head, ready to splatter his brains everywhere if he hurt Martina.

I was the one who was impressed now. I was putting a lot of trust in this stranger, but something inside me told me it was the right thing to do. And just when I needed it, I felt Mama Anne's presence guiding me to trust my gut.

"Okay," I said, lowering the shield.

A blast of heat wafted off Martina, and smoke filled the room. Erryn lifted her shirt to cover her nose, the gun still trained on Zeke, while I shooed Nova and Sybil from the doorway. I had my face in the crook of my arm as Zeke, the Sleep Demon, sucked a mass of black smoke from Martina's ear, like sipping soda through a straw.

Slowly, my sister calmed and the flames engulfing her body died down. Zeke slumped to the floor looking gluttonous and satisfied, like a fat, happy kitten. Erryn grabbed a blanket from the chair on the side and covered my sister's body, for which I was grateful.

"Wow. That was a big sucker," Zeke said, and he sounded a little drunk. "I got it though. Anyone else here having bad dreams?" he asked hopefully.

"No. Leave," Erryn said, showing the Demon the door.

"Damn Err, I thought we were friends," he growled, but he sounded more like he was teasing than truly affronted, so I paid him no mind.

"Davi?" Martina's voice was raspy, as her eyes fluttered open.

"I'm here, kiddo. You're okay. Go back to sleep," I whispered, smoothing her hair off her forehead.

The room was no worse for wear, though she would need new bedding. Again. Erryn came back, and asked what she could do to help, and I asked if she wouldn't mind changing the bed while I lifted Martina.

"Just pile the burned sheets and blankets on the floor," I whispered and gave her directions where to find the clean stuff.

Erryn worked swiftly, even using magic to suck up the ashes and clear the smokey smell. I was impressed, and it dawned on me she was very much like my sisters. I had questions. So many questions, but it was late, and we were all spent.

I tucked the other girls back in and bade Erryn goodnight before going to my room. My mind wouldn't quiet down, though. And that night I dreamed, and fuck, it was sweet.

Erryn and I lying in a tangle of sheets and limbs. Ecstasy writhing through me. Magic calling to magic. Our hearts beating. Our home warm. Together. We belong together.

"Davian?" her voice woke me, and I opened my eyes as the first light of dawn filtered in through the curtains.

"Erryn? What's wrong?"

"I have to show you something."

"Okay. One second," I mumbled, stumbling a little as I got out of bed.

When I washed my face and brushed my teeth, I joined Erryn by my desk. She was sitting at my computer, her fingers speeding over the keyboard as I watched her pull up the secret project, I had been working on for months now.

"What are you doing? How did you find that?"

"I think I know why you were targeted for elimination," she mumbled, her purple eyes luminous as she looked up at me. "And I think I know a way to call it off."

My heart stuttered in my chest, and I spared her one long glance before closing the door to the bathroom. As surprised as I was at her statement, I was even more shocked that she wanted to stop it from happening.

I'd been vulnerable a thousand different times in her presence. If she'd really wanted to kill me, she could have. I knew it. She knew it. But for some reason, she decided against it.

A small bud of hope unfurled inside me, and it was about half a second from blossoming completely. This feeling was new and wondrous, and I wanted to explore it, but it was better to experience than theorize, right? Hell if I knew, but there was only one way to find out.

Go to her.

CHAPTER TEN

ERRYN

SLEEP CAME HARD FOR ME, especially after the night we'd had. I didn't know what was in the healing potion Davian had given me, but my leg was about 98% healed up, and I felt great. Awake and alone, I tiptoed through the house and found the computer where I'd watched Davian work all day.

His system was sweet, and my fingers itched to take it for a spin, so I did. Maybe I should have asked permission or waited for him to wake up, but once my fingers hit the keyboard, my magical talents took over and there was no stopping it.

Two hours and miles of code later, I gasped at what I found. Davian Harbor was not just some average programmer working a side gig. He was a damned genius. It was early still, but I needed to talk to him.

"Davian?" I whispered his name, drinking in the sight of him sound asleep.

He was beautiful. A strange word for a male, but it was fitting all the same. Tall and lean, he had strong arms and defined musculature like a swimmer's. I appreciated his smooth skin, and the fine smattering of chestnut hair on his chest that matched that on his head.

He smelled sweet and gentle, and I wondered if that berry scent was more his powers or the fact that he was good to his toes. I'd met evil men in my life, and Davian Harbor was anything but that. His name said it all, really. He was safety. He was home.

Um, to his sisters. Not me.

I didn't fit in there. This family was patched together from multiple parts, but somehow it worked. They worked. And I would never endanger them.

I knew it was wrong, but my inner beast purred, growling softly as I neared him. I wanted to touch him, to feel the warmth of his skin, and I did with just my fingertips. I allowed myself one moment's indulgence, tracing a line from his eyebrow to his chin.

My heart was thudding, and it was like something had broken open inside of me. For the first time, I wanted something other than freedom. I felt desire, need, and a wave of unbridled fury at the injustice of it all.

The director wanted me to kill this man, and by doing so, I could set into motion the thing that would free me forever. But my inner beast begged me for something else entirely.

Not kill, protect. Not leave, stay.

The truth was, I wanted Davian Harbor as my own. Owning that broke my heart. Wanting wasn't having, and how could I ever be worthy of someone as pure and good as he was?

"Erryn? What's wrong?" he muttered, breaking my reverie.

I blinked, adopting a bland expression. How embarrassing to be caught gawking!

"I have to show you something," I said, my voice low.

"Okay. One second," he replied, getting out of bed without any embarrassment.

He wore only a pair of underpants, and I admired the view as he walked into the adjoining bathroom. I was an Assassin, not a saint, and Davian had a fantastic backside.

He joined me at his desk, where I sat at his computer, my fingers flying over the keyboard. I pulled up the code he'd been working on in secret, practically drooling as I read it again. It was a hacker's dream. The most innovative spyware I had ever seen.

"What are you doing? How did you find that?" he asked.

"I think I know why you were targeted for elimination," I told him, flicking my gaze to his. "And I think I know a way to call it off."

Davian pulled up a chair and sat down beside me. I had already rigged my own mini system to his, setting it up on a side table.

"I was just going to do it, but I wanted to show you first. You see, on Icarus, the director has hordes of information on his clients, targets, creators, handlers, and, of course, his assassins. If any of this information got out, he would be finished. Hell, the whole fucking thing would blow up."

"That's good, no?" Davian asked.

"Well, no, because there are people there. Children. Who knows what he would do if cornered?"

"Would he really harm children?" Davian asked, aghast.

"Oh yes. He has done it before. My job was to come here to kill you, Davian. And I think this is why," I confessed.

"My spyware? But I didn't even know he existed."

"Maybe not," I explained, "but someone somewhere felt this was a threat, and they wanted you gone. I was even ordered to bring your work back with me."

"Shit! He probably wanted to take it for himself," Davian growled, and I had to agree.

"Yes. That is something he would do. Even his mate, Ava, was not above targeting children."

"So, what do we do?"

"First, I have to tell you something," I said, facing him. "I had planned to carry out this mission—"

"To kill me?" he asked, eyebrows raised.

"I told you, I am not a good person. I have killed before. It was why I was created, but spending just one day here, I feel called to a different purpose. You see, Davian, I was going to complete this mission and run away. I had the plans in place, but something changed when I saw you," I whispered.

Fear of rejection was a helluva thing, but I was not so cowardly as to deny how I felt about him.

"Talk to me, Erryn. Please," he said, and his gaze warmed me as he leaned closer.

I'd never felt such heat or welcome from anyone in my whole life and it brought tears to my eyes. Davian deserved the truth. So, I gave it to him.

"From the moment I saw you, I knew my life was going to change," I said, letting my tears fall as I fumbled to tell him what I thought was true. "My inner animal whispered a word I had never thought to hear."

"What did she say?" he asked, reaching out with one long-fingered hand to cup my cheek.

He wiped my tears and his other hand joined in holding my face as I told him my deepest, darkest, most precious secret.

"She said *mate*."

Me, the outcast, the Hybrid cur had found my mate, and I never wanted to let him go. Even as I admitted it to myself, I knew I had to do something to protect him and his sisters, including leave them if need be.

"Erryn," he whispered, and his lips crashed into mine.

I had never been kissed before, and I was not sure what was supposed to happen, but this was beyond any of my wildest dreams. Davian filled all of my senses, like I'd just jumped into the deep end and was now completely drowning in him.

His lips were surprisingly soft, and skilled as they coaxed mine into opening. I wasn't ready for his tongue, but even as he slid it inside my mouth, I knew I wanted it and more still. Wrapped in his strong arms, I should have felt like he was crushing me, but instead I felt cradled, cherished even.

For someone who'd been deprived of affection her whole life, I was taking to this like a fish to water. Davian led me in a merry dance of lips and hands and bodies until he was sitting on the couch with me straddling his waist.

"More," I whispered, holding his face while I kissed, and kissed, and kissed him some more.

"Erryn," he murmured, saying my name with something akin to reverence.

He slowed the pace, and I was just as taken with the sensual pace as I was with our headlong rush to get into each other's arms. He was so good at this, and I wanted to match him. My inner beast was purring, the sound reverberating through my chest, and Davian's shocked eyes met mine. He grinned, dropping another smacking kiss against my lips, and pressing his forehead to mine as we tried to catch our breaths.

"The girls will be waking up soon," he said, and I nodded.

He was right. We had to stop, even if my inner beast was about to tear a hole right through me to get to him.

Mine.

"How about I make breakfast and you tell me your plan?" he asked.

I nodded my head, sliding off his legs and missing the feel of his hard body beneath mine. Davian stood, smiling at the look on my face and lowered to give me one more, too-short kiss.

"We will finish this later, okay? Now, I left you some clothes on my bed. You shower, I'll cook, then we will discuss. Alright?"

"Alright," I agreed.

After I was clean and dressed in a pair of Davian's sweatpants, which were about a foot too long, and a tight thermal shirt, I met him in the kitchen. Good thing my boots held up the bottoms, or I'd be tripping over my own feet.

With my holsters off, I felt naked, vulnerable, but I would not need guns for this. Davian had already shown me the cabinet where he kept his own rifle and ammo, and allowed me to use it to store my weapons. I did as he asked, grateful he would allow such things in his home.

Platters of food lined the table, and I dug in, starved as usual. I moaned around a crisp ration of bacon and sighed as I sniffed the heavenly aroma coming from the coffeepot.

"Don't you have coffee where you are from?"

"We do, sort of. But I confess, of all the realms I have ever visited, the cuisine on Earth has always been my favorite," I confessed.

"Really?" he asked and grinned at me, cradling his own coffee mug in his hands.

"Yes. See how you hold your mug? On a subconscious level, you know it too," I said, only slightly teasing.

We laughed a bit, talked of nothing, and I came to appreciate his nerdy, shy guy personality. Yeah, it conflicted with the male Witch who knew his shit last night, but that's what made him so appealing.

Davian Harbor was full of intricacies and contradictions. Everything about him called to me, and I was greedy for more time with him.

"So, what you were saying before? If you used my spyware to break into the Compound's computers, you could clone everything and use it to get free and stop the contract on my life?"

"Yes, it would be like holding a gun to the director's head," I explained.

"Isn't that dangerous?"

"It is. But it is the only way I can think of to help you," I said honestly.

"Alright."

"Just alright?" I asked, surprised.

"I trust you, Erryn."

"But I came here to kill you," I said, completely baffled.

"You did. And you were honest about it. But you also helped my sister last night when you didn't have to. Not to mention the fact, you let me stick my tongue down your throat only a few minutes ago, and I sure as hell want to do that again. So, if this means getting us both free of that monster, the director, then I say, alright."

Davian dropped the hand towel he'd been holding

on the table and leaned down to kiss my lips in a too-quick brush that was actually perfect since the sounds of three girls racing down the hall had just reached my ears.

"Sit down, heathens, I have breakfast," he shouted.

"Davi!" Martina cried out, running to her big brother, and hugging him tightly.

I smiled at the exchange, but almost fell off my chair when she turned and treated me to the same wickedly strong embrace.

"Thank you for helping," she whispered, and I nodded, struck dumb by her emotional display.

"Mama Anne would beat you with a wooden spoon if she heard you call us heathens," Sybil snarked.

I wasn't prepared for that level of trust off the bat, and I didn't know whether to whack him on the head for being so careless or jump for joy.

"What's for breakfast?" Nova asked, sniffing delicately.

My heart pounded, and I felt my magic swirling around me. I could not believe it, but I understood then what was happening. These four people had just stamped themselves on my very soul. Accept me or send me away, it no longer mattered. My animal had imprinted on them.

Mine. Mine to keep. Mine to protect.

Shit. I wasn't sure what to do about this new and

sudden turn of events, but I felt warm. Too warm. My skin tingled and sweat dripped from my pores. Cramps assaulted my stomach, and my fingertips and jaw ached.

Shit, shit, shit.

"Um, she smells like fur," Nova said, tugging on Davian's arm.

He turned around quickly, eyes riveted to me.

"Take your food inside, girls," he instructed, walking over to where I was now crouched on all fours.

My animal did not require me to shift as often as others I knew, and this was the first time in a very long time the creature was refusing to obey my commands. I needed him to back away, but all that came out was a low growl when I opened my lips.

"Easy, I'm just gonna untie your boots," Davian said, and though I was grateful for his thoughtfulness, I needed him to move.

It happened quickly. One moment, I was me, and the next my beast came ripping out of my skin. Davian fell back on his ass with the force of my change, his eyes riveted to me, and I growled, hating the look I knew I would soon see. All my life I had been the outcast, the Hybrid, and now the one man I was sure the multiverse had made for me was about to be disgusted by what I was.

Helluva nasty reveal, I thought, pissed at myself for not being strong enough to stop it.

"Erryn?" he whispered, eyes wide as he looked over my furry form.

I growled, angry that this had happened, and still warring with my beast for control. The Badger Mountain Lion part of me was always pissy when she first came out. I should have warned him not to come near me, but it was too late.

I saw myself reacting before I could even think to stop it. Davian reached out to touch my hide and I turned my head, jaws wide, going in for a bite right on his hand.

"Ow," he hissed, pulling back almost in time.

Almost being the key word. A small slice from one fang was all it took. I licked the tiny drop of his blood and felt my entire world shift.

Mine.

CHAPTER ELEVEN

DAVIAN

FUCKING HELL.

Erryn had just finished shifting in the middle of breakfast, for some reason she'd been unable to control it. I sent the girls inside with their food, gave them instructions to stay there.

I felt helpless as I watched the woman, whom I was becoming increasingly attached to, turn from a human into a sort of mountain lion. Only the coloring was wrong. She had the shape of a cougar, but her fur was jet black with thick white stripes—*just like her hair.*

"Erryn?" I whispered, and stupidly reached out to touch her.

I should have known from the girls, she'd be feeling dangerous and not yet in control. Anyway, I learned my lesson after she turned her head wickedly fast and tried to bite me. I almost got away unscathed, save for one fang that broke skin.

"Ow!"

Erryn's Lion's eyes widened, the same purple color as her human's, and I knew she was there with me. She backed away, tail tucked as if she were scared, and I raised my hands.

"Easy, sweetheart. You're okay. We are both okay," I whispered and stood up slowly.

I opened the door and watched her dart outside, hoping she would be careful and would come home soon. There was nothing else for me to do but wait, so I called the girls back in and we finished breakfast before they left for school.

I went over what happened last night with Martina. My sister was a little shaky but wanted to go to class, so I let her. After I loaded the dishes into the washer and started some laundry, I sat down and looked at all the code Erryn had left on my computer.

If my spyware could help her free herself and get rid of the target on my back, she was more than welcome to use it. My chest ached, and I rubbed it while I worked on ways to make the delivery more efficient. This needed to happen soon, tonight even. I couldn't live with a threat hanging over all our heads, and I needed to talk to Erryn about the future.

Maybe it was crazy, after all, we only kissed, but I

was pretty sure she was the girl I was going to marry, or mate, or both. She was it for me. The second I acknowledged it, I knew with unwavering certainty my suspicions were correct. Even my magic reveled in the idea of being with Erryn. Blue and white sparks danced along my fingers, and I grinned at how easily just thinking about her got a rise out of me.

I wanted Erryn to stay here with me, *well*, with us. My sisters and I were a package deal, but maybe, if I said it all correctly, she wouldn't mind. Anyway, if we were going to hack into the system of a corrupt psychopath, like the director who lived in another realm, I needed to get the girls to safety.

There was only one Witch I would ever trust to watch them, and lucky for me, she was in town. Sherry Morgan was a powerful White Witch with a long history of magic embroiled in legend and myth. She was a pip, that one. Her multi-colored eyes and hair were just one manifestation of her powers.

"Sherry?" I asked when the ringer stopped.

"Davian Harbor, my friend, it has been a long time," she said in her lightly accented voice.

I had almost forgotten she was psychic, but didn't let that rattle me. Mama Anne was a good friend of Sherry's and had trusted the Witch with all our secrets.

"I need a favor," I said.

"Ask away then, my boy."

So, I did. I explained everything that had happened in the past twenty-four plus hours and was greeted with a long whistle.

"You have been busy. Yes, well, I will pick the girls up from school, just let them know I am coming."

"Will do, Sherry, and thanks."

An hour later, the back door opened, and Erryn walked in, head down and completely naked. I stood up slowly, my breath completely stolen as I tried not to look, but failed miserably. Fuck, she was beautiful. Her skin was scarred from past battles, but they only made her more stunning to me. She was so strong, so brave, and without conceit as she lifted her gaze to mine.

"Erryn, are you alright?" I grabbed a towel from the laundry basket I had just brought in to fold later.

"I'm so sorry. I lost control. And I bit you, and you don't know what it means, but I will find a way—"

"Shhh," I said, wrapping her up in the towel.

I lifted Erryn in my arms and closed my eyes at how right she felt there. She was trembling and mumbling stuff and nonsense, and I could tell she was about a second away from a full-blown panic attack.

"No, you have to listen. My animal wanted you, so she claimed you, and that means, well, it means—"

"Am I yours, sweet assassin?" I asked, unable to stop my grin.

"What? You know about claiming?"

"I do. Earth Shifters, and sometimes Witches, do the same thing. So, your beast claimed me, then?"

"Yes," she said, her gaze never leaving mine.

"Good. Because from the second I saw you, I knew you were meant for me," I told her, swallowing her sigh as I pressed my mouth to hers.

This time, when we started touching, I knew there would be no going back. But I didn't want our first time to be rough and tumble on the couch. I wanted it to be slow, thorough, and oh so sweet, so I lifted her once more and brought her to my bedroom.

"Are you sure?" she asked as I pulled my shirt over my head and took my pants off.

"I am. Are you?"

Erryn nodded, sitting up in bed and removing the towel from her body. Fuck. She was lush and tempting, with womanly curves and secret places I could not wait to explore. Her purple eyes glowed in the dim light of my bedroom. It had been done all in green with natural wood furniture, and I smiled at the contrast between the earthy setting and her ethereal beauty.

"I want you, Davian," she whispered as I crawled over her.

Never in my life had I coveted someone as I did this strange, beautiful creature, and I knew the moment we touched with intent, I would never let her go.

"I claim you as mine, Erryn, here, now, with my

magic, with my blood, with my body, heart, mind, and spirit."

Erryn's eyes glistened with unshed tears as she cupped my face and brought my lips down to hers.

"And I you, Davian Harbor. You are my home now, my retreat, my safety net, and I will protect and love you with everything I am and have from now until I am no more."

I accepted her vow, felt the power of our bond stretch and cover us like an ethereal blanket. Bending down, I kissed Erryn thoroughly, sliding my tongue into her mouth as I explored every hill and valley of her luscious body.

Her berry-tipped breasts beckoned me like a moth to flame and I indulged my hunger, feasting on one, then the other. Every mewling moan, every gasping whimper was fodder urging me on. Her nails raked down my back, marking me up as I slid further down, pressing my lips to her belly, hips, and thighs.

"Davi," she moaned, legs spreading wider of their own accord as I inched closer to her slick sex.

Her dewy desire greeted my kiss with a heated flavor so intense, I growled against her flesh as if I were the Shifter among us. Erryn bucked against me, but I was nowhere near finished. I lapped at her like a starving animal, ravenous for the woman I coveted above all others.

I used the thick, flat of my tongue to part her further, searching for and finding her hard little nub. Once I had it, I concentrated my efforts there. Sucking on her clit while my fingers explored her intimately. By the time she started coming apart, I was already sliding up her body, cock in hand, I pressed into her willing heat, hissing at the sensations rolling over me.

"I feel your magic touching mine. Oh Davian, it's good, so good," she moaned, and I nodded, unable to speak.

Yes, I felt it too. I felt so much it was damn near my undoing. I hadn't been ready for how good it would feel to have my dick buried deep into her tight little sheath. Fuck, the woman was a virgin, and I hadn't realized that at all. But we were so far gone, she didn't seem to mind me pushing past her barrier.

I slowed my pace, kissing her mouth and whispering words of encouragement and praise. I would never hurt her, not for all the world, and I needed her to know that.

"You won't break me, Davi," she said, a grin splitting her face. "Please. Need you."

Who was I to deny her? She sucked on my tongue and slapped her hands on my ass, lifting her hips to meet mine. Fuck, that was good. I grunted and moved. I was being buried under an avalanche of sensation and I loved every second of it.

Erryn was no passive partner, she was with me every step of the way. Lifting her hips to meet my thrusts, moaning to let me know what she liked, kissing me when the mood struck, and gasping when she was overcome with pleasure. She was so fucking perfect.

How could anything feel this good? Fuck, I didn't know, but I never wanted it to stop. I felt her pussy tighten around me and I knew she was moments from coming again. This time, I intended to join her in reaching ecstasy.

"Look at me, Erryn," I commanded, and her wide-eyed gaze met mine.

"It feels so. I can't. I'm gonna—"

"I got you, Erryn. Let go. Lemme watch you come. We'll go together this time, baby. I got you. That's it, that's it!"

Fuck. Me. Did we come! And loudly.

The shout that left Erryn's lips shook the damn house, or maybe that was me. It took years before I felt strong enough to move again, but when I did, it was to find Erryn staring at me with so much love glowing in her eyes for the first time in my life I felt whole.

"I love you too," I said, though she had not said the words.

"But how can you? You don't know who I am and what I've done?"

"I know who you are, Erryn. You are my beautiful

hybrid assassin from another realm. You are my fated mate. My lover. And I am hoping you will stay here with me. Be my partner. Help me raise my sisters, and any other young we might have or adopt. I know this is a lot, but what I am saying is, will you?"

"Will I what?" she asked, tears falling helplessly now.

"Will you stay?"

CHAPTER TWELVE

ERRYN

I COULD NOT BELIEVE IT. He wanted me to stay. Me. A nothing. An outcast who had never belonged anywhere before.

"Well, you belong here, Erryn. With me. With the girls. Life is going to be different now, better. If you want it," he said, dipping his gaze.

I could feel his uncertainty, and I frowned. Of course I wanted it. He was offering me a future I never dreamed possible. Nodding my head, I tackled him with a powerful hug and was greeted with a laugh and a sigh. That nuzzle led to more, and after another round of tempestuous lovemaking, we napped a bit and ate sandwiches when we woke.

"What is this called?"

"Grilled cheese. You like it?"

"Very much," I said, sighing as I noted the time.

"It is time, isn't it?" he asked, and I could feel his anxiety about me leaving through our new matebond.

"Yes, but only for a little while."

"Go over it with me again," he said, and I did.

I needed to get back to the Compound, to one of the hidden server rooms beneath the director's office to upload the spyware. With the upgrades I made, it should instantly clone the entire system over to a virtual server I created in the cloud. After that, I just needed to get out and get back to Earth.

Treya had already sent me detailed instructions from her connection on how to locate and remove my tracker, and Davian had helped me with that earlier.

"Let me check the site," he murmured, standing, and taking the bandage off the base of my neck where he'd located the grain of rice sized device a little while ago using the finder, we pieced together with pieces of tech he had in his workshop.

"I think it is healed already," I said, and he grunted, placing a kiss there before returning to his seat.

"If they can't track you, this should be safer, right? Why don't I come with you—"

"No. You don't understand. Even though there are many who want to be out from under his thumb, the director has many loyal to him. I will not put you in danger."

"But I am supposed to be fine allowing you to walk right into it?" he asked, and I could feel him struggling with it.

"I was trained for this, Davian. I can do it. Besides, the girls need you more than they need me."

"We all need you, Erryn."

"Then I will return to you all, I promise," I said.

I'd never felt the burden of others depending on me before, and I had to admit, it was a heady thing. Tough, but good. I meant every word I had said, I would be back. They were mine now and my beast would not rest until I returned.

Even now, she hissed and spat, angry at me for having to go. This was the only way I knew to erase the target on Davian's back and free us both.

When it was time to go, I put on a pair of borrowed pants and made sure to add my holster and guns. Yes, my tracker was gone, and I had added some special customizations to my Comm unit that would allow me to emit a sort of blocker that would shield me from the security systems at the Compound.

"Come back quickly," Davian murmured, kissing me on the forehead.

"I will."

"I love you," he whispered, and I closed my eyes tightly.

It seemed so unfair, having found this miracle of my

very own, only to have to risk it all just to keep it. Ugh. I wasn't even making sense, but I just shook my head and wiped my eyes.

"Piece of cake," I growled, winking before I walked to where Zeke was waiting for me on his baby blue Vespa.

"I wondered what kind of motorcycle I heard last night," Davian muttered, scratching his head.

"Like her?" the Sleep Demon asked.

"I have to admit, Zeke, I was not expecting that," my mate said and chuckled.

"She's a beaut, right?"

"She's ridiculous, Zeke. Let's go," I growled.

I just wanted to get this over with. Davian walked over to where I jumped on behind Zeke and kissed my head, and I allowed myself to feel the warmth of the man and his magic one last time before I tapped the Demon's back, urging Zeke on.

"I'll be waiting here, Err," Zeke said after we made it back to the first portal in record time.

"I will hurry back."

Another jump, and I was back at the Compound just as night had fallen. Revulsion snaked through me as I crept around the main building where the director's office sat. Beneath it were the hidden rooms where the server housing the entire system sat behind guarded doors.

Good thing my talents lay where they did. I snuck inside, timing the guards' movements as I stalked my way through the winding maze of hallways and hidden doors. Finally, I found it and was in and out with the system cloned and loaded in minutes.

Of course, that was the easy part. The hard part was when I crept past the dormitories. Silly sentimentality brought me back to the coded message I had left on the wall of the locker rooms. I wanted to add something else to it, to let the assassins who wanted out to know that I could help.

After all, I had found a miracle on the outside, and who knew? Maybe others could as well. My multiversal transponder could come in handy for others, and I felt as if it were my duty to try to pay it forward. So, I tagged the wall, and went to leave just as the last fucker in the world I would ever want to see walked inside.

"I thought I saw you, ERR394N, but why wasn't I alerted to your arrival? Was the assignment complete?" H67, my old handler, asked.

His beady eyes roamed over my body, and I could not contain my growl. The bastard always got to me, and he knew it, judging by the satisfied smile that split his repulsive face. Typically, I was able to hide my dislike for him, but something had changed inside me.

Now that I was mated, my inner animal did not care for this male's unwelcome looks and stares. She cared even less for the way he moved forward, crowding my space.

"You will answer me, ERR394N!"

"The hell I will," I hissed, and pushed past him, hurrying down the hall.

I should have known that wouldn't be enough, but I hated being anywhere near him. He sounded the alarm, and far too soon, I was surrounded.

"You think you are so smart?" he growled, and grabbed my head, scanning the back of my neck.

"You removed your tracker. The insolence! Well, we will see what the director has to say about this!"

An hour later, I stood in the director's office, bloodied, and bruised. H67 was not about to let me get away with disrespecting him, so he brought some to the ring and had some of his assassins practice on me. Of course, they took my guns and bound my hands, but I did alright.

It was pretty fucking hard to hurt a Badger. Even a half-Badger.

"What is the meaning of this?" the director spat as he glided across the room and sat down behind his desk.

"Sir, ERR394N, has removed her tracker, she has gone rogue. I request permission to reprogram her my way," H67 said, practically vibrating with anticipation.

Growling low, I snapped my jaws when he moved to

touch my hair, and the man was at least smart enough to move back. The director lifted an eyebrow, and I held his gaze.

"ERR394N, I recall you were sent on a mission. Has it been completed?"

"Before I tell you, sir, I think you should clear the room."

"You think? Ha! Keep a civil tongue, you cur," H67 spat in my face as he reared back and slapped me across the cheek.

"Just look at your private messages, sir," I said, speaking to the director only and ignoring my former handler.

Nothing could get a rise out of a bully, like ignoring him. Sure, I wanted to retaliate, to break free of my handcuffs, and kick his miserable ass. But the pain from a beating would be far too fleeting for the horrible male. Much better to inflict a lasting mental anguish, in my not so humble assassin's opinion.

"H67, you are dismissed. I have things to discuss with the Hybrid," the director said, his voice shaking me from my reverie.

The handler straightened his back. He looked like he wanted to argue, but must have thought better of it since he skedaddled out of the room. I did not blame him. Ava had just joined us, and the director's consort was a vile bitch if ever there was one. Her thirst for blood rivaled any Nightwalker's in the realm.

"How?" asked the director.

"It wasn't hard," I replied. "Do you mind?" I asked, jiggling my cuffed hands.

"Release her," he commanded, and the guards did as they were told.

"Explain your terms."

"It's simple. If anything happens to me or mine, all of this goes public across all the realms. Every client you ever had. Every relative or associate of everyone who has been made deceased by your assassins. All the vile deeds of this place will all be public."

"What? She can't do that!" Ava yelled.

"Correction, I won't do that, but only if you allow me to walk away."

"We could just kill you now," Ava hissed, crossing the floor and facing off with me.

"Stop," the director said, his voice mild, though I could tell by his eyes he was paying attention.

That was good.

"The target. He is yours?"

I nodded.

"And all you wish is sanctuary with him—"

"And everyone we care for, His sisters to start with."

"I see. Or else?"

"Or else, like I wrote in that message, the information will be sent automatically. You see, I am the only one who knows how to get into my deeply encrypted, not to mention magically protected, files to access the reset switch, and that must be manually reset every twelve hours. You kill me, or anyone I care about, and I will not reset the switch. Understand?"

Ava was sputtering, and the guards looked uncertain, but they were not my main concern. The director held all the cards. He was the one I needed to agree to my terms. Finally, after several long moments, he nodded.

"Leave, Err304N, and do not ever come back."

I shook my wrists, trying to get the blood flowing once more and wiped the blood trickling down from the split lip I'd received courtesy of H67, that piece of shit.

"My name is Erryn, and don't worry, director. You keep your end of our deal, and I will never have to come back here."

His eyes flashed with anger, but I stood my ground. Waiting for his nod before I started out once again with six hulking guards on my tail. Ava told them to escort me to the portal, and I was fine with that. I just wanted to get back to Davian.

My safe harbor. My home.

Outside, H67 was waiting for us. I growled a warning, but the man was dumb as fuck.

"Well, he has let you walk out, so I assume command of your person once more. She is with me now," H67 said to the guards, but they did not move.

"She is free to go," the lead guard said, and I watched with a grin as H67 lost his shit.

He was so out of control, the vile bastard tried to muscle his way through the males. A right hook from one massive guard was all it took to send him flying, and I was on my way once again. It was delicious knowing I would never think about that piece of trash again, though I knew he would think about me for a very long time.

Good riddance.

EPILOGUE

ERRYN AND DAVIAN

A FEW WEEKS *later in Maccon City, New Jersey.*

"Davi, Err! Dinner is ready," Martina shouted from the back door.

I turned around from my perch on the hammock Davian had hung up in the yard, and smiled as he pulled me back down. We liked to lay out there together in the afternoons after the girls came home, offering them a bit of privacy to get their giggles out after the long day of school.

Winter was fast approaching but with our magic and my Shifter blood, we were snug as we huddled close and kissed and talked the minutes away.

"I wonder what they made tonight," I mused.

"I just hope it's not burgers again," Davian said, scratching his chin.

Burgers had been the entrée three days counting, and I agreed I could use a different source of protein.

Sniff. Looked like we were shit out of luck. Burgers it was. But I wasn't going to tell him, though.

We'd started a new tradition, allowing each of us to take command of dinner one night a week. Weekends were kind of a free for all.

I could not believe this was my life now. I'd gone from outcast and wretch, to mate, big sister, and protector of this little patchwork family. I had even started training the girls in self-defense, and with some help from a kind White Witch, we were working on their magic, too.

Keeping hidden in Maccon City was difficult, There were changes coming, I could tell, but I could not be sure what they were. All I knew was this was exactly where I was supposed to be and I would do everything I could to protect my family.

Every twelve hours, I logged into the secret code to reset the timer that would explode the director's world. And every time I even began to wonder if I did the right thing, I just had to look at Davian and the girls, and I knew I had.

I never said I was a good person. In fact, I had said the opposite many, many times. I was not the hero who would sacrifice that which she loved more than anything in the world to save it.

Not me. I was the bad guy. I was the villain who would blow up the fucking world, *or not*, to save what was *mine*. That was the choice I made. The League of Supernatural Assassins was behind me now.

I was a part of something else now. Something bigger and more important than I could have ever dreamed. It seemed Hybrids were outcasts everywhere but here. Not at Harbor House with Davian, Martina, Nova, and Sybil.

Here we were simply family.

I frowned and worried about all I had to catch up on to even try for a normal lifestyle, but I wasn't worried. Not really. As if on cue, our special little Fire Wolf flicked her gaze right to mine. She was showing some alarming growth in her magic, which included certain psychic aspects. It was incredible, truly. Even so, I worried.

"You know," Martina said as she pulled out our chairs. "It's okay if you missed stuff before, Erryn. I don't care about any of that. We can learn it all together."

"Thanks, kiddo," I said, grinning at her.

"Oh, did I tell you guys I have a name for us? I drew a picture and everything. Hang on!" Nova interrupted, as she placed a jar of pickles on the table.

"Burgers again? You knew, didn't you?" Davian whispered in my ear, and I elbowed him playfully.

Sybil was scooping patties with melted cheese onto buns, and Martina was pouring cups of cola for everyone. We were chatting and waiting for Nova to return, and she did, looking breathless and happy with a piece of paper in her hand.

"It's gotta be a secret for a while, but what do you think?"

She turned the paper around, and everyone fell silent. Sketched out with unerring perfection were Davian and me at the center, with all three girls surrounding us. Behind us were our creatures, Badger Mountain Lion Hybrid, Wolf, Snow Fox, and River Dragon, and swirling lines which I assumed were Davian's magic.

Beneath the drawing, in perfect script, were the words *Witch Shifter Clan*.

"Wow, Nova!" Martina exclaimed.

"That's amazing! But why am I so short?" Sybil asked.

"You are short, though." Nova frowned.

"Nova," Davian said in a hushed whisper, and walked to take the paper from her. "This is beautiful."

"You think so?"

"Yes, I do. We'll get it framed and hang it up in our training room so no one accidentally sees it, okay?"

She nodded, and I stood, watching in awe.

"Erryn? What do you think?"

"I think it is perfect."

And it was. I had never heard of a Witch Shifter Clan, but I was more than proud to be part of this one. That night, I showed Davian just how much he meant to me without words, sharing gifts and secrets only lovers could with touches and kisses meant for us only.

"Are you glad you stayed?" he asked me as I tried to collect my thoughts and catch my breath.

The man had magic in his fingers, and elsewhere, that had the power to make me feel things I never thought possible. Being with him was everything, and I never wanted to imagine being without.

"Davian, you are my mate. I only ever want to be with you and the girls, our own Witch Shifter Clan," I said, loving it the more I repeated it.

"Good, I am, too. I love you, Erryn."

"I never thought I would have a home, a life, a mate, a future, but you have given me everything," I told him, resting my chin on his chest as he rubbed my shoulders and arms lovingly.

"You won't miss the excitement of your old life?" he asked.

I knew it was something he was worried about. I simply smiled and shook my head.

"The realms are each of them special, different, wild, fierce, deadly, and more beautiful than we have the right to bear witness to. But I am here, on Earth, with you, and I have staked my claim. This is the life I want, Davian. I love you."

"Good," he growled, hugging me tight. "Because I am claiming you right back. Your place is here, Witch Shifter Clan all the way."

My heart sang with happiness, and I cried, knowing finally what it meant to belong. It was here. With Davian, the girls, and this place.

Harbor House used to be known as a safe place for supernatural runaways and delinquents, the unwanted. Now it was my home, just as much as Davian and the girls were. I would help to keep Harbor House safe. I would carve out this life for myself and make sure my family never suffered because of me.

I was part of something here. Part of the Witch Shifter Clan and I protected what was mine.

"I can see your mind working, and I need you to know I love you, Erryn. I will protect you, too."

"I know. My mate," I whispered, and we kissed.

Who knew what the future would hold? The fact that I even had one was a miracle. I couldn't wait to see where it took us just as long as we were together.

THE END...FOR *now*.

Thank you so much for reading this story! I hope you enjoyed Erryn and Davian's quick journey to love and family.

Please keep an eye out for the Witch Shifter Clan books, starting with Fire Wolf, where we will hear Martina's story. Thank you and happy reading!

Hang on a sec...

Did you know I am launching a special campaign for an exclusive print edition the entire Witch Shifter Clan books?

Lend your support here: https://www.kickstarter.com/projects/cdgorri/witch-shifter-clan-collectors-edition-hardcover-spicy-pnr?ref=1mqo6f

Welcome to the Witch Shifter Clan!
Do you love a **paranormal romance** book with a **badass heroine** who speaks her own mind and goes after what she wants?
How about 4 of them?
4 interconnected standalone paranormal romance stories in one exclusive book.
Yeah? I knew I liked you!
These paranormal urban fantasy romances feature

Shifter Witch Hybrids and their fated mates. Get ready for powerful heroines who speak their mind and kick some serious butt while forging their own paths to their HEAs.

Emotional, gripping, and exciting adventures await. The illustrated chapter headings, new cover, and character art are so beautiful and I am hoping we can meet stretch goals for the diamond foil hardcover with painted edges.

I can't wait for you to meet the Witch Shifter Clan. As a storyteller it is my dream to reach as many readers as I can, in as many mediums as I can manage and Kickstarter has just the kind of book community that I believe can make a difference.

Your support means everything.

Thank you so much.

del mare alla stella,

C.D. Gorri

OFFER AVAILABLE FOR A LIMITED TIME

C.D. GORRI

FIRE WOLF

WITCH SHIFTER CLAN 1

FIRE WOLF

Secrets. Magic. Forbidden Passion. This Wolf is breaking all the rules!

With her thirtieth birthday fast approaching, Martina Harbor is coming home to celebrate the day she shares with her two sisters. Little does she know her big brother and his mate have invited the whole dang town to join in the festivities.

Things might have changed with the local Wolf Pack, but after spending her entire life hiding what she is from the very Shifters she's eating cake with has Martina more than a little confused. Is she just supposed to forget about the past?

Why were her siblings okay with this? And who the heck was the hunky guy who kept sniffing her whenever she walked past?

Could someone explain what the actual heck was going on?

Mitchell Truman is a Wolf Shifter comfortable in his own skin. Happy go lucky, that's his vibe. He had friends, money, and was always a shoe in with the ladies. But one look at Martina Harbor and his bachelor days are a thing of the past! He knows she belongs to him. With his inner beast scratching against his skin, there is no doubt in his mind the female is his fated mate. But there's more than meets the eye with this fiery Wolf.

Will Martina brush Mitchell off, or will they light fires together?

PROLOGUE

HARBOR HOUSE. **About twenty years ago…**

Nova beckoned me and Sybil to her side. She showed me the piece of paper, and I felt my magic and my Wolf tremble. This was important. She ran inside to where Davian and Erryn waited for us, and Sybil and I followed, our hands clasped together.

"It's gotta be a secret for a while, but what do you think?" she asked, blue eyes wide and bright.

She turned the paper around, and everyone fell silent. Sketched out with unerring perfection were Davian and Erryn at the center of the image, with me, Sybil, and Nova behind them. Behind all of us were our animals. A Badger Mountain Lion Hybrid for Erryn, a Wolf for me, a Snow Fox for Nova, and an awesome

River Dragon for Sybil. Swirling lines surrounded us to represent Davian's magic.

Beneath the drawing, in perfect script, were the words *Witch Shifter Clan*.

"Wow, Nova!" I exclaimed.

"That's amazing! But why am I so short?" Sybil asked.

"You are short, though." Nova frowned.

"Nova," Davian said in a hushed whisper, and walked to take the paper from her. "This is beautiful."

"You think so?"

"Yes, I do. We'll get it framed and hang it up in our training room, so no one accidentally sees it, okay?" he asked.

Nova nodded.

"Erryn? What do you think?"

"I think it is perfect," Davian's new mate said.

I liked Erryn. In fact, I had named her. She felt big to me, important. Wolf liked her, so I did too.

Witch Shifter Clan.

That was what Nova had named us, and something about it made my insides warm and my Wolf howl with joy. This was a good thing. I just knew it. And someday it would be everything. My Wolf growled softly inside of me, and though I had yet to meet her, it made me smile that she agreed with the sentiment. The Witch Shifter Clan was important.

I slept that night in the same room as my sisters, with Davian and Erryn in the bedroom they shared, and for the first time my magic and my Wolf were content. It would not always be that way. My animal and my powers often fought on another.

Harbor House was the first place we ever belonged, and I knew it was one of those special places I'd read about in one of the many books lining the shelves in the reading room Mama Anne had set up for us when we were kids.

It would always be the place I came back to. Mama Anne built Harbor House for supernatural runaways and delinquents. Those of us who were unloved and unwanted. But it was so much more than a soft spot to land. It was home. My first home. Just as much as Davian, Erryn, Nova, and Sybil were my home.

I would leave there someday. That was inevitable. But Harbor House would stay with me. The place, the memories, that feeling of belonging. They would always be special to me. Just like the drawing Nova did of us.

Witch Shifter Clan.

That was our name. It was where I belonged. And someday everything would fall into place. I didn't know what that meant, but my child's heart felt it with the absolute surety only an innocent could claim. I had things to do yet. Adventures to go on and experiences to have. But home would always be there waiting. Just like Mama Anne said.

Harbor House would always be my home.

CHAPTER ONE MARTINA

"FUCK A DUCK," I muttered and kicked the flat on the brand new Tesla Model Y I borrowed from Phillip.

Phillip was sort of my boyfriend. We'd been dating on and off for six months, and our relationship sort of felt like a hamster on one of those spinning wheels. In other words, we were always moving but never really going anywhere.

Phillip was easy on the eyes, smart and not at all needy. He'd just made partner in the law firm we both worked for and was busy with a sudden influx of added responsibilities. I was happy for him. Really, I was. He worked hard and earned the job. Besides, changes were coming for me. Changes I hadn't shared with anyone. Not yet.

I'd been thinking about this thing with Phil for days

now, mulling it over. No, I was not mad about his dedication to his job. In fact, I really didn't care. It was just, his sudden promotion was the reason I was headed home alone. Typically, we accompanied each other at family events. But this was just another indication of where we were going, in separate directions.

I hadn't told Phil what I was planning, and I doubted he would approve. It didn't matter. I would do what I felt I needed to do with or without him. I didn't need permission from any man to follow my path, much less a man who spent more time on his skin care routine than he did on making sure I came. I mean, really. Who the fuck did that?

Reminded of my sexual frustrations, I growled and grabbed my cell phone, calling the insurance company to send a tow. Fucking Tesla. Electric cars might be the wave of the future, but for all their gas saving blah blah blah, they still used rubber tires. And as I just found out, running over six-inch-long rusty nails were hazardous to all vehicles, regardless of all the fancy tech shit.

So there I was, an hour late to my own damn birthday party and stuck on the Garden State Parkway just two exits away from my hometown. At least I had heat. I checked the temperature gauge and frowned. Sixteen fucking degrees was too damn cold, I didn't give a shit what anyone said about *majestic blankets of white across forests* or *winter wonderland photo ops.*

Despite the enormous midnight black Wolf inside me, I did not appreciate winter. Like at all. I turned the heat on full blast, snuggling into the seat as I waited for the tow truck. It was fifteen minutes away, which wasn't bad. Of course, as soon as I had that thought, the battery light went from green to red and within thirty seconds, the damn car shut down on me.

"Motherfucker," I snarled, tapping my long fingernail on the damn thing.

It was no good. The car was dead. I had no heat. And my phone just chirped, letting me know the tow truck was delayed, and I'd be sitting there for the next two hours if I didn't do something. Gritting my teeth, I called my brother.

"You're late," he said jovially, and I could just picture the goofball smiling wide as he scolded me.

"I'm stuck," I countered.

"Are you safe?" Erryn asked, having grabbed the phone from Davi.

Her tone was more than concerned, and I knew her eyes were probably glowing purple with her Hybrid beast. God, I missed her! Actually, I missed both of them. Erryn and Davi raised me and our sisters. They were the best people I knew. Caring and protective, but also loving and fun. The two of them were so in sync, I used to stare at them in awe. For the past six years, I lived in Manhattan, and I never came across another couple like them.

"Yes, I'm fine, Err. Phill's car just—"

"That fancy electric thing I told you not to drive?"

"Yep, that one," I mumbled, feeling like I was twelve all over again. "Anyway, I got a flat, so it wasn't the car's fault," I grumbled.

"Then why are your teeth chattering, Marti?"

I closed my eyes and huffed a sigh. Dammit. Nothing got past Erryn.

"Because after I got the flat, the car shut down and now, I have no heat. There. You happy?" I barked, trying to stop my teeth from chattering.

"Of course, I am not happy. Just vindicated," she replied, and I heard a muffled laugh that told me Davi was listening.

Ugh. Incorrigible. There was nothing like looking like a fool to make you feel like a child again. I cleared my throat and tried for patience.

"Why don't you use magic to fix the flat?"

"Because, Erryn, as you know, I'd be more likely to make the damn car explode. Besides, fixing the flat wouldn't matter. The engine is dead!"

"Still having problems with your powers, pup?"

I ignored her probing question. I knew she meant well, but I didn't want to get into it.

"Am I walking or are you coming to get me?" I asked, finished with this conversation.

"Stay put, pup. I'll send someone to get you."

Erryn hung up before I could respond to her cryptic statement, and my rumble filled the tiny car. Something was totally up with my Wolf. Ever since the Curse of Natalis had been broken a few years back by a tenacious teenager named Grazi Kelly, I'd been able to communicate with my inner animal faster and clearer than ever.

But living in the city was hard on Wolf. Hell, it was hard on my magic, too. Truth was, I'd been so busy pretending to be normal with my human boyfriend and my human world job, I'd lost touch with my supernatural self. What was I supposed to do? My entire life, I tried so hard to just fit in. Years of hiding my magic from the Macconwood Wolf Pack had taken its toll. How long could a person live in denial, anyway?

The sign to Maccon City loomed in the distance, but with Wolf's help I could read it just fine. A bitter wind shook the idiotic, pretentious automobile, and I shivered, but not because of the cold. Something was coming. A change. And I wondered if I was ready for it.

My phone buzzed, and I saw a text from Phillip, but I really was not in the mood. He probably got an alert his precious car had stopped working. The man was ridiculous about material possessions. I knew he grew up poor and was proud of how far he came, but sometimes it felt like I was just something else he'd acquired.

After all, with my Hispanic heritage, my noticeable curves, and my own hard knock life background, far as he knew anyway, I checked off more than a couple of the boxes he needed to appear a super guy. The first time I met him he greeted me with some badly accented Spanish, and I had to tell him I didn't speak a word.

That was when he really got interested. I guess I'd had a weak moment, or seven. I mean, Phil was a nice guy, if a little vanilla. He'd been a good listener though, and hearing about how I'd been abandoned and put into foster care, he didn't judge me. In fact, he seemed to admire how far I'd come. Maybe we were alike in that way, but something was very clear as I sat in his overpriced car a few hours away from where I left him.

I did not love Phil. Not even a little. What was I doing with this guy? He was human. He knew nothing of my real life. Even the physical aspect of our relationship had taken a huge nosedive. And it wasn't all that to begin with.

Shit. I really needed to break up with him. I'd told him in the beginning, this would not be a forever kind of deal. He'd thought I was issuing a challenge, playing hard to get. But he had to know I didn't love him. And he sure as fuck didn't love me. We hadn't even had sex in months! I grabbed my phone and scheduled a reminder for later that week.

Break up with Phil.

What? Don't judge me!

I was bound to get sidetracked by family shenanigans, and this had to get done. Shivering in earnest, I checked the time. What the heck was going on? Fifteen minutes had passed, and the temperature was dropping.

I thought about the welcome I would get when I walked into Harbor House and my Wolf perked up. A long while had passed since I'd come home. Ever since Davian and Erryn, my adoptive brother and sister-in-law, had taken to globetrotting, it seemed kind of pointless. Sybil and Nova were busy with their own lives, and I was doing fine with my law career, living in the Big Apple.

Some life, huh? I was living the dream, or so I told myself. But the truth was my Wolf was out of sorts and my powers were wonky as fuck. The second I got the call from Davian asking me to come home to celebrate the birthday I shared with our two sisters, I knew I was going to say yes.

How could I say otherwise? My big brother did everything for me. For all of us, really. Davian Harbor was a saint. Okay, maybe not a saint. He was a Witch. But he'd raised Sybil, Nova, and me after our foster mother, Mama Anne, passed away, and that meant a shit ton of sacrifices on his part. He wasn't perfect, but none of us were, and Davian loved us just the same.

When Erryn came into our lives—literally from another world—we were struggling a bit. But after they took care of a couple of goons who wanted to hurt us, Davi and Err put all their strength into raising the three of us. But that still wasn't why I said yes to coming home for a visit.

It wasn't out of obligation. No way. That was a copout, and I was not into lying. Not even to myself. I was coming home because I needed to recharge. My life was going according to plan, but lately I had started to wonder—what if the plans were wrong? What if I was supposed to do something besides help wealthy businesses cheat the government?

Did I mention I worked in corporate law? It was challenging at first and fun, but lately, it seemed to have lost its appeal. My Wolf yearned for something else, and the way I kept setting the sheets on fire at night—because of bad dreams not super smexy times—all pointed to one very obvious thing. I was homesick.

Our little makeshift family was anything but normal, and that was exactly how I liked things. But coming back to Maccon City? That left me feeling kind of iffy. I had a complicated relationship with the town where the biggest, baddest, and most powerful Werewolf Pack in the entire world had its headquarters.

See, back in the day, Witches were a big no-no to those guys. The problem was, I was one of those guys. A Werewolf, or Wolf Shifter. But only half. The other half of my DNA was pure Fire Witch. Of course, that sort of magic was something most covens feared, and therefore hated.

So, there you have it. Outcast on both counts. Hated by Wolves. Feared by Witches. I was left to rot on the outskirts of town, which was exactly where Mama Anne had found me almost thirty years ago to the day. God, I missed her. She was the kindest, most giving person I had ever met. Her example was a strong one, and somehow, I felt that I disappointed her with my life's choices.

Before I could get too maudlin, however, an enormous, cherry red pickup truck pulled in behind me and out of the driver's side came the tallest, widest man I had ever seen. He had a thick scruff of beard covering his face, a skullcap pulled down tight over his head, and a pair of reflective sunglasses covering his eyes.

Wolf, my inner beast growled, having sensed his animal before I even had time to register, he was coming towards me.

The stranger wore a thick, hooded sweatshirt. It was one of those brands people who worked outdoors favored, and it molded to his powerful chest and arms perfectly. He had dark blue jeans on his long legs and work boots, and the prints they left on the snow-covered ground had to be at least twice the length of mine.

"You gonna come out or what?" he asked, his Jersey accent brisk and no nonsense.

Fuck. I startled hard, grabbing my chest before I remembered myself. Motioning for him to step back, I opened the car door and gasped as the freezing wind whipped against me.

"Did Davi send you?" I yelled above the noise of the traffic and bitter January weather, and the man nodded.

He hadn't backed up a step either, which meant I had to push him a little with my hip to wiggle out of the car.

"Excuse me," I mumbled, and the man bent down.

"What for?" he growled.

Damn, but that accent of his was so familiar. Jersey natives tended to drop r's so *what for* became *what faw*, and so on. It took me a really long time to get rid of my accent, which was a necessity in the legal world. I bet I'd have it back in an hour, being home.

Sexy voice. Good body.

"Oh, just—hey! Did you just sniff me?" I asked, shocked at his bad manners.

I knew the Macconwood Pack had stopped its ban on Witches and magic, but that didn't mean I liked this big, strange Wolf sniffing at me like I was a bag of Cheetos, for fuck's sake.

"Smell good, sweetheart. Got any bags?"

"Yes. Two in the back, and I am not your sweetheart," I growled, stomping my way to his truck.

I stopped short, certain I heard him say "not yet" but when I glared at him, he totally ignored me. I noted the stenciled logo on the truck door and frowned.

Truman Contracting LLC? It couldn't be! Could it? The Truman boys had been in school about the same time as me and my sisters. I'd had a crush on Timothy when I was ten, but this wasn't him. This man was too big, too dark to be the delicate blond boy I'd once known.

Didn't Tim have a brother?

I gulped. Oh crap. Yep. He had a brother named Mitchell. And I remembered him.

Mitch Truman had been every teenage girl's dream in high school. If I remembered correctly, he'd played varsity basketball as a starter freshman year. The guys had talent. But he was one of those beautiful, popular boys. The kind who never paid attention to me.

Now, Nova, she'd had her pick of the boys at Maccon City High, but my sister was ridiculously beautiful. She never dated the Werewolves, though. None of us did. But I wasn't a teenager, we were not in high school anymore. That meant I had options.

Wait. What?

CHAPTER TWO MITCHELL

MY BREATH HUFFED OUT in streaming clouds, but I was far from cold in the cabin of my truck. With the beast I had inside of me, it was a wonder I didn't fog up the windows all on my own.

"Where are you?" I mumbled to myself, checking the sides of the road as I drove carefully, looking for a broken down vehicle.

Of course, I didn't know what I was in for when Davian Harbor called me and invited me to his little sisters' birthday party. I vaguely remembered the girls from back in school. They'd been pretty, smart, and a few years younger than me.

It was odd to be invited to their party since we weren't friends, but I owed the man a favor. Davian Harbor was one of those super smart computer guys, and he'd been recommended to me by a member of the Pack after our brand-new top dollar computer system ate all our files. My brother and I own and operate a construction firm, mostly renovations.

Tim studied architecture in college, as for me, I just liked to work with my hands. Anyway, our system crashed, I called Davian, and he came through for us. So, when he sent the invitation via text, I figured what the hell? I liked parties as much as the next Werewolf.

Of course, it never occurred to me when he called a second time that I'd be picking up one of the guests of honor on my way to Harbor House. Davian shared her location with me, and I frowned. The woman had gotten stuck with her car just a few miles away from the house. She could have shifted and ran home—I knew they were all Shifters, the sisters, having gone to the same school as them even if I was older.

Maybe she'd been anxious about her luggage. Or the car itself. Females always carried a ton of crap with them. But I had to admit the hoity-toity, super geek ride was not something I had expected from Martina Harbor.

Sure, I knew electric cars were the future, but what could I say, I was a throwback. I loved the classics. I'd restored my 1972 Chevy C/K and made tons of modifications towards making it more environmentally responsible, as well as comfortable for me and any guests, of which *she* was the first.

Talk about a classic. The woman was petite and curvy, with skin that looked as smooth as silk, and a creamy tan complexion I was dying to touch. There was something unusual about this she-Wolf. Oh, I knew what she was, alright, but she didn't feel like Pack. I'd have to call one of the Wolf Guard, maybe the Pack Beta, Seff, to ask him what he knew about little Martina Harbor.

I grabbed her bags out of the trunk of that toy car she was driving, shaking my head at her choice of vehicle. Oh well. I didn't expect her to be perfect. What was I thinking? I didn't expect anything from her. She was a stranger. I didn't know her from Eve—my Wolf snarled, and I froze, listening to the beast's long, drawn out rumble.

Mine.

Fuck.

Elation warred with caution. Mine? Could this tiny, curvy, little female really be mine? It was definitely a possibility, and I was more than open to it. In fact, I had to adjust my dick in my jeans because of how open I was to the possibility that Martina Harbor and I might mean something to each other.

Grrrr.

She smelled good. Like cinnamon apples with hot

honey drizzled across the top. My favorite dessert. I knew better than to tell her that. Women today didn't like to be compared to food, but what better compliment was there than that? The fact I was already imagining licking her from head to toe was a testament to the fact I found her absolutely fucking mouthwatering. It was a wonder I didn't need a bib.

"Cold?" I asked, noticing her shiver.

That was odd. She was a Wolf Shifter like me. She shouldn't be cold enough to shiver unless temps went below zero. I frowned and turned the heat on, not waiting for an answer.

"Thank you," she replied stiffly, and I grinned.

Oh, but she was a feisty one. I recalled Davian saying something about his sisters taking over the world. One was a scientist. The smart one, Nova, I recalled her name from school. One was a social worker. And another was a lawyer.

One look at little Marti Harbor and I knew which one she was. Everything about her from her expensive clothes and the top dollar luggage she carried with her said big city rich. She was no social worker. She'd been known for her razor sharp tongue back in high school, and it seemed she put it to good use.

Good for her.

Pride filled me and I couldn't stop the shit-eating grin from spreading across my face if I tried. Seriously, for some fucking reason, I wanted to fist pump the air and give a victory shout. This little badass was doing strange things to me, and inside me my chestnut brown Wolf was simply taking it all in.

"I live on the edge of town, down Devilwood Lane," she said and told me the directions.

"I know where Harbor House is," I replied easily, wanting her to be comfortable with me.

"Oh. I guess Davian told you where to bring me?" she asked.

"Your brother sent me, didn't he?"

"Yeah. About that, um, thank you."

"My pleasure." It really was. She just had no idea.

Her warm cinnamon scent filled the cabin of my truck and my Wolf practically fucking purred at how delicious and tempting she smelled. Animal instincts were harder to control on full moon nights, and wouldn't you know it? It was a full moon tonight.

The Wolf Moon, actually. Which was kind of a joke around town, seeing as how most of the Macconwood Pack, especially members my age, had grown up playing the online game of the same name created by one of our very own. WolfMoon was still going strong, had its own fandom and everything.

"By the way, happy birthday," I said, needing to fill the silence before I did something stupid, like reach for her.

"How did you know it's my birthday?" she asked and turned her luminous violet eyes on me.

Fuck. They were beautiful. More purple than blue. There was something different about those eyes. Special. But maybe that was her Wolf. I knew mine turned gold when my beast was near to the surface, otherwise they were just a muddy hazel color. Nothing like hers.

"One, I was invited to your party—"

"Why? We aren't friends. You don't even know me."

"I would know you anywhere, Martina Harbor," I said, and my voice was rough with my Wolf.

She narrowed her eyes, arms crossed across her chest, and damn, but she was cute when she got fired up. My Wolf studied her while I concentrated on driving. Sure, my reflexes were supernaturally enhanced, but January meant ice-slick roads and there were plenty of humans driving two-ton death machines who didn't have my senses.

Steady does it.

"I'm sure Davian put you up to this, but I am not in the market for some pity date, got it?" she growled and this time, she'd shocked me.

"Pity date? I'll have you know I am a very well sought after bachelor in Maccon City," I told her.

"Oh, I bet, Mr. Truman."

"First of all, gross. Mr. Truman is my dad. I'm only like three years older than you. My name is Mitch—"

"I know," she said softly, turning her head towards the window.

But it was too late. I already saw it. A grin was peeking out at the corner of her mouth, and she'd averted her face to hide it. The woman was teasing me. And there went my interest, skyrocketing up a few more notches, as if it needed it. She was intriguing.

Fiery little badass.

"We went to school together, didn't we?"

"You remember that?"

"Yes, I remember that. Damn, woman. I wasn't just a dumb jock back then. Besides, the Harbor sisters were the prettiest girls in town when we were in high school. Not that you grew up too bad," I added.

"Well, gee, thanks. I'm speechless," she replied, and rolled her eyes.

But her scent told another story. She was nervous, And maybe a little interested. I took the exit and drove slowly, trying to drag out this bit of time we had together. I was becoming more enamored with the woman with every second that passed. It wasn't unnatural for me to want to prolong this first reunion.

Score one point for Mitch Truman.

"Seriously though, weren't you a senior when we were freshman?"

"Junior, actually, and your sister was in my AP Calculus class that year. She got top marks, if I recall correctly. Made me feel a little dumb to be honest," I told her.

"Hmm. Yeah, Nova makes everyone feel a little dumb. But that's usually because she looks like a supermodel and has a brain like Einstein," Martina replied easily.

I detected no jealousy, or snark like I did whenever my siblings got to chatting about each other. I came from a large family. Four sisters and a brother. In fact, I was pretty sure the Harbor girls were in Tim's class in grade school.

"She was definitely smart," I said, wanting to keep the conversation going.

"And pretty. I mean, her eyes alone have been known to stop traffic," Martina said.

Was she fishing? I inhaled and tried to determine what she was angling for, but she was concealing something from me, and it made my nose less reliable than usual. Hmm. That was odd.

"Blue eyes, right? Yeah, I remember. I'm partial to purple, myself," I said in a low voice.

Take that, I thought with a tiny grin. I didn't want her getting too comfortable now. Best to keep her on her toes. Her breath caught in her throat, and I pulled to a stop at a red light. Two more minutes till we'd pull up at her door. I turned my head towards her.

"Shouldn't you be looking at the road?"

"Hard to look at anything else with you sitting here."

"Yeah, right," she said and snorted.

Oh, my God. She actually snorted. Fuck. She was cute.

"I'm serious. Look at you, Martina Harbor, sitting in my truck all grown up."

"What are you talking about? Like you ever wanted me in your truck."

"I did. But I was shy—"

"Okay, I call bullshit."

"Yeah, you do that for a living, right?"

"Excuse me?"

"Isn't that what it means to be a lawyer? Calling bullshit," I asked, enjoying the fact I surprised her.

"Okay. You know who I am and what I do. What else do you think you know about me, Mitch?" she asked, and I could see her moving back, calculations forming in her brain.

She was an overthinker. Probably had something to do with trust issues. I understood that, not from personal experience, but because I was a thirty-three-year-old man and I didn't live under a fucking rock. Besides, like my mom always said, anything worth having was worth waiting for and I could be patient.

I was a Wolf, after all. An apex predator. A natural born hunter, and hunters needed to have an unlimited supply of patience to catch their prey. Not that I thought of Marti as prey—okay, yeah, maybe some small part of me did. But only in a *I wanna get to know you better kind of way* not the *hey, bunny get in my belly* way.

"What else do I know about you? Well, I know I like what I see so far. And I know I want to get to know more about you," I said.

"Is that so?" she asked, one eyebrow quirked up.

She was shivering again, and I wanted to warm her up. In fact, I was desperate to. My growl started slowly, building up inside my chest, and filling the whole damn cab of my truck. Desire and need raced through my veins, and I was hypnotized by her, drowning in the crystalline violet pools of her eyes.

"Oh, yeah," I replied.

A horn honked behind us, breaking the mood. It was all I could do not to leap out of the car and beat that fucker with his steering wheel. I should have kissed her already, but she was skittish, and I wanted more than a stolen moment.

"So, you still playing basketball?"

"Ha! So, you do remember me? Okay," I replied, grinning in earnest now.

There was simply no stopping it. I liked this woman. I was interested. And I was not afraid to let it show.

"Hardly," she muttered, but it was too late for take backs.

I pulled up outside the long line of cars filing up the driveway of her childhood home, noting with surprise the big party tent set up outside and the loud thrumming of a guitar.

"Holy shit. What did they do?" she muttered, eyes wide as she leaned forward to get a better look.

I barked a laugh and shook my head. Looked like the whole Pack was there, and from the sounds of it, everyone was having a good time. The tent was fashioned for outdoors. Heaters were placed strategically throughout, the music was live, and I smelled the mouthwatering scents of food and drink dancing on the air.

Yep. This was some party, all right. I got out of the truck and went to the passenger side, opening the door for her. She was still stunned and seemed unsure of her next move. So, I stole it from her. I was a Wolf, not a saint.

I took her elbow and helped her out of the truck and cupped my hand around the back of her neck and crashed my mouth to hers in a hot, rough kiss that left my dick hard and her heart thundering inside her chest.

My eyes were glowing gold with my Wolf, their reflection shining in the window of my truck behind her.

Martina held on to my shoulders, dazed from our kiss, and damn, but that made me feel ten feet tall. I growled and dipped my head again, sniffing her neck before stepping back. Fuck, she smelled good. I needed to distance myself before I pushed too fast, and it was torture, but I managed it, turning around one last time to flash her a Wolfish grin before I vanished inside the tent.

"Welcome home, Martina Harbor."

CHAPTER THREE MARTINA

"YOU'RE HERE!"

Sybil tackle hugged me before I got my bearings. I fell backwards, hopefully denting that asshole's truck. How dare he? Imagine kissing the hell out of a woman then running off to party. Oh, I saw the fucker. He was dancing with some tall blonde she-Wolf. Not that I should care, but for some reason I did. Even more shocking, I wanted to rip her damn head off.

"Of course, I'm here," I growled, hugging Sybil back.

"Let's get Nova," she squealed, grabbing my arm and pulling me forward with more strength than necessary.

My sister was a badass River Dragon, the only one of her kind as far as I knew. She was super fucking strong, making her petite pixie-like appearance the perfect camouflage. Within seconds, we found Nova in the throng of people, and I was just flabbergasted.

First, I missed my sisters. We hugged and screamed and kissed and jumped up and down, which was what sisters did. We'd always been connected, if not through our shared birthday, then through our bond as former foster kids who'd grown to depend on each other for anything.

They had my back, and I had theirs. And dammit, I missed this. Living in New York City was not what I'd hoped. I'd been lonely and cut off from them for too long. My Wolf was sick. I hadn't told them, but she was. Something was wrong. But being with them, even for just a few minutes was, well, it was magic. I felt better already.

Tell them, my Wolf urged, but I zipped my lips.

Now was the time for reunion, not secret telling. Besides, I wanted to feel them out before I mentioned what I was really doing home. There were a lot of moving parts and I wanted to make sure I dotted my i's and crossed my t's first.

"I am so glad to see you," Nova said, and hugged me tighter.

"Yeah, you look like shit," Sybil yelled over the music, and I frowned as ten pairs of Wolf eyes shot a curious glance at me.

Fucking Shifter hearing.

"Where's Davi and Err? And why the fuck is the Pack here?" I growled and felt old angers rise.

The motherfucking Macconwood Pack had made my life hell when I was a kid. Back when Zev Maccon was the Alpha, he'd outlawed witchcraft and had no use for half-bloods or mixed offspring. Wolves were encouraged to mate with other Wolves, anything else was considered a violation, a weakening of Pack bonds.

He was a fucking medieval monster, and I hated that prick. It was because of him my parents had given me up. His stupid prejudices against Witches and magic made my childhood hell. I had to hide who I was at every turn. In fact, no one except for family knew I was both a Witch and a Wolf.

That was my secret. Mine and Sybil's and Nova's. Each of us harbored a beast inside, along with our Witch blood. But while Nova and Sybil had their own demons to contend with, mine had been very real and in my face on a daily basis. I had my family, but I was a Wolf without a Pack, and my animal had felt that loss keenly.

Shit. I'd really messed up everything, hadn't I? Moving to the city. Dating Phil. What the heck was I doing with my life? My heart stuttered in my chest, and I felt panicked for a moment.

"Hey, you're safe, Marti. You're here with us," Nova

whispered, and I felt her minty magic seep into me, bringing calm and coolness.

I always thought about things in terms of food. Maybe that was why I had such a fat ass. Seriously though, Nova's striking beauty was just one of my sister's attributes. She was a certified genius, worked for some secret government agency as some mad scientist. I always pictured her with goggles and elbow-length gloves, laughing maniacally as she poured chemicals into tiny vials. I know, I know, my imagination was totally fucked.

"Here, take this," Sybil said, her blue hair glittering under the disco lights.

She was so damn cute as she offered me a shot glass of some dark liquid. Of all of us, Sybil had the biggest heart. She'd followed in Mama Anne's footsteps, becoming a social worker, and helping kids who needed it. I admired the shit out of both of them, and I was proud to be their sister.

"There you girls are!"

Davian, our brother, came running towards us and lifted me in a huge bear hug. He squeezed me tight and fuck, I felt like crying. I was so happy to see him. I felt Erryn embrace me on the other side. She smelled like fur and gun oil, as always, and I snorted a laugh through my tears.

"Good to have you home, little Wolf," she murmured and kissed my head.

"More shots!" Sybil yelled and came back with two more for them.

"Okay, we down them in one, two, three—Happy birthday!" she shouted, lifting her shot into the air.

Davian, Erryn, Nova, and I did the same. We clinked glasses and everyone cheered as we tossed them back. I still didn't know why the fuck all those people were gathered to celebrate our birthday in a huge fucking tent outside our childhood home, but for a moment there, it seemed totally normal.

People came over, clapping hands on our shoulders and wishing us well. There was a live band playing some country cross over and I giggled as a big, lumber-jack looking fucker took Nova's hand and asked her to dance. She looked horrified, but Sybil double-dog dared her, and off she went.

I laughed and shook my head when Davi tried to drag me onto the makeshift dance floor. The party was jumping. I recognized dozens of people from town. Mostly Wolves, and my chest felt tight again. The Wolf whined, but I shushed her, quieting my beast was just second nature. Chills ran through me, and I felt slightly nauseous.

Shit. I hadn't told them yet that there was something wrong with me. Later. I'd get to it later. My gaze drifted over the crowd, landing on a pair of gorgeous hazel eyes. Shit. It was him. Mitch raised his longneck in some sort of a salute, and I offered him a two-fingered wave. I tugged on the bottom of my sweater, crossing my arms when he started to amble towards me.

Shit. What did one say to a guy who stole a kiss then left immediately after like he was on fire? And he wasn't. I checked. Besides, my magic was not exactly reliable these days. I suspected my fire had gone out, and to someone with my kind of Witch blood, that was not good. Like at all.

But I had no time to ponder that with Mitch Truman headed my way. He did one of those long-legged slow walks guaranteed to make the girls turn their heads, and quite a few did. I didn't even realize I was growling until I saw his eyes widen and that panty-melting grin of his spread across his face the closer he got.

"Hey, you," he said, clicking his bottle to my empty shot glass.

I'd taken four already, and that was pretty much my party limit. Shifters had supernaturally enhanced metabolism, but I was only half Wolf and that meant liquor hit me almost the same as it did normals. Four shots and I was happily buzzed, but not drunk. I didn't like to be drunk.

Losing control had never been allowed when we

were younger. Keeping a leash on my emotions and behavior had become second nature. It was ingrained in my very soul. Right then, I very much needed to stay in control.

There was something about Mitch Truman that reminded me of a caged beast. An untamed, wild thing. And if he was set free, well, I worried what he might do. Pounce on me, perhaps?

Yes, please.

I rolled my eyes at the predictable bitch my Wolf was being. He was so damn good looking, it should be illegal. Tall, dark, tempting. Dangerous, I should have led with dangerous. He was sensuously enticing, but I hadn't even ended my non-relationship with Phil yet. Shifters moved fast, but I was not ready to go there with anyone.

"Are you having a good time?"

"Yeah. why? Don't I look like I am?" I asked mildly insulted.

He raised his eyebrows, and I wondered what I did to bring about that expression. Then I realized I was just being myself again. Defensive and antagonistic to hear some tell it.

"You look a little pissed off, actually," he said, and once more, I was taken aback by his bluntness.

"You know, there's this whole thing people do. It's

called being polite and not pointing out the faults of others," I mumbled, angry, but not quite sure if it was at him or myself.

"Yah, but that's a rule for normals, sweetheart. We aren't that," he replied, clinking his bottle to my empty glass again before taking another long pull.

Dear God, how could a man guzzling a beer look so fucking hot? I had no idea. But there was just something about the way his lips curled around the bottle and his throat worked as he swallowed that had me quivering in places I didn't even know could quiver.

"Just so you know, I kind of have a boyfriend."

"Kind of?"

"Actually, I made a note on my calendar to break up with him. I suppose I'll do it tomorrow when I tell him I left his car stranded on the parkway," I mumbled.

"That was his car?"

"Yeah. Why?"

"Good, means I like you even more now because you didn't buy that piece of shit."

I smiled then. How could I not? Looked like Mr. Sexy hated the Tesla almost as much as I did. Not that I hated the concept of the car, just the actualization of it. It was downright weird looking, and the fact was, it didn't work. Not well enough for me to trust it to drive as far as I did. Maybe they were just a city life car.

Maybe the next edition would be better. Who could say really?

"Did you say you like me?" I asked, unable to help myself.

"Yep."

"Even though I have a boyfriend—"

"You said he's a *sort of boyfriend*, which is girl code for someone who means less than your favorite ice cream—which is?" he asked, and I felt compelled to answer.

"Strawberry. But only if it's Hagen Daas. Otherwise, my favorite ice cream is always chocolate. Wait. What?"

"Besides, you're breaking up with him. Tomorrow, in fact," Mitchell continued.

He clinked my glass again before taking another sexy sip and I stared, mouth hanging open. I must have been more desperate for male attention than I knew if I thought some man slurping beer was hot. Okay, he didn't slurp. But what the fuck? I wasn't some needy little coed looking for attention and this wasn't a 90s movie, either.

God, he was so hot. Like the kind of hot I was only used to seeing on billboards in the city. He could be an underwear model easily. Of course, he was probably too big for the industry. And I meant that in a purely observatory sense. Werewolves, Shifters, were large in general.

I'd almost forgotten that. I mean, yeah, there were supes in New York City, but not many in corporate law from what I'd seen. The men in my current circles were thin, lean, average height. It had been a long time since I'd felt tiny around a man, if ever. But Mitchell did that to me. He made me feel petite, and his hungry gaze did wonders for my self-esteem. Even if the constant sniffing was a bit strange.

I didn't mind my curvier than average frame. In fact, I was pretty fond of my ass, which some had compared to fabulous booty award winners such as J-Lo and a certain Kardashian, though mine was gained *au naturel*. Likely from a lifelong romance with Ho-hos and other snack cakes.

Anyhoo...

"Why do you keep doing that?" I barked the question, wincing at how rude I sounded.

"Doing what?" he asked, one dark eyebrow raised.

"Tapping your bottle to my glass. It's empty. I don't have another drink," I said.

He made me so frustrated. I felt inadequate and silly, and dammit, I did not like that. Of course, that part was all me. Mitch hadn't done anything wrong. And if I was being honest with myself, he intrigued me more than anyone else of the opposite sex had done for a very long time.

"It's for good luck, sweetheart. Can I get you a drink?"

"No," I began, then shrugged.

Fuck it. It was my birthday, and I was entitled to live a little dangerously once in a while, right? I nodded.

"Yeah. Yes. I mean, sure, I'll have what you're having."

"Be right back," he said and winked.

Sizzles seemed to spark through me at that sexy little gesture, and I rubbed my arms. What was going on? I'd been freezing my butt off lately, but five seconds with Mr. Tall Dark and Scruffy and I was warming up all over. And I meant all over. This was dangerous territory, but I was in it now.

"Hello little Martina," a lightly accented voice flitted towards me.

I turned my head to see a beautiful Sherry Morgan smiling widely with a handsome man, *sniff*, Werewolf, on her arm. That was a shocker. I didn't know Sherry had settled down, and I was surprised it was with a Wolf. She'd been part of my childhood, a local White Witch who'd helped me and my sisters learn to control our powers. That she was the descendent of the first Morrigan, and now held the powerful title herself, was something I didn't learn until I was much older.

"Sherry! I didn't know you were here," I said, and gave her an awkward side hug.

I was trying to avoid touching the male who had an arm firmly around her waist. I frowned. Possessive much?

"Seff, be a good boy and let go. You're making my young friend here nervous," she told her man.

The Wolf was handsome, I'd give him that. He grinned at her indulgently, whispered something in her ear before releasing her. He leaned close and kissed her temple before he turned to acknowledge me.

"Sorry, I can be a little protective of my Sherry. The name is Seff, Seff McAllister," he said and offered me his hand.

I stared. My heart was pounding, and my Wolf whimpered deep inside of me. This man wasn't just a Werewolf. He was the motherfucking Beta of the very powerful, scary as hell, Macconwood Wolf Pack.

"Easy, I mean you no harm," he rumbled, and I saw his Wolf in his eyes. "You are upset, and my animal is protective. Please be at ease, Martina. I am a friend."

"We'll be okay, Seff. Leave us a second," Sherry said, and he nodded, backing away with his head cocked to the side as if he were baring his throat to me.

But that couldn't be. Why would a powerful Wolf bare his throat to someone as insignificant as me? I shook myself out of whatever trance that whole meeting had put me in and looked up into Sherry's worried gaze.

"You're sick, little Wolf. Tell me what is wrong," she whispered, and I gasped.

"You could always see right through me. Please keep it quiet, Sherry. I haven't told the others," I said, gripping her hand.

I was desperate for her to keep my secret, and she frowned, but nodded. In the nick of time, too. Mitch just returned with our beers, bowing low to Sherry and I realized things had changed a whole lot since the last time I was around.

"Hey Sherry," the big male said and grinned.

"Hello there, Mitchell. How are you now? I see you'll be taking care of our girl, then, yes?"

"Looking forward to it," he replied, and I was fucking lost.

I watched the exchange like I was watching a foreign film. I heard their words, but they made no fucking sense, and without subtitles, I had no idea what was happening. Sherry smiled widely, then whispered something to Mitch whose eyes went gold before he nodded once, hard.

"Come see me soon," Sherry told me. I nodded, watching her float away towards Seff.

"What was that about?" I asked, truly baffled.

"Nothing much. Come dance with me," he growled, and took my half-drunk beer from me.

He put both bottles on a nearby table and pulled me

onto the dance floor before I even had the chance to respond. He was taller than me. Like a lot taller. But for some reason, that didn't seem to matter when he wound his arms around me and pulled me in to lean against the curved muscles of his body.

"You could have asked me to dance," I said.

I was trying hard to stay grounded when all I wanted to do was drift away on the wave of desire I felt for him, rising like the tide from somewhere deep inside me. Mitchell Truman was magic, and not in the sense that I or my sisters were. No, this was something purely physical. Like an animal magnetism I hadn't been expecting nor was I prepared for it.

"And risk you turning me down? Fat chance, sweetheart."

"You're light on your feet," I murmured, allowing him to lead me around.

"Mom made us take lessons when we were pups," he confessed, and I laughed.

"Really?"

"Yep. My brother, you remember Timothy, right?"

I nodded, and he continued.

"Well, she had the two of us taking lessons and teaching our sisters to dance before we could even tie our own ties."

"That's awesome," I said, laughing.

"Are you making fun of me?"

"I wouldn't dream of it. Really, you dance well, Mitch. I like it."

And I did. Apparently, so did my Wolf. My usually reticent beast peeked through my eyes, a deep, satisfied growl sounded beneath my breast.

I like him.

CHAPTER FOUR MITCHELL

SPINNING MARTINA HARBOR around the dance floor last night was like something out of a dream. Kissing her goodnight at her door, well, that was like a memory of something I never got to do. It was strangely sentimental, but perfect all the same. I'd wanted more, of course. But I wasn't some horny kid trying to cop a feel just so I could have something for my spank bank when I got home.

I mean, yeah, I was interested, but this was different. She was special. After what Sherry had whispered to me before the knowledgeable White Witch had walked away, I knew I'd been right about the woman. Martina was important. She was big. And I needed to proceed with caution.

So, instead of putting the pressure on last night, I

decided to take it off. I danced her and her sisters around the dancefloor. Acted as their own personal waiter, I got them drinks and snacks from the endless buffet. When it came time to blow out the candles, I cheered her on from the sidelines and accepted the forkful of chocolate deliciousness she held out towards me.

Hell, I felt like I'd known her for years. I guess I had. Even if it was the first time, we'd hung out like that. Martina was not what I thought. She was funny and sweet, smart as a whip, and not the hardass she actively presented to the world. It was like that persona was a suit of armor she wore to protect herself, and last night, after a few more rounds of shots with her sister, that armor had come down.

She was a puzzle. An enigma. Someone I wanted to know more about with a hunger I'd ever known. I knew she had secrets, but we all did. I was no different. I wanted to earn them from her. To build her confidence in me, in us, and yeah, I knew I sounded like a fucking idiot. But I guess that's what love did to someone.

Yeah. I said it. Love. There was no other explanation for it. I knew all about fated mates and the instant lust one Shifter felt for his or her or their true soul mate, but this went beyond my wanting to bend her over the nearest surface and fuck her until my cum ran down her plump thighs—though, fuck, yeah, I was down for that. Did I mention my obsession with the woman's perfect apple of an ass?

"Enjoying yourself?" Erryn harbor, Davian's wife, had asked me at some point during the night's festivities.

"That I am, Erryn. Thank you for the invite."

"Our pleasure. Just know this, if you hurt her, I've got two guns in our cabinet at home that have been itching for some target practice."

Eyebrows raised, I nodded once at the terrifying female. Her purple eyes were light and glowed with an eerie vibrance as she stared me down. I had no quarrels with the female, and I appreciated her looking out for Martina. So, I nodded and bared my throat, showing her where words couldn't that as far as Martina was concerned, I was not a threat.

Hell. The woman had no idea how safe she was with me. My eyes coveted her as she and her sisters giggled and danced together on the makeshift floor. I had to hand it to Davian, that party tent was off the charts. Lights and disco balls hung from the frame, sending a rainbow of colors dancing across Martina's beautiful, tanned skin. She and her sisters jumped up and down, shimmied, and shook their asses, and damn, but I loved watching her.

They were tipsier than I'd have thought after only a

handful of shots. Other Wolves and Shifters had very high tolerances for alcohol, but Martina, Nova, and Sybil were lightweights. Hell, they were almost like normals, getting their buzz on after what amounted to a few thimbles full of liquor.

It surprised me, but I was always good at rolling with the punches. I made sure no one bothered them or got too rowdy, and everyone seemed to have a ball. Davian cornered me at the end of the night, doing his brotherly duty and all, and I told him like I told Erryn and Sherry.

"You don't have to worry about me, Davian. Your sister is perfectly safe."

"What does that mean exactly?" he asked, and I felt a power buzzing beneath his skin I hadn't noticed before. Interesting, but no concern of mine. His sister, however, that was another story.

"What that means, Davian, is no one and nothing will ever harm her while I am around. Martina is mine," I said, my voice dropping a full octave.

Davian's eyes glittered with emotion before he clapped a hand on my arm and squeezed, giving me a nod. It meant something that he approved, even though I hadn't been looking for that. Davian was a good man, well liked and highly respected in town. His mate was scary as hell, but again, Erryn was someone I held in high esteem.

The band wrapped things up around three am, and the cold was positively bitter by then. Davian and some others were using magic to clean up, and I volunteered to walk a tipsy Martina to the door like a mother-fucking gentleman my mama raised me to be.

Fuck, she smelled like heaven. Cinnamon apples and hot honey spice. I wanted to lick her from head to toe, but I made do with a sweet, soft kiss that made my Wolf purr like a fucking kitty cat.

"Mmm, I think I like you, Mitchell," she'd said before closing her eyes.

I caught her before she fell to the ground and carried her inside. Sybil directed me to their childhood bedroom, and I laid Martina down, kissing her head before I did something stupid, like climb in beside her.

That was last night. And I'd had a hell of a time trying to sleep after leaving her. The beast took my skin, and I barely made it to the shed before he went full on monster mode. Other Wolves were able to just take to the forests when they needed to run, and usually, that was enough for me. But Martina had my animal all riled up, and he needed more than just a run. He needed to burn.

"Dude, pay attention!" Timothy barked, tossing a sledgehammer at my head.

My motherfucking little brother had a death wish or something. I growled and snatched the heavy thing out of the air, putting it back inside one of the many work vans our company, Truman Construction LLC, used. Business was booming, but we typically handled all projects involving the Pack personally.

Of course, he knew I'd catch the thing. Our reflexes were sharp and though the hammer was heavy, I caught it as easily as I would have a piece of paper. I was strong. Stronger than most Shifters, but that was because my Wolf was a touch different from others. I had a sort of genetic quirk, *er*, a sequence of DNA that skipped generations, or so I was told. It took years to control, but I managed it. Barely.

With my focus on Martina now, the beast was more anxious than usual. The idea of having a mate, some-thing to protect and cherish, was very attractive to my Wolf. He needed that. It was good for him. Good for me. Hell, Martina was good period. But having a mate was excellent for both sides of my being. She gave me a higher purpose, and I couldn't wait till the day I claimed her as mine.

"Where is your brain today, Mr. Pouty Pants?" Tim asked, and I rolled my eyes heavenward, praying for patience with my idiot brother.

"Fuck you, Tim."

"Ooh, testy this morning, aren't we, big brother?" Tim, the idiot, asked as he waggled his perfectly tweezed eyebrows.

Fucker.

"No, *we* are not fucking anything, Tim. You and Peter were probably wrapped around each other all fucking night. I imagine you are happy as a clam. Meanwhile, I went home alone, knowing the woman meant for me was sleeping on the other side of town. Without me," I grunted.

Aside from being my brother, Timothy was my best friend. Naturally, I told him all about meeting the woman I believed was my fated mate just last night. That we both knew the Harbor girls was just a bonus. Tim was happy for me, but since he was newly mated to the love of his life, a Wolf Shifter from Hope Falls named Peter, he was all about spreading the joy.

"Yeah, that's accurate," Tim replied. "So, what is your plan, big bro? How you gonna woo her?"

"Woo her? Did we time warp back to the seventeenth century or some shit? I ain't wooing anyone."

"Yeah, I mean you must have a plan," Tim said, staring at me like I had any fucking idea what he was talking about.

"I don't know. I was thinking I'd just swing by and ask her if she wanted to grab a slice or something in town—"

The sound of Tim's sharp hiss almost brought me to my knees. How the fuck a Werewolf could make such a noise was beyond me. I shook out my eardrum and glared at the little pissant clutching his chest like he was having a heart attack.

Drama king much?

We'd just finished giving an estimate for a remodeling project on one of the abandoned strip malls on the edge of town. Cat Maccon-Nighthawk, the sister of our Pack Alpha and one of his Wolf Guard, had just purchased it. She was turning it into one of the several Macconwood-Nighthawk Teen Outreach facility centers that were now found across the country.

I was one of the many Shifters she'd helped in town when she had opened her first center. You see, Werewolves used to be cursed to only connect with our animals during the full moon. The rest of the month was pure agony. We were cut off and weak from wanting our Wolves. Think of it as being starving and staring through a window where a buffet of all your favorite things were spread out. So close, but so far. In other words, it was fucking torture.

Then the curse was ended by a spunky she-Wolf, who was now a major contender for High Alpha—that was like the Alpha badass of all badass Alpha Wolves—but it left a major gap in our Wolfy education. Suddenly, a whole bunch of us were hit hard with bonds to our animal we'd only ever felt at their weakest level. It was rough, learning control all over again, trying to curb our animalistic tendencies. If not for the Cat's program, I don't know what I would have done.

But back to the present and the reason for my recent turmoil. Last night, I'd met my mate. But Tim was right. I needed a plan. I wondered why Martina's Wolf wasn't pushing her towards me the way mine was insisting I go to her right this minute. Shit. Maybe I was wrong.

No. Mine. Mate.

Well, that answered that. I ran a hand over my face, scratching through my beard. It was getting out of control again, but it was only going to get colder over the next few weeks. The beard was a buffer between my face and the wind.

"Ohmygawd, Mitchell!" Timothy snapped. "Look, I love you. You are my brother. But if you are going to land a sophisticated she-Wolf like Martina Harbor, then you are going to have to step it up."

"Step what up?" I asked.

"Hello! I am talking about your style. I mean really, Mitchell, you need help."

My brother walked around me in a circle and shook his head. He was wearing the same damn thing I was. Jeans and a work sweatshirt. Only, well, his outfit looked sort of better. Like it had been tailored to his lithe body. And his hair was styled perfectly, blond waves falling just so across his forehead, emphasizing those brilliant baby blues.

Fucker.

"Is this one of those cockamamie schemes you and Peter get up to when you binge watch those damn DIY remodeling shows?" I growled, hands on my hips.

"Um, no, this is more like blue collar meets project runway. Ohmygawd, Mitchell, that would be an awesome show! I am putting this down on my *Timothy's Awesome Ideas* board on Pinterest."

"What are you doing?" I asked, really worried now.

"Hush. I told you about Pinterest. Anyway, now I am texting Peter. Yay! He had a cancellation this afternoon. Come on."

"Come on, what, Tim? I don't want to go see Peter—"

"You need this, Mithcell. Please. let us help you," he said, and I sighed.

My brother could sell clothes to a nudist colony if he put his mind to it. Resistance was futile. I knew. He knew it. So, eventually, I nodded. Thoughts of Martina and her sexy little ass crept up in my mind, and I grinned. I was ass struck by the woman.

"What did you say? Ass struck? HA! That is fucking awesome, bro," Timothy said, and fuck, I realized I'd said all that aloud.

"Well, she's a ten, Tim. I mean that. A perfect fucking ten, and I want her. Badly."

"And you will have her. Well, with a little work."

"The fuck—"

"Don't be such a bore. Let's see what my Petey can do to improve this blue-collar chic look you've got going on."

I rolled my eyes. There were some things I was not willing to change about myself for anyone. But Peter, my brother-in-law, was a damn good barber, and I could do with a cut and shave. Even if it was cold.

"I'll get a haircut, Tim, but that is all. This woman means more to me than even I understand. She's special, but I'm not going to trick her by pretending to be something I am not."

"Mitchell, you don't ever have to do that. I was just teasing. You know how I love a guy makeover," he said, shoving me in the shoulder.

He was right. I knew Tim didn't really think I needed to change. At least, not on the inside. But anyone worth anything to you deserved you at your best. That's what our mom always told our dad when she wanted him to dress up and take her out for a night on the town. He did too. Reluctantly. But they were the best couple I knew, and if their example didn't inspire me, nothing else would.

It was eleven hours since I'd left Martina in her bed,

and my Wolf was eager to be with her again. Yeah. I could sit through a haircut.

"You drive," I told Tim and grabbed my phone.

Davian had texted me Martina's number yesterday before I picked her up from that broken down POS car she'd borrowed from her now, hopefully, ex-boyfriend. My Wolf didn't much like that she'd been seeing someone, but it was in the past and I wasn't such a Neanderthal that I couldn't handle the idea of her having had a life before meeting me. Besides, it wasn't like I was some pure as snow virgin, either.

"Are you texting her?" Tim asked, grinning from ear to ear. "Tell her you've been thinking about her all day! No wait, say something sexy! Ask her what she's wearing!"

"Jesus, Tim, is that what you think women want to hear? I thought you were supposed to be sensitive and shit," I said.

"Oh yeah, I'm sensitive, and you're just a football loving, Coors drinking, nacho loving motherfucker, right, Mitch?"

"Fuck football. You know I watch soccer. I prefer IPAs. And I know you know that nachos give me gas," I replied, my smile matching his.

I loved teasing my gay brother with all that stereotypical shit. He gave as good as he got, and it was just one way we bonded with each other. Men were men regardless of who we were sexually attracted to, straight or gay or bi, it didn't matter. Basically, men were idiots.

But as long as we stayed within the boundaries we set, everything Tim and I said to each other was all in good fun. I couldn't say whether or not that was true for everyone. And I didn't know if we had a special bond because we were relatives, or maybe it was because of the fact we had the same point of reference for our senses of humor. Growing up in the same house, raised by the same parents, tortured by the same sisters, Tim and I were best friends, as only brothers could be. Were we politically correct? Probably not. But it worked for us.

"Are we done generalizing?" he asked.

"Yep, I think so," I replied, trying like hell to figure out what to text.

"Good. No, just text her something she'll likely remember from last night. Like a picture you guys took together or something," he suggested.

That was actually a good idea. There was one selfie we took together that was promising. I clicked open the photo album on my smart phone and scrolled down to the picture I wanted.

Martina's cheek was pressed against mine and she had a small, secretive little smile teasing at the corners of her pretty, pink lips. Her violet eyes shone with hints of purple and I was looking down at her, a grin on my face. Damn, she was beautiful. And we looked good together.

Send.

Three tiny dots appeared at the bottom of the screen, and I was so intent on waiting for her reply, I didn't realize we'd arrived at *Pete's Place.* The name of my brother-in-law's barbershop was simple, but it was effective. It really was *the place* all right, with a waiting list a month long. Pete was a fucking artist. Tim was pulling me out of the car and leading me up the stairs and inside to Pete's chair while I stared at the screen like a zombie.

"What's wrong with him?" my brother's mate asked.

I ignored him, watching those three dots without blinking.

"He's been *ass struck* by a woman," Tim informed him, and I barked a laugh, still not taking my eyes off the screen.

Fucker.

"Ass struck? I see," Pete replied.

I grunted. The place was jampacked, but it was Saturday and I expected nothing less. Pete and Tim chatted while he wrapped a small towel around my neck, then whipped a shiny black cape around my chest, and snapping it closed. Finally, a message appeared, and my heart pounded like mad inside my chest.

Cute.

"She replied!" I shouted. Tim screamed, and Pete jumped, sharp as fuck scissors in hand.

"Baby, please! I could have killed your brother," he grumbled.

"What did she say?" Tim asked.

He leaned over my shoulder opposite where Pete was cutting my hair. Fuck. I didn't tell him what I wanted. Not that it would matter. He was what I liked to call a mood barber. In other words, the haircut you received at *Pete's Place* depended entirely on his mood. He looked at my brother with love and indulgence on his face, and I knew I was gonna get a good one.

Thank God.

Once I'd gone in there after he and Tim had argued and I wound up with a fucking mullet. Trendy again or not, mullets were so not my jam. But I didn't have the heart to complain, and that fucking thing took six long weeks to grow out. And that was with more changing into my Wolf than usual just to encourage the hair growth.

"Cute? Okay. We can work with this," Tim said and began pacing.

"Tim, I'm just gonna ask her out," I growled.

The sound was a little more aggressive than usual

for me, but that was because Pete was pushing my head around and my animal didn't much care for it. Tim looked at me like I was an idiot, and I rolled my eyes.

"Shush up," Pete growled back, and I stopped.

It dawned on me there were too many normals in the place for that shit. My Wolf needed to calm the fuck down. But the animal was excited. He wanted to see her again, and maybe Tim was right. Maybe I needed help not to fuck this up.

"Fine. What should I say?" I asked.

"I'll tell you, but only if you say, *Guide me, great and wise Timothy. Help me achieve my heart's desire, oh wonder of wonders, you sex god guru genius!* Yes, say that first. Come on, chop chop," my idiot brother said and clapped his hands together.

"Tim, if you don't help me, I'm going to eat you," I growled instead.

Pete laughed, and my brother glared at him. Uh oh. That was bad for my hair.

"Seriously, I am your brother. Help me out," I said, turning his attention back to me.

"Fine. I will help you. But only because Mom wants grandkids, and she's given up on the girls and me and Pete won't be ready for that for at least another year," he said.

"Now, type this exactly."

"Okay," I said.

I closed my eyes, willing myself to calm down. The Wolf was right there, scratching at my skin, begging to be released. He wanted to hunt her down, bite her, and give her the mating mark. But I had a feeling that would be bad. After all, consent was real. And I needed hers. I highly doubted the beautiful and brilliant she-Wolf would appreciate me just going all furry on her sweet ass.

Snip snip. Snip snip.

The sounds of Pete's scissors working their magic on the back of my head were oddly soothing and when I opened my eyes, I saw Timothy had turned serious. Baby bro was done fucking around. He was about to get serious, and that was good. I didn't want to fuck this up. It was too important. She was far too important.

"Ready?" Tim asked.

"Yes. I am ready."

"Okay, text her this," Tim began.

I listened and smiled as Tim told me how to start a conversation with this woman. Oh, he really was smooth. And after he gave me the idea of how to begin, the rest came straight from me. Martina texted back immediately that time. A laughing emoji.

So cute.

I grinned.

Mine, growled my Wolf.

But she wasn't. Not yet.

CHAPTER FIVE MARTINA

"WHAT'S HE SAYING NOW?" Nova asked.

She was sitting on the couch, munching on a bowl of crisp green grapes straight from the refrigerator. Erryn and Davian were out doing some shopping since apparently, we still ate them out of house and home. Sybil was out on an emergency case. So, it was just the two of us.

"I don't know. The three dots are going, but nothing has come through," I replied.

Yes, I realized I was acting like a teenager and not like a woman who just turned thirty. We were both sporting gnarly green mud masks on our faces and had deep conditioning treatments on our hair. We also had boob masks beneath our wrap around towels, had to get the girls looking all perky, and my toenails were currently sporting a brand-new coat of hot pink polish.

We looked like a couple of extras for the Go-Go's *Beauty and the Beat* album cover Sybil framed and hung on her side of the room years ago. It was still there, and I adored the cover and the tracks. The nostalgia of being home kinda, sorta wrecked me, but still, I felt better than I had in months.

"Marti! Something came through," Nova screeched, looking over my shoulder.

"Ouch! Wolf ears," I growled and pulled back abruptly.

Of course, I dropped my phone and accidentally kicked it under the couch. We both dove for it, giggling and snorting as we tried to get to the thing before it stopped buzzing. Too late.

It stopped vibrating, but I finally got to it. I tried to catch my breath as I read the flirty little message.

"Well?" she asked.

"He's asking me out," I said.

Yes, I wore a huge grin by then. My Wolf was growling softly, and my magic was pulsing gently inside me. Sick or not, that was the best I'd felt, the most at peace I'd been with both sides of myself in a very long time.

But was it fair to start something with the man if I might not be able to finish? I told no one about my suspicions yet. That something was wrong with my Wolf or my magic, or both. The idea of it filled me with dread. What if something was really wrong with me? I frowned hard. Thirty wasn't old enough. But I was just being overly cautious. At least, I hoped that was the case.

"Hello, Martina? I said where does he want to take you?"

"Oh, um, dinner and a movie."

"Oh my god, that is so high school," she snarked, but I just shrugged.

It was kind of high school, But to a girl who didn't get out that much back then, it was sort of perfect. My animal had been much harder to contain when I was a teenager, and while Nova and Sybil enjoyed things like cheering and dating, I was always working on hiding what I was. It was imperative the local Wolves didn't see me lose control.

The rules had changed for the Pack somewhere down the line, but I was wary and uncertain. If I dated Mitch, did I tell him what I really was? How much of myself was I supposed to reveal? Especially when something was wrong. It was all very confusing. I popped a grape in my mouth and chewed, looking at the photo Mitch sent. I remembered when he took it last night. How good it felt to snuggle close to him and let his warmth seep through my chilled bones.

The party Erryn and Davi threw for us was wild. I hadn't had a night like that in a long time, if ever. People I never expected to see at a birthday party for me and the girls wished me well, raised their glasses, and ate cake to celebrate our collective birthday. It was surreal.

"Are you going to go, Ti?" she asked, using one of the many horrible nicknames we gave each other as kids.

"Yeah, Doc, I think I am going to go out with him," I said, surprising myself with my answer and pissing her off by using the name she hated most.

"Don't call me Doc. Anyway, you know he's a contractor, right?"

"And? I'm not a snob like you, Nova," I said, narrowing my eyes at her.

"I am not a snob! But you've lived in New York for a while now, Marti. And Jersey boys are a different breed."

"Please, Doc. I grew up here the same as you. Besides, I like him. He's different."

"Different how?"

"I don't know, I just felt good hanging out with him."

"Fine. You can go out with him," she began.

"Gee thanks. I didn't know I needed your permission."

"Well, you have it. But be careful, okay? I don't want

you rushing into anything. Especially since you feel so," she started, scrunching up her nose. "I don't know, it's like I see your energy but it's off. When are you going to talk to me?"

"I will, Doc. I promise. And don't worry, I won't have sex with him on the first date—"

"Oh, no, have sex with him. Have lots of sex with him. Like buckets of bowchickawowow boinking time! I just meant don't fall for him," Nova clarified.

"Oh my God, you are the worst sister," I said, jaw hitting the floor when she started twerking in the middle of the living room singing Nikki Minaj way off key.

"Please stop. I have to do something, and it requires a modicum of propriety," I said, tossing a pillow at her still-shaking ass.

"Oh, you mean operation let Phil down? Yeah. Bummer."

"Yes. So, please, hush."

"Fine. But put it on speaker."

A few minutes later, I was holding my head in my hand as I explained to Phil why our relationship sucked and how I was having his car towed back to him. Nova was on the floor, hiding her giggles behind her hands. I kicked at her, but she couldn't shut up, and I couldn't blame her. The man was crying. Like sobbing. And why? We didn't even like each other that much.

"Phil, I have to say I am surprised by your emotional display," I said.

"But pookie," Phil began, and I cringed at the pet name he'd insisted on calling me. *"I thought we were really going places. Now that I made partner, I was even considering ring shopping."*

"Oh," I said, completely shocked. "Well, I'm glad we settled this sooner rather than later. Goodbye Phil. Also, um, I am resigning and leaving town. The other partners already have my resignation letter, I guess I just didn't feel like it was real until now," I said, watching as Nova's eyes went huge as she stared at me.

"That is surprising news. Fine. I guess you aren't who I thought you were, Martina. Good luck to you."

"Bye, Phil."

I hung up the phone and met Nova's stare. My chest was heaving, and thunder roared in my ears. This had been weighing on me for a while now. Even knowing I was leaving the firm, I hadn't really pictured what was coming next. Except now the cat was out of the bag. Shit. Sybil would be fine with it. She was a big softie. And I already knew Nova was more than a little concerned. What would Davi say? And Erryn?

Would they be disappointed in me? I knew they loved to talk about what successes the three of us turned out to be, but what would they think of me now that I was essentially a quitter?

"So, you're coming home for good, then?" Nova asked, and her brilliant blue gaze pinned me to the spot.

"I mean, I want to. For however long I have," I whispered, and that's when the first tear fell.

Nova wrapped me up in a familiar hug, and I cried in her arms. Spilling my deepest fears of what was wrong with me to her was the only thing I could do.

"How long since you shifted?" she asked.

"I haven't changed into my Wolf since the last time I was here," I confessed.

"Marti! That was two years ago! How? Why? Is that even possible?" she asked, and I knew it was bad.

"I've been working, and it's been so hard. I'm surrounded by humans day in and out. I thought it was what I wanted, but I-I just want to come home."

The front door closed with a click, and I saw Davi and Err standing in the doorway. Twin expressions of worry and tear-stained cheeks met my stare, and I ran to them, seeking the sort of acceptance and comfort I'd come to expect.

"We got you, little Wolf. it will be okay," Davian whispered, tightening his arms around me.

After I cleaned up the emotional vomit I had spewed all over everyone, I explained the situation as I knew it. I'd been denying my Wolf my body for two years—a feat that should never have been possible. With that, I'd also been stifling my magic. After all, what use was a

Fire Witch in the middle of New York City? I'd told my siblings that I'd found a local Coven to chill with and let loose, but that wasn't exactly one hundred percent the truth.

"Martina Harbor, you promised you had people who were working with you," Erryn snarled, and I exhaled slowly.

"I know I did, and I was hanging out with a group of Witches for a little while, but that just isn't my thing. I don't I can't—"

"Trust is hard for us, Davi. You know that," Sybil injected, having come home in the middle of my spiel.

"I know, but we're family. You should have told us," he insisted, and he wasn't wrong.

I felt ashamed. Like I'd let them down, and maybe I did. Nova was standing over me, collecting some blood samples to run in her lab. She didn't bother giving me a bandage, and I was pretty sure she tried to hurt me on purpose. I deserved it, though. I had them all worried, and it sucked.

"Alright, I will have this back in about six hours," she said.

"Um, shower first. Don't you think you should?" Sybil asked, and I snorted.

Nova looked between the two Yof us in our matching towels, face masks, and other beauty paraphernalia and heaved a sigh of disgust.

"Fine. Me first," she snarled.

Nova shoved me aside when I went to make a dash for it. I stomped my feet and howled loudly. The brat.

"Dammit, Nova, my date!"

"Date?" Davian asked.

I sat back down at our crowded, but well-loved kitchen table and explained about Mitch and my date. Davian looked grim, and Erryn was rubbing his shoulder. Her white streaked black hair was pulled back in a ponytail, and she listened attentively while I spoke.

"Well? Do you think it's okay?" I asked, biting my lip.

"For you to date? Yes, I think it is fine. In fact, I think it is great," Erryn replied.

"Look, Martina," Davian began, and I knew I had upset him.

That was something I hated doing, but couldn't seem to help ever since I was a child. I looked up at the man who was more like a father than he was a brother and waited for him to finish his thought process.

"I don't know what you were thinking denying your Wolf and your magic, and we will get to the bottom of all that, but this place is your home. You aren't dying, Marti. You might be a little sick, but we will figure it out. But most importantly, you are always welcome here. Harbor House is your home. The fact you didn't know that tells me you really stayed away far too long, little Wolf."

He opened his arms, and I ran into them, needing that bit of reassurance from him. He was right. Whatever I broke inside myself, I would fix. It might take a little time, but it was possible. I guess I just needed someone else to believe that could happen before I could even start.

"So, who are you going out with?" Sybil asked as I waited for my turn in the shower.

"Mitchell Truman."

"Mitchie? OMG! Didn't you crush on his brother Tim as a kid?"

"Shut up! Davi, make her stop," I snarled, and everyone started laughing.

"*Mavi, make mer mop,*" she mocked me.

Even me. It was just like when we were kids. She blew a puff of Dragon smoke at me and I chomped my jaws, pretending to bite her. I was not about to trust myself to use magic. Erryn separated us, and Davi sent a splash of water across the kitchen from where he was rinsing dishes to splash us in our faces. We sputtered and fell into a heap of giggles on the floor.

"God, I didn't realize how much I missed this," I said, struggling to stop laughing.

It really was good to be home.

CHAPTER SIX MITCHELL

THE SECOND I saw her wearing that long velvety skirt and tight little sweater I knew I was fucked. Shit. I should have made reservations at a fancy restaurant instead of my usual booth at *Roll Over*. It was the best sushi place in town. Maybe that would count for something.

"This looks good," Martina said, and I could hear the truth behind her words.

"Good. I was counting on you being more of a quality over luxury kind of woman. This place has the best sushi," I murmured.

"I like sushi," she replied, her dark violet eyes flicking to mine.

I smiled as we scanned the menu. We chatted and laughed, and I was ridiculously pleased when the waitress came over and Martina asked if I wanted to share one of the biggest sushi platters on the menu with her.

"Yeah, that sounds great. Can we have a couple of orders of hibachi rice and noodles, and beef negimaki, also?"

"Ooh, that does sound delicious," Martina said after the waitress left.

"It sounds like a lot, but I do have an appetite."

"And I don't? Actually, this is refreshing. You know, it's been forever since I went out with someone who was sort of like me," she whispered.

"Sort of like you," I repeated.

She had no idea the monster I really was, but again, I was not worried. Destiny led me to Martina Harbor, but that was just to create the spark. This insane attraction I had towards her was growing by the second, and that was all her.

"I, um, noticed you got a haircut and a shave. Was that for me?" she asked, grinning.

"Maybe. Or maybe it was just time," I replied evasively.

"If I confess I spent most of today in face masks and doing my nails, will you tell me the truth?"

"Face masks? Clay or gel? My sisters like this peel off cucumber shit, and they did that to me once, but it got all caught in my eyebrows and facial hair. Fine, I got a haircut and shave to impress you. My brother said I looked like a lumberjack."

She laughed then, and I smiled. My chest puffed up like a proud peacock, and the animal inside me rumbled pleasantly. It felt good being the cause of her smiles, the reason for her laughter. There was something sad behind her eyes, and I wanted her to share it with me. But I wouldn't rush her. Trust was a slow earned thing for Martina Harbor, but I was gonna win hers. It was a promise I made to myself and my beast.

"Well, I happen to love lumberjack romance novels, so tell Tim to mind his own business next time," she replied, after her giggles had died down.

"Is that so? I've got a flannel in the back of my truck I could put on for you—"

"You're incorrigible! But maybe later," she murmured, and her cheeks turned a dusky rose color I really liked.

After dinner, I drove down to the old movie theater everyone in town still went to. I held her hand, and Martina allowed it, sending chills of awareness rippling through my body. Her spicy cinnamon apple scent was driving me crazy, but her constant shivering had me worried.

"Cold?" I asked while we waited in line for tickets.

She smiled tightly, looking down as if she were embarrassed by that fact. Hell no. I was not okay with that, so I wrapped my arm around her and tucked her into my side, letting her feel some of my own natural heat.

"Wow, you are really hot," she whispered, and I grinned.

"You ain't so bad yourself, sweetheart."

"That's not what I meant," she replied and rolled her eyes, but she stayed put. And that meant everything to me.

"Popcorn?"

"Oooh, yeah. Popcorn, and a box of Snowcaps, and Sour Patch Kids. Oh, and a large Fanta," she ordered and pulled out her wallet.

"Nope," I said, grabbing it and tucking it into my back pocket.

"But it's my turn. You paid for dinner," she said, frowning.

I knew I'd struck a nerve with her, but I could not help myself. There were just some things a man didn't allow a woman to do, and one of them was pay for his movie theater candy.

"I asked you on this date, so I'm paying. Of course, you could wrestle me for your wallet," I said, eyebrows arched in open invitation.

The cashier chuckled, and Martina sighed. She rolled her eyes again, and I sizzled inside. It was fast becoming one of my favorite expressions on her. Damn, but she wore exasperated well.

Sexy woman. I got my eyes on you, sweetheart. 100%.

The movie was one of those comic book action flicks, and I worried she wouldn't like it. But that changed the second she started shouting at the screen and clapping with the rest of us. The theater itself was older, and the crowd was mostly local kids, but I only had eyes for Martina. She was laughter and light. And when her hand touched my leg or brushed against mine when we went to grab popcorn at the same time, hell, I trembled like a kid on his first date.

We sat together while the credits rolled, waiting for the little Easter egg at the end of the film. It was a good one, promising more from the series of super funny superheroes. Martina chatted on and on about what she thought of the actors and the story line, and I was shocked when she pointed out the not so obvious flaws in the plot line. Smart as a whip, she was.

"You know, you sound sexy as hell when you talk comic books, woman," I growled, and my eyes raked over her possessively.

She was taking up space in my head, planting roots in my heart. I wanted her with a ferocity that was damn well frightening, but I worked hard to control that part of me. Of course, there was nothing I could do about the raging boner clearly outlined in my jeans, and yes, I caught her staring.

"See something you like?" I teased.

"Oh my God, I was not just staring at your dick," she muttered, and I laughed out loud. "So," she declared with false brightness. "I liked the movie!"

"Well, looks like this hometown boy is full of surprises. And here I thought you were going to turn your nose down at my taste in food and movies, Miss New York City," I said, teasing her as we walked hand in hand back to my truck.

She froze in her tracks, brows furrowing, and I knew I'd made a mistake. But what had I said?

"You really think I'm a snob?" she asked and fuck, she looked hurt.

"No! I think you're smart and cultured. You're a lawyer. You live in Manhattan, Martina. Shit, I don't know. I guess I was worried about making the right impression on you because I never left Maccon City. I never went to college. Just started my business right after high school. Anyway, I guess I assumed you spent your free time going to museums and shit," I growled, suddenly uncomfortable.

"Wow. So, you think I'm a snob? You think I couldn't enjoy a date with a man unless he takes me someplace flashy and spends a lot of money?"

"What? No, I didn't say that—"

Fuck. This conversation was going way off course. I'd obviously upset her. She let go of my hand, and I felt pained by the absence of her touch. I unlocked the door and held it open for her, offering my hand, but she didn't take it. She was short though, petite, and perfect in my not so humble opinion, and it snowed some during the movie. With her long, tight skirt on, Martina couldn't quite get into the damn seat.

She was cold. I knew it. I could see her shivering again. After watching her fumble a second time, I snapped. Hands on her hips, I lifted her up and closed the door, ignoring her shocked gasp. My hands burned where I touched her, and my animal was snarling at me for letting her go so soon. At the rate this was going, I would need to shift in the shed again tonight.

Fucking hell.

Timothy had warned me not to fuck this up, and my brother was right. But he was wrong, too. He'd told me to act a certain way, to step up my game, but the best time of the entire night was when I was just myself with her.

After my fuck up, I felt about two inches tall. Martina didn't care about a lot of the things I'd expected. But she cared what I thought, and that was a sign. I mattered to her. That was all the encouragement I needed to try to fix this.

"Martina," I began, starting the car and turning the heat on for her. "I did not mean to say that before."

"Why? I'm happy to know what you really think of me, Mitchell," she replied, anger and hurt staining her words.

"Shit. No, I didn't mean that. I don't think anything bad about you, woman, I just want you to—look, I don't wanna fuck this up. I am doing a bang-up job of it, though. But hurting you or insulting you was never my intention," I growled, biting back the pain of my Wolf tearing me up on the inside.

"I like you, Martina Harbor. I really like you. I want to know more about you. I'm sorry if I acted like a judgmental ass. I didn't mean it. I swear."

"I guess I am being a jerk now, huh? No, it's okay. Don't apologize," she said, and heaved a sigh. "This was a mistake. Just, would you mind taking me home?"

"Wait. Please, give me another chance. Don't, don't leave like this," I said, turning towards her.

"It's not your fault. I have a chip on my shoulder, especially about your Pack."

"My Pack? But you're a Wolf and this is the Macconwood Pack's home territory. I have wondered and I guess now I am asking, why isn't it your Pack, too?"

"It's just not," she said, and her words felt heavy. "I grew up in Maccon City, but I lived under a cloud. The

Macconwood Pack left my family alone, but I was never one of them. Never accepted."

"Because you grew up in Harbor House?" I asked, confused.

She shook her head, and tears swam in her deep violet eyes. It was breaking my heart to see the hurt there. I unbuckled her seat belt and tugged her towards me, and she allowed it.

Thank God.

I couldn't stand the idea of hurting her anymore. It was making my beast feel all kinds of protective. All I wanted was to wipe the hurt away. To wrap her up in a bubble of good feelings and sweetness. To kiss away the pain and make it all better.

Good idea.

"Hey," I said, holding her face with one hand and wrapping my arm around her waist. "Please don't cry, sweetheart. I never meant to upset you. I just wanted to take you out. Be with you."

"Why did you ask me out?" she asked, canting her head in a way that reminded me she was a Wolf, too.

But she didn't smell like a regular Wolf. I couldn't find any hint of fur on her at the moment Just the smoky, spicy scent of cinnamon and apple pie, and dammit, I wanted her with a hunger I'd never known. I leaned towards her, brushing her nose with mine, my chest rumbled with the power of my beast.

"I want to kiss you, Martina," I whispered, so close to her lips, but needing her consent before I took this thing a step further.

I was playing with fire, and I knew it. I just didn't care. Barely able to keep the leash on the furious desire I felt for her, I growled, my gaze intent on hers. Her soft curves pressed against me, and I hated the clothes between us. I needed to kiss her. Hell, I might die without it. But I waited.

"So," she whispered, her breath mingling with mine. "What are you waiting for?"

That was all the permission I needed to claim her lips beneath mine. Finally, I had this woman's mouth on mine, and I kissed her with all the pent up passion I'd been feeling since I laid eyes on her again yesterday evening. I growled, swallowing her soft whimpers and moans, and put all of my energy into our kiss. She tasted better than I imagined, and, oh, I had imagined plenty.

To me, kissing was better than sex. I realized that made me an oddity among men. But this act meant more. It was more intimate than fucking. Sexier than head. And her mouth was the best fucking thing I had ever felt working in tandem with mine. We were good at this. At kissing each other, and I felt elated. Like I'd been waiting my whole life for this woman, and I supposed I had been.

Mine. Mine. Mine.

The word was on repeat as I kissed her harder, forcing her head back and plundering her mouth with my tongue like a man on a mission. And I was. She was my mission. My reason. Being with her was everything to me.

Some part of me was aware we were sitting in my parked truck outside a movie theater, fogging up the windows of my truck, but another part of me did not give a single fuck. Her mouth was hot and delicious, and she was kissing me back. Me. Mitchell Truman. A guy who worked in construction. Not a fancy pants lawyer or doctor. Just me with my calloused hands and my rough manners.

Were we a good match? I would bet my fucking life on it. Yeah, she was brilliant and beautiful, but she was more than that. She had a monster inside her, too. Right then, I could feel her Wolf moving inside her, rising up to meet me and my beast. Contrary to the always shivering Martina, her animal radiated heat, and it rivaled mine.

"Mitchell," she moaned my name and my cock pounded against my jeans.

I wanted her so damn bad. Needed her. I placed sloppy wet, biting kisses along her jaw and down her throat, tugging on the neckline of her sweater to get better access to her silky soft skin. My soul burned for her, and so did my body. Following an instinct, I'd never felt before, I growled a low deep, possessive sound, my hands roaming her body with a possessiveness I couldn't control. I wanted to devour her, time and place be damned.

The inside of the truck was like a fucking sauna, and I thanked God I had parked in the furthest corner of the now empty lot. While everyone else had driven away after the movie, I'd been busy fucking up our night. But now we'd moved past that, and kissing and making up was definitely the best part of the whole evening.

I pulled the lever on the side of the seat, pushing it back so I could pull Martina onto my lap. She climbed right on, straddling my hips, and the sound of her skirt tearing was loud. Neither of us cared enough to stop our lusty explorations, and I made a silent promise to buy her a new one.

Her sharp fingernails clawed at my shoulders, and I hissed, finding her panties with my hands. I growled deep and rough once my hands were on her ass, and fuck my cock grew even harder.

"You have such a perfect ass, Martina. I wanna bite it," I growled, squeezing her ripe globes. I raised my hand and slapped her left cheek, holding her in place with my mouth on her neck.

"Next time you look in the mirror and see my handprint, you're gonna remember this, sweetheart," I told her.

I wasn't sure if I went too far, but she pressed her fiery core against me, and moaned sweetly, and I knew she liked it. A little pain mixed in with pleasure wasn't unusual for creatures like us, but I shut down that thought as soon as I had it. There was no room for jealousy here. No room for anything but pleasure, but thinking about Martina with another man was liable to make my beast homicidal, so no. I was not going there.

Martina grabbed my face and pressed her mouth to mine, and I was so fucking turned on by her show of aggression precum leaked from my slit. Between that and the way she was soaking through my jeans, I was going to be a fucking mess when I went home. Thank fuck I'd moved out of my parents' house years ago.

"Need, fuck, Mitch, I need," she growled, grinding her sweet pussy against me, and my response was immediate.

I mean, I nearly lost my mind. Sliding her lacy panties to the side, I cupped her sex, loving the rumbling growl that spilled from her lips.

"So wet for me, sweetheart," I growled.

Good girl. Very good girl.

Her pussy was hot and soaked and so fucking tight, I didn't think I could even get two fingers inside her, but I needed to. If I wanted even the chance of fucking her without hurting her, I needed my little Wolf primed and ready.

Waves of pleasure flooded my senses as I began pumping my fingers in and out of her slit. Martina moaned, holding on to me like her life depended on it. Hell, I felt like mine did, too. I circled her clit with my thumb, curling my fingers inside her channel till I found the right spot and angle.

"That's it, sweetheart. Fuck my hand. Let me see you come."

Martina moaned, gasping now, hot tears trailing down her cheeks. She started to quiver and tremble, but this time I knew it had nothing to do with the cold outside. Hell. She was on fire for me. Wait. Fuck. She was on fire!

"Martina!" I shouted as flames erupted over her body.

Pained eyes met mine, and she shoved the door open, stumbling out into the cold. Before I could even comprehend what was going on, much less move, Martina's enormous midnight black Wolf ripped through her skin. The beast darted one glance my way, her purple eyes glowing before she lifted her lupine face towards the sky and loosed a mournful howl before taking off at breakneck speeds.

What. The. Fuck.

I sat there speechless with my dick literally in my

hand. One minute, we were making out like a couple of love struck teenagers, and the next, poof. She was gone. By the time I came to my senses, it was too late to go after her. A security officer had already driven by, asking me for my license and registration.

I was already zipped up and had the remnants of her clothes all tucked away in the trunk by the time he'd stopped his car. But that didn't stop the wanker from wasting a good fifteen minutes of my time.

"Alright, you have a good night now, son."

"Thanks," I growled at the rent-a-cop.

It wasn't his fault I'd had a shitty night, but I wasn't in any mod to mince words. Confused and circling the drain on full out devastation, I drove straight to Harbor House and raced to the front door. I'd fucked up some- how, maybe moved too fast, even though I was sure at the time Martina had been with me every step of the way. It didn't matter. I would apologize, grovel, beg, hell, there was not much I wasn't willing to do just to fix whatever went wrong.

I knocked for what felt like hours but was likely only minutes only to be denied entry by Martina's brother. The rejection hit me hard, but I told myself to chill. It wasn't coming directly from her, so there was no need to lose myself to my animal. I sucked in a breath, nearly choking on the sharp tang of magic in the air. Davian Harbor had come out as a Witch years ago, but I never really thought about his powers. How strong they were and what not. It might have been a good idea to think about that before showing up half-crazed and banging on his door, but it was too late. I was already there, and my Wolf was desperate for any drop of information he had about our unclaimed mate.

"Is she here? Is she okay? I need to see her," I asked, trying to calm my Wolf. But there was no getting the animal out of my voice.

"She doesn't want to see you, man," Davian said, and he looked exhausted with sadness and worry.

"Why? I don't understand—"

"I know you don't. But it's her secret to tell, Mitch. I can't do it for her. She is safe, though. That's all you need to know."

"I have to see her," I pleaded, but he shook his head and before I could move the fucker had me pinned to the spot with some sort of magic spell. "Fuck. Let me go, man."

"You know what I am, Mitchell, and I know what you are. You will not get in this house until she is ready, if ever. Do you understand?" he said with quiet strength, and my Wolf raged.

"You can't keep her from me," I growled, my beast roaring inside me.

I was about ten seconds from going feral and lighting everyone up in that fucking place, but I knew it wouldn't help me. So, I reined in the monster, and tried for calm when all I wanted was to howl my misery and surrender to the darkness.

"I don't want to keep her from anyone. She needs time, Mitch. If you are the man for her, give her some time."

Fuck. Davian was right. I'd promised myself before that I would earn her trust, but I had to admit, I didn't expect what had happened. I had no explanation for it and I was full of questions, but Davian made a good point. It was Martina's decision now.

But I would show her I was worthy. I'd prove myself, somehow. The Wolf in me agreed with a long, guttural growl. The beast understood assignments and purpose. If I wanted to win Martina's trust, her affection, and love, then I would need to give her time.

Be a patient hunter, I told my monster. *Just be a little patient with her.*

Grrrr.

CHAPTER SEVEN MARTINA

THREE DAYS after the date from hell, I came out of my room. The house had been buzzing with activity since Sybil was dealing with a pretty terrible case where a foster child needed to be removed from his home because of alleged abusive behavior by the parent there. She was excellent at her job, and I didn't doubt her for a second.

Nova was busy working with whatever secret government project they had her doing, and she'd hardly been home except to give me the results of my blood test. I was too sick at heart to even open them, but since she didn't demand it I knew they were fine.

Noise from the kitchen caught my attention, and I walked inside, not sure what I expected to see. Whatever it was, it surely wasn't that. Erryn and Davian were frowning as they typed numbers into a laptop. They didn't even look up when I came in, which was weird. But even stranger was the pair of long legs sticking out from beneath the sink.

"Got it," a familiar voice said. "One more second," he grunted.

"Mmm."

Erryn grunted her reply. Davian said nothing, still busy tapping away at the keyboard. I stood there, waiting for someone to say anything, but no one did. Finally, the stranger slid out from under the sink, and I was greeted by a shocked gasp from a blond-haired, blue-eyed, slender giant of a man.

"Well, good morning, Martina," the man said, walking over to give me a quick, hard hug.

"Who—oh my God! Tim? Is that you?" I asked, startled but eventually hugging him back.

"It sure is. Want coffee?" he asked, as if this was his house and not mine.

I came out of my stupor and went to grab cream and sugar. I had to move Erryn's arm, and she growled, as she sometimes did whenever she and Davi were working on something that required all their focus.

"Oh, don't mind them. She gets a bit snappy when focused," he told me, as if I didn't know. "Our accounting program went wonky again, and I came over so they could troubleshoot it. While they were fixing that, I figured I could do something for them, and what do you know, garbage disposal was broken," he explained.

I admit I was shocked as hell to see the boy I once had a crush on, not to mention he was the brother of the man I ran out on a few nights ago, in the middle of my kitchen. Tim sure was pretty. He wasn't as big, muscular, or devastatingly handsome as Mitch, but you could tell he was related.

"I see. Um, well, did you fix it?"

"Oh yeah. This was stuck," he said and picked up the half-bent spoon he'd retrieved from the disposal unit.

"Hmm. That was probably Sybil," I murmured. "She's always in a rush and doesn't always pay attention. You know the type, big heart, but not big on details."

"Sweetheart, I have a man at home just like that," he said, and my interest piqued.

"You might not have heard, but I am out now, have been since after college. You know, Rafe taking over the Pack made it easier for anyone with an alternative lifestyle to live in the open. You know, cause I'm gay," he said, spelling it out for me.

"Oh, um, I hear he's a good Alpha," I replied, sipping my coffee and trying not to choke on it.

This was a lot of information to take in. Zev Maccon, the former Alpha, the one I remembered, was a fucking asshole. He'd hated everything that wasn't like him. I'd always assumed the anti-anything different culture the Wolf Pack had was eternal, but maybe I was wrong. The possibility beat slowly inside me, more like a whisper of a breath. Like a bud of hope had suddenly unfurled, and I lifted my gaze to Tim's.

"Oh, he is, Marti. Rafe Maccon is an inherently good man, an excellent Alpha. He offers sanctuary to any who ask. Even going so far as to allow other supes to settle in his territory," he said.

I was feeling simpatico with Tim and I got up and grabbed some cookies from the jar, dropping them onto a plate for us to share while we drank our coffee and gossiped like old friends.

"I didn't know that," I said, clearing my throat.

I was a little uncomfortable, after all, Tim was trashing all my preconceived notions about the local Pack, and it was doing terrible things to the barriers I'd placed around myself. Walls I had built years ago so I would not feel the sharp sting of rejection quite so keenly.

I'd built the Macconwood Pack into something evil in my mind, and it made it easier to hate them. But Tim and Mitch, they weren't evil. In fact, everyone I'd met at our birthday party the other night didn't seem bad either.

"So, um, tell me about you," I said, changing the subject.

I needed time to process all that information before I decided my feelings about the Pack. Even if Rafe Maccon was a saint, that didn't mean my Wolf wanted to pledge fealty to the Pack he ruled. It didn't mean I wanted to live under his thumb.

"What have you been up to, Tim?"

"Me? Oh, honey, where to begin. After high school I went to college, studied architecture a bit. But I missed my family. My parents are the best. And you know how sisters are. Maureen, Celia, Peggy, and Lynda practically begged me to come back. And of course there was Mitchell," he said, grabbing a chocolate-covered graham cracker from the dish of goodies I'd spread between us.

"My brother is my best friend," Tim added, and for a split second the jovial male was replaced by something else.

Protector, my Wolf whispered, and I understood. He was worried about Mitch. Little did he know I was, too. I was worried I'd hurt Mitch with my fire the other night. And I was too scared to ask him. Too afraid to have to see the results of my loss of control.

My powers had been unreliable for years, and for the last few months they had been almost nonexistent. The other night was the first time I'd shifted in so long,

I couldn't believe it. It was like he had pulled the Wolf from my body, but with her, my magic went too. But with my powers, pain often followed. Fire was like that. Uncontrollable and so very deadly.

Please don't be hurt.

"How is he?" I asked, leaning forward but not looking Tim in the eye.

"Physically? Perfect. The guy has got a demon Werewolf inside him, honey. Emotionally? I'd say Mitchell is hurt and confused."

That brought me up short. Yeah, most Wolves joked about their inner monsters, so I ignored that bit. Shifters often had super healing abilities and what not. It was different for my sisters and me, but I was still glad he was not injured.

"You know, I used to have a crush on you," I confessed.

Timothy's big blue eyes danced with laughter as we traded stories about junior high and eventually high school. His laughter was like Mitch's and my heart squeezed inside my chest as I thought about all the texts he'd sent over the past few days.

Like a scaredy cat, I'd ignored each and every one of them. And his calls, too. I was too afraid to answer. Too scared to hear the judgement in his voice. Nervous as hell of what he would think after I ran like that. Shit. I owed him an explanation. After all, he'd been nothing but sweet to me. Our date was the best one I'd gone on in years. He was charming and fun, sexy, too.

Memories of that hot petting session we'd shared in his truck have haunted me ever since. I wasn't sure why my powers reacted like that, and I was embarrassed. But I could have hurt him, and that thought was simply unbearable to me. Yeah, I needed to explain myself and to tell him why I couldn't see him anymore.

"I knew all about your crush back in grade school. Your sister told me," Tim said.

"She did not! Who? Nova or Sybil?" I gasped and threw a cookie at him in mock outrage.

"Crumbs," growled Erryn, still not looking away from the laptop she and Davian were working on.

Tim and I exchanged glances, and we covered our giggles with our hands as I swept the crumbs up with my napkin. It wasn't like I would have left the mess there, anyway, but a happy Erryn meant a happy Davi. So I cleaned up my mess, and I did it with a grin.

"Sybil, but only because she was trying to gauge my feelings for you. I was flattered, truly," he said.

"I am going to kill her," I growled.

"You sound like Mitchell. You know, he has a temper, too," Tim replied and laughed.

"Mitch? No way. He's so sweet and kind."

"To you maybe. That boy houses a monster inside him, and I don't mean in his pants, so get your mind out of the gutter, thank you," he said, and my cheeks burned.

Fine. I went there.

"Anyway, I plan to rib my brother relentlessly about how his woman liked me first. You know, he is such an easy target now that you have him all ass struck and everything. He is gonna be so pissed. But as for me, I am happily mated now to a wonderful Wolf from Hope Falls named Peter. He owns the barbershop—"

"Back up. Did you say *ass struck?*"

"Honey, my brother has got a fixation on that beautiful booty of yours. Lunges?"

"What?"

"Do you do lunges?" he asked, and I shook my head. "Hmm. Just gifted, I guess. Lucky so and so."

"Okay, Tim, we found the bug," Davian interrupted us.

"Great! Now maybe my brother will stop snarling at me. Although, I don't think that will happen until a certain *booty-ful* Miss Thing—see what I did there? *Booty-ful,*" he asked, and I rolled my eyes.

"Yes, I see, Tim, but can you explain—"

"Explain what? How I am a genius? Honey, I do not have that kind of time. Anyway, all you need to do is answer his phone calls before half our crews quit, please and thank you. Poor Mitch is behaving like the Beast himself. He's acting like a bloody tyrant,

Martina, and only you can bring him to his senses," Tim said.

"Me? But why? We just went on a date. One date. I'm nothing to him," I whispered, my heart damn near pounding me to death.

"Oh my God, are you listening to me? Is she hearing me? What kind of Wolf Shifter doesn't recognize her own fated mate?" Tim snapped.

"My what?!"

He looked over at Erryn and Davian and I noted their red cheeks and guilty expressions. Something was going on, and those two were in on it. My Wolf growled, and I wondered at how close she felt. Sparks started at my fingertips, and Tim's gaze dropped to them.

"You're not just a Wolf," he said, shocked as he sat back down.

"Tim, we got it from here," Davian said.

He put himself between me and my, er, *my Mitch's* brother. A heated discussion broke out between them, but I could not hear a word of it. Instead, my mind was racing inside of me. My Wolf, that midnight black monster howled a long, solitary note, and I fell to my knees. Her heartbreak filled me, and I gasped at the pain. She was mourning the loss of something. No, not something, someone. A missed opportunity.

Mate.

She wanted her mate. The truth slammed into me like a derailed train, and I could hardly breathe for the weight that was crushing me. Could Mitch really be my fated mate? We'd only gone out once, but I understood that kind of bond could happen instantly between souls fated to each other. This separation had been painful, but I thought it was just guilt causing me to feel that way.

But I'd been wrong. My Wolf was angry, sad, despondent. Oh God, what had I done? This was impossible.

"Martina? Martina!" Erryn was kneeling in front of me, her worried eyes on my face.

I heard Davian and Tim arguing in the background, but I felt no danger from either of them. They weren't trying to hurt each other, Tim was protecting his brother, and Davi was protecting me.

"Stop. STOP! This is between me and Mitchell."

"He's my brother," Tim said.

"And she is my sister. I won't have her under Pack scrutiny," Davian said.

"He won't tell, Davi. That's for me to do."

"What?" my brother asked.

"It doesn't matter right now. First, I need to talk to Mitchell. Where is he?"

"He's at the old strip mall. We're renovating it for Cat Maccon," Tim said.

I nodded and grabbed the keys to Erryn's Vespa. Yeah, it was cold as fuck, but after years of hearing Zeke, my honorary Uncle who was also a Sleep Demon, wax poetic on his fondness for the tiny motorbikes, Erryn had caved and gotten one of her own. It was the same shade of purple as her eyes, and though I'd never driven one before, I was totally convinced I could do it.

There wasn't much choice, really. I had to get to him. I had to see if the things Tim and my Wolf said were real. Was Mitchell really mine? There was only one way to find out.

I took off like a bat out of hell down the slushy streets of Maccon City to the old strip mall that had sat abandoned for years. The wind was bitterly cold, but my powers were back, and I felt just fine. Hell, I hadn't even grabbed a jacket.

I was wearing fleece lined leggings and knee-high boots with a gray hooded sweatshirt and my hair in a careless ponytail that had come loose somewhere along the way. I looked like a lunatic. I was sure of it, but I didn't care.

CHAPTER EIGHT MITCHELL

IT WAS ALMOST NOON, but I had already dismissed the crew for lunch. I rubbed both my hands over my face and growled in frustration. The place beneath my breastbone felt hollow and empty. Fuck, was this what rejection from your mate felt like?

I hated it. Hated knowing I'd done something to break whatever bond had already started to form between me and Martina. I knew she was my fated mate, but despite her being a Wolf Shifter, she didn't seem to have the slightest inkling. Did that mean I was wrong?

No, my Wolf snarled. And I rubbed my chest, trying to soothe the monster. I'd spent the last three nights locked in my fur, pacing the length of the shed. I was grateful for the help of Sherry Morgan, the Pack Beta's mate, and the most powerful White Witch to walk the earth.

She'd used magic to make the interior of the otherwise normal looking ten by twelve-foot structure to be much larger for my changes. Damned family curse. My Wolf snapped his jaws, and I chuckled at the ornery fucker. Fine. It wasn't his fault, but still. Life would have been easier without the constraints I was forced to live under. At least with Rafe Maccon as Alpha, I didn't have to hide what I was.

That train of thought reminded me of Martina. Puzzling woman. She'd talked about living under a cloud when the old Alpha was in power, and what little I recalled of Zev Maccon confirmed what she'd said. But she was a Wolf, so why the hatred? I wished she was there so I could ask. One look at my cell phone told me she hadn't sent a reply to any of the sixteen texts I'd sent over the last three days.

Fuck. I looked desperate. But it was fitting. I was desperate. Like a fucking dog sitting at her feet, hoping for a scrap. I was pathetic. But I was owning that shit. Waiting her out wasn't working. Despite my promises to Davian, tonight I was going to see her if I had to break down the fucking door.

The slight sound of a motor reached my sensitive

ears, and I turned my head to the front of the trailer. Tim always insisted we have one for the two of us when working on a site. But the fucking thing only had two windows, and they were facing the other way. I stood up, walking to the front door and narrowly missed being slapped in the face with the fucking thing.

"What the—"

"Mitch!"

Holy shit. It was her. I stood stunned as she barreled into the trailer, frowning when I noticed the absence of a coat.

"Fuck, sweetheart, it's twenty degrees outside," I growled and grabbed her hand.

I closed the door and pulled her up against me, intending to warm her with my body heat. Only when I touched her, I realized she was hot. Not her usual sexy as fuck hot, I meant hot to the touch.

"Sorry, I'm, uh, a little riled up," she said, easing back from my hold.

I wanted to roar and squeeze her even tighter. My Wolf was riding me hard, and it was all I could do to finally release her. Holding onto my raging animal was difficult, but I managed. Barely.

"Um, what are you doing here? Not that I am not thrilled to see you, I mean. Shit," I said, rubbing my hand over my head.

I bit my fucking tongue in an effort to keep my mouth shut.

"I just saw your brother," she began.

"My brother?" I asked, confused.

"Yeah. He was at the house. Um, I used to have a crush on him, actually, never mind. Davi and Err were fixing some computer bug, anyway, he, um, he said something," Martina whispered, her words running together.

I made a mental note to kick Tim's ass later, but first I needed to figure out what the heck was going on here. She was wringing her hands and pacing as little as the space allowed, making me anxious as fuck. I tried to be calm, but there was something wrong and the beast in me demanded I fix it.

"Hey, let's sit down," I said, and grabbed a couple of waters from the small fridge by the desk.

We had a three-cushion sofa against one wall for naps or guests to sit in case a meeting was necessary when either Tim or I were working in there. It wasn't fancy, but it was sturdy and a hell of a lot better than me just standing there like a total idiot.

"Here," I said, offering her the water.

"Thanks. You know, Mitch. We don't know each other well. I mean, there are things about me I could never tell anyone, and even if I can now, you don't know them and if you did, you might not like—"

"Hey, slow down, sweetheart," I said, touching her hand.

Chills danced up my arm and down my spine. The woman gave me chills, and I growled, wanting more of her skin against mine. She was an addiction now, and I was fast becoming obsessed.

"Would you hate me if you knew my secrets?" she whispered.

"Martina, I could never hate you. And I want you to trust me enough someday with all your secrets. I won't steal them from you. Don't you know what you are to me? I can wait till you're ready to tell me whatever's on your mind, sweetheart. And I swear to you, I will keep them safe. I'll keep you safe. You're here already," I said, touching my heart.

Martin exhaled sharply, blinking back tears. She opened the bottled water and took a small sip, not looking at me yet. I suspected she was going over whatever it was she wanted to say in that pretty head of hers, and I was helpless to do anything but wait.

"I know there is a lot about me you don't understand, and that's because I haven't told you. This thing, um, whatever this is, I don't want to assume, but anyway, it's just really, really fast. Faster than I expected," she explained, and I tried really hard to follow. "You see, I wasn't expecting anything, actually. Not to meet you, well, meet you again since we knew each other from school. But what I mean is—shit, is it true? Am I your, your mate?" she asked.

The entire world seemed to stop moving the second she said those words. Her deep violet eyes were liable to swallow me up as she stood, facing me, head tipped back, waiting for me to say something. The scent of spicy cinnamon apple pie grew stronger, filling my senses and making me dizzy.

I reached out with one hand, cupping her cheek. Her skin was so incredibly warm beneath my fingers, I shivered in delight. My monster craved heat. Hell, he was born of it. Her breath caught in her throat as I moved in closer, giving her ample time to back up. She stood her ground, though, and pride sizzled through me along with something else.

Brave, beautiful, brilliant girl. My girl.

"Yes, you're mine, Martina Harbor. I knew the second I saw you again."

Her lips curled up into a breathtaking grin. She placed her hands on my chest and reached up on tiptoe to press her lips to mine. Soft, soft, so fucking soft. She kissed me and I was falling for her harder and faster than I thought possible. She kissed me, and I never wanted her to stop. Moaning softly, she pushed me back, and I sat down on the couch, reaching for her. Fuck, I was hard beneath my jeans, hungry for her, and desperate to finish what we had started the other night.

"Mitchell," she moaned, climbing onto my lap.

We were frantic then. I wanted to, *no*, I needed to possess her, to mark her with my scent, my bite.

"Are you telling me yes, sweetheart? Is that what this is?" I asked.

I hated myself for being so damn needy. But I had to know. I couldn't do this and walk away, and I needed her to understand that.

"I want you," she whimpered, leaning back, so she had room to pull off her sweatshirt.

Holy. Fuck. She was bare beneath it. Her beautiful, tip tilted breasts were perfect with dusky nipples puckered just for my lips. I couldn't resist. I bent my head and sucked one hard nub into my mouth, growling as her hands wound through my hair. Thank God Pete had left it long enough for her to have something to hold on to. By the time I was finished, I was likely to be bald.

This tiny little she-Wolf shattered me with her ready submission. But even as she granted me access to her precious body, her nimble fingers were working to divest me of my clothes. I was burning for her, and I didn't care if she knew it. Hell, I wanted her to know it. No one else had ever wrecked me so completely, and all we were doing so far was kissing. Her pants and moans increased and soon I'd kissed my way down her soft belly to her covered sex. Growling and impatient, I used my claws to slice off her thick leggings.

"I fucking love red," I growled, my face up close and personal with her red lace panty-clad pussy.

Her eyes widened, and she gasped as I closed my mouth over her covered mound. Sucking on her secret place through the sexy little garment was erotic as fuck. I used my tongue, growling to add some vibration, as I tested the texture of the soaked material.

"Oh fuck, yes," she whimpered.

It wasn't enough. I was kneeling on the floor between Martina's splayed legs, but I needed her completely bare. The animal in me would brook no arguments. I wanted to sink into her heat. To fill her with my cock. Make her come a time or ten before sinking my fangs into her flesh and claiming her as mine. I tore her panties right off her, grabbing her thick thighs and placing them over my shoulders.

"Mine," I growl, sending trembles through her whole body before I buried my tongue inside her tight heat.

I squeezed her legs, holding them open while I fucked her on my tongue, swallowing down every drop of her spicy cinnamon flavored nectar. She was so fucking sweet, so hot, and so fucking mine. Martina rolled her hips in time with my tongue, and I damn near lost it.

"Mitchell, fuck, yes, I'm coming," she cried out, arching her back.

I stayed with her every step of the way, stroking my tongue inside her slick heat, and lapping at her swollen clit until she rode every tremor and wave till the very last one.

"No more, please," she whimpered, and I took pity on her.

"Rest a minute, sweetheart, but I'm not done with you yet," I said, grabbing the water from the floor and helping her take a sip.

I switched our positions. Sitting on the couch, ignoring my boner, I picked Martina up and had her cradled against my chest. She sighed and snuggled, contentment and satisfaction rolling off her, scenting the air. I leaned down and sniffed her neck. God, I love her smell. She giggled and turned towards me, a smile on her face as she kissed my lips.

"Mmm. What about you?" she asked, her gaze flicking down to where her bare pussy sat right on top of my denim covered cock.

"What about me?"

"You know," she said, "I wanna take care of you too."

"Oh, so you think I licked your pussy till you were screaming my name just for you?"

"Oh my God, don't say lick your pussy," she said, and covered her face with her hands.

"What should I say? Ate you out? Either way, sweetheart, that wasn't only for you. That was for me too," I told her and winked. "Your mistake is an assuming people don't have ulterior motives for what they do. But of course you are wrong. Everyone has a motive."

"Oh yeah, what's yours?" she asked, sitting up and giving me an eyeful of her gorgeous tits. "Hey, eyes up here while we're talking!" Martina snapped her fingers in my face, but I still stared at her tits. I couldn't help it.

"Sweetheart, you know what my motive is," I growled and pressed my lips between her two beautiful mounds.

"Oh my God, Mitch," she said like she was exasperated, but I heard the moan as I started sucking on her right nipple. "Can you not think about your dick for like five minutes?"

"But honey, if you just let me show it to you, you'd see why that's the case," I said, only half teasing.

At that point, my dick was so fucking hard I wondered if I broke it with wanting this woman. Martina raised both eyebrows. She leaned back and I could see where her naked sex was pressed against my dick. There was a wet spot on my jeans and it was growing, and fuck, that was hot.

"Are you saying if I see your dick, it will be all I can think about every five minutes?" she asked in what I assumed was her lawyer voice.

Shit. That was hot. So fucking hot. My lips twitched. So did my cock.

"Yep," I replied, slapping my hands on her ass and squeezing. "That's what I'm saying."

"You are so fucking conceited," she growled, winding her fingers through my hair, and kissing me again.

Fuck, I was mad for this woman. Completely out of my mind. There were so many facets to her, I was always learning something new. And I couldn't wait to discover more.

"It's not conceit if it's true. To put it plainly, I am packing, baby," I growled, thrusting my tongue down her throat.

I held her face in my hands, wrapped one around her neck as I kissed her hard and long. When I finally let her up for air, her eyes were glowing, and I was completely captivated by the purple flames I saw dancing there.

"Okay, Mitchell. Let's see you back up that boast."

"What?" I asked, still caught up in her eyes.

Martina scooched off my lap, and I growled, reaching for her again. She wagged her finger and nodded towards my lap.

"Drop your pants."

"Martina," I began.

Lunch break was almost over, and I knew we

needed more time than we had to finish this here. My plan had been to get our asses in my truck so I could take my mate home to claim her. But that wasn't going to happen if I took my dick out.

And yet, I wasn't ready to stop all this yet.

"Mitchell," she countered. "Drop. Your. Pants. Now."

CHAPTER NINE MARTINA

WHOEVER SAID DESIRE WAS A LIVING, breathing thing had obviously met Mitchell Truman. My entire body seemed to throb to the beat of his drum, and I was putty, soaking wet, horny as fuck, putty in the man's very large and capable hands.

I'd searched him out at the construction site Timothy had said he'd be at with the intention of speaking to him in a calm, adult-like manner. Of course, that lasted all of two seconds. It was like just knowing the tall, sexy as hell man was possibly my mate had fried all my circuits. I couldn't do anything other than slam my mouth to his and drink down every drop of that smoky, spicy masculine essence that was all him.

We were both breathing like marathon runners by

the time he'd finished eating me out. The man knew how to use his tongue and I appreciated that, sincerely and deeply. That sort of talent should never be wasted, and while I'd had lovers in the past, no one had a goddamn thing on Mitchell Truman.

Holy. Hell.

Even then, I felt my magic sizzling beneath my skin. My Wolf was standing at attention, both supernatural sides of me watching as our mate ravaged me with his impossibly soft lips and incredibly versatile tongue. Desire flooded my brain and pulsated through my core, even though I just orgasmed minutes ago.

The fact he was still the same charming, sweet, and funny man as before, even after he'd wrecked my body, just made me fall a little faster. Our easy banter turned into a contest, and soon I was standing in front of him demanding he drop his pants.

What the hell was wrong with me? I knew he was working. Knew it was lunchtime, and he was probably expecting someone at any minute, but I could not seem to help myself. I'd been sitting on top of that thick, long, hard a steel bat beneath his jeans for the past few minutes, and the idea of seeing him, naked and wanting, was doing the naughtiest things to my body.

He was good at teasing me. I never knew sex could be playful and funny, something to be thoroughly enjoyed in every sense. And no, we hadn't actually had inter-course yet, but we were going to. Every nerve ending I had sparked with anticipation at the thought. My skin warmed, and I closed my eyes, using all my strength to control the fire I felt sizzle just beneath the surface.

"Martina," he growled as if in warning, but that just made my blood burn hotter for him.

"Mitchell," I growled. "Drop. Your. Pants. Now."

His hazel eyes glowed gold, and I saw something huge and chestnut brown in his gaze. Was that his Wolf? I paused, shocked. I thought I saw flames, but maybe that was a trick of the light. Mitchell hissed out his breath, chest heaving as he unbuttoned his pants and dragged the zipper down slowly. Then, in a move so swift he seemed to blur, Mitchel shoved down his jeans and briefs, and holy mother fucking shit, the man was not conceited or boastful.

"It won't fit," I whispered, eyes bulging as I watched him grip the base of his enormous dong.

"It will fit, sweetheart," he growled.

His cock was so primed and hard. Thick veins and ridges covered the thing, and oh my fucking shit, he was pierced. Three thick barbells were just under his mushroomed head, a Jacob's ladder and I wondered who did them. My Wolf snarled, and his head canted to the side.

"I pierced myself," he growled, his voice deeper than ever before.

Under my rapt gaze, Mitchell started stroking himself and I felt moisture pool between my thighs. I stepped towards him, but he shook his head.

"No touching yet, baby. First, I'm gonna sit down, then I want you to stand on the couch, right above me," he commanded.

Nerves assailed me, but there was a part of me that liked him taking command and telling em what to do. I watched as he kicked off his boots and clothes, completely naked, he sat on the couch, his big, thick thighs spread as he cupped his balls and stroked his massive erection. My mouth was watering, and I could not keep my eyes off his ministrations.

Mine.

"Up here, baby," he grunted, and I moved, standing on the couch beside him.

He stopped touching himself long enough to position me where he wanted me. I felt exposed and open, my pussy right at eye level. Arousal dripped down my thighs, and Mitchell breathed in deep, his heated gaze meeting mine. The smile on his lips was feral and wicked, and I shivered in response.

No one ever looked at me like that before. Like he was the Big Bad Wolf, and I was Red Riding Hood. Only, I was a Wolf too. Big and bad in my own right.

Mitchell's growl grew louder as his tongue snaked out of his mouth and found my clit. How he knew exactly where to touch me, I had no idea, But his fingers dug into my hips and my ass, and I was a goner.

"Oh fuck," I moaned.

I had nothing to hold on to but him, nothing to steady me, and he knew it, the fucker. I felt his smile as he licked at me in slow, long swipes of his tongue. My legs shook and I could hardly stand, which seemed to suit him just fine. He grabbed one thigh and draped it over his shoulder, trying to do the same to the other.

"I'm too heavy, I'll suffocate you," I said, *er*, gasped really since he hadn't let up.

"Get up here, sweetheart, or you won't get what we both know you really want."

I frowned and tugged him by the hair, using it as leverage to pull myself up onto his shoulders. Mitchell just grunted. His eyes were bright with his Wolf and they locked into mine before he buried his face between my legs. I never thought I could do anything in that position. But Mitchell was built like a god, and he held me up and ate me out until I came again, harder than before. Thrusting his tongue into my tight slit and using his nose to rub my clit until I screamed with my release.

The sound of engines in the distance worried me. We would have to stop soon. But they didn't even slow

Mitchell down. He just lifted me off his face, apparently done devouring me, and I slid down his body, leaving a trail of my slick and his saliva down his rock hard pecs and incredible abs.

The animal inside me loved that I'd marked him with my scent, and while my human side might think it icky later, I had to admit it was a serious turn on. Mitchell was just so damn gorgeous. All his worry about my not being into him because he was a construction worker was ridiculous. Also, he owned his own company. That took brains and skills, not to mention courage and a certain amount of grit.

There was nothing about him I didn't find attractive. The fact he wanted me, while baffling, was enough to earn my interest. But it was the rest of him that made me want to learn everything I could about him. I burned with a need to be near him, hated the last few days without him. True, I'd felt positively sick and I could only explain it as our semi-formed matebond kicking my ass so I would go back to him to finish the job.

"Mine," he growled, holding me high for just one more second before he slammed me down onto his cock.

"Yours. Mitch. Yours. Please. More, Mitchell. Gimme more. Gimme all of it."

I didn't know what I was saying, but I meant every

word. I needed him like I never needed anything. It was like all the missing pieces of me were suddenly being pulled from the very recesses of my soul, but I wasn't scared. I rejoiced in the feelings he was conjuring inside me.

Mitchell Truman. Mate. Mine.

Yes, that sounded right. It felt right, and my Wolf howled inside my mind's eye, hoping to reach his beast. One big hand gripped my hip, and the other held me by the neck so he could kiss me while he moved me to the pace he set. It was too much too soon, and before I had even started to match his rhythm, I was already coming.

"Oh Go—"

My words cut off, and I was incapable of speech as Mitchell really took over then.

His thick length stretched me, splitting me open, as he lifted me and slammed me back down, fucking me on his dick. I felt so full, so complete, it was difficult to know where I ended, and he began. Maybe we were just one being, separated by atoms, and forced back together during sex to our true state. For real. That could be true. I'd have to ask Nova. Fact was, I had never felt more like myself than I did with him inside me.

"Mine, mine, mine," he growled over and over again,

owning my body as he took me with a ferocity that bordered on violence.

I'd never expected to find a mate. Never thought I would share myself with anyone else. Maybe it wasn't fair because he didn't know the truth yet. But I swore I would tell him everything.

There was something to be said about the Fates. When they matched up pairs, they did it perfectly. It was like Mitchell's body had been made just to fit mine. His cock stroked inside me, hitting my g-spot every fucking time, and I was sobbing by the time my next release hit.

That time, Mitchell's need had caught up with him, and he jerked upward his roar muted by the fact he had my neck in his mouth and that was when he struck. Biting my flesh, he sank his fangs deep, and the pain was blinding. But it was followed by a release so strong, I went blind, deaf, and dumb for a full minute.

It was like he had shattered my reality, ripped it to shreds, then reassembled the pieces only this time they were changed. He was embedded in every cell. And as he pumped his hips, filling me with his release, I saw flames, and they were beautiful. Still panting, Mitchell looked up, a tiny trail of crimson spilled from his lips, and I went to wipe it, feeling wonderful and loved.

Tears blurred my vision, and I reared back. Fuck. How had this happened again?

"Sweetheart," he murmured, eyes wide as he watched the flames spread from my hands across my skin.

"I'm sorry. I'm sorry." I whispered, stumbling over our discarded clothes.

"No, no, no. Dammit, don't you do it," he growled, but I knew what I had to do.

"No, Martina, wait—"

The sound of someone traipsing up to the trailer gave me all the distraction I needed to start my shift, and by the time Timothy opened the door, I had already Wolfed out. I bumped into him as I raced outside, the sound of Mitchell's roar echoing in my ears.

I darted through a crew of men and women, ignoring the gasps and snarls from the ones I startled. I supposed it made sense Mitch would hire Shifters. But that didn't matter right then. My vision was all reds and oranges and I knew I was seconds away from flaming out. That kind of uncontrolled use of my powers hadn't happened to me since puberty.

Usually, it was extreme stress or emotion that brought my magic out to play when I wasn't ready. Over the years, Davian, and Erryn, and sometimes Sherry Morgan, had worked with me to use my Wolf to stop the magic from consuming me. Wolf could handle my little fire bug tendencies. Whatever force controlled these things had made sure when I was born with both

Fire Witch proclivities and a beast inside me, they granted protection to my animal.

My fire could not hurt my Wolf. But that didn't ring true for anyone else. How many bedding sets had I burned through in my youth? How many times had I put my sisters, Davi, and Erryn in danger because of my powers? No. I could not risk doing the same thing to Mitchell.

Devastation had me howling as I ran through trees and bushes. The pine barrens were like this vast series of forests in South Jersey made of gnarly looking trees and shrubs. To the normals it looked probably half the size as it truly was. Supernaturals had started masking the world's precious places centuries ago, and this place was no different. What seemed like acres to the human world could be miles and miles to us supes.

All I knew as I ran in my fur were the trees looked like giants, and I felt small and hollow. Flames blazed across my fur, and I prayed like hell the cold and snow would stomp them out before I did any harm to this magical place.

Where I ran, I saw mostly pitch pines and several varieties of oaks, mostly black. Maccon City was surrounded by them on one side. So many legends involved this place, and I felt the power and magic of it as I ran in my Wolf form. How many of them were true? I didn't know, though I'd heard the Devil, the

Jersey kind and not the Prince of Hell, and his family lived there still.

Harbor House sat at the edge of the barrens, on the outskirts of Maccon City, and I don't know how long it took, but eventually I recognized the special stand of scarlet oaks that stood like sentinels at the back of our home.

My Wolf was snarling and snapping, the animal torn between needing to go back and needing to protect him. Protective instincts won out and even my flames died down as I crawled through our backyard, broken and angry.

The back door flew open, and Nova and Sybil ran out. It was too early for either of them to be home, and yet, there they were, and the pain and sympathy on their faces were too much to handle. I shifted to my skin and screamed.

"Martina, I am so sorry," Sybil whimpered and ran to me, covering me with a blanket as she hugged and cried with me.

"Come inside, Marti. I have tea waiting and we can talk," Nova whispered, her expression dark and full of concern.

"Davi and Erryn aren't here," Sybil added, holding onto my hand like a lifeline.

I allowed them to usher me inside, needing the comfort of my family around me. They didn't pause in the kitchen like I expected. Instead, they shoved me right towards the shower, and I supposed they were right. I was covered in mud and soot. That sometimes happened when my fire came out unexpectedly.

I washed my body and shampooed my hair to get the smoky smell out. Then I simply stood still, letting the hot water sluice over my body as I tried to make sense of what had just happened. The Fates were fucked up. Giving me a mate only to show me it was impossible for us to be together.

Seriously. What. The. Fuck.

I was already resigned to the fact my career was over. I no longer wanted a life practicing corporate law in New York City and dating men who could never know me. I wanted to come back home. To be with my family and figure out a way to bring balance to my Wolf and my magic. That part was settled.

So why did Mitch have to walk into my life and change all my plans? Why did everything have to get so fucked up? I sobbed and sank down to the bathtub, shoulders shaking hard as I poured out all my wretchedness and misery and allowed it to wash right down the drain.

"Talk to us, Marti," Sybil implored.

I knew the girls were sitting on the bathroom rug side by side, waiting for me to explain, just like when we were kids. So I talked. I told them everything. Well, mostly everything, but they didn't need all the details. I told them the gist of things and that Mitch had claimed me and I thought it was okay. Then my Wolf went dark, and my powers came out and I almost burned down his whole fucking trailer.

"But you didn't actually hurt him?" Nova asked, and I could almost see her scientific cogs turning inside that pretty head of hers.

"But I could have."

"But you didn't. You stopped. You got out of there," Sybil said,

"That's not the point," I argued, standing up and turning off the water.

Nothing motivated me like anger, and they were pissing me off. I couldn't have Mitch. Period. Why beat a dead horse? I grabbed a robe and towel, wrapped it around my body then my head.

"But Marti, you are so lucky. You found your fated mate. I don't think you should just quit," Sybil said, and I growled my fury.

"Quit? You think I want to quit?"

"Well, it's not like you're fighting for him," Nova pointed out, and I screamed again, walking out of the bathroom.

What happened to the comfort they were supposed to bring me? I shook my head, stomping towards our bedroom, both of my sisters hot on my heels. I turned around and snapped my jaws, and they slowed down, but continued to dog my steps.

This was not helping. I dressed angrily, shoving my feet into socks, and pulling on a pair of pajama pants and a tank top. I angry-brushed my hair, and yes, it fucking hurt.

"Maybe ease up before you tear it all out, Marti," Nova murmured, and I snarled again.

At this rate, I was going to Wolf out again in no time. Fuck it. That was not important. Nothing was. The only thing that mattered was I could never have a mate. I was a total fucking hazard. A danger.

"Sweetie, you are not a hazard. Mitchell would be lucky to have you—"

"Mitchell can't have me! No one can," I yelled, and stomped my way through the house to the living room.

Sybil and Nova raced behind me, but I was so done with them. I didn't want them talking to me about possibilities that were not possible at all! It was making me crazy. Couldn't they see that it was gutting me to do this? It was killing me to admit that I was so fucked up, I had to leave my fated mate to save him.

"Did you even tell him the truth? Did you tell him what you are?" Nova asked.

"No. I didn't."

"So you're telling me you decided you are this

danger to him and therefore you know better than the Fates themselves?"

"Yes. No. What? Nova, I have the worst fucking headache in the world right now and my heart is literally broken. Fuck whoever set this thing in motion if it's the Fates, then yes, fuck them. I do know better. How the fuck could I live with myself if I hurt him? It isn't worth the risk."

"So, you are drawing the conclusion that your Fated Mate is better off without you, and you aren't worth the risk without even testing your hypothesis? That's just sloppy work, Marti," Nova said and tsked.

Fucking scientist.

"Marti, you should talk to him. At least give him the chance to decide what he wants," Sybil argued.

My blood was boiling. I could feel my magic sparking inside of me, and while it was nice not to be dead inside anymore, to hear my Wolf and feel my powers, I was so not about to hurt either of them. Even if they were kind of asking for it. I spun on my heel, cracking my neck as I inhaled and tried to remember those breathing exercises I used to do when I was a kid.

Inhale. 1, 2, 3. Exhale. 1, 2, 3.

"Look, I know you want to help. But you can't."

"But you only just came home," Sybil whispered, tears welling in her eyes.

Fuck. I hadn't even considered that I would have to

leave. That Harbor House could not be my home anymore. There was no way I could stay in Maccon City and risk running into Mitchell at every turn. Fuck. Fuck. FUCK.

"I'll figure that out. You know I can't stay here," I replied, letting my own tears run down my cheeks.

"No. There has to be another way," Nova yelled, and I knew she was mad.

Almost furious. Wind whipped around her, making her black hair fly this way and that. Sybil gasped, and I growled. Shit. We were about to have a full on magical fucking frenzy if I didn't diffuse this shit.

"Stop," I said.

But Nova was breathing too rapidly, and the air around her was crackling with energy. Sybil's reaction was worse. Green scales started to pop out on her skin and if she shifted into her beast inside, well, the house would be fucking destroyed.

"STOP!" I roared, and power infused my command.

Both of my sisters covered their ears and bent their heads, averting their gazes while I tried to rein in whatever the fuck that was. They looked frozen in place, and that scared the shit out of me. The very air seemed to sizzle with power, and I was stunned and scared, but I thought maybe it was my emotions that were setting the scene.

So, I did my breathing thing again. My arms were

already open, hands raised like Moses parting the Red Sea, and I lowered them, forcing myself to calm down. After a moment, both of my sisters were able to move. They looked at me, shocked but not angry.

"Wow, Marti. Did you just command us?" Nova whispered.

"She totally did. Oh, my God! You know what this means, right?" Sybil asked, and she seemed really fucking excited for some reason.

"What?" I asked, for some reason I was always late to the party.

"You're the Alpha. We always figured you would be," my petite sis added, and she was all but glowing.

"What?"

"Sybil is correct," Nova said, brushing her hair back with her fingers. "You're our Alpha. The leader. The one calling the shots."

"What the hell are you talking about?"

"Witch Shifter Clan!" Sybil shouted and clapped.

"What?"

"Witch. Shifter. Clan." Nova enunciated like I was hard of hearing.

I'd heard her all right. I just didn't believe it. My heart thundered inside my chest and the door opened and closed behind me. I couldn't face Davian and Erryn just yet, so I continued to give them my back.

"You can't leave us, Marti. You're the Alpha of our

Clan. We need you," Sybil said, and something inside of me clicked.

"That's right. We do. Besides, you and Mitch have to work this all out."

"I-I, no, I mean, Alpha?" I whispered, shaking my head.

But it felt right. My Wolf growled and my power surged. Both sides of my being seemed to know this was the right place for us. I stared at the wall opposite where I was standing and flicked my gaze over the bookshelves and old pictures hanging up. Harbor House was my sanctuary, and it would be wonderful not to leave.

But what about Mitch? My heart hurt, the pain so bad I gasped as I placed my hand over my chest. Nova and Sybil stepped closer, and both put their arms around me. Any other time, I'd just shrug them off, but I needed them. The bickering and the arguments were nothing serious. Sometimes you had to shout to be heard in a gaggle full of girls. It was this, the comfort and support that my sisters gave me that I truly needed and loved them for.

We'd always been peas in a pod. The three Musketeers with Davian and Erryn cheering us on and helping us grow. God, I was so lucky. Even when I was in denial about who I was, they were there for me. Always having my back and letting me find my way.

How had I stayed away so long? New York was exciting at first, and different. There was no pack to hide from, and no one to call me on my bullshit. New York was easy. That was why I'd stayed. But look what I had missed? My heart was constricting so damn hard I could hardly breathe.

"Do you love him?" Sybil asked.

Love? I'd never thought I was the type of person to fall in love or have a mate. Fated mates were just fairytales, made up stories, they told little Shifters before bed. I never expected the Fates to pay any attention to me, and maybe they shouldn't have. Maybe my heart wouldn't be breaking if they had just left me alone.

My Wolf howled and the pain I felt from my powers hit me right in the gut. I gasped, but I could only nod. Nova squeezed my shoulder, and I knew she wanted to argue some more. But there was nothing to say. Alpha or not, I couldn't hurt him.

"He might surprise you, you know," she whispered.

"Even if he was fine with me being a Wolf and a Fire Witch, I couldn't ask him to live like that. I mean, who would want a mate who could potentially burn the fucking house down every time she got angry, or happy, or horny?"

"That is a lot, but if the sex is good, could be worth it," Sybil teased.

"Come on. Seriously, who the fuck would be crazy enough to want me in their life?"

"Me."

The sound of a deep, masculine voice behind me brought all the hairs on the back of my neck standing straight up. I covered my mouth with my hand, body tensing, and tears pricking my eyes. Sybil and Nova released their hold on me, and I spun around.

When the front door had opened, I expected Erryn and Davian to be there, had even scented them. And they were there, standing in an embrace as they witnessed the entire drama that was my life unfold.

But I wasn't expecting *him* to be there. Seeing him standing not ten feet away, looking better than anyone had the right to, Mitchell Truman simply stole my breath away. His hair was tousled, and he had on a t-shirt and jeans, his boots unlaced. It was freezing out, but he didn't have a jacket.

He smelled like fur and the elements, and that smoky, spicy scent that I loved that was all his and his alone. Had he run out in the cold after me? My gaze ran over him from head to foot, but I'd been avoiding his face. When I finally found my courage to look at him, I gasped.

Mitchell's eyes were red and his frown deep as he stared at me with such longing and tenderness on his face. He held his hand out and for one second, I was completely frozen. Then I was running and jumping towards him, leaping into his arms. He caught me, of course, hands on my ass as he slammed his mouth to mine and claimed my lips in a kiss that rocked my entire world.

I barely heard the cheers and wolf whistles of my family as Mitch spun me around and around, kissing me until I forgot all my worries, all my cares, everything, and anything except him. Only him. My him.

Mate.

CHAPTER TEN MITCHELL

THE MONSTER inside me was about to rip right through my skin if I didn't make myself known. But I couldn't. Not yet. Martina was in the middle of something huge, a moment of complete self-awareness, and there was no way I was going to interrupt her. Yeah, my heart had cracked a little when she'd run. Leaving me alone after a second and even better encounter that left my dick aching for her and my brain so fucked up, I couldn't even think straight.

Fuck. She ran. Again.

The monster demanded my skin, and I gave it. Tracking her through the woods like a homing pigeon. But this was no ordinary hunt. Martina wasn't some fluffy bunny I was chasing down, intending to gobble her up for a midnight snack. Not that I wouldn't mind eating the woman.

Grrr.

But baser instincts aside, she was my mate. My woman. And I already gave her my bite. She belonged to me. Forever and always. I just had to prove I was the right man for her. The only man who could handle everything she could dish out, and from the sound of things, that was a whole fucking lot. My woman packed a powerful punch, and it was my favorite fucking kind. Fire.

Fire Witch. Wolf. Fire Wolf. Mine.

Davian and Erryn stood silently beside me, wrapped in an embrace I was so fucking jealous of I couldn't even look at them. Martina had just showered, her hair was still wet, and the sweats and tank top she wore hugged her curves in ways I only dreamed about being able to do. Her back was towards me and I almost laughed at the joke the universe was playing on me.

If there was one surefire way to catch my attention, it was with that ass. Seriously, all that female had to do was flash her backside in my direction. Fuck yeah. She had the perfect ass. Perfect face. Perfect brain. Perfect heart. And I didn't mean in the sense that she was better than everyone else. Martina was just perfect for me.

She was my mate. My everything. And the only

thing I needed. Martina Harbor was without a doubt the one soul in the universe that matched mine. And after hearing her deepest, darkest fears and secrets, I knew we were a match in every single way.

My Wolf cried out for me to go to her, but a hand on my arm stilled my progress. I glanced down at Erryn who shook her head, beckoning me to wait. Good thing it was her who'd touched me. The female had always struck me as someone not to fuck with.

She nodded towards where Martina was in deep discussion with her sisters, and my gaze snapped back to my mate. I watched her shoulders slump and my heart pounded hard beneath my ribs. This was killing me. Watching her suffer was like the worst kind of torture. I wanted to go to her to soothe her and reassure her. I'd never expected to meet my mate, but now that I had, I never wanted to let her go.

Patience. Be patient.

I waited a beat longer, my fingers itching to have her in my arms once more. I wasn't cut out for this waiting shit. I wanted her here, now. I needed to tell her she was wrong. That we could make it if she'd just give us a chance. Then she asked her sisters the one question guaranteed to make me break my silence.

"Come on. Seriously, who the fuck would be crazy enough to want me in their life?" she asked and fuck, my pulse started racing.

"Me," I said without hesitation.

Me. I was crazy enough to want her in my life. Her and any magic or mischief she brought with her. I held out my hand, and she looked at me with her gorgeous violet eyes filling with tears. Was I too late? Did I stay quiet too long?

Then her nose twitched, and she moved, ran actually, till she was right in front of me. And did my girl pause for even a second? Fuck no. My badass mate jumped right for me, knowing I'd catch her, and yeah, I fucking did. I would always catch her. Slamming my lips to hers, I kissed her, desperate to devour as much of her cinnamon apple flavor as I could with that one meeting of mouths.

I didn't care about our audience or the fact her family was losing their minds, cheering, and whistling at us. They were great, but all that extra needed to wait. All I cared about was how right it felt to have her in my arms. And I had important business to tend to.

Now. Right now.

"Come with me," I growled, carrying her outside to my truck.

"Wait," she said, but I was not about to let her go for anything.

"No," I grunted, stomping through the icy slush that had fallen after my arrival.

But my monster was riled, and I was feeling like the

motherfucking post office. Neither rain, nor sleet, nor snow, hail, or a motherfucking supernatural disaster was going to blow us off course this time. My sexy little Fire Wolf had run out on me twice now, and now that I knew her little secret, I was jumping up and down inside.

A Wolf and a Fire Witch? Holy fucking shit. No wonder she drove me wild. Sexy little badass. Woman of my heart. God, I fucking loved her.

"Mitch? Mitch? Where are we going?" Martina asked, her violet eyes wide as I sped down the back roads to my place.

"I got something to show you," I growled, my voice deeper than usual.

My beast was riding me hard. The monster inside me had gone completely fucking ballistic when Martina took off like that. I hoped it was the last time, but you never could tell.

Eventually, I found her at her house, and when I knew she was safe, I went back for my truck. My plan was to kidnap her ass and keep her coming on my dick till she was too damn exhausted to run away. I know, I know, kidnapping isn't okay, but I was desperate at the time and not thinking very clearly. Anyway, I didn't do it.

After hearing her confess to her sisters what she thought was an impediment to our mating, I wanted to jump for joy. Then she said she loved me, and my heart fucking exploded. I loved this woman so damn much. She had no idea. But I was going to show her. If it took the rest of my life, I was going to show Martina Harbor exactly what she meant to me.

I pulled into the gravel driveway of the single-family home I bought a few years ago and renovated. It wasn't a bad house, pretty nice actually. But I would sell it in a fucking heartbeat and move wherever the hell she wanted if it meant I got to live with Martina. Besides, it wasn't the house I wanted to show her.

"This your place?"

"Yes," I growled, jumping out of my seat and running for her door before she had time to open it herself.

"Thanks," she whispered, ducking her head.

Sweet, sexy woman was acting shy and nervous, and that made me one protective motherfucker. Because I couldn't help myself, I backed her against the truck and lifted her till she was eye level, then I kissed her again. Deeply, slowly, and thoroughly, I kissed her until both of us were breathing like we'd just climbed a fucking mountain. That's what it felt like to me. But I would do more than that to win this woman. I would do anything.

"You have a nice house," she said.

I relished the feeling of her pressed against me.

Every soft curve seemed to mold to my body as I let her slide down until her feet hit the ground. She smelled delicious. Spicy cinnamon apples mixed in with my smokier musk, and fuck, I loved the heady combination.

"Thank you."

"Um, where are we going?" she asked when I grabbed her hand and practically dragged her behind the house.

"Shed."

Fuck. I was speaking in one-word answers. The woman had me so damn crazy I couldn't think long enough to form a complete sentence. My dick thumped inside my jeans, and I growled.

"What's in the shed? Mitch? Oh, my—"

She gasped and stared in wide-eyed wonder as I revealed my secret place to her. Martina was not the only one keeping things under wraps. I had one whopper of a secret myself. And it was time I showed her.

"Mitch, look, I am happy you came back for me, but I have to tell you. I'm messed up. You don't understand why I left, but I was scared I'd hurt you. I don't know whether I'm coming or going. I thought I was sick, maybe dying. I know it was silly, but my Wolf and Witch powers were gone, and I really felt like I was lost, but then you came into my life and both of them are back, and raring to go. I'm torn between being happy and scared. I could hurt you—"

It hurt me to see her so upset. She was trying so hard to tell me everything, but she needed to hear my truth first. I needed her to listen.

"I promise, baby, it will be okay. Just watch."

The rustle of my shirt was loud in the shed as I took it off, my shoes next. She was watching carefully, looking side to side, and fuck, I loved her. Loved how brave she was. How honest. Oh, she didn't think she was, but just look at everything she'd done. Spilling her guts, trying to keep me safe. She was the best damn woman I had ever met, and I was so proud I caught her attention. I intended to keep it, too.

This fierce, proud, hardworking female deserved to have someone in her corner. And that someone was me. She needed time yet, and a constant, steady love, and I planned to give that to her. When she was ready, this woman was going to shine. Her sisters had called her Alpha, and I fully believed them. She was a leader. A caregiver. A nurturer with a heart like gold.

"What is this place?" she asked, facing me.

"It's a safe place. Like Harbor House is for you. This is my shed. It's a place I can change without fear or worry."

"What do you mean?"

"Sometimes the animal needs something other than

the typical Wolf run with the Pack. Sometimes I need more."

"I don't understand, Mitch. Look, we have a lot to talk about—"

Martina walked right up to me, placing her hand on my chest and fuck, it felt so good to have her touch me. Her luminous eyes were like two velvet pools of purple, and I wanted to sink right into them more than I wanted anything. But first, she needed to know. I had to show her.

"We do, sweetheart, I agree. But first, let me show you my secret, Martina."

"Okay, Mitch, and I promise, I'll keep your secret safe," she whispered, kissing my chest where her hand rested.

She stepped back, a frown on her face, and I moaned at the loss of her touch. The woman was hell on my nerves, but before we got to the kissing part, she needed to see. I stripped off my clothes, smirking when I caught her staring and laughing softly when her cheeks burned pink.

Sexy little Wolf.

Usually, calling my monster Wolf took a minute, but I was more than ready for my sweet mate to meet my other side. My change was fast and rough, and Martina yelped, falling back on her ass. I growled as smoke and ash swirled around my monster's body.

During normal shifts, my Wolf was like most Were-wolves. Big, muscular, strong, and fast. But there were nights when my *other* needed release. When the monster came out to play.

"Mitchell," Martina whispered as I stalked over to her on four legs.

Her eyes were wide with wonder, and I opened my jaw, chuffing and growling softly. I did not want her to fear me, so I moved slowly with caution. I never allowed anyone in my space except for Timothy, and he wore protective gear to ensure I didn't hurt him.

"Wh-what are you?"

I allowed her to look her fill and stood frozen when she finally reached out with trembling hands to stroke my flame-covered fur. A few more strokes, and I was done for. I needed to feel her hands on my skin, so I swapped places with the monster, allowing him one small lick across her cheek before I was back in my human body.

Changing was always accompanied with a certain amount of pain and sensitivity afterwards, but I didn't give a fuck. I needed Martina in my arms, but I had to know how she felt about this.

"I should have told you—"

"I have so many questions," she said, talking over me.

Her excitement was contagious, and I thanked the

Fates for blessing me with such an incredible woman. We were both on our knees on the compact dirt floor of the shed, and suddenly I felt bad about it.

"Come here, let's sit and talk," I said.

I stood up and took her hand, leading her to another area of the magicked shed where I had a futon and blankets for nights when I wore myself out and crashed there instead of in the house. Martina sat down on the edge and I grabbed a blanket and wrapped it around my waist, figuring it might be easier to talk if my dick wasn't waving around trying to get her attention.

What could I say? I was only human.

Kinda.

"Okay, first question, what was that?"

"My shift?"

"Very cute, wiseass. I mean what exactly are you, Mitchell?" she asked, and I love that she hadn't lost any of her sass.

"I'm glad you asked, gorgeous. You see, I'm a Wolf Shifter, just like you. But like you, I have a little something extra in my bloodline. It skips around the family tree, but every now and then one of us Trumans pops up with it."

"With what?" she asked, and I chuckled.

"Patience, sweetheart, I'm getting there," I teased.

"Mitchell Truman, if you want to see this ass

without clothes again, you will stop fucking around and tell me," she growled and stood up.

Martina was standing right in front of me, a vision of furious beauty. Sparks shot from her fingertips the more annoyed she got, and my dick grew even harder. Biting my lower lip, I grabbed her by the waistband of her sweats and pulled her close.

The scent of her cinnamon flavored arousal filled my nostrils and my chest rumbled in response. I couldn't wait to have her riding my face again, those thick thighs spread for me so I could lick her until she was screaming my name.

Want. Now. Grrrr.

"Nope. There will be none of this until you explain all of that," she quipped, but she was smiling too and when I locked my arms around her, she didn't fight it.

"That was my Hellhound side, sweetheart."

"Hellhound?"

"Yep. Like I said, it skips a generation. But I just got lucky. Sherry Morgan helped magic this shed for me so I would have a safe place to run when my monster needs to ride the dark flames," I explained.

"You're not a monster," she whispered, cupping my cheeks and nuzzling my nose with hers.

"It took a while but me and the Wolf have an understanding, Marti. And now, I know why I was given this bit of extra. You see, baby, I'm fireproof. Seriously, my skin is tough. Nothing you can throw at me, fire balls included, will hurt me. My Hellhound just eats that shit up."

Her lower lip trembled as she looked at me with such emotion filling her eyes.

"What is it, sweetheart?" I asked, scooping her up and gathering her close.

"I fucked up. I ran away—"

"No. You didn't know, and it's my fault too, for not just telling you in the beginning. Please, baby, give us a chance. I know we were meant to be together."

I kissed her tears from her cheeks and swallowed her moan as she tipped her head back and allowed me access to her precious mouth. Our kiss grew frantic in no time at all, and we were pulling off blankets and clothes, kissing, licking, touching everywhere we could reach. This time, I had no intention of stopping. The room was dark and warm from the heat we created between us.

Martina gasped, head tilting back, granting me access to her throat, and I kissed her there, on that special secret spot that made her pant and moan. Fuck, I loved the way she gave her all when it came to loving. Fucking was a physical thing, but this was different. This was a communion of bodies and souls, an intimacy I'd only ever felt with her. I wanted her to take it all. I freely gave her all of me and I was driven by the need to bring her pleasure and peace.

She was a wild thing, writhing around me, filling my head and heart. Hell, I might as well get used to it. The woman was going to be a permanent fucking resident right smack there.

Beautiful. Perfect. Fiery woman.

She seemed to burn with passion, and the hotter she got, the harder I got. Her skin burned like flames, and I was addicted to the feel of her. Power pulsed in the air, and it smelled of cinnamon and spice, fur, and musk. I wanted to be part of that, part of her.

"Love me, fuck baby, love me please," I growled, catching her nipple between my teeth, not even aware of what I was saying.

"I love you so much, Mitch. I love you," she moaned.

"Make me yours, sweetheart. Mark me with your fire and your bite. I can take both," I growled, cupping my hand around her neck as I brought her face to mine. "You're mine, Fire Wolf. My mate. And I am yours. I match you. I can take it all. Give it to me," I begged.

"Need you, Mitch," she nodded and fuck, I was a goner.

She was fire. And I needed fire. Martina was it for me, and I worshipped her with my body, coveted her. Sweet, precious, perfect mate.

"I need you too, baby. You match my soul. Look,

look how perfect we fit," I grunted, pressing my hard length inch by inch into her hot, wet sex.

"See, baby. See how good we fit. I belong to you, and you belong to me. Mine. Our wolves know it and I know you know it too," I growled, moving in earnest, growling with pleasure as I pumped into her harder and deeper.

I didn't know it was possible, but I swear my dick swelled and swelled, stroking along her tight, quivering sheath until my darling Wolf was scoring my back with her claws. Head tipped back, sweat coating our skin, Martina moaned, long and loud, her sex gripping me tight as she started to come.

Fuck, yes. My fangs lengthened, and I bit her again, claiming her on the opposite side where I'd struck before. Hell, I'd probably claim her ten more times before the night was over. The beast demanded it. The man in me loved it. Loved her.

Mine.

"And you are mine, Mitch. You're mine," she growled.

Then my sexy, snarly mate struck, marking me right over my heart. That bite of pain was exactly what I needed to fall over the edge, and I stiffened above her. Our matebond wrapped around us, a flame covered chain that pulsed with love and power. When I opened my eyes, we really were wrapped up in that flame. My beautiful Fire Wolf's eyes glowed purple as she reached up and stroked my face with her flame wielding fingers.

"All my life I thought love was forbidden to me," she whispered.

"You were wrong, and that's okay. I'm wrong like nine and a half times out of ten," I said and smiled, kissing her flame-tipped fingers.

"I love you, Martina. That's the truth of it, and I want to build a life with you."

"I want that, too. I love you, Mitch," she replied, and smiled so wide my heart completely flipped over.

We loved each other slowly after that. Slowly, and thoroughly, all night long. Never once did she hurt me with her flames. Never once did I expect her to. And finally, I felt her open up to me. The bond between us burst wide open, and I felt her love, her desire, and her power pulsing through.

I growled contentedly and held her tight. This was just the beginning.

EPILOGUE MARTINA

"OKAY, SO HERE IS THE PLAN," I said, looking each of my family members in the eye before continuing. "I want to build Harbor House into something bigger. Something more."

"What, like an addition?" Nova asked, face scrunched.

"I suppose we can," Davian started, but I cut off my brother.

"No. I don't mean another bedroom or bathroom. I mean, an extensive renovation project. I have the money. There is nothing to worry about there. And luckily, I happen to know a guy in construction," I said, winking at Mitchell who sat at the table with a wide grin on his handsome as sin face.

"Do you mean," Davi started, surprise making him gasp. "You want to reopen Harbor House."

"You do? You mean like sign up to foster kids, only, we'd help supernaturals who need guidance," Sybil said, clapping her hands with glee.

"Rugrats? Here?" Nova growled, but I could see she was open to the idea.

"This could be good," Erryn murmured, and her eyes darted to my brother.

I knew they could not have children, and this was a way for them to give more of that love they had stored inside them to help others. After all, they'd done a pretty good fucking job with the three of us.

"That means you'll stay and be our Alpha! The Witch Shifter Clan is official!!" Sybil shrieked and the Wolves in the room hunched our shoulders.

"OW! Look, I need to talk to Rafe Maccon about that since it is his territory, but I understand the Pack is a bit more relaxed now," I said, eyes darting to Mitchell's.

After a few more minutes of talking logistics, I took out the plans Timothy had drawn up for us and let everyone go over them. This was still our home, and my sisters and brother and Erryn all had a say in what would happen. But I was excited, and I knew this was exactly what I was supposed to do with my life.

At Harbor House, I knew what it was to have a home. My Wolf and my powers felt better when I was there. And now that I had Mitch, there was nothing I couldn't tackle. He was the perfect man. An amazing cheerleader, and the best lover I had ever had. Like holy fucking shit, I didn't know how he did what he did, but my body seriously thanked him.

He made me feel so good. And not just in the *hey, that was an extra special dicking you just gave me there, pal, thanks* kind of way. More like he made me feel good about myself on the inside and out kind of way. He was a wonderful man, an exceptional mate, and I was one lucky Wolf, er, Fire Wolf. That was the name Mitchell had given me, and I really liked it. So did my beast.

"Hey, sweetheart. You're thinking loud again," he rumbled, kissing my temple and gathering me up in his arms.

I loved that he always needed to touch me. And the kisses. Fuck, yes. I was so on board with his obsessive need to kiss me.

"I think Sybil is going to want more bathrooms, but Davian and Nova, and Err seemed fine with everything," he said.

"Yeah. That's okay, we can try to work another one in the budget," I whispered.

"This is some dream you got, sweetheart. I am damn proud of you," he said, tucking me into his massive side.

I slipped my arms around his waist and hugged him tight.

"Thank you for being willing to support that dream."

"That's easy. I support *you,* sweetheart. You. Period. All dreams included."

A warm feeling filled me, and I recognized our mate-bond flaming up between us. I could see it now, bright and blazing in my mind's eye. My midnight black Wolf and his chestnut brown Hellhound curled around each other in the metaphysical plane where they waited till called.

"You know, you're my favorite dream, Mitch. And you've already come true. You've given me so much," I said, looking up into his glowing hazel eyes.

"You're my fire, baby. I can't live without you."

"I love you."

"I love you so fucking much."

Then he kissed me, and my soul burned with love for him. I sighed, wondering what a fool I'd been to think coming home was hard. I mean, it wasn't easy, but nothing worth it ever is.

Our story was just beginning. The Witch Shifter Clan was in its infancy. And Mitch and I were just starting out. But I had faith in us, in my Clan, my family, and I knew we would reap what we sowed.

Power and fire, beast, and human, we would be a

sanctuary for those on the outside. The ones looking in from the cold. I was determined to honor Mama Anne and Davian and Erryn. And I would devote myself to this, to Mitch, to those we could help by being better and stronger, and fuck knew that meant being together. Oh yeah, this was the beginning, but it was already better than I expected.

"Let's go, sweetheart."

Mitch took my hand and led me outside to his truck. We had an Alpha to see, and a Clan to get recognized by the Council. I didn't necessarily mind the politics of the supernatural world, and my corporate law background actually gave me a leg up on the paperwork I needed to fill out just to get this meeting. Nerves assailed me, but I had Mitch at my side and my family behind me.

The Witch Shifter Clan was about to be official. And we were off to a banging start.

The end.

Thanks for reading Fire Wolf! I hope you enjoyed Martina & Mitchell's story. Please consider leaving a review so other readers can find their story, too.

Have you read The Hybrid Assassin: A Witch Shifter Clan

Prequel yet? To find out more about Davian and Erryn, download their book today
& you can continue the series with book 2 in the Witch Shifter Clan, Snow Fox, here: https://www.cdgorri.com/books/snow-fox/.

Happy Reading!

USA TODAY BESTSELLING AUTHOR
C.D. GORRI
SNOW FOX
WITCH SHIFTER CLAN 2

SNOW FOX

She's a genius with a secret. He's an agent with a grudge.

Being pretty isn't all it's cracked up to be. Nova Harbor would much rather be known for her brain than her symmetrical facial features, stunning bod, and eye-catching coloring.

As a research scientist for the secret section of the US government known as the Division of Paranormal Creatures & Activities, or DPCA for short, getting the big boys to notice her achievements is a heck of a lot harder than getting them to notice her *assets*. She does all she can to stay professional, but frustrations run rampant when she's forced to work with a snobby feline and his oversized ego.

Working for the DPCA has always been Asher Donnelly's dream job since he was a tiny cub. When an investigation leads to evidence of illegal experiments being done on Shifters, Asher is assigned to the case.

He'll do anything to find the culprits, even if it means working with her, the woman the entire DPCA calls *the face*. Asher has no patience for the female whom office rumors say slept her way to a cushy job. The only problem is his Lion is quite taken with the beauty. But Asher has better things to do than chase her fluffy white tail.

Nova is aware of Asher's low opinion of her. But this Snow Fox has nothing to prove. Especially not to a stubborn, butt-sniffing, litter-box-using overgrown house cat!

Will prejudices keep these two from solving the crime? Or will they become more than just co-workers?

Trigger Warnings: The fictional characters in this book deal and discuss heavy issues such as infertility, kidnapping, experimentation, and plots to destroy a species through chemical terrorism. Violence, steamy scenes, and also some over the top obsession and possessiveness between the main characters. This is a paranormal romance where the focus is always on love and HEA, and everything inside these pages is pure fiction. It is not real or intended to harm. This book is written for entertainment. As always, please take care of your mental and emotional health.

PROLOGUE NOVA

DEPARTMENT OF PARANORMAL CREATURES *& Activities. Approximately 3 years ago.*

I'd just finished my first month working for the DPCA as a scientist in their research lab, and I was stoked. The head of the department just informed me he was impressed with my work and was looking forward to watching me grow. It seemed I was exactly what they'd been looking for, and Mr. Anderson assured me I was well on my way to my new position and would have my team running by the end of the quarter.

I thanked him and shook his hand, pride filling me as I left his office. I worked damn hard to get where I was, and it was nice to be appreciated. I had shitty luck with bosses in my past, but Mr. Anderson seemed perfectly fine. It helped that he was older, happily married, and looked me in the eye when we spoke rather than at my body.

When I left his office, a coworker stopped me and said a group of them were headed out to a local bar after hours, I said count me in. *The Thirsty Dog* was a favorite among supernaturals for drinks and apps. It was run by a Werewolf Shifter, a member of the local Pack, and even though I was a Fox, I still thought it was a good idea for me to go.

"Sure, I'd love to. Thanks, Gabe," I told the young male, Gabriel Markovsky, who I'd been shadowing all month.

Shifter friendly establishments were typically rare, but Maccon City was a hotspot for supes. Having grown up on the outskirts of town, I knew the place well. Living at home again after spending the last decade traveling and attending various universities, where I'd earned several degrees and studied under cutting edge scientists and geneticists, was not the letdown I thought it would be. In fact, I was pleasantly surprised by how grounded I felt being back.

Especially after Laz. Ugh. What a douche canoe! Lazarus McNeil was my ex. He was tall, thin, handsome enough to catch my eye, and smart. Very smart. He worked for the same company I interned with in Europe, and we met on the job.

For a while, I thought he was the one. He'd been complimentary and attentive at first. But that mask slowly faded, and I learned the truth about Laz. Along with his nerdy cuteness, he was also petty, cruel, and a master manipulator. It didn't take long to figure out he was using me for my brain, stealing bits of my work and passing it off as his own, then acting surprised when our supervisor praised him for his innovations.

Once I knew he was playing me, I stayed long enough to catch him in the act and out him to our peers. He was furious when asked to prove how he'd reached certain conclusions he stole from me only to discover I'd fed him the wrong information. But that was his problem.

Fucking jerk was too dumb to check the math himself and that was not my fault. I mean, I had every right to be angry. I actually changed myself for that man, playing down my appearance because he was never happy about the attention I received from other men and women. I allowed his insecurities to control me, and it was something I vowed to never do again.

Leaving Prague and that prick behind was the best decision I ever made. Something about being home again settled something inside of me. Like a missing puzzle piece that just sort of clicked back in place. It wasn't perfect, but it was better. Still, making friends was not my forte, but with this job I was determined to try.

I had already promised Sybil I would, and my sister was nothing if not relentless when it came to keeping promises. With Martina, our other sister, living in New York City, Sybil and I learned to rely on each other for painful truths and no holds barred critiques.

"OMG Nova! YES! Just forget that stuck up asshat and go make some friends!"

Sybil's assertiveness only ever appeared when she was talking to either me or Martina, and I grinned as I recalled how she yelled at me when I texted her earlier to ask if I should accept the offer to go out drinking with my co-workers. I was becoming a hermit, and that was not acceptable. But what was even worse was I hadn't had sex in over a year. Hence, the second voice-mail from my sister.

"And while you're at it, get yourself some DICK!"

After my last dumpster fire of a relationship came to a screeching halt, I had to admit this dry spell was longer than expected. As a Witch Shifter hybrid, I had to be more careful about those kinds of things. Keeping the peace between my Snow Fox, who was jumpy as fuck, and my magic, which was unreliable at best, was of the utmost importance.

I'd only just discovered the truth about my inherited Witchiness, and it was not good. Apparently, whoever dear old Dad was, he'd been at least a partially elemental Witch. On its own, that would be fine, except that wasn't where my sperm donor stopped with the good news.

Nope. Apparently, along with my prowess with air magic, I've seemed to have inherited a serious attitude problem—*as in, when my attitude gets out of whack, watch out, world!*

I had to admit I was a little touchier than any of my siblings. Davian, my older foster brother who raised me, along with my sisters, Martina and Sybil, said it was because of the way I perceived attention. Not that I didn't get any. I mean, I wasn't an attention whore or anything. In fact, I preferred to be left alone. But that was exactly what he meant.

"You think the world can't see past your face, kiddo. I concede there is some truth in that statement, but you're a lot more than your looks, Nova. Never forget that."

"What if I do?"

"Then me and the rest of you terrorizing triplets will be here to remind you, and to kick your butt if you need it."

I smiled sadly at the memory. After the breakup with Laz and the mess that came after his thievery was revealed, I was simply depleted. I needed some time to heal my soul, and my ego really needed a boost. Coming home was the right decision.

Davian was the best big brother a girl could ask for.

He still teasingly called me and our sisters triplets. We weren't, but it was fitting since we all shared the same birthday and formed a bond that I believed could rival any biological siblings' bond any day of the week.

Family was awesome. And mine was better than most. I was ashamed deep down because my beast craved more. My magic needed more. Something was missing inside of me, and I was desperate to find it.

So, I went to The Thirsty Dog with some of my peers, and I tried to psyche myself up for the outing. Determined to try to form relationships with my coworkers, to step out of my comfort zone, and to be part of a team. Well, as much as I could be, since they didn't really know, I was going to take some of them to start my own research project for the DPCA.

I couldn't divulge anything about that or why I'd been sought by the heads of our department. But I could shoot whiskey with the best of them. In fact, I was on round three when things got complicated. I'd thought hanging out would help endear me to these people. Just another step in my plan to regroup and establish myself there. To be the best me I could be.

What I wasn't counting on was *him*. Asher Donnelly, a thirty something year old Lion Shifter who was also a top agent for the Division of Paranormal Creatures & Activity. The second he walked through the door of the bar, all my attention was focused on him. He had more muscles than any one person should have and a face that looked as though it were carved by angels. All thoughts of work fled my brain when I saw him. And that was a first.

"Oh no! The new girl is awestruck by our very own Ashman!" Drew, one of my colleagues, snorted as he put down his empty shot glass on one of the tall tables our group occupied on one side of the jumping establishment.

"Ashman?" I'd asked, curious about the newcomer.

"Yeah, like Batman or Superman, but he's Ash, so it's Ashman!" Gabe, a shorter, stouter research scientist who I'd been shadowing all week explained.

I smiled and shook my head. These guys were nerds, but I was used to that. Smart people tended to be on account of the whole socializing made us freak out thing. So yeah, comic books and cult films were our bread and butter. Even me, though I admit I was more a Charmed fan than I was a Marvel or DC kinda gal.

"Aww, come on, Face. Don't look at him like that," Drew said, and his voice had taken on a whiny note.

"Face?" I scoffed. "And look at him like what? Who is that?"

"That's Ashman," Gabe said again and giggled, sounding a lot like a twelve year old girl. I knew because I used to be one.

Sigh.

"Yeah, Face. That's what we call you behind your back," Drew continued, pushing his glasses up his nose. "Although, this is your front. So I guess we're calling you that to your front, too," he said with a dumb little smile as he stared at my boobs.

I tried to let that little jibe slide, but yeah, it bugged me. What were these guys going to do when they discovered I wasn't just there to join their team, but to lead it? The big guns at the DPCA wanted me to lead a team of my own to help with investigations targeting Shifters and other supes, and as I shadowed these guys, I was actually choosing who would be a part of that team.

Drew was seeming less and less likely. Gabe, on the other hand, was okay. At least he wasn't drooling over my tits. I cleared my brain and pushed a glass of water towards the guy. A cheer went up around us, and I turned to see a trio of flighty young things attempting to drag the newcomer onto the dance floor.

Ashman, or whatever his actual name was, extricated himself from their hands smoothly, and something loosened inside of me. I hadn't even realized I was stressed, but there it was. My Fox peered through my eyes, intent on the group of females touching him. His gold eyes locked onto mine and all the noise in the bar seemed to dull. Frowning, he stalked over to the tall table where I was standing between Drew and Gabe.

"What the hell is going on here? What are you two doing out drinking? It's a work night."

"Hey Ashman!" Gabe said, raising his hand for a high five, which the man didn't even acknowledge.

"Whose idea was this?" he asked, his voice deep and stern, sounding a lot like a high school principal and making me all tingly in places I'd ignored for way too long.

Can you say role play? A sudden vision of me bent over a desk while Mr. Ashman spanked me for being tardy to class filtered through my brain and heat filled me. He must have scented my sudden arousal because his eyes found mine again, only he wasn't smiling.

"I don't know who you are, Miss, but these are two of our finest minds and I would rather you didn't mess with their heads for funsies," he growled.

"Did you say funsies?" I asked, stunned by his verbal attack.

"That can't be the only thing you heard from my statement."

"Well, no, but I don't understand," I said, frowning at him.

"Apparently not," he growled, eyes narrowed as he raked me from head to toe with his golden stare.

"Ashman, she works with us. This is the new girl," Drew said, draping an unwanted arm across my shoulders.

I shrugged it off.

"You work for the DPCA?" the newcomer asked, one perfect, golden eyebrow raised.

"I do. Nova Harbor, I'm a scientist. Hey, would you like a drink?" I asked.

I was mesmerized by his masculine beauty. So much so, it apparently short-circuited my brain. There was just so much about him I found intriguing. His direct manner, his intense stare. I just couldn't help myself.

"Do you always invite coworkers out to get drunk during the work week? What was your plan? To lead these two on and then what? You know, I don't know who you got to *know* to get this job, but for the rest of us, the DPCA is more than a means to an end. If you're looking for entertainment, I suggest you look elsewhere and do it discreetly," he hissed and glared down at me like I was an insect.

I swallowed. I was a fucking idiot. While I'd been completely undone by his calculated gaze, practically panting for Mr. Tall Gold and Sexy AF, he was busy making up his mind about me. And none of what he'd decided was good. How stupid of me to mistake his cold assessment for interest, but it was too late now to correct my errors.

Gabe and Drew watched the entire byplay with their mouths agape, and I felt my face burn with embarrassment. I'd been called a lot of things, cold, calculating, and stuck up. But I'd never been called whatever it was he just called me.

Whore?

It was difficult to say since he only made innuendos and references to how I could have gotten my job.

Douche.

"Ashman, you got it wrong. This is *Nova Harbor*. We call her the Face, cause I mean, my gods, have you ever seen such symmetry? She's a total brainiac, and she works with us in the research lab. Oh, and *we* asked *her* out to celebrate her first month—" Drew started to explain.

But I didn't stick around to hear the rest of it.

CHAPTER ONE NOVA

DEPARTMENT OF PARANORMAL CREATURES *& Activities. Present Day.*

"Are you shitting me?" I muttered under my breath.

I just finished adding some new figures to the computer program I had Davian build for my latest research project. But nothing was adding up. People always said numbers don't lie, but this couldn't be right. No way.

"Miss Harbor," a youthful voice interrupted, and I noted Steve, the new intern on his rounds to deliver lunches.

"Doctor," I said, correcting the young man.

"Huh?" Steve squeaked.

"Dr. Harbor is a stickler for rules," Gabe told our intern, and I rolled my eyes at him.

"He's not wrong, Steve. Call me Dr. Harbor. Not Miss. I hold several doctorates on top of being a certified MD."

"Wow. So you're a real doctor?"

"Yes. I am a real doctor. I am also your boss. So, when you address me, call me Dr. Harbor," I said, enunciating clearly.

Poor Steve just stared at me, unblinking, and I swore I could hear his heart beating a mile a minute. Where did they find these guys? I stopped myself rolling my eyes in his face, not wanting to give the kid a complex, but what the heck?

"Sandwich," I said.

"What?"

"Steve, she ordered a roast beef sandwich for lunch. You are here to deliver it, right? Give Dr. Harbor her sandwich," Gabe said, gently patting Steve on the shoulder.

"Yeah, Miss Doctor, um, I mean, Dr. Harbor," he mumbled.

I would have felt bad about embarrassing him, but he'd interrupted my work, and I was a very busy woman. His cheeks were a burning bright pink color as he dug through the enormous cardboard box, he had balanced on the top shelf of a utility pushcart, with dozens of drinks stacked below it. It took him a minute, but he found my sandwich, wrapped in paper, and labeled with the obnoxious nickname the guys in the cafeteria gave me.

The Face.

"Tell that jerk Eddie that unless he wants me to slip something in his water supply that will make all his hair fall out to use my actual name and not this BS next time, got it?" I growled.

"Oh, boy. Okay, Steve, let's leave the doctor alone now," Gabe said, tugging on the kid's arm.

Steve nodded, swallowing audibly as his gaze roamed over me in my fitted black pants and lab coat. It was hardly sexy attire, but if at thirty I wasn't used to being ogled, I guessed I never would be.

Sigh.

"Thank you," I said, waiting for the gangly young man to back the cart out so I could close *and lock* the door. "Gabe, can you please?"

"I am trying," muttered my lab assistant. "Steve?"

"Huh?"

The intern was just standing there. His eyes had that daydream quality to them, all shiny and bright like he wasn't even aware of his surroundings as he stared at my tits, or really, the place where my tits were, since I wore my lab coat buttoned practically to my throat. There was absolutely nothing provocative about my attire. Neither Steve nor anyone else could see a damn thing. Even so, he was staring as if I were laid bare like a goddamn centerfold.

Oh, for fuck's sake.

"Steve!" I yelled his name, and he squeaked, and finally, his eyes met mine.

"Yes, Face. I mean, Miss, *er*, I mean Doc—"

"Get. Out." I said through clenched teeth, and he nodded, taking off like a bat out of hell.

"Sorry, Dr. Harbor," Gabe muttered, following Steve and mumbling something about having to chase his own lunch down the hall.

My stomach growled as the scents of rare roast beef and sharp cheddar cheese with coarse mustard, lettuce and tomato on a French baguette filtered through to my nose. Yum. I was starving. I hadn't eaten anything all day and after being in the lab since four am working on my research, I was definitely ready for a break.

"Well, I see some things never change," a growly, familiar, not to mention irritating, voice said.

I froze in the act of closing the door, wanting to slam it shut. I recognized the speaker. Of course, I did. It was *him*. The bastard who'd basically accused me of earning my job on my back and my knees rather than because of my brains and hard work.

Sure, I was the youngest person to lead a laboratory in the whole history of the DPCA, but that didn't mean I wasn't qualified. Something Asher Donnelly had to learn the hard way. Like when I broke one of my framed degrees I had hanging in my office over his fat Lion head.

Seriously, didn't his neck get tired of having to hold that thing up? Never mind the added weight of all that ridiculously long, flowy, golden hair. Stupid sexy Lion Shifters and their stupid sexy manes.

He must go through a ton of conditioner a week.

"Scientists and philosophers would argue everything is always in a constant state of flux," I quipped.

"Then why do they still call you *the Face*, Hotshot?" he asked in that same voice I wished I didn't find so damn attractive.

I would never let him know how much that voice got to me. And I meant that in every sense of the word. Squeezing my thighs together whenever he was around had become a habit. Thank fuck for the *Emotoblock* spray I used every day before coming into work.

It was a little invention of my own. A spray that could block the particular scents Shifters and other supes identified with certain emotions. Really, how would it look if every male in the office knew how much I was repulsed by them? And on the flip side, this sexy as hell, totally infuriating house kitty was never going to find out just how much he turned me on. Not if I could help it.

"Did you need something, Donnelly? Or did you just

come to stare at my big brain like the rest of your cohorts?"

Okay, I was being hella snarky, but the bastard brought it out in me. Really, it wasn't all my fault. The man ruffled my fur like no one else ever could.

"Now, Hotshot, we both know that ain't what they're staring at," he said with a pointed look at my legs.

"What? I'm wearing pants," I balked, looking down at my slate gray ponte pants, and ignoring that fucking nickname.

For someone who'd basically accused me of being inappropriate with colleagues, he had no problem calling me whatever the fuck he wanted, as long as it wasn't my actual name. Like Nova was hard to remember.

"Yeah, you're wearing pants. They're just painted on like a second skin," he grumbled, followed by something that sounded like *woman's got legs a mile long,* but maybe I imagined that.

Having him in my workspace was bad enough, but having him witness that little exchange was downright humiliating. I wanted to be taken seriously, and that was difficult when everyone looked at you like they were surprised you could speak and stand at the same time. What was it about pretty people that everyone expected you to be dumb?

This asshole.

"Oh, please. Like you should talk with your man-jeggings," I retorted, secretly loving the way he filled out his jeans with super thick thighs a professional rugby player would envy.

I was through with allowing men to dictate how I dressed. I'd changed myself once for a man, and there was no way I was ever doing it again. So yeah, even after the whole bar incident when I'd just started at the DPCA, I dressed the way I always did. I liked fashion. Sue me.

But I always steered clear of leggings and skirts, finding they caused way too much unwanted attention in the lab. Paired with my white lab coat, I saw nothing wrong with the thick, stretchy material of my fitted yet stretchy pants. They were professional and comfy. A total win-win in my book.

"What the fuck is a jegging? These are Levi's," he growled, staring down at the denim straining to contain his enormous legs like he couldn't figure out what I was talking about.

"Oh, um, you got a little," he muttered, looking back at me and I squeaked as I grabbed my napkin.

Fucking. Squeaked.

My inner Fox hung her head in shame as I hurried to clean myself up. What the hell was I doing?

Drooling, Nova. You were drooling, my Vixen seemed

to say from that space inside my mind's eye where she existed until I swapped skin for fur.

Shit. I wiped my mouth and cleared my throat, looking back at my sandwich. I really didn't want to get caught ogling his man parts in all that dark denim, but good lord, I had eyes, dammit. How was I supposed to ignore all that smexy?

The man was seriously built. If I didn't know any better, I'd think he spent all day at the gym, but nope. That magnificent body of his was just another perk of being an apex predatory Shifter. Lions were top of the food chain everywhere, and there was no doubt in my mind Asher Donnelly was king of his jungle.

Why that irked me, I didn't want to know. I had some sense of self-preservation to keep my feelings guarded even if from myself. Animal attraction I could handle. It wasn't like I was in charge of my body's natural reactions to a person. I could only be held accountable for my actions in response to those reactions. So I made sure I didn't act. Not ever.

Anything having to do with Asher Donnelly in a non-work scenario was strictly off limits. The man hated me. He could not stand me at all. The one and only time we interacted outside of the office, I'd barely asked him to have a drink with me and not only had he shot me down cold, but he did it loudly and in front of the whole damn office.

That stuck up pussy cat went so far as to report me to human and non-human resources department. Nothing happened, really. But I was given a warning about the inappropriateness of workplace romances. The research department was drooling for my input on their projects, so they let it go. Chalking it up to me not having had any knowledge of the DPCA's policy on interoffice dating.

Since the supernatural world ran on magic and mates could pop up literally anywhere, there was no official ban on office romance. Apparently, you could date a co-worker as long as he or she or they were not in a position of power and only if both parties consented—which was weird to me because how did you date someone without their consent?

Anyway, I was also told I couldn't flirt or even talk to a co-worker about anything other than work if he or she or they did not want to. Also, if she or he or they was an unbelievable asshat.

Guess which one Asher was? Did you say asshat? WINNER WINNER!

Seriously though, I was humiliated one month into this job and for the past three years, I did my work and went home. The end. No more after office hours drinks. No parties. No socializing. In fact, I did everything I could to avoid any interaction with DPCA officials, but mostly, I just wanted to steer clear of the big, stupid pussy.

"Did you have anything else you wanted to talk about or was it just pants? Perhaps you'd like to criticize my shoes or my blouse?" I asked, picking up my sandwich and taking a large bite.

"Anyone ever tell you to take human bites?" he asked, eyebrows raised.

"Not really, since everyone around me is supernatural," I replied with my mouth full of meat and cheese.

Normally, I had better manners than that, but screw him. He didn't deserve my manners. In fact, I doubted he'd recognize what they were.

"I didn't come to talk fashion, Hotshot, though I'm sure you're more than competent."

I sucked in a breath at the insult. Was that all he saw when he looked at me? He knew damn well how qualified I was for this position. But it wasn't enough. Some people thought being pretty meant everyone handed you everything, but they didn't realize there was a dark flip side to that little quirk.

You see, people don't forgive pretty people for not being perfect. They tend to judge and criticize. When you are under a microscope, everything you do is ridiculed. I recalled the pressure of my younger days. High school and college were the worst.

Being smart wasn't enough, and it did nothing to ease the social pressures of looking the part. Asher

Donnelly should understand. He should be more sympathetic. He was born a Shifter, and not just any Shifter, but a Lion Shifter, and I knew what that meant. He was a prince among his people.

The fact I only grew curious about Lion Shifters after I had met Asher Donnelly was a secret I would take to my grave. I knew all about their Prides and politics. Talk about barbaric. Sure, like wild lions, Lion Shifters lived together in groups called Prides, but unlike their wild cousins, they allowed multiple males to remain under one group.

The need for diversity in order to breed healthy young was a must. Arranged pairings for the sole purpose of making cubs was a practice that still occurred in the 21st Century, and I shuddered to think how many times he'd been put out to stud.

My magic hummed in my veins, but I closed my eyes, willing it away. I kept my Witch side under wraps, force of habit from back when I was a child and the local Wolf Pack had put a ban on magic. No one at the DPCA asked about my status as a hybrid, and that was fine by me. I wasn't exactly bosom buddies with anyone there, and some stuff was simply personal.

"Come on, Hotshot. Let me at least see that face when I talk to you—"

That was it. I'd had enough. This judgy motherfucker had an entire Pride full of females taking care of his furry ass and he was going to give me shit for something I had literally zero say in. He could fuck right off.

"Well, since all I am is glitter, it makes me wonder why you're even here. You know what? Scratch that. I don't give two shits what you're doing here, it's my lunch break, Donnelly. Don't let the door hit you on the way out!" I growled.

"Look, I came here for a reason—"

"Too bad, so sad. Out to lunch."

"You're not out," he corrected, and I rolled my eyes.

"My body might not be, but my mind is."

I'd opened my reading app on my phone and scrolled, doing my best to ignore him, while I pretended to be engrossed in the book I was currently reading. Of course, I'd stopped the deliciously smutty billionaire romance book at the precise moment the hero had the heroine naked and writhing beneath him. I tried not to let it affect me as I took another massive bite of my sandwich.

Fuck. It was good. But not even the perfectly balanced culinary delight could make me unaware of him.

"What are you reading?"

Asher's spicy male scent grew stronger as he moved closer to me. The rumbling hum in his chest sent vibrations through the air, but I'd learned to school my features not to react. He was just so big. So much. So everything. It wasn't fair that he had this kind of effect on me, but life was rarely fair. Asher Donnelly was a real man's man. All the men wanted to be him. All the women wanted to fuck him. Come to think of it, half the men wanted to fuck him, too.

I had no idea what his personal life was like, and it kind of bugged me I didn't. I mean, was he one of the guys who got asked to go for drinks with the crew every weekend? Probably. Did he take dates to those bars? Maybe. I wouldn't know. Aside from the occasional invitation from a few acquaintances, I was one of those people no one wanted as a friend. Especially not my peers. Gabe said it was because I intimidated people. But whatever.

The sound of him clearing his throat reached my ears, and I paused in the act of taking another bite and looked at him slowly. My face was devoid of emotion, and once again, I thanked the gods for giving me the brains to come up with *Emotoblock*. It was the best damn invention I'd ever made, allowing me to hide my emotions from super sniffing Shifters.

"Look, I know you have something important to do, so can you say what you have to say and leave? I only take like ten minutes to eat."

"Dammit, Hotshot," Asher grumbled, wiping a hand over his face. "I didn't mean to start an argument—"

"And yet you always do," I replied.

"Can't figure out why yet?" he asked, golden eyes glowing with his beast.

"What are you talking about, Donnelly?"

"Why don't you ever call me Asher?" he asked, canting his head.

"What are we friends now or something?"

He stood a moment longer, just looking at me like he was disappointed or waiting, but I had no idea why or what for. I refused to put my sandwich back down. I had no appetite left and was really just using it as a bread wrapped meat and cheese shield.

"No, Hotshot. We aren't friends," he whispered, and his words cut like a blade. "But I need you dressed and ready tonight at 8."

"What?!" I yelled, but he just kept walking away.

"8 o'clock, Hotshot. On the dot."

And poof, the fucker was gone.

CHAPTER TWO NOVA

"GABE, what's with the test results for series B? Oh, and I got another complaint from finance saying our supplies and the bills they have don't add up, I need you to call them," I told my assistant.

"On it," he replied.

Fucking bureaucracy. I hated it. I had no time for it. I was a scientist, not an accountant. I looked down at the latest batch of testing of the antidote I developed to counter that garbage GHA was pushing into Shifter's veins. As far as I understood it, their injection was freezing a Shifter into one shape or other, depending on what skin they wore. It accomplished this by eating away at the DNA sequence mutation that allowed for the change.

My antidote was countering it by creating a shield around that sequence mutation. But using the blood of the latest victim, a poor young Hyena who'd been taken from a local club and released back into the zoo in her animal state, my antidote was currently failing. It was like they knew exactly what I was trying to do and countered it accordingly.

"This makes no sense. It's like they know exactly what I am doing and designing their formula to specifically combat what I am doing!"

"What do you mean?" Gabe asked.

"It's like these assholes had a blueprint for my antidote and were already working on ways to counter it before I even finished thinking about it. How can that be?" I muttered.

"Who knows? The GHA is completely insane. Anyway, let's talk about you going into the field with Ashman, *er*, I mean, Agent Donnelly?" Gabe asked with his mouth hanging open.

"That's what they tell me," I muttered, allowing my displeasure to be known.

"Ohmygawd!" Gabe screeched.

"Volume," I said, covering my ears and glaring at him.

He made a face like he was a *real housewife of NJ* instead of the nerdy research scientists who still lived in his Mom's basement and did a little wiggle while chanting that stupid nickname he gave Donnelly.

"Ashman. Ashman. Ashman."

"Ugh, Gabe, come on," I moaned, shaking my head.

Not that it mattered to me where Gabe lived, but I couldn't help but shake my head. The guy was seriously crushing on almost every single one of the DPCA agents we came into contact with, which admittedly, since most of them were Shifters, they were hot. There was just something in the genes. That superior physique that made them attractive even if only on a primal level.

"You're so lucky! I mean, the guy is always warning people away from y—um, nothing. I wanna know how this happened."

"What? No, what were you saying first?"

"Nothing. Never mind. Just, okay, just tell me every-thing," Gabe demanded.

What a weirdo. I rolled my eyes and shrugged, telling Gabe everything that had happened earlier that day while I packed my things and cleaned my workspace. I'd never worked in the field, and I was a little nervous, especially since no one told me exactly what I'd be doing.

After this afternoon's surprise visit, I was called into Mother's office. Mother was a code name, of course, for one of the directors of the local DPCA office. There were any number of them, but red tape and security levels varying meant you never knew for sure exactly who did what.

The man was powerful, even her magic sensed something not quite average about him. He was just under six feet tall, stocky, but she doubted it was fat. Not all Shifters were muscular as Donnelly, but the half-Chinese half-African American male was intimidating without all the extra definition.

"Dr. Harbor, thank you for coming. We're experiencing a shortage of female operatives and we're this close to catching the assholes behind the Global Human Alliance, also known as the GHA, who've been kidnapping and experimenting on Shifters," Mother said, leaving no room for inquiry.

"I understand Agent Donnelly already requested your aid for his current assignment. While we would not typically send a scientist such as yourself out into the field, I believe having you on hand will benefit both Agent Donnelly and any victims of the GHA you might come into contact with. I understand you've made some headway in creating an antidote for the anti-Shifter drug GHA has been working on?"

"Um, yes, sir. I've found a way to halt the drug's progress in shutting down the DNA sequence that allows for Shifters to swap bodies. The GHA drug is designed to make shifting impossible from one form to another. They haven't been able to make the change permanent yet, but they are close, sir."

"Outrageous," Mother growled in an impossibly deep voice.

"Agreed, sir."

"And that is why you and Agent Donnelly will stop them."

"Can you believe he wouldn't even let me speak? I mean, I don't even want this assignment!"

"Oh puhleeze," Gabe replied, rolling his eyes. "Everyone wants to work with Ashman."

"Not me," I said, shaking my head and grabbing my jacket.

It was officially Spring, but New Jersey hadn't caught up to the calendar yet and I wasn't going to freeze my ass off just because. Shrugging into my fluffy NorthFace, I waved goodbye to Gabe, ignoring his pleas for me to send him pics of my outfit choice for tonight.

Driving back to the home where I grew up and now lived once again with my brother Davian and his mate, Erryn, my sisters, Sybil and Martina, and Martina's new mate Mitchell, was a lot nicer than it sounded.

I'd been back in Maccon City for three years, but having all of us under one roof again was recent. With Martina's return from New York City and her subsequent mating to a Werewolf/Hellhound who handled her Witch side just perfectly, plus the fact we'd officially announced to all and sundry that we were the Witch

Shifter Clan now, our own supernatural organization, I had to admit I was still finding my feet.

"Your back!" Sybil announced as if everyone hadn't heard my car pull into the driveway.

Construction had ceased for the day. Thank goodness. I mean, I loved the new plans for Harbor House, but it was a lot. A lot of noise, a lot of people in and out, and a lot of mess. Still, I was shocked at how much progress Mitch had made with the additions we were putting in on the house and grounds. The Witch Shifter Clan was official, and returning home to them, to my family and my Clan every day did something wonderful inside of me. It helped soothe the anxiety I felt in both my magic and my Fox after being cooped up in the lab all day.

I mean, I loved my work, but the stress was real. After my meeting with Mother, I went back over all my recent discoveries on the drug DPCA agents had found in the bloodstream of Shifters' bodies they'd recovered from various places strewn across the country like so much trash. Indignation and fury filled me at the Global Human Alliance. That entire organization was based on pure hatred.

What a stupid fucking name! Supes might not be only human, but some of us were partially human. So what if we were different? Scientific evidence proved supernaturals existed as long as, if not longer than homo sapiens, walking the Earth for hundreds of thousands of years. If humans, or normals as we called them, had even the smallest inkling of what was really out there, of the multiverse and the many creatures that existed beyond what their tiny brains could comprehend, I imagined their whole world would simply implode.

The Global Human Alliance was just one of many heinous groups whose existence was a foul stain on humanity. How they knew about supernaturals I had no idea. But the DPCA had been closing in on their hunting grounds. I understood from Mother that one of their recruiters, the slimeballs responsible for targeting individuals, had been recently caught.

In a terrible twist of events, the man was the father of one of the DPCA's longtime handlers, Jennifer Dylluan. I didn't know her well, but I'd worked with her a time or two, providing the support of the research lab where applicable. The biggest impediment I saw in this case wasn't in identifying and neutralizing the chemical agents these bastards were using to suppress or freeze Shifters in one state or other.

That was the kind of thing I could figure out in my sleep. It wasn't conceit, it just was. I had a big fucking brain, and I knew how to use it. But my anger, the simmering rage at what these fuckers were doing, now that was going to be a challenge. This was more personal than Mother knew. Closer to home than anyone knew.

Unlike Martina and Sybil, I wasn't an infant when Anne Harbor rescued me. I was older, and being precocious even as a preschooler, I had vivid memories of my life before I came to Harbor House. Secret memories that I swore to take to my grave. But this case, this fucking case, was bringing them all back to the surface. Magic pulsed beneath my fingertips and my inner Fox growled deep and low.

"Earth to Nova!" Sybil snapped her fingers in my face, and I was ripped from my unpleasant past and thrust back into the present.

"Hey," I said noncommittally. "Sorry, I was thinking."

"Yeah, no shit," she said and laughed. "Did you see Martina's email?"

"What email?"

"She's so fucking cute, taking her position as Alpha of our Clan into the 21st century by creating a newsletter," Sybil said, tearing up a little and I rolled my eyes.

She was always so emotional. Dutifully, I took out my phone and scrolled to the email from our sister. I bit my lip to stop grinning as I read the very detailed and organized missive. Martina was a lawyer, so it kind of went with the job, but I couldn't deny the note of pride that swelled inside of me. It was official. She'd registered the Witch Shifter Clan with the Shifter Council, giving us both protection and status among supes.

With the permission of Rafe Maccon, the Alpha of the Macconwood Pack, we were allowed to take root in Maccon City, so long as we respected Pack boundaries, which, of course, we would. Only complete morons would pick a fight with the biggest Wolf Pack in the world over something as dumb as territory.

We already owned our plot of land. It was left to us by Mama Anne. She'd built Harbor House for supernatural runaways and delinquents, the outcasts, the unwanted, and the trafficked. That last bit caught in my throat. I'd been rescued from a group that hunted Shifters for sport. The similarities of what that now defunct organization had tried to do was too close to the Global Human Alliance for me not to be affected.

The Shifter Child Abduction Ring, or SCAR as it had been known, was once the greatest danger known to Shifterkind. They'd planned the eradication of Shifters from the face of the planet by perverting our DNA with one result in mind, infertility. The GHA wanted to steal our animals from us, and SCAR wanted to make sure we could not pass on our Shifter genes. Both groups were monsters. Both deserved to be wiped off the planet.

Bloodthirsty? Maybe. But after what they did to me, I couldn't really be blamed, could I? Tears pricked my eyes as I thought of the very real consequences of my kidnapping. I could never have children. That was my deepest regret, my darkest secret, and another reason I would never, ever take a mate.

"So, are you coming to the meeting?" Sybil asked, catching my attention once more.

"Meeting?"

"Yeah, our first official Witch Shifter Clan meeting! It's tomorrow night," she said, following me to our old bedroom.

We were sharing it until construction was complete. Thank fuck for Mitchell. Martina had really lucked out with him. Adding several smaller buildings, including a dormitory, indoor gym, and outdoor recreational center was going to do wonders for this place. I was also looking forward to having my own space again. Not that I didn't like being home, but between Davian and Erryn constantly kissing and touching, Sybil's nonstop chatter, and Martina and Mitchell pawing at one another, I was getting a little claustrophobic.

"Yeah, tomorrow should be fine. I think. Actually, I don't know," I mumbled.

"What do you mean, you don't know?" Sybil asked.

Just then, my phone buzzed, and I grabbed it, frowning when I read the message. Shit. It was from Asher. He was going to be there in twenty minutes to get me, and I hadn't even showered.

"I'm going to be doing some work in the field, um, undercover actually," I said, looking through the closet for something to wear.

"In the field? Holy fuck, Nova! But you're a nerd, not an agent," Sybil pointed out unhelpfully.

"Thanks, dufus," I growled, rolling my eyes. "I won't be alone. It's important."

"Who's going with you? Ohmygawd, please say it's that hot Lion Shifter you won't admit you like," she said, eyes bright with mischief.

"I don't like him!"

"Yes, you dooooo," she replied in her annoying singsong voice. "Now, spill!"

So, I did, bringing her, and then Martina who crashed into our room a few minutes later, up to speed. I blew out a gush of air and turned to face them in my bar appropriate outfit.

"Well?" I asked, and both my sisters just gaped at me. "What?"

"Are you going undercover as a sex worker?" Sybil asked, eyes wide.

I looked down at my pleather miniskirt and thigh high boots paired with a silver halter top and sighed. Fuck. She had a point.

"Shit. What do I do?"

"Okay, let's fix this before you get arrested for indecent exposure," Sybil muttered, shaking her head.

"Come on," I growled. "It's not that bad."

"Not bad? Honey, I can see your hoo ha from here. We want Agent Donnelly to swoon, not have a heart attack," she said.

"I do not want him to swoon!" I lied.

Fine. Maybe I did want the man to swoon over me. Just a little. Fuck.

"Enough, you two. Okay, Nova, keep the top on, they make the girls look great," she said, wagging her eyebrows and nodding at my boobs.

I did have pretty great boobs if I said so myself. I was human enough to have my own insecurities and while I was more accustomed to nudity than the average female because, *hello Shifter*, that did not mean I was completely comfortable in my own skin. But yeah, I liked my boobs. They were a regular c-cup, perky enough to forego bras when I had to with certain outfits, such as this one.

"Take those boots and that skirt off and put these on," Martina said, coming to the rescue.

I grabbed the high-waisted, wide-leg pants from Martina and shrugged them on, sliding my size nine feet into the silver wedge heels she tossed on the floor. It certainly wasn't my go to, but the second I put them on I felt deliciously feminine and pretty. The pants were made out of some sort of soft shimmery fabric that was almost see-through from right below my panty line, but only if you pulled the fabric apart or stared really hard. When I walked,

it gave tantalizing glimpses of what I looked like beneath the fabric, but it still managed to be modest.

"Holy shit," Sybil said, and I had to agree with her.

Holy shit, indeed.

CHAPTER THREE ASHER

I DIDN'T GET a lot of downtime, but when I did, I was addicted to reading those AITA stories. You know the ones. *Am I the asshole?*

They were blog posts where folks asked if they were the asshole in a situation. The poster would often go on to explain what happened in a long-winded, sometimes utterly ridiculous story, and a billion people would then comment and criticize and offer their POVs because the internet was a cesspool of self-righteous people hiding behind avatars, saying shit they didn't have the balls to say in real life.

Whatever.

Everyone was entitled to whatever the fuck they wanted these days. I didn't judge. I didn't care. And it was just my guilty pleasure that I liked to read those fucking posts. They were entertaining as hell. And more often than not, they gave me a good, long laugh, one of those fully belly kinds, whenever life was throwing a curveball at me. Like today's fuck-fest.

Nova fucking Harbor. Of all the fucking people in the world, I get told I was partnering with Nova Harbor on what was the biggest assignment of my career. Taking down the Global Human Alliance meant everything to me. Those fuckers were responsible for more misery than I cared to think about, but couldn't get out of my brain if I tried. Not even with a scorching hot poker.

But the Face? Really? What had I ever done to anyone to deserve that kind of torture?

It was my fault. I'd fucked up with her from the first minute I'd met the unbelievably gorgeous woman. But it wasn't like I was one of those guys in the AITA posts. You knew those dudes were the fucking asshole the second you started reading their whiny ass posts. They just could never admit it.

Now, normally, I knew I was the fucking asshole because I was. I meant that to my core. That's what I did. I was an agent for a secret government department that dealt with supernatural activity. Nobody paid me to be nice. They paid me to be efficient. They paid me for results.

So yeah, most of the time, I was the fucking asshole.

But not this time. This time, the fucking asshole wasn't me. It was the motherfucking Fates. They were the assholes! Why? Did you ask why? Well, the answer was fucking easy. Because out of all the women in the multiverse, those tricky motherfuckers paired me up with the Face.

Nova fucking Harbor was my fated mate. I only scented her once, but that was all it took for my Lion to make up his mind. The animal wanted her, but I couldn't have her. For so many fucked up reasons, all of which would normally make me the asshole. But I wasn't. I swear, it was not me this time.

It was them. Why the fuck would the Fates do this to us? Nova did not deserve this. I was not in control of who I wound up with. Didn't they know that? They fucking had to. The Fates knew how we worked. Lion Shifter Prides operated in very tight circles. Big Cat Shifters were a lot less common than most other subspecies. Therefore, our breeding schedules were highly scientific.

Cooperation amongst Prides allowed for my kind to continue on this planet by making sure we had the best chances for successful breeding by genetic pairing. It was almost my turn to be matched with a female for the sole purpose of making cubs. I always wanted to be a father, but ever since I saw Nova, that plan had changed. I wanted to father young with her, not some faceless Lioness.

So the question was why? Why had the Fates paired me with the most beautiful woman I had ever seen, who was not only *not* a Lioness, but was also a fucking genius on top of being physically superb? The answer, I had no fucking idea. And that made them the assholes. The Fates. Not me.

Nova was so much better than anything I could have ever dreamed of. So much better than I deserved. And when I met her, I acted like a total ass. Basically accused her of exchanging favors for her new job. Yeah, that was something I really regretted. And every time I saw her since that day, I knew she remembered my cruelty and I knew she hated me for it. As if I needed a reason to feel even more like shit about myself.

How could I do that to her? I couldn't forgive myself. I couldn't make her forgive me. And maybe it was better that way. I still had an obligation to my Pride, to my people, to my fucking mother, who ran the whole damn breeding program.

Every single day was a test. Every minute, I struggled to resist the pull I felt to her. Nova Harbor. She was perfection personified. I tried to put in for a transfer once, thinking it would be easier, but I couldn't do it. Even if I knew I could never have her, the idea of never seeing her again just didn't sit well with me. So, for three years, I'd been her shadow. Her stalker. Secretly watching her when she didn't know it.

She'd started using some sort of scent blocker almost immediately after our first encounter, and I regretted it so fucking much. The memory of her peppermint and rosemary fragrance was so damn precious to me. I wanted it again. Wanted to breathe her fragrance from the source, but I knew I didn't deserve it. I knew I couldn't give into that desire.

The number of agents and DPCA workers I'd subtly and not so subtly warned off asking her out was getting higher and higher, but somehow Nova did not seem aware. She ran her own lab nowadays, and I was thrilled with her progress, but sad that she allowed my stupidity to stop her from forming any lasting friendships at work.

Gabe Goodman still worked with her, second only to Nova who ran her own lab. He was a decent guy, always good at providing me with information on her. He had a bro crush on me, had even given me a nickname with his former partner Drew. They called me Ashman, and I did my best to ignore it. I didn't lead him on or use him. I let Gabe know exactly what our relationship was and would be. Work associates. Period.

Drew no longer worked with Nova, so he fell off my radar. There was a new intern, Steve Chamberlin, a Rabbit Shifter from upstate New York. He just finished grad school at Princeton and Nova scooped him up and brought him into the DPCA after reading his thesis on biological development and inheritance applied to gene theory. I read it myself, but doubted I understood more than half.

With no other recourse, I'd admired Nova from afar. For the past three years, like a fucking psycho, I watched, I listened, I collected every hint I could about her likes and dislikes. And I admired from afar, fuck, yes, I did. I admired Nova Harbor. I was even proud of her to some extent. Oh, I heard the naysayers. The ones who, like me at first, thought she got her job based on the fact that she was stunning.

I was embarrassed by my bad behavior and could only hope someday she would listen to my apologies and accept them. She was better than that, and she deserved better. Folks in the office called her the Face, but she was so much more than her appearance. And anytime I came within hearing range of anyone talking shit, well, I let them know that simply was not allowed. Ever since the first time I'd insulted her so badly, I tried to make it up to her by shutting down all the gossip and jibes.

Nova Harbor got her job based on merit. Not only that. My little Vixen was headhunted for this position. The higher ups sought her out because of her extensive knowledge and the impact her studies were making in the field of genetic research. The DPCA did well to hire her.

She ran a tight ship. She kept her lab personnel small, but efficient. They did more work in one year than the others put together. Nova was just that good. Her assistants enjoyed her leadership, and I couldn't imagine looking at her all day was a hardship either. But that kind of thinking was exactly what she didn't need.

Still, guilt assailed me every time she turned down an invitation for an after work drink or dinner. Guilt and satisfaction. My Lion was pretty proprietary over the brilliant Snow Fox. Anyone who wanted to date her would do well to keep that shit to himself. What could I say? I stayed away from her because it was better for both of us, but I wasn't a fucking saint. Gabe was good for telling me when one agent or another came sniffing around her lab, and then I did my thing in quiet afterwards. I'd corner them and let them know how much the DPCA frowned upon intra-office fraternization.

It was bullshit. But it worked. No one was getting near Nova while I was around. It was fucked up of me, but I wasn't looking too deep into that slightly obsessive aspect of my personality.

Fine. I was smitten. There, I admitted it. I was Lion enough to acknowledge my unhealthy fixation on the woman who pretty much hated my fucking guts. But, really, who could blame me?

Wickedly smart. Incomparably beautiful. Sexy little Snow Fox.

I pressed down on my growing cock as I took the street that would lead me to her door. Thoughts of Nova filled my brain, but they always did, so I wasn't distracted. When Mother handed me this assignment and said I'd need to get a woman to work undercover with me, her name came out of my mouth before I could stop myself.

"Nova Harbor? She's a scientist," Mother stated the obvious.

"Yep. That means she'll know how to counter this fucking drug GHA has been shooting up victims with," I'd said, as if that was why I'd picked her.

It was true, of course. She had been working with the samples from the victims we'd recovered. I didn't know how GHA planned to get away with what they were trying. I mean, how did you wipe out an entire species one injection at a time? But whatever. That wasn't my purview. I just needed to shut them down.

Did I like the idea of putting Nova near GHA? No. Not one fucking bit. But she was a Shifter, and I wouldn't underestimate her. Besides, I would never let a single hair on her head be hurt. My Lion would go fucking ballistic. I might not be able to claim her, but I could work with her, keep her safe, and maybe sate some of my need to be near her.

This was my one shot to satisfy my beast's need and my human side's curiosity about Nova Harbor. I knew in the end I would have to walk away from her, knowing somebody else would have her someday. Dealing with that was going to suck. But I would take what I could get. Not because I was the asshole, but because the Fates were the assholes. I should be fucking canonized for managing to stay away from her, knowing I had nothing to give her.

When we first met, I'd played a part. I was rude and cruel. But I didn't want to be rude or cruel anymore. I wanted to get to know her. I wanted to see what I would spend the rest of my life missing. Why? Maybe I was a sadist.

I sure as fuck must be, I thought as I rolled into her driveway. I pulled up to the door and forced myself to stay in the car. This wasn't a fucking date. We were on assignment. I couldn't allow myself to forget that. I honked the horn, and seconds later she came outside.

Fucking. Hell.

I knew she was beautiful. Hell. Everyone did. But this was my first time seeing her dressed up, like really dressed up, for a night on the town. My cock thumped against my jeans and my Lion froze inside me. Nova Harbor was a goddess. She was draped in silver and black, the fabric shimmered as it swirled around her long, luscious limbs.

She was at least half a foot shorter than me, which put her about five nine, tall for a woman. Her legs were long, shapely, her thighs just right. She had a perfect hourglass shape. More Monroe than Mansfield, but with that same 50s era classic beauty. It was her midnight hair, crystalline blue eyes, red lips, and creamy pale skin that made her so jaw dropping.

That was why they called her the Face. She usually wore an average amount of makeup, and her clothes were always fashionable and neat, far as I could tell. Tonight she'd gone all out. Her lips were painted red, and she had smoky liner and glittery shadow framing her eyes. That damn halter top was going to give me fits, as I wondered if she wore anything underneath.

Geezus. She looked hot as fuck. I adjusted my dick quickly and feigned annoyance as she opened the door to my car, sliding into the passenger seat as if she'd done it a hundred times.

"Ready, Hotshot?" I asked, keeping my gaze carefully averted.

"I guess. Mother didn't explain much, just said we were going to set a trap," she said.

"That's right. We're going to *Quenched*," I said, naming a new bar that was trending amongst supes and, apparently, the GHA.

"Quenched? Where is that?"

"About a half hour north. Whispers are it's a favorite place for GHA scouts."

"Scouts?"

"The guys who sniff out Shifters and target them to be kidnapped."

"Okay," she said, and nodded, her small hands fidgeted with the bag sitting in her lap.

"Hey, I won't let anything happen to you," I felt inclined to add.

"Good," she said. "I didn't expect you would, Agent Donnelly."

"Asher," I corrected.

"What?"

"Call me Asher. No one will believe we're a couple of civilians out for a night on the town if you call me Agent Donnelly."

"Right," she murmured and nodded her head. "Okay then, I will call you Asher."

Fuck. Me. Hearing my name on her lips was even better than I imagined. I wanted to hear it under different circumstances and damn the repercussions. Good thing she hated me, otherwise I'd never be able to stick to my guns. I couldn't have Nova for keeps. But maybe, maybe I could have her for now. Just the possibility had my Lion standing at attention.

Rrrrr.

CHAPTER FOUR NOVA

I WASN'T sure what to expect tonight, but Donnelly, *make that Asher,* was certainly a surprise. He'd been attentive and almost sweet, except for the fact he rarely smiled. But even without that, he made this feel more like a date than it had any right to.

"Is your drink alright?" Asher asked, and I blinked up at him, having been immersed in my own thoughts for the last few minutes.

"Yeah. Thanks," I said, and tried to smile, but it came out more of a grimace.

He'd appropriated a cozy booth for us in the back corner, far enough away from the DJ that we could talk without screaming. The lights were dim and the sound of glasses tinkling and people chatting filled the space. I traced the bar's logo on the small napkin and tried to get a handle on my runaway emotions. Quenched was a popular place. There was standing room only left and the dance floor was jam-packed.

"So, how does this work? I mean, is just sitting here supposed to do something?" I asked.

"It's part of it. We're going to have to frequent a few more places like this over the next couple of days or weeks. Let people see us together, make them think we're a couple. From what our intelligence has gathered, the GHA likes to target couples," he explained, and I couldn't believe it, but he wasn't even being rude.

Imagine that.

"Why would they do that? It seems a rather simplistic plan, and far too risky on their parts," I said.

"Believe it or not, bad guys aren't all masterminds. But targeting couples makes it easier. We aren't sure how they can tell a Shifter from a normal, but we suspect it has something to do with scent."

"But Shifter couples are too volatile, aren't they?"

"Not every couple is mates, Nova. But take it from the kidnapper's point of view. You have a man and woman, and they are on a date at a bar. So, they just started dating. Then, throw in some barroom drama. A fight, some jealousy, whatever. A stranger swoops in to rescue or flirt with one of them, woman or man, it doesn't matter, and bam, you got a kidnap victim."

"Really? That seems highly convoluted," I replied, frowning.

"And yet, it's been proven to work. Lonely people are easy to fool, Hotshot. Just show them a little something shiny to divert their attention, and anyone is a potential victim," he said.

I tried not to bristle at his statements. I didn't know if I was part of *the lonely people* or the *shiny something* that diverted attention. Either way, I hated both descriptions.

"Okay, so back to how do they know we're Shifters," I said, whispering that part.

"Not sure how they are picking up on that bit, but we can't rule anything out and that's why I'm going to tell you something right now you might not want to hear, Hotshot," he murmured.

I braced myself for whatever his next criticism might be. Shoulders back, I met his golden gaze head on, readying myself for whatever he might say. It was ridiculous for this man to have such an effect on me, especially when this was the most we'd talked since I met him.

"I need you to stop using that spray you wear," he said, and I froze like a deer in headlights.

"You know what I'm talking about, Nova. But if the GHA picks up on Shifters via some scent scanning device—"

"An olfactometer?"

"Yeah, that. Anyway, I can't have you wearing that odor blocking spray you came up with, however revolutionary it is."

Holy. Shit. How the fuck did he know about my *Emotoblock* spray? Goddamn it. I knew the answer before I even finished the thought. Gabe that rat!

"I can see by your face you know how I know, but don't blame Gabe, Hotshot. It's unnatural for a Shifter not to have a scent."

"Yeah, well, I'm not just a Shifter," I mumbled, grabbing my drink, and tossing it back.

"I know, Baby. Snow Fox and Witch, your powers include air magic, and I imagine are the reason you have such an affinity for chemistry," he said, stunning me for the second time, and not just because he called me Baby.

"What else do you know about me, Asher?"

"Not enough, Nova Harbor, but I'm a quick study," he growled.

"Can I get you something else from the bar?" the tall, slender server asked, interrupting what had turned into a staring contest between me and the growly Lion.

"Yeah, we'll have another round," Asher said, handing the guy a wad of rolled up bills.

He stood up as the server left and offered me his hand. With no thoughts of self-preservation, I took it, allowing Asher to pull me up from my seat. Damn, he was big. Tall, wide, and muscled, and this close, he smelled insanely good.

Like sunshine and sand. Fur and musk. And man. Definitely man.

He tugged me close to his body, crowding me as he took my hips between his hands and moved with me to the pounding bass. The man could dance, and predictably, science geek that I was, I couldn't. But I was half-Shifter and counting on my natural physical grace to make up for my lack of ability, I pressed myself against him and let Asher do all the work.

And work he did. For a big man, he was smooth, flexing and tilting, twisting us both in a manner I found highly arousing. I swallowed, glad I still wore the Emotoblock, even though he basically told me I couldn't anymore after tonight. I felt his chest rumble with his growl and the vibrations seemed to stretch all the way down to my core, creating an ache deep inside I knew nothing would ever fill.

Well, nothing except for him. But Asher didn't want me that way. Not really. This was just a job. A role we were playing. Just make believe. As long as I told myself that, I wouldn't fall under his spell. At least, I hoped I wouldn't.

We stayed another hour, dancing and making small talk, and keeping the server happy by ordering round after round of drinks. Shifter metabolism was such it would take a helluva lot more than a few glasses of watered down alcohol to get us drunk. Though, admittedly, I had a far less tolerance for alcohol, seeing as I was only half-Shifter. Not that it mattered. Drunk or not, I trusted Asher to take care of me. He wasn't even buzzed by the time we left.

"Buckle up, Hotshot," he said, his voice deep and growly.

I obeyed. Of course, I did. What idiot didn't use a seatbelt?

"Are you hungry?"

"I could eat," I replied honestly.

Asher made a humming noise in the back of his throat, one I associated with approval. For some reason, that pleased me, and I wanted to slap myself in the head for having such a ridiculous reaction. I shouldn't give two shits for his pleasure. Asher Donnelly had been nothing but careful with me tonight, but his typical M.O. was that of a man who cared very little for the feelings of others. As a scientist, I found him interesting. As a colleague, confounding. And as a woman, devastating.

Asher Donnelly had a very special brand of power over me. One I would never admit to out loud. I wanted him. Craved him. Needed him. His was the face I envisioned on those cold lonely nights when I resorted to self-pleasure to release all the tensions building up inside me. Dangerous. That was the word I would use to describe him if asked.

Asher Donnelly was dangerous. He presented a very real problem for me. Especially after tonight. Before this, I had him carefully cataloged as a supercilious dickhead. A total douche bag who didn't deserve to have me even think about him, let alone masturbate to his image.

But tonight he'd held doors open for me, touched my lower back when I passed, swayed me on the dance floor, ordered me drinks like he knew what I liked, and he'd been right every time. He was witty, charming, and fun to talk to. Even now, as he held my chair out for me inside the old diner off Route 35, I had to hold my breath to steady myself. He put my entire sense of inner peace in jeopardy. It made sense in the bar where we might have been watched by anyone from the GHA, but not now. Here, his manners did nothing but confuse me.

"What can I get ya?" an older woman asked, staring at her pad while she waited.

"Good evening. How are you tonight, Rose?" Asher asked politely, waiting for the waitress, Rose, to meet his gaze.

"Oh, um, hello, I'm fine," she said.

When she did, she smiled and blushed like a schoolgirl, patting her hair and straightening her apron. Asher grinned even wider. The brat. He knew exactly what he was doing to the woman, and the effects he had on females everywhere. Must have been a Lion Pride thing, but I just rolled my eyes and watched.

"Can we have two cheeseburgers, make them deluxe, medium rare, with extra rings and slaw? One seltzer, and a cherry coke," he said, handing her the menus.

"You got it, gorgeous," Rose said, and winked.

My Fox snarled at that, and Asher's golden eyes flicked to mine. He canted his head, a grin starting at the corner of his lips, but I cleared my throat, playing it off.

"What if I wanted something else?" I asked, annoyed suddenly for no reason.

"Did you? We can add more to the order," he began, frowning as he looked around for Rose.

"No, it's fine," I relented.

"If it's fine, Hotshot, what are you complaining about?"

"I'm not complaining. But you seem to have an uncanny ability to know what I like," I said, giving away far too much before I realized it.

"Is that so," he growled, and the heated look he gave me made me squirm in my seat. "Well, I look forward to discovering what else you like, Vixen."

Vixen? That was new. Better than Hotshot, at any rate. My inner Fox yipped and barked, vying for more of his attention. But I knew better. Asher Donnelly wasn't something I could keep, and it would be dangerous to form any attachments to him. Something I told myself on repeat during our meal. We ate in relative silence, and I was surprised to find it comfortable. He was a neat eater, too. Something I appreciated.

"How long do you think we'll have to do this until GHA acts?" I asked.

"Sick of me already?"

"No! I mean, no," I said, clearing my throat. "It's just I was wondering. You know, I think I broke down the formula they used on the last victim. They're getting closer to finding a way to put one side of a Shifter permanently to sleep, Asher. It's dangerous. They need to be stopped," I said, suddenly growing quite serious.

"We will stop them, Nova. You and me and the whole DPCA. I don't know how long it will take. A few weeks till someone bites. Then when they attempt a grab, we'll catch him, and he will lead us to the real bad guys."

"So, that's the plan? Just wiggle the bait and see who goes after it," I said, biting my lip.

"Hey, nothing will happen to you," he said, eyes blazing into mine.

I nodded, wiping my cheeks of imaginary tears, and

smiling brightly. Too brightly if the way he was frowning at me was anything to go by. There were secrets I had that no one knew about. Terrible nightmares of being kidnapped and sold, of the real monsters who wanted to "cure me" of my Shifter disease. Those sorry assholes didn't suspect I was more, and that was why they died.

"What's going on inside that brain of yours, Nova Harbor?"

"Who me? Nothing. I'm boring. Just a nerdy scientist, remember?"

"First, nothing about you is boring, and I highly doubt there isn't something going on inside that pretty head of yours every second of the day," Asher said, giving me a slow once over that made me shiver. "Second, I already know all about you at work. I know you're a fucking genius. A real hotshot, Hotshot. But I wanna know something else. Tell me something personal."

"Personal? What for?" I asked my mouth going dry at the very idea he wanted to know about me.

"Because I asked, and if you tell me, then I'll tell you something," he said, and color me intrigued.

"Fine. I have two sisters, Martina and Sybil, and we actually just registered with the International Shifter Council to be recognized as our own group. We're the Witch Shifter Clan," I said, waiting to see his response.

"Fuck, Hotshot, that's awesome. Congratulations," he said, surprising me for the millionth time that night.

"You aren't put off by the fact we wield magic?" I asked, trying to gauge the validity of his response.

"Not at all. Lion Prides actually work a lot with Witches. I wasn't raised with the prejudices many of the Wolves in the area have as a result of that asshole old Alpha of theirs," he explained, and I had to admit he was right.

"Okay, well, I told you something, now tell me something."

"I just did. Lion Prides and Witches work together a lot," he said, and I shook my fry at him.

"Cheater," I teased, trying not to swoon when he caught the fry in his mouth, closing it over my fingers as he slid the fry from my grasp.

Gulp.

The feeling of his warm lips around my flesh sent shivers racing up and down my spine. He was so damn sexy, and he knew it, too. His hooded eyes glowed gold with his beast as he watched me from across the table.

"You finished, Hotshot?"

"Uh, huh."

"Good. Check, please," he called out, not bothering to wait for it while he put another pile of bills on the table.

The ride home went by faster than I remembered,

the air between us seemed charged with a newfound awareness.

"Stay," he grunted as we rolled up.

And I did, like a frigging dog, while he rounded the car and opened my door. I exhaled a nervous breath and stood up from his vehicle, watching Asher as he watched me.

Being the subject of someone's unwavering stare was something I'd gotten used to over the years. But I never cared about anyone else's opinion before. So when he did it. It was different. I knew what everyone thought about me. That I was pretty, therefore conceited. But everyone had issues with their self-image. Even people everyone else thought were pretty and perfect.

I wanted Asher to like what he saw when he looked at me. I wanted him to like me. But was I fooling myself? Was I building castles in the sky?

"I'll pick you up earlier tomorrow. We'll have dinner first," he growled, cupping my cheek with his big hand.

I thought he was going to kiss me when he leaned forward. I even tilted my head, readying for it. Asher moved right into my space, crouching down, but our lips never touched. Instead, he grabbed something from the seat behind me, holding it out while his lips curled up in a grin. My bag. He'd bent down to retrieve my bag.

"Oh, um, thanks," I said and took it from him, scurrying around the door and refusing to look back.

"I'll be back tomorrow at five, Hotshot," he said, and I didn't have to turn around to see the grin I heard so clearly in his voice.

Stubborn, butt-sniffing, litter-box-using, panty-melting, overgrown house cat!

CHAPTER FIVE ASHER

IF ONE MORE OF *these sorry motherfuckers looks at her, I'm going to lose my mind.*

I didn't know how many more of these fake work dates I could take. It was the third weekend in a row since we started this undercover gig, and I still couldn't get my cock under control around her. Three weekends of Nova dressed to the nines, without her *Emotoblock* spray, and I was so damn hard every time she came near me, I could hardly walk.

The woman was divine. Her scent was ambrosia. Peppermint and rosemary. Juniper berries and orange zest. She smelled like winter. At least, she had the first time I met her, and I would bet anything she tasted even better.

My nightly habit of jerking myself to images of her

flashing through my head did nothing to take the edge off. In fact, I wanted her more than ever. This was getting ridiculous. I needed the GHA to make a move, show their hand already. My phone buzzed, and I grabbed it, frowning when I saw who it was from.

My mother. Of course, my mother would text me when I had Nova on my brain. Who needed cold showers when you had nightly interruptions from your mother? Ugh. Seriously though, Mom was the Queen of our Lion Pride, and a fierce matriarch. She was responsible for over one hundred breeding pairs, and that was quite a feat among Big Cat Shifters.

I knew what she wanted from me, and it didn't make things any easier. The Spring breeding cycle was coming up with the next moon, and she fully expected me to do my duty as her son and a prime male in the Pride to try to impregnant one or more of the females during their heat.

Rrrrr.

My Lion snarled. The animal was so not on board with that plan it was not even funny. I silenced my phone, deleting her message, and muting the contact. I didn't need that shit when I was working.

My eyes scanned the crowd. Nova was driving herself to meet me at Quenched tonight, as she had every night after that first time. She always had the perfect excuse. Tonight she had to stay late in the lab, going over her latest round of testing on the antidote she derived to counter that GHA poison.

Apparently, she found a way around their latest batch of nasty. Good on her. I knew she would. It wasn't like I didn't trust her to figure shit out. She'd already managed to return the Hyena female we'd recovered last week back to her human skin, and so far, the woman had no trouble passing back and forth between shapes.

Nova Harbor was a fucking genius. I understood that better than most, having spent hours of my life going over her file. The woman was my obsession. She took up more headspace than I'd care to admit. And no, I was never going to say that out loud. I looked down, tapping my empty tumbler of whiskey on the bar and catching the bartender's attention. He poured a generous refill, and I held the glass halfway to my lips when I felt her re-enter the room.

"Hi Asher," she said.

Damn. I loved hearing my name roll off her tongue. It was easy as pie now that she'd gotten used to it. Much better than Donnelly or Agent. My Lion growled pleasantly inside my mind's eye. The animal was pleased to see she was growing more and more comfortable around us.

"Hey, Hotshot," I murmured, my eyes just eating her up.

"Would you mind holding this? I have to use the restroom," she added, not even waiting for my reply before she pushed her purse into my hands.

She'd excused herself to the restroom when she arrived, and it was all I could do not to follow her. Tonight she wore a pair of low slung jeans that looked as though they were panted on and when she'd turned around, I caught a peak of a tattoo curling just around her hip.

A tattoo. A motherfucking tattoo.

Of what, I had no idea. And it didn't matter because that little secret beauty was for my eyes only. I wanted to take off my shirt and wrap her up in it. Hide her gorgeous skin from inquiring eyes. And yes, I fucking knew what I sounded like. A lunatic! A possessive alphahole moron. But what was I supposed to do?

I stood there at the edge of the bar, willing the crowd to part as I watched the door to the ladies' room like a fucking creeper. I felt on edge, angsty, and I knew exactly why. Fuck. How long did I think I could go on like this? Being near her and not touch her except for a few casual swipes of my hand on her back, or those few times we moved together on the dance floor.

Nova wasn't really into the party scene like me. She seemed to enjoy herself more when we were cozied up at a table, just talking or sharing some food. I liked the fact she ate. She might look like a movie star, but she ate like a real woman. Just one more thing for me to like about her.

Shit. I liked everything about her. Putting her in danger every weekend was not sitting right with me. I thought we'd have these GHA bastards by now, but they were behaving cautiously for whatever reason. I didn't know if I should thank them for making me spend more time with her or kill the motherfuckers for torturing me once I found out who they were.

My breath caught in my throat as Nova walked out of the restroom, looking down as she moved. I saw the big asshole lumbering towards her before she did. He'd already been vetted by me and my guys and was just another lonely, horny regular at Quenched. I couldn't hear what he said, but her frown was enough to get me moving.

The bass was thumping, and the crowd of people seemed to move and sway in time with it. It was dark, but that was nothing unusual. It was the blood red color tinting my vision that was different. That and the constant growl in my chest. The one that grew in volume when I watched the soon to be dead asshole put his filthy hands on Nova's ivory wrist.

"Move," I growled, standing right behind the sweaty motherfucker.

Nova's gaze flicked right to mine, and I saw relief mingled with something else. Heat maybe? Fuck. I really needed to talk to her in private. In fact, I'd been wanting to get her alone since she stopped wearing that fucking *Emotoblock* spray of hers. But every time we went out, she insisted on meeting me there. She'd been avoiding me. And that shit stopped right now.

"Back off, Ken," the clueless fuck said.

"I won't tell you again, Pal. The lady is here with me, now get your fucking hands off her before I remove them from your body," I growled, slapping my hands together to stop myself from ringing that fucker's neck.

"Well, maybe she wants to come with someone else," the asshole said, smirking as he closed his beefy hand around her wrist and yanked her into his sweaty body.

"Let me go," Nova growled, trying to push off the man's hand.

Something was going on with my little Vixen. She was growling and her eyes were glowing almost white in the dark hallway. I almost felt bad when I started to smell ozone in the air, but not really. That asshole was still holding onto her, and he deserved everything he had coming. Suddenly, there was a flash of light, and the distinct smell of ozone increased.

"Ouch!" he screamed, releasing her hand as a small bolt of lightning seemed to strike right where he'd been holding her.

I grabbed his neck, pinching his nerve and putting him to sleep, calling for the server to come over before a crowd began to form. Lucky I was strong as I dragged the heavy bastard over to the wall and propped him up against it. Nova was panting, and I knew I had to get her the fuck out of there.

"What the hell happened?" the server asked.

"This idiot dropped his drink and touched the outlet as he stood up. Must have got a shock," I told him.

"Oh wow, okay, I'll get the manager," he said, and ran off.

I looked around, making sure we were alone before I reached out for Nova.

"Hey, Vixen, come on. We gotta go," I said, but she was zoning out on me.

She was breathing heavily, in great big gulps of air. Her eyes were glowing inhumanly, and I knew it was only a matter of time before someone pointed it out. Shit. She still smelled of ozone and rain, but beneath that was that peppermint rosemary fragrance I only ever associated with her. Must be her soap or something. I didn't know. I just knew she smelled good.

It was the first time I'd gotten that close to her in weeks, and definitely the first time since she stopped wearing that spray that blocked her scent and hid her emotions. I wasn't ready for my reactions to the onslaught of her feelings. I mean, holy fuck, was she emoting!

Rage, fury, desire, and fear.

Above all else, she smelled like fear, and my Lion was two seconds from losing his fucking mind. I really did not like it when she was afraid. It made me want to break things. To hunt down whatever it was that caused such a reaction in her and wipe it off the fucking planet.

"Asher," she whimpered my name, and I unfroze from my position, moving towards her until we were touching.

Everything and everyone else forgotten. All I could see were her bright eyes, and I wanted to help. I needed to make it better.

"It's okay, Baby. I got you. Come here," I whispered and reached out slowly to touch her. She nodded, and I took that for the assent it was.

"I'm gonna pick you up, okay? I got you," I continued.

"Asher, I didn't mean to—"

"Not your fault, Baby. It's okay. I'm sorry I wasn't fast enough. Fuck, I should have been faster," I murmured, bending my knees so I could pick her up, princess style.

So many things were going through my mind when I witnessed what was going on between Nova and that asshole. I was so damn afraid I wouldn't be able to stop if I laid hands on that man. My vision turned red, for fuck's sake, and the last time that happened, hell, I didn't even want to think about it.

But now I had her in my arms, shivering and clinging to me, something just clicked. The rightness of it all. The way she fit perfectly against my body. Her scent. Her softness. Her unrivaled beauty. Her. Just her. Before I could stop myself, I breathed the one word I should have never said out loud when it came to Nova Harbor.

"Mine."

CHAPTER SIX NOVA

USING my magic was not something I was ever really comfortable with. Maybe it was because my scientific mind preferred situations where the outcomes were predetermined based upon a set series of variables. Magic was not like that. It could not be controlled in quite the same way, especially not when it ran off emotions.

Typically, I kept that side of me on lockdown. My Fox and I had a much stronger relationship than I had with my Witch side. My magic always came in bursts of temper or when I was in a highly emotional state. I did my best to not be in situations like that, but these last few weeks were stressful for me.

I never dreamed in a million years I would work on an after-hours undercover assignment. Especially not with him! True, it was the kind of mission I could not turn down. The Global Human Alliance was responsible for the deaths and pain of so many people, they needed to be stopped. Just like SCAR.

I began to shiver uncontrollably as memories rushed through my brain even as I sat safely in the warmth of Asher's car. The custom Camaro SS was roomier inside than I'd imagined, and the sleek performance seats hugged my back and hips as he took turns at breakneck speeds.

"Easy, Baby," he growled.

His voice was impossibly deep and scratchy. The notes struck a chord deep within me. Fuck. I flicked a cautious glance in his direction. His eyes were glowing gold. The striking color was anything but human, and it made me tingle in places that really should not be tingling around this man.

Mine. He said mine.

Shaking my head, I pushed the thought out of my brain. I was a mess. Shivering and feeling reckless after expelling my magic in such a way. That always happened to me after I used my powers without preparation. Still, I felt bad for having stirred Asher up.

Protective instincts ran deep with certain predatory Shifters, and for a male as dominant as Asher was, his reactions were inevitable. His Lion was genetically predisposed to defend a female regardless of her abilities to take care of herself. And really, what had just occurred outside the restroom of that bar proved I was not exactly great at that. Sure, my magic packed a punch, but just look at what happened after.

"Wait," he growled, and I realized we were parked.

"This isn't my house," I said, but he was already gone.

I followed him with my gaze, taking in his long strides as he rounded the hood of the vehicle and pulled open my door. Asher didn't wait or say anything else. He bent down and scooped me out of my seat like I weighed nothing at all. I gasped and clutched his shoulders, shocked by how tall he really was.

By modern standards, I supposed I was a big girl. I mean, I wasn't as rounded as my sisters, but I wasn't small either. Also, there was the whole Shifter thing, so I knew I was heavy. But Asher didn't so much as increase his breathing while carrying me up the path to his front door.

"Asher."

I said his name, trying to think of something to say. His muscles tensed as he typed something into the keypad and opened the door, shaking his head and the rumble inside his chest was enough to shut me up. Once inside, I expected him to place me on my feet, but he didn't. He walked straight back to what I assumed was his bedroom, and farther still, till we entered an enormous bathroom.

Once there, he sat me down on the enormous vanity and closed his eyes, pressing his forehead to mine. I didn't know how long we stayed like that, but I was powerless to move. There was something about being eye level with him standing between my open legs, his enormous hands cupping my hips, while he tried to regain control of himself that made my heart squeeze so damn tight inside my chest, I thought it would explode.

"Are you hurt?" he asked, finally breaking the spell between us.

I raised my eyes slowly, shocked to see the genuine concern on his handsome face. Shaking my head, I reached out to touch his face, amazed that he allowed me.

"I'm okay. You got me out of there. Thank you," I said, but he was shaking his head again, turning away from me.

"No. I didn't do anything. I am so fucking sorry, Nova," he whispered, and I heard it then.

The strain. The shame. The anger.

"You did. You helped me. You stood up for me, Asher, and no one has ever done that before unless they were related to me. You helped when no one else did," I said, and it was the truth.

"I should have done more," he replied, teeth clenched hard.

"You did a lot. Thank you. Really, thank you. I don't know why you did it. You don't even like me," I said, trying to play it off with a laugh, but it came out sounding like a sob.

Embarrassment filled me, and sadness too. Dammit, I knew he could scent it now that I'd stopped wearing the *Emotoblock*. It was my one defense against him and anyone who could pick up on emotions through scent.

"Don't like you? Is that what you think?" he asked, and I could see in his eyes he was bewildered.

"Of course you don't like me. You reported me to human and non-human resources after the first time we met."

"What? No, I didn't," he said, and he was telling the truth.

"It doesn't matter. You don't have to like me, Asher, I'm a big girl, I can take it," I said, needing to assert my position somehow.

I mean, he already saw me falling apart. He witnessed me in my weakest moment. There was no way I was letting him know how badly I'd been crushing on him for the past three years. Shit. I needed to think about something else. Anything else. Not the fact I was alone with Asher Donnelly in his bathroom with his big body irresistibly close to mine.

Shit. Recite something. *The Expression of the Emotions in Man and Animals* by Charles Darwin usually did the trick, but even that heady work could do nothing to get my mind off the fact that Asher Donnelly was staring at me like he wanted to eat me.

"You got it all wrong, Baby. I like you. This is how much I fucking like you," he growled.

One second, he loomed over me, hard and aloof, like a giant marble statue of some god or ancient hero. The next, Asher had one hand cupping the back of my neck and the other on my cheek as he pulled me towards him and slammed his lips to mine.

He barely came up for air, and I didn't mind it one bit. Asher Donnelly was kissing me, and it was the best kiss I had ever experienced. People assumed I was some sort of sex goddess because I was good looking, but what that really meant was most men found me unapproachable. Add to it the fact I was a genius, and well, there you had it. My sex life left a lot to be desired.

"So fucking sweet, Baby," he growled, stroking his tongue between my lips.

I mewled and pressed myself against him. My nipples ached and my core clenched on air. I'd never felt anything close to the desire I felt for him. The bright lights overhead should have been uncomfortable, but as he leaned back, tearing off my shirt, then his, I appreciated them. Asher moaned, fusing his lips back to mine as his giant hands roamed over my body. Sitting on the top of the vanity in my tight pants meant I had a slight belly roll hanging over my pants, and normally I would balk at letting anyone see that, but Asher made me feel so damn good with his whispered praise, constant pets, and the Lion glowing in his stare, I couldn't feel anything but good about myself.

"I guess you do like me," I teased when he started unbuttoning his pants.

"Guess? When I'm done with you, you won't have one fucking doubt how much I like you, Baby," he growled and lifted me off the vanity, heading for his bedroom.

His pants were down around his hips, giving me a tantalizing view of the dark blond happy trail leading into his black boxer briefs. He wasn't watching my eyes, though. Oh no, his gaze was glued to my hip as he pulled my tight jeans off my body.

"You're fucking killing me, Hotshot," he growled, nostrils flaring as he traced the tattoo I'd gotten when I was in college.

It was about a foot long, maybe longer, starting on my thigh and moving up my hip. The design was vines and spirals and swirls in thin black ink, all interconnected. The artist was a friend back in school and she drew the image from something I had done in my notebooks on one constant line, never breaking it so it would look better as it healed.

Of course, she didn't know I was a Shifter, and the healing went rather quickly. I also swapped out her basic ink for one I knew would take on a Shifter's skin.

"Who did this?" he growled, and from the way he paused, I had the feeling he wasn't in the market for a tattoo himself.

"A friend."

"His name?" he growled, and I almost laughed.

Was he serious? And why the fuck did that turn me on?

"Why? Did you want to get one to match?"

"Nova," he growled, his enormous hands squeezing both my hips. "Give me his name."

"No. And I won't give you any old boyfriends' names either," I said, not so secretly liking his jealousy.

It was silly, maybe immature. But there was just something about a man getting all possessive and growly that made a girl feel special. Even as a die hard feminist, I couldn't deny seeing his little green monster sitting on his shoulder was hot as fuck.

"What boyfriends? How many? Names and last known addresses," he growled.

"Oh my fucking gods, that is not happening," I muttered.

I gasped when he licked a trail from my neck to my

mouth, rocking his hips so I could feel all his delicious hardness as he flexed against me. But the damn pussycat lifted his head before I could kiss him the way I wanted to.

Fucking tease.

"You will give them to me, woman."

"Asher," I said calmly, running my hands up his arms, all the way to his shoulders.

"What?"

"Do you want to talk about our exes, or do you want to fuck me?" I asked, needing an answer.

His eyes heated, and the slow growl that had been simmering inside his chest rose in volume until I felt the vibrations running through him and to me. Asher was done fucking around. He pressed me down onto the mattress and claimed my mouth in a kiss that left me gasping and panting, begging for more.

"I think I'll fuck you, Baby. But you will tell me what I want to know, eventually."

"Oh gods, that feels soooo. Asher, please!"

"What do you need, Baby? Tell me," he growled, closing his mouth over one taut nipple, and sucking it into the hot cavern of his mouth.

I'd never understood foreplay. But maybe it was because I'd had so little of it. Most guys were so damn eager they hardly made it across the finish line with me. More often than not, they simply did not know what to do with a woman. But not him. Asher knew exactly what he was doing, and he made me yearn.

It had been so long since anyone touched me there. Longer still since I wanted anyone to, and even then, it was never like this. I whimpered against his sensual onslaught and threaded my fingers through his thick, glossy mane. It was so silky and smooth, I pulled, liking the way he mimicked the move by sucking more of my tit into his mouth.

Liquid pooled between my legs, and I knew he could feel it against his stomach, but I wasn't embarrassed. Sex was always messy. And if it was good sex, it was even messier. This promised to be good sex. My body was ready, my mind willing, and as for my heart, well, I wasn't going to overthink it. I was finally in Asher Donnelly's bed and there was no way I was going to ruin it for myself by admitting how much it was going to crush me when he moved on.

Live in the now, Nova. Live in the now.

CHAPTER SEVEN ASHER

SO TIGHT. *So fucking tight.*

I could hardly breathe as I pushed my cock into her dripping pussy. She was so fucking wet. So warm. And so tight, my balls squeezed high, ready to explode after just one thrust. But I was not about to blow my load without feeling her slick heat pulse around me,

"Fuck, Baby, you feel so fucking good. That's it. Take me. Take all of me," I growled, pushing deeper, and angling her hips so I could stroke her just right.

Her nails scratched down my back, and I growled, my Lion loving her animal side. Nova was so different from any woman I'd ever known. And I didn't mean just because she was a fucking knockout. It was everything combined.

Her brains, her beauty, her magic, her beast, her wit,

her insecurities, her confidence, her scent. Her. Just Her. It was always her. The way she opened to me was like a homecoming. She welcomed me with her body as I fed her inch by inch of my dick until she held my entire length inside her quivering sheath, and nothing had ever felt better.

Mine. Mine. MINE.

I pushed her knees further apart, needing her nice and wide so I could watch as I filled her again and again, thrust after thrust.

"Play with yourself," I commanded, and she didn't offer one protest.

Nova merely ran her hand down my stomach, making me tense as she circled the base of my cock with her fingers, moaning as she felt every thrust and pivot of my hips. I didn't know a woman could be so mesmerizing. Maybe it was witchcraft. Maybe it was just her. My heart thudded and my pulse raced.

Her rosemary peppermint fragrance permeated the air, mixed with my own male musk and the scent of sex. So good. So damn good. I watched as Nova dragged her fingers higher, sliding along her wet folds until she found her clit.

"Good girl," I grunted, and she was. My good girl. My sexy Vixen.

My eyes were fixated on where she circled her swollen nubbin, harder and faster according to my thrusts. So sexy. Such a good girl. Listening to my commands. She was so damn good at taking my cock. Shit. I was gonna come.

"Faster, Baby. That's it. You like that, don't you? Now, be a good girl, and come on my cock, Nova," I growled and felt her squeeze all around me.

"Asher," she moaned my name.

"Come for me. Now."

I growled as her pussy squeezed and quivered around my cock as I spurted my release inside her. My fangs descended. The need to claim her with my bite was so fucking strong, but I pulled back, needing her consent before I did anything close to claiming her. I couldn't stop moving. Not for a long while. Dragging out our pleasure, I rocked my hips against hers until I felt every last sweet squeeze and pulse of our orgasms still.

It was so fucking quiet in the house, but to me, it was loud. The sounds of our breathing and the pounding of our hearts, not to mention my Lion who was roaring like a motherfucker inside my mind's eye. I pulled out of her slick heat, eyes down as I watched as a trickle of my release slide down her inner thigh.

Not thinking clearly yet, I swiped it with my finger, sliding it back into her hole and rubbing it inside, wanting to keep it there. Nova whimpered, eyes closed as she shivered with the intensity of what we'd just shared.

Fuck.

I removed my hand and rolled onto my back, trying to catch my breath. My heart was pounding so fucking hard and Nova, she was panting as well. My Lion snarled, the beast angry at me for withdrawing too soon.

Fuck. Fuck. FUCK.

We laid there side by side for several minutes before either of us moved, and she did first. I was still stunned. Shocked by what happened, I expected her to be flippant or rude, to scream at me for taking advantage, or something. But she did none of those things. It was like a wall dropped between us, and she slid from my bed and went into my bathroom.

I didn't have to be a Shifter to know something was wrong and that it was my fault. I should have handled that better. But how could I know touching her was going to change everything? My phone buzzed from somewhere on the floor, and I ignored it, standing up and going to the bathroom door. I touched the handle, expecting it to be locked, but that didn't make it hurt any less.

"Nova?" I said her name.

No answer. Fuck.

I heard the shower come on, and I frowned. If she

wanted to get washed, she just had to say so. But why not answer me? No. Something was wrong. I grabbed the doorknob and without overthinking it, I crushed the thing under my hand and pushed my way inside.

"What are you doing?" she asked from inside the shower stall.

Her eyes were wide, and tear tracks were visible down her cheeks. I frowned. I made her cry. Maybe I was the fucking asshole.

"You got out of bed too soon," I said, joining her in the stall.

It was big enough to hold both of us and still have some feet of space. There were multiple shower jets, but she'd only turned on the main one, so with a little adjusting of temperature, I put them all on. Nova gasped, and I grinned, pouring some body wash onto a loofah.

"Turn around," I instructed, but she frowned at me. "Turn. Around."

"No. Look, it's obvious you were upset in there, and I get it. The real thing isn't always the fantasy—"

"What the fuck are you talking about?" I asked, stunned.

"There's this quote I read once from Rita Hayworth. Do you know who she was?" she asked me.

She stared up at me with her clear blue eyes so damn big and pretty, her hair all slicked back and wet, I almost forgot what she was saying. But I nodded. My mother was a classic movie buff, so yeah, I knew who Rita Hayworth was. I was also something of a thriller reader and Stephen King had quite the story about the Hollywood icon. Curiosity held me in its grips as I wondered what the hell my sweet Vixen was going on about.

Patience, I told myself. I needed to tread slowly if I wanted this thing to grow. I knew rushing her was a bad idea. But once Nova understood where I was coming from, maybe she could wrap her gorgeous brain around the fact that I was the only man for her. Even thinking it, I knew it was true. I'd had a taste of my Vixen, and I was not giving her up.

"Well, she said every man she ever slept with went to bed with Gilda, probably her most famous role, and woke up with her. So, you see, I'm saying I understand, Asher. You had all these expectations of me—"

I couldn't listen to another word. Did she think I was fucking disappointed? Shit. I really was the asshole. Shaking my head, I grabbed her face and pulled her to me, claiming her mouth with mine. She pulled back, as if she wanted me to stop, but I wasn't going to. No fucking way. I kissed her harder, demanding she let me in.

Finally, she stopped struggling, and instead of pushing me away, she pushed herself into my arms. Our bodies were slick with water, but I was a mother-fucking Lion. When I grabbed my woman, there was no way I was letting her fall. I hoisted her up, my palms on her ass, and she wrapped her legs around my waist.

"You think I was disappointed? You think I was expecting more than that?"

"Weren't you?" she asked, panting against my lips.

I growled, stepping out of the shower, and I walked with her in my arms back to my bed. I was enraged. I was horny. And no, I did not bother with towels. I had to prove to Nova how I felt, and I was a man of few words. So, I fell on top of her instead. Pressing my body into hers right on the rumpled blanket where we'd just fucked.

"You stole the breath from my body, Baby. I've been wanting inside your tight little pussy since the first day I saw you. Even then, I knew you were mine. But I let other shit get between us."

"What? Y-you wanted me since then?" she asked, her eyes wide as I notched my cock right at her entrance.

"Every fucking day since then. I've dreamed of this pussy. Longed for it. Warned others at work to stay the fuck away from you. I made you fucking hate me," I growled and pressed in another inch, spreading her wide and groaning at how good she felt.

"But you do hate me—oooh!" she moaned as I pressed in deeper.

"Hate you? Does it feel like I hate you? Look how fucking hard you make me, Vixen. Only you do this to me. Hate you? I couldn't hate you if I tried. You. Are. Everything," I snarled and buried myself to the hilt inside her tight pussy.

"Fuck, you're soaked for me, Baby," I moaned when I felt how wet and hot she was.

"Asher," she whimpered as I held myself still. "Need you."

"What do you need me to do? To fill this pussy? I am. I'm right here. Feel me," I growled, licking a path from her neck to her mouth.

Fuck. This woman. I needed to own her. To fill her with my seed, my scent. And yes, to mark her with my bite. Maybe three years was long enough.

"Your mine, Nova, tell me," I said, flexing my hips and loving the feel of her walls tighten with every slide and stroke.

"Yours. I'm yours."

"Nod your head if you mean it, Baby. That's it. You're mine. No one else's. Just mine."

"Yes. Yours, Asher. I'm yours," she moaned, clinging to me, and scratching my shoulders, breaking the skin there, and fuck yes, I loved it.

"Come for me, Baby. Tell me what you need to come."

"You, Asher. I just need you," she said, and that was it.

"You got me, Baby. You got me, always," I growled, and struck, biting her between her neck and shoulder.

Her pussy squeezed my dick as her orgasm pulsed through her and I didn't bother holding onto my own release. No, instead, I chased her right into oblivion, spilling my seed and reveling in our matebond as it wrapped around us.

Mine.

CHAPTER EIGHT NOVA

SUNLIGHT STREAMED through the blinds covering the windows facing out towards Asher's backyard. My body ached in places that had gone unused for far too long, until last night, of course. I sighed and snuggled into Asher's big, warm body. He was something of a cuddler, and since I hadn't had much of that in my life, I had to admit I enjoyed it.

Waking up in the middle of the night with a sexy blond giant wrapped around me was new, but awesome. A girl could get used to it, for sure. In fact, I raised my hand to my neck, lightly brushing over the still sore scar of his bitemark, and I exhaled shakily.

"Mmm, morning, Baby," Asher grumbled, gold eyes blinking down at me then flicking over to where my fingers were still touching my bruised flesh.

"Lemme see," he said, and carefully began to inspect my skin.

"It's going to leave a big scar," I murmured, not really minding.

"I'm sorry if I was rough, but I can't say I'm sorry about the scar. Want everyone to know who you belong to," he said, eyes glowing with possession.

I bit my lip, liking this way too much than was normal, but we weren't that, so I wasn't worried. He leaned down, his soft lips brushing against mine, and I fell into his kiss much like I had last night. It was all super-fast, but at the same time, it was really, really slow.

I mean, we'd been dancing around this for three years, but last night everything came to a head. We fucked. We talked. He claimed me. All in all, it was a pretty big deal. I needed to get home and tell my family. Asher pressed his nose to my skin and breathed in deep, making me lose my train of thought.

"Fuck, Baby, I love that I can smell you now. Wicked girl, hiding from me for three years," he grumbled and sucked on my neck, sending shivers down my spine.

"Mmm, I thought you hated me. Can't blame a girl for trying to salvage at least some of her pride," I confessed.

"You're mine now. No more hiding, Baby. Come here," he grumbled, pulling me tight to him.

My body swelled and heated, the proof of my sudden arousal pooled between my thighs. Asher was so damn big and handsome, and he looked at me like no man ever had. He saw past my picture perfect beauty and my armor. Past my big brains and my multiple insecurities. Asher saw deeper than most. He saw me, and he still wanted me. Hell, I think he wanted to devour me, and even crazier than that, I wanted him to. I wanted him to claim me as his own and I wanted to claim him, too. That was the scariest thing of all, admitting how much I wanted him to belong to me.

The sound of the front door opening and closing, followed by several pairs of shoes had Asher jumping up from bed in time for the door to swing open.

"See, he's home! And look, he's ready to perform his duties for the Pride!" an older woman said, unabashedly pointing at Asher's slowly deflating erection.

I sat up, anger and jealousy making my Fox hiss and my magic tingle. I growled, ready to fight this bitch when Asher said the one word, I would have never guessed in a million years.

"Mom!"

"Asher, who is that woman? Get rid of her, now. Alexis is here for you to service, and she is ovulating, darling, so let's go," his mother said, snapping her fingers and pointing at a tall, thin blonde woman.

"Mom, you can't just barge in here," Asher growled, still standing defensively in front of me.

"The hell I can't. You, female, you must leave at once. My son has duties to fulfill, and Alexis can't wait. Take your clothes off and get on the bed," Asher's mother instructed the blonde. And wouldn't you know it? The woman started to unzip her skirt.

"What? Stop!" Asher yelled.

"Oh my gods, what the hell is happening here?" I asked, too shocked, and upset to control myself.

My magic was getting all zappy, and the scent of ozone started to grow. Asher stood to his full height and turned to face me hands raised like he was soothing a wounded animal. I wrapped the sheet tight around me and backed up a step, needing the distance.

"Easy, Baby. I have no idea what my mother is doing here. But I will straighten it out," he started.

"You know very well what I am doing here, Asher Calvin Donnelly! It's breeding season and we have to get our numbers up. The Blue Valley pride has had a twenty percent increase in their population, and there is no way those lice riddled pussies are going to have larger numbers than us! Now, I don't care who you screw for fun, but this is your duty," the polished older woman said.

"Mother, this is my mate, I will not be breeding with anyone but her!" he snarled.

That was it. The straw that broke my back. At least Alexis had stopped taking off her clothes. The vapid woman was on her cell phone, ignoring the chaos around her and me, I simply closed my eyes and tried to ignore the voices and the yelling, but it was no good. All I saw when I did that was the physical report I'd received following my rescue from the SCAR laboratories.

Victim was found in a cell with a group of females who were treated with SCAR labs drug InFer XXI. Side effects of this treatment include disruption of the menstrual cycles, hormonal imbalance, fallopian obstruction, ovarian degeneration, and permanent infertility.

"You have a duty, Asher!"

"I have a mate, Mother!"

"Stop! Stop fighting," I said, exhaustion and defeat making me weary. "Asher, can I talk to you a moment?"

"Anything you have to say you can say in front of me," his mother hissed, her gold eyes cold and angry. So unlike her son's.

I was such a failure. Shame and an overwhelming sadness filled me. I had a mate. Finally. For all of a few hours, but when I finished telling him what I needed to tell him, he was going to regret his hasty decision to mark me with his bite. I knew I was wrong for not stopping him last night. But I'd hoped maybe our bond would be strong enough to get over this hurdle.

Only over the last few minutes, as I listened to his mother harp on about his duties, and then to Asher saying he wanted young with his mate, my heart just broke. I fucked up. I lied by omission. He needed the truth, and he needed it now.

"Baby, I am so sorry. My mom means well, but the Pride isn't like other Shifter groups. We have extensive breeding programs, but I swear I want nothing to do with that," he tried to explain.

I listened, appreciating the fact he had wrapped the blanket around his waist while he talked to his mother. But it was my turn to talk, and what I was about to say was going to kill me.

"I think you should do it," I said, trying for a calm I did not feel.

"What?" he asked, and I could see he was stunned and hurt at my words.

Fuck. It was gutting me to say those things. But what could I do?

"Yes, you heard her. Your mate is right. Do it for the Pride!"

"Shut up, Mother. Nova, what the hell are you talking about?"

I turned to face him, forcing myself to look unaffected while I died on the inside.

"I can't have children, Asher," I said, just letting it roll off my tongue simple as that.

"You mean you don't want kids?" he asked.

His handsome face scrunched like he was trying to make sense of my words. I could hear his mother muttering in the background, but I ignored her. No, this was not ideal, but the truth had to come out somehow.

"No, Asher. I just can't have them. When I was a toddler, I was kidnapped by SCAR, you remember that group, the Shifter Child Abduction Ring that Tony Leeds busted years ago? Well, I was rescued from one of their labs, but not before they exposed me to some of their more nefarious treatments. I can't have children. I should have told you," I whispered the last.

Wiping my eyes, I tried not to react when I reached for him, and he flinched away, stepping back from me. Fuck, this was so hard. It was one thing to have everyone treat me differently because of my appearance, but quite another when they did it because they found me lacking. I did not like the feeling. Not one bit.

"Anyway," I continued, trying for nonchalance, and failing miserably. "Your mother is right, if you want cubs, you should do this. Do her. That, uh, that Alexis chick. This is your chance. Excuse me, will you? I have to go to the lab," I lied, pushing past him.

I'd half hoped he would stop me, but Asher didn't. He seemed frozen in place, which was just as well. I had no car and no clothes, but it didn't matter. As soon as I was outside, I called on my beast and swapped my skin for snow white fur.

Allowing myself one brief howl of misery, I looked back once, expecting to see Asher, but he wasn't there. He was probably inside, inside her, that lucky Lioness who was whole and complete and could give him what he wanted.

Young. Cubs. A family.

This was too much for me to unpack all at once. I knew logically not being able to have children did not make me less of a woman. It did not make me any less real or important or whole. But I wasn't thinking logically. I was reacting, and I was feeling. Allowing emotions I had buried deep inside me to surface for the first time in my adult life.

Asher represented everything I ever wanted. A mate. A man to call my own. Someone who could give me the things I craved. The need to feel desired for who I was not just how I looked. Someone to offer me safety. To talk with. To be with. To love.

Fuck, I loved him. My heart squeezed and my stomach heaved. I loved him, and that was why I was going to leave. That was why I was going to let him fuck that pretty Lioness so he could pass on his gorgeous genes and be a Dad. Yeah, I loved him so much, I was going to let him go, and break my own heart in the process.

The bright morning sun was beating down on me as I raced off into the woods behind his house. I ran and ran, pushing onward until my legs burned. I didn't stop, not once. I just ran until I made it back home.

Harbor House loomed in front of me, and as the door opened, held wide by my brother Davian. He'd always been there for me when I was a kid and had a problem. It was an uncanny ability of his to read my moods and really, it shouldn't have surprised me anymore. I ran inside and changed into my skin. Davian was there with a blanket, and he draped it over my shoulders as I sobbed my misery, collapsing on the floor.

"What is it?" I heard Erryn, his mate, ask.

"Shh, it's okay, sis," Davian whispered, petting my head.

Next, Mitchell and Martina came in from outside, my sister gasping when she saw me. She called for Sybil who must have been outside doing one of her early morning meditation thingies.

"Oh my gods, Nova! Did someone hurt you?" the River Dragon asked as she kneeled down beside me, her hand on my shoulder.

"Should I call someone?" Mitchell asked, his alarm evident.

"No, no. Just give us a minute," Martina told her mate.

"I did. I hurt me," I said, sitting up and taking stock of the people who cared about me no matter my flaws.

They were my family. My Clan. And it was time I told everyone the truth.

CHAPTER NINE NOVA

"HOW DID I NOT KNOW THIS?" Davian asked, one hand covering his mouth as he tried to absorb all the information, I'd spent the last few hours sharing with everyone.

The skies were already growing dark outside, and I had to remember it was only Spring. Sunset was still pretty early in the northeast. There was a chill in the air, and I snuggled deeper into the pajamas I'd eventually changed into.

"Mama Anne thought it was best for everyone if we just tried to forget it and move on. I agreed," I whispered.

"Here, drink this," Sybil said, handing me a steaming mug.

I was so wrung out, I needed the pick me up and her teas always had a healing quality to them. Erryn sat quietly in the corner, her instinct to hunt and kill anyone who hurt any of us must have been in overdrive because she was cleaning her guns, and we already knew they were immaculate.

"Sweetie, your phone is ringing again," Martina said, but I just shook my head.

"I don't want to talk to anyone."

"Look, I don't know about Lions, but I can tell you about Wolves. There is no way a mated Wolf would ever touch another person as long as his mate breathed air," Mitchell said, and I hated to say it, but yeah, it soothed something inside me.

Images of Asher fucking the blonde Lioness had been flashing in my head for hours. My stomach threatened to turn in on itself every time I thought about it, and I had to bite my tongue to keep from dry heaving. He had every reason to want out of this, whatever it was we did. It had only been one night, after all. And technically, I only scratched him, I didn't bite him back yet. Was planning to when we'd been interrupted.

Kismet? Maybe. Fuck.

"Well, are you going to go back to work?" Sybil asked.

"Don't see as if I have a choice," I muttered. "The

GHA is still at large. We were supposed to be setting up a trap."

"Can't say as I'm fond of the government using my baby sister as bait," Davian huffed, and it made me grin.

"No worries, brother. It was my choice."

"Okay, I think we should all go out for a drink. Just Clan."

"Um, I don't know if I am up for that," I mumbled.

"It will be fun. We can color coordinate our outfits like we did in school," Sybil said, clapping her hands.

"Yeah. We can do that! Come on, Nova, we need the bonding time," Martina said. "Do I need to make it an Alpha order?"

"Ugh. So bossy," I said, allowing Sybil to drag me off the couch.

We spent the next hour showering, doing our hair, putting on makeup, and eventually dressing for our first Witch Shifter Clan outing at *The Thirsty Dog*. I had to admit, it felt good being with my sisters again. I'd missed being with them like this. Just having access to them whenever I wanted. The comradery we used to share on the daily, the feeling of belonging, it was soothing and healing, and I needed both.

Mitchell drove us there in his giant pickup. His brother Tim was already there with his husband, Peter, and they'd snagged us a table, having already ordered apps and drinks.

"What is this?" I asked, sniffing at the brightly colored liquid inside the martini glass.

"An Aviation! It's amazing, try it," Tim said, pressing the bottom of the cup and tilting it.

I had no choice but to sip and swallow and was pleasantly surprised when I did. I tasted the sweet violet liqueur immediately. After that were hints of lemon, bringing a brightness to the cocktail, and complimenting the bouquet of whatever top shelf gin the bartender used. I knew Tim, and he didn't do bottom shelf anything. I grinned and tapped my glass to his.

"Cheers," I said.

"Cheers, Foxy," he replied and winked. "Now, let's get our gin on!"

We went through the first round of booze and appetizers fairly quickly, but we were Shifters, so that was to be expected. As the afternoon passed into evening, I realized we were having a helluva time. *The Thirsty Dog* was always a fun place with virtual games and a dance floor, a DJ booth, good food and drinks, pool tables, pinball machines, and more to keep us supes entertained and jovial. After winning my fourth round of e-trivia, I was banned from playing.

"Oh my gods, Nova, you are such a fun sucker. Right Erryn?" Martina teased, tossing her napkin at me.

"You are a bit of a know it all," Erryn agreed, and

Davian just grinned at his mate like she was the cleverest thing ever.

"Ha! You should talk, Marti. Hey, Mitchell, do you know what we used to call your mate when she was little? Marti tattles, cause she always cried to Davian whenever me or Nova did anything wrong," Sybil said, and we all laughed.

It was true. Martina went through a period of tattling when we were about seven before Davian explained the difference between telling to keep someone safe and telling to be a brat.

The rest of the night went much the same. It was a good time spent with friends and family, cracking jokes, and making memories. Maybe if my heart wasn't broken, I would have enjoyed it more. As it was, I'd spent the last few hours ignoring my cellphone, and pretending I wasn't dying on the inside.

"Hellllooooo! Incoming hottie at five o'clock!" Sybil whisper-screamed, being her wonderful, happy-go-lucky self.

I laughed and turned my head, freezing in place when I saw who'd just walked in. Fuck. I was not ready to see him just yet. Thoughts of what he'd been doing the past few hours tried to claw their way into my carefully closed off psyche, and I whimpered. Fucking whimpered.

"Hey, are you alright?" Martina asked, her eyes glowing with her Wolf.

She had much better control now that she'd claimed her position as Alpha and found her fated mate. But I still did not want her getting riled on my behalf. I nodded.

"Yeah, uh, I-I'm fine," I said.

"Who is that big blond dude headed this way? He looks like he wants to eat you," she pointed out unhelpfully.

"Who wants to eat Nova? Oh, Mr. Big Blond and Burly? Well, if it's the *happy smexy fun time* kind of eating, I am all for it," Tim said, giggling as his husband slapped a hand over his mouth.

"Sorry about him. Gin is his kryptonite," Peter said and shook his head. "Let's go, Honey."

"But I want to watch Nova get eaten!"

"Now, now, we can go home and watch all the Food Network you want, okay? See you guys later," Peter said, holding onto his mate as he left the bar, passing Asher on the way.

Tim said something that had the Lion Shifter's eyebrows disappearing into his hairline, but whatever it was, it didn't stop him from zeroing in on me once more. I braced myself for whatever he was going to say. The insults, the anger, the hatred I felt I'd deserved for keeping my secret from him. I braced myself, not even trying to hide the warring emotions swirling inside of me. I was so damn happy to see him. He looked angry and a little rough, but still so damn handsome in his black shirt and pants.

Asher's golden eyes were glowing with his Lion, his mane looked as if he'd been brushing it back with his fingers, and his short beard seemed longer than it had been that morning. He was the best looking man I had ever seen, and my heart cracked a little more, thinking of what I'd lost.

"Hello, I'm Martina Harbor, Nova's sister," my sister said, moving in front of me with her hand extended.

"Asher Donnelly," he growled. "Nova's mate."

Nova's mate. He said he was my mate. What the heck?

"Oooh, okay," Martina said, her eyes bouncing back and forth between me and Asher.

I was just as clueless as to what was happening. Power seemed to roll off Asher in big, crushing waves, and it was all I could do to hold his steady stare. He was so heavy. So dominant. And so fucking pissed.

"Um, hey, everybody, let's move this party to the dance floor," Martina said, giving me and Asher space.

Not that I wanted it. I was freaking out without making a single sound. His eyes roamed over me from head to toe, and I shivered with desire. How could he do that? How did one man have the power to turn even my brain to mush with just a little look?

"You left me."

It wasn't a question. But I felt the need to answer.

"Yes."

He huffed a breath, the rumbling in his chest was audible from where I sat across the table. I felt his anger, his pain, and it hurt to experience. I sucked in a heavy breath, my eyes filling with tears.

Did he hate me? Was he there to tell me off?

I closed my eyes, letting the tears go as I waited for him to do whatever he needed to do. I wasn't going to run or leave, I deserved whatever it was he had to get off his chest. But I wasn't ready for him to touch me, and when his big hand closed over mine, turning it so we were palm to palm then squeezing it tightly, I wasn't ready for the wave of feeling to crash into me.

"Never again. You hear me?" he asked, his voice cracking. "You will never leave me again."

I gasped, raising my eyes to meet his, and the raw emotion I saw there was my undoing. Asher stood and pulled me up, crushing me to his chest as he kissed my head, my cheeks, my lips, drinking in the tears that ran down my face.

"You are mine. You said so. Never again, Baby. You stay with me. You belong with me," he growled.

He ran his hands over my shoulders, cupping my

neck, and my face, hugging me so tightly as he repeated himself over and over, saying more than I ever hoped to hear before he crushed his lips to mine and kissed the hell out of me. I was a goner. I completely swooned, leaning into him, daring to hope he left that woman untouched and came after me instead.

Should I ask him about that? Is that too much to hope for?

"You crazy, gorgeous, brilliant, infuriating woman. I could never touch anyone who isn't you. I haven't touched anyone since the first time I saw you! Didn't you know?" he growled, cupping my cheeks in his hands, and forcing me to look at him.

"You mean? For three years!"

"Three long years I waited for you to be ready to hear me out, to listen to my apology. I've got you now, Baby, and I am never letting go."

"But what about cubs?" I whispered, hating that I couldn't be everything for him.

"First of all, I need you, Nova. Nothing else, no one else. Just you. Second, I read that report three years ago."

"You knew I'd been taken by SCAR and they used that garbage on me?"

"Yes, I knew. I also know you haven't been to see a reproductive specialist. Have you tried getting pregnant before and failed?"

"What? No!"

"Then you don't know what that drug did or if it had lasting effects," he said reasonably and I paused, shocked. He was right. I never did get tested, I always assumed it was what it was.

"But what if—"

"Baby, you can *what if* until the cows come home. I don't give a fuck. You are my fated mate, Nova. I knew it the moment I met you. That's why I acted like a dick. I was jealous of those fucking lab coats hanging all over you."

"Who? Gabe? He's gay," I said and shrugged.

"Actually, Gabe is bi. Drew is straight. And even if he didn't wind up working for you, I still fucking hated him back then."

"So, wait, I'm your fated mate," I said, trying to catch up.

"That's right, Baby. You are my destiny. But even if you weren't, I would still pick you. I will always pick you, which is exactly what I told my mother when I tossed her and that female out of my house."

"You kicked your mom out of your house?"

"Yep, and more. I left the Pride. That's what kept me tied up all day. I'm officially a rogue Lion. I tried calling you and texting, but you didn't answer. Made my Lion fucking nuts. Oh, here," he growled and picked up my hand.

"What is it?" I asked as he slid a ring on my finger.

"It's a ring."

"I know that, but—"

"You already wear my bite. But since we live in a world filled with normals, I figured you needed something to show them you belonged to someone. To me. That is an engagement ring. Never take it off."

"Oh, um, typically you ask a girl when you give her one of those."

"Is that right? Well, maybe good little girls who don't run away from their mates get nice proposals. But not you, Vixen. I'm telling you, you're gonna marry me. You are going to take my name. Gonna wear my ring. And my bite, and you're gonna ride my cock every night and sleep by my side because you are never getting rid of me," he growled, nuzzling my face, kissing my lips, licking my neck, and finally, nipping my earlobe between his teeth throughout his entire, lengthy, and sexy as fuck speech.

I was a trembling, needy mess by the time he raised his head. My panties were damp, and from the heat I saw in his eyes, he'd already scented my arousal.

"Maybe now you'll start to understand what I mean when I say you're mine, Vixen. Now let's get the fuck out of here so I can show you."

"Okay."

"Okay," he nodded.

"Let me tell my sisters I'm leaving, then we can go," I said, feeling completely intoxicated by him.

Asher Donnelly was truly a force to be reckoned with, and I had to admit I had no idea what I was in for when we came together the previous night. But now I knew. Now I knew, and I craved more. I loved the possessive way he watched me and the filthy words that came out of his mouth.

No one ever talked to me like that before. I'd been told I was beautiful, sexy, hot by a lot of people in my lifetime. But with Asher I felt that way. He made me believe I was all those things, and that belief made all the difference in the world.

I kissed him once, pressing my mouth to his before turning to find my sisters. It was the first time I'd initiated a kiss, the first time I'd touched him without cajoling or provocation, and I liked it. I liked the way he let me, and I fucking loved that he looked so damn pleased and turned on by my small display of possession.

I was through waiting. If he still wanted me with all my damage and all my baggage, I was more than ready to next level this thing. Tonight was the night. I was going to claim Asher Donnelly as my own.

With my mind on that, I wasn't paying attention to where I was going when I pushed through the crowd to find my sisters. I didn't get a chance to scream when I felt the pinprick on the side of my neck. By the time I understood what was happening, paralysis was already settling in, and I was being dragged backwards through the side door. And all I could think about was him. His face when he told me how he felt when I left.

Would he think I ran? Would he forgive me again when he found the truth? Would he forgive himself?

Asher, I am so sorry.

CHAPTER TEN ASHER

FIVE MINUTES PASSED. Then ten.

I checked the time on my cellphone. What was taking so long? I knew how sisters could get when they started chatting, having three of my own, but Nova and I had some unfinished business. Like her bite mark on my neck. Nice and fucking high for everyone to see. That was where I wanted her to put it. I was tired of acting like she didn't own me, body, heart, and soul, because she did.

As I'd explained to my mother earlier, Nova Harbor had the fealty of my Lion, the soul of my human side, and all the pieces of me that had ever or would ever exist. She was my all. My everything. My only thing.

I didn't give a fuck about anything else as long as I had Nova. And like I told my sexy sweet Vixen when I saw her sitting at that goddamn table in the middle of the crowded bar, her expression so sad and vulnerable, so fucking beautiful it hurt to look at her, she was never leaving me again. Not ever.

I adjusted my cock and swiped up on my phone, unlocking it. I was determined to send my errant mate a text to get her ass over here when I saw two things that should not have been possible. Sybil and Martina Harbor, the two sisters Nova went to find, and they were headed towards me, laughing arm in arm. But Nova was nowhere in sight.

"Hey, what are you doing here?" Sybil asked.

"Yeah. Where's Nova? Did your super hot reunion go okay?" Martina added.

A grin split her face as she bumped Sybil with her hip, but her smile fell right off once she saw my expression. Fear gripped me as I turned my head, trying to catch sight of her. But no. Nothing. No black-haired, blue-eyed Vixens about. My heart stuttered in my chest, and I felt the walls closing in on me.

"She was going to find you to say goodbye, then we were leaving after that. Did you see her?"

"No," Martina shook her head as Sybil gasped and looked around. "We never saw her—"

"Check the front. Tell the DJ to shut off the fucking music and ask for her by name now!" I yelled and ran towards the back.

Fuck. Fuck. FUCK.

I didn't wait to see if they listened. I knew they would. They loved their sister, and Martina was her Alpha. There was no way she wouldn't help look. I heard Sybil's voice over the speakers, she must have grabbed the mic from the DJ. She was asking anyone who saw her sister leave to come forward.

I ran to the lot scanning the rows of cars, then I saw something out of place. Some big fuck was tossing something in the back of a blacked out SUV. I started running towards them, but they were too far away. The car peeled out before I got anywhere near them and an earth shaking roar left my throat.

"NOVAAAAAAAAA!" I roared, my hands clenched into fists so tight blood ran from my palms.

"Asher! ASHER! Did you see her?" Martina shouted, running towards me.

"Get in," Mitch growled, and I vaulted inside the truck.

Sybil was already there with Davian and Erryn. The scary female had two strange looking guns in her hands, and she was focused on checking her ammo. Thunder pounded in my head as we scanned the highway for any sight of that SUV.

"I don't see it anywhere," Mitch said, slamming his hands on the steering wheel.

"What about DPCA headquarters? Would they have anything?" Sybil asked.

"What? No, fuck, wait—the ring!" I growled, wanting to slap myself in the head for not remembering immediately.

"What ring?" Davian asked.

"The engagement ring I put on your sister's finger twenty minutes ago. It's got a tracking device embedded behind the star sapphire," I explained, pulling up the app and calling Mother.

"She loves sapphires," Sybil murmured, but I didn't acknowledge her.

Truth was, I bought her the sapphire because it reminded me of her sparkling blue eyes. That it was her favorite just cemented the fact we were made for each other. The blue of her eyes was so deep and true, I'd never seen anything like it in another living creature. That she kept her eye color when she shifted into her Fox was just another thing I loved about her. Fuck. I loved her. And if they fucking hurt one hair on her head—no, I couldn't even bear to think about it.

Two halves making one whole. She was my everything, and I would burn the whole fucking world down to get her back. I wondered briefly if the GHA had any idea what they'd done. They took what was mine, and I had no intentions of playing fair when it came to getting her back.

Fuck DPCA protocol. Those motherfuckers knew all about Shifters, right? Then they should be prepared for what was coming. Somehow, I didn't think so. And that only served to whet my appetite for their total destruction.

"*This is Mother,*" my boss' voice spoke through the speaker.

"They grabbed Nova. I'm headed there now."

"*Hold on, Donnelly. You'll need backup.*"

"Sorry, Mother, but I'm not waiting. I'm sending you the coordinates now."

"*Dammit, Donnelly, you will wait—*"

"She's my mate, Mother. I. Am. Not. Waiting," I growled.

"*Fuck. Fine. Try not to make too much of a mess.*"

"No promises," I grunted and clicked end, pulling up her location on the tracking app. "Make a right off exit 37a. Then go about a mile down the road," I said, watching the tiny blinking dot that represented my entire world as it flashed on the small screen.

"By the old Hanshaw place?" Mitch asked, and I barely recognized the name of a rundown farm that'd been for sale for years.

Shit. Why hadn't we looked there? There were several dilapidated buildings spread out across the land. A barn, a silo, a greenhouse, tool shed, an old farm store, and the old Colonial where the Hanshaws had lived. My thoughts strayed back to Nova. To the woman who owned my whole heart.

Why had I waited so long? I wanted to curse and kick myself right in the fucking ass for being such a dick. Three years I wasted. Three whole years of longing and watching and waiting like a fucking stalker when I could have had her by my side. I felt like such an asshole. I was the fucking asshole. Dammit.

No. This was not where we ended. I was going to get her back. If I had to burn the whole world, I would get her back. I would not accept defeat. Looking at us, the big blond DPCA agent, and the drop dead gorgeous genius scientist with her Snow White coloring and her kickass snark, we couldn't be any more different. But Nova was the embodiment of everything I ever wanted in a woman. She completed me. The dark to my light. The brain to my brawn. The logic to my fury.

As a dominant male Lion, I had a short temper. I was possessive and aggressive. I could be a real fucking brute. But Nova gave as good as she got. Over the years, our verbal sparring had been a kind of foreplay. And now that we actually got around to really have some foreplay, I was not letting her go.

Fuck that.

I watched the dot on the app obsessively, growling when I noted it stopped. We were so fucking close. Minutes away. I prayed to whoever might be listening to just get me there in time. My Lion scratched at me from the inside out, tearing at me to free him from his confines. But I couldn't do that yet.

"When we get there, my Shift is going to rip through me," I explained so the others could do what needed to be done. "I don't have a choice. But here's my phone," I growled and handed it to Martina. "The dot is her location. If you can, open doors or whatever might be in my way. If not, don't worry about it. I'll just go through them."

I ignored their gasps and scoffs. They didn't understand. I was not the average Lion Shifter. I was the son of a Queen. An African Lion Shifter. When changed my beast was twice the size of the largest recorded wild male lion. Sixteen hundred pounds and fifteen feet of pure muscle. Now picture that enraged and desperate to get to his mate.

That's what I was. Oh, I'd heard all the kitty cat jokes growing up. Some of them were even funny. But I was no pussy. I was death, and I was going to crash right through Global Human Alliance's front door.

My Lion stilled inside me. Two minutes out. Two minutes of Nova in their grasp. Whispered words filled my head, and I hoped like hell my mate could hear inside her heart and mind.

I'm coming, Baby. I'm not leaving till I have you in my arms. You hear me, Nova? I'm coming for you.

Mitchell stopped the car, and I saw it. The SUV that grabbed her parked alongside the old barn. I didn't bother to wait for anyone. I jumped down, taking my first step as a man. But by the time my other foot lifted in the air, BAM, I was my Lion, and the earth shook beneath my paws as I ran towards the place where those bastards took my mate.

CHAOS ERUPTED AROUND ME. I saw men shuffle out of buildings, guns raised as they took aim. The scents of fear and sweat mixed with gunfire, and I think one or two bullets may have even hit me, but I didn't stop moving. I couldn't. I had a singular focus.

Get to the barn. Get to Nova.

I heard Erryn yell a warning, and I moved my body to the right as she raced beside me, wielding her guns with expert precision, and taking out their snipers. I roared my thanks, and she nodded, her purple eyes glowing. To my left I saw a bright pink Dragon take to the skies, and an enormous black dog like beast taking down more men as they filed out of every fucking hole on the farm.

Like sewer rats, they ran from the fire Martina rained down on the outer buildings with her powers. I knew the Harbor sisters had magic, but I'd never seen it in action. I had no time to waste now to watch, but I appreciated it and them. Davian followed behind his mate, using his magic to watch her six. There was a van in the center of the field where shots were being fired from, I didn't bother watching it for long. They could shoot me all they wanted, my hide was tougher than it looked.

Screams and gunshots, magic and Dragonfire filled the air, but all I needed to do was get to that barn. The place they'd taken my Nova. I trusted the Witch Shifter Clan to take out the small militia of GHA troops. Those bastards wanted to destroy our people, but their time was up. They'd failed, and now they had to pay.

The Global Human Alliance was nothing but another hate group. A band of small-minded assholes who wanted to destroy that which they didn't understand. Shifters weren't a threat to humanity. No supernatural was. Hell, we'd been here just as long as them, if not longer. Their hatred was pointless and their mission statement stupid.

"Asher, I'll shoot the lock, then you should be able to go right through," Erryn yelled and took aim.

Two heartbeats later and I slammed my front paws into the heavy wood door, crushing it beneath my weight. I roared loudly, shaking the rafters with my rage.

"Asher," Nova moaned my name from where she was strapped down on a metal table.

My Lion's vision was different from my human's, but I could tell she'd been drugged. Her crystalline eyes were glassy, and her face was paler than normal. I growled threateningly and took out the first man who attempted to stop me with one swipe of my claws across his chest, splitting him open like a can of tuna.

"Shoot him! Shoot him!" someone screamed.

"Stop! Why won't you die?" another asshole asked, trying desperately to shoot me with his Glock.

Moron must have loaded it with BBs because it didn't even slow me down. Another swipe of my claws and he was disemboweled, bleeding out on the ground next to his buddy.

"You idiots! You brought them right to us!" a man yelled, and it sounded familiar. "Someone kill him!"

I turned my head to the corner where the bastard was cowering and snarled. He was the last person I expected to see, and I admit I was stunned I recognized the piece of shit. Gabriel Markovsky stood pointing at me with a shaking hand. DPCA research scientist. A man Nova had called friend. And the motherfucker whose head I was two seconds from biting off.

But really, why wait?

I didn't see the needle in his hand, not that it would have stopped me. I heard the others filing into the barn, taking out GHA operatives left and right. Target in sight, I vaulted across the last couple of feet separating us and wrapped my jaws around Gabe's puny fucking head.

Then, with only the slightest amount of pressure, I crushed his skull between my massive Lion's teeth, and I jerked back, ripping his head clean off his body. I didn't stop there. My vision was red, and I was filled with bloodlust. By the time I was done with him, Gabe was a gory mass of bloody pulp and splintered bones. Unrecognizable as human, let alone as the man he once was.

"Asher?" Nova's voice brought my head up, and I turned to see my whole fucking world stumble towards me.

She looked a little worse for wear, but I swore to the gods GHA would pay for every tear track and bruise on her perfect precious body. Her hands wove into my mane as she pressed her face against me, weeping softly and murmuring stuff and nonsense. It was okay. I understood. My emotions were still running high, too. I bumped her with my nose, sniffing her all over to make sure she wasn't bleeding anywhere. I'd kick my own ass if she got hit with a stray bullet or something of the like.

I couldn't wait to hold her in my arms, and I tried but something wasn't right. I needed to shift. Needed to turn back into my human form. But I couldn't. Fuck. This was wrong. I growled, shaking my head, and she stood back, her eyes roaming all over me.

"Asher?" she whispered, but it was a question, not a statement.

A tendril of panic slithered through me, and I tried, but I couldn't find that magical thread, the bond that linked beast and man. I growled as my worry increased. Nova's eyes widened as she reached into my mane and removed something from my skin. I grunted, but was careful not to move too swiftly. Panic started to flare once I saw what she held. A single syringe, the plunger already depressed.

I might have killed Gabe, but the motherfucker had damned me to a half-life.

Nova. I'm so sorry.

CHAPTER ELEVEN NOVA

IT TOOK four hours for the DPCA to clear out the old Hanshaw farm. After a thorough search, they located holding cells where a half dozen Shifters, three of which were children orphaned by the GHA's experiments. It was all in their records, which were surprisingly thorough. But I guessed maybe that was because I was the one who'd trained Gabe and I was nothing if not diligent in my record keeping.

That fucking prick. I wished he were still alive so I could kill him all over again.

With Mother's help, the orphaned children were placed in Sybil's care, which was perfect timing since Harbor House was just about ready to reopen. I gave everyone physicals, making sure to draw their blood to test for anything the GHA might have injected them with since most of them couldn't remember much about their time there. I was grateful they mostly suffered from ordinary bumps and bruises. Nothing lasting. Nothing like what that bastard did to my Asher.

It seemed Gabe, that piece of shit, had been working for the Global Human Alliance all along. Siphoning supplies from my lab and stealing my notes. Luckily, we had arrived on scene just in time before the next round of injections. Unfortunately, Asher got the first one, and it was another variation of their formula. Gabe had taken measures to counter all the advances I'd made in my research, and it was going to take some time to fix this. But I wouldn't give up. Not now, not ever.

To think this all happened because of the total fucking ineptitude of the goons working for Gabe or his GHA bosses. From what I understood, the DPCA team who'd been tracking their movements found the leader and his minions, and they got them all. Every last one of those hateful fucks.

The leader of the Global Human Alliance turned out to be this piece of shit Warlock with a beef against Shifters. The fucker resented the Supernatural Council, and the Shifter Council, for denying his request for a separate entity to police Warlock and Witch magical practitioners. His whole mission statement was to out the supernatural world to humans and to takeover. The madman believed supes were superior and therefore destined to rule the world.

He was hardly original in his grand scheme, but whatever. His name was Michael Smith, or Smithers, or some shit. I didn't care. But his story was so fucking stupid. He didn't get what he wanted, so he went and found himself an army of scared, worthless, hateful jackasses with access to weapons. How he managed to convince Gabe to work for him, I had no idea. Regret filled me as I readied another vial of the latest antidote I'd been working on. I didn't regret Gabe dying, I regretted the fact I hadn't recognized him for the sniveling two-faced prick he was.

The sound of claws scraping against the cement floor brought my head up, and I smiled at my mate as he stalked towards me in his Lion form. Six weeks had passed since Asher and my Clan rescued me from Gabe's clutches. Six weeks since I last saw him in his human skin. Not that I didn't love his beast, but I needed my man. I had to get him back.

Please gods, please help me get it right this time.

"Are you ready to try again?" I asked Asher, watching his Lion for any sign of distrust or discomfort.

Shifters were dual natured creatures, but the animal's sentience was different from their human awareness. Even Shifter animals ran on instinct, and I never wanted to get Asher's hackles up. Especially not when he was more than half a ton of powerful Lion.

He sat down on his haunches directly in front of me, his big gold eyes never leaving my face. I shivered at that stare, feeling his love and adoration wash over me. Gods, I loved this man. I sucked in a breath, turning back to look at the vials, checking dosages and jarring a few notes to make sure I had everything ready.

Lucky for me, my brother-in-law was a construction guru. He'd outfitted me with a lab of my own in the back of the new Harbor House construct, complete with enough space to house a Lion, and a smallish bedroom area for me to crash with him. I hadn't left Asher's side for more than a few minutes since we got out of that GHA hellhole.

I felt a gentle swoosh across the back of my head and turned to see Asher's tail caressing me. It was a gesture he made often, one that made me feel safe and loved. One that told me it was okay if I failed again. Only, it wasn't okay. Not really.

"Here we go," I said, keeping my voice light.

I ran my left hand over his giant leonine head, giving him a good scratch and smiling as he closed his eyes and purred, pressing his head more firmly against my touch. He was such a pussycat with me. A big pussycat, but still a pussycat. I had no doubt he'd curl up on my lap if he could fit. I was just glad he didn't try. I did not feel like adding crushed by Lion to my list of shit I never expected to do this year.

I used the flat part of my hand to press down on his thick, glossy mane until I saw his skin. Aiming for the same patch where I had injected previous versions of the drug I'd made to counter GHA's poison, I stuck Asher with the needle and closed my eyes as I pressed down on the plunger.

Now, I was a scientist, and my brain was hard wired for logic. But these past few weeks, I think I prayed more than I ever had in my entire life. Even then, I prayed, whispering promises, offering bargains, wishing with everything I had that this worked, that I would bring him back. But nothing could have prepared me for the absolute relief that flowed through my body when I felt human hands touching my face.

"Baby, you did it. You did it! I'm back. Baby, I'm back!"

Asher's voice sounded deep and husky, but I was so fucking happy to hear it I couldn't stop from sobbing as I flung myself at him.

"Asher? Oh fuck, thank the fucking gods, Asher, you're back!" I repeated, crying hysterically as he held me tight to him.

"I knew you could do it, Hotshot."

"I'm sorry it took so long," I cried, hoping like hell

he would forgive me, but he was shaking his head, hushing me as he pulled me tighter against him.

He smelled like fur and dominance, Lion and man, and musk, and I wanted to roll around in it, *in him*. As if he understood, as if he felt the same, Asher pulled me by the back of my neck and pressed his mouth to mine. He kissed me hard, and rough, with a desperation I felt down to my toes. And it was exactly what I needed, what I wanted, what I craved.

Lust and love slammed into me with all the force of a wrecking ball, and it wasn't long before I was helping him tear my clothes off. He groaned appreciatively, running his big, firm hands over my curves, testing the weight of my breasts before rolling the nipples between his fingers as his teeth scraped over the claiming scar he'd given me.

"Gonna fuck you now, mate. Gonna claim you again with my bite. Remind you and everyone who you belong to," he growled, and I squirmed as a fresh wave of arousal pooled between my legs.

"Want that, mate?" he asked, and it was clear he was waiting for an answer.

I felt his cock against my belly, hot and heavy, and hard as steel. I couldn't think, I was like one throbbing hormone. But this damned man was not going to budge until I said it, was he? So, I scratched my nails down his back, grabbing his ass and squeezing as I told him exactly what I wanted.

"Yes, Asher. I want you to fuck me, claim me with your bite, fill me with your cock, and I want to claim you back, mark you as mine," I said roughly, almost choking on my emotions.

"Yes," he growled, eyes glowing as he cupped my face and slammed his lips to mine.

I had zero time to adjust to his lips, as they were off me as fast as they'd been on. Asher's entire body was vibrating with his growl, and the sound seemed to rush through me, straight to my clit. He turned me around till I was on all fours, his big hand pressing down on my back as he lined himself against my entrance from behind.

"Can't be gentle now, Baby. Gonna take you hard this time," he grunted, and I nodded, needing it rough, wanting him any way I could get him.

"Fuck, you're so wet," he said, rubbing the tip of his cock along my soaked seam.

Sensation after sensation tingles up and down my spine as he continued to coat himself in my juices. His big hands were holding onto my hips, but he moved them down to my ass, cupping the cheeks before spreading them wide.

"What a pretty little rosebud, Baby. Can't wait to

fuck you there too," he growled a split second before I felt him bend.

I moaned loudly when I felt Asher's tongue between my cheeks, licking at my asshole before he turned and bit me right on my butt. I didn't think I could like such a thing, but like everything else when it came to him, I was so turned on, I didn't think I would ever be turned off again. He moved again, and I felt his thick head pressing inside one inch, then withdrawing. Again, deeper that time, then withdraw.

"Please," I begged.

"Please what, Vixen? What do you need?"

"I need you to fuck me, Asher. Now, right now."

Apparently, that was the right thing to say because he was done messing around. He pulled my hips and slammed into me from behind, making my whole body shake with the force of his thrusts. He filled me so good, so right, stroking that special place inside me that no one else ever touched before until I thought I'd spontaneously combust. Nothing ever felt so good, well, until he reached around with his long fingers and started plucking at my swollen clit.

"Oh gods," I moaned.

"My name, Vixen. When we fuck, you say my name," he commanded, caging me in with his enormous body.

His hips never stopped pistoning, and I did as he

asked. I said it. I fucking shouted it as he drilled into me, making me feel better than I ever had before.

"Asher. Asher! ASHER!" I screamed, my orgasm skyrocketing through me just as I felt his teeth pierce the skin across my left shoulder.

"MINE!" he roared.

I groaned loudly as I felt the first pulse of his warm release filling me. Turning my head, I caught his bicep between my teeth, and I bit down. Hard.

Mine indeed.

CHAPTER TWELVE ASHER

AFTER CLAIMING my mate on the hard floor of the office, shed, or whatever the fuck that building was, we showered and moved to the bed. Facing me on her side, I traced every inch of Nova lovingly with my eyes first, then my hands, and eventually my lips.

"You know you have me, right? I mean that, Baby. You have every inch of me, and I am never letting you go," I whispered and dragged her body closer to me.

I dropped a kiss on her temple, enjoying the way she leaned into me. Poor little thing was exhausted. After making her come on my tongue, fingers, and cock several times in a row, I understood. But I wasn't through with her yet. All those weeks I spent trapped inside my Lion's body, I ached for her. It would be a good long while before I sated the need to feel her slick sex pulsing with pleasure around me.

"Good. I don't want you to let me go," she whispered back, kissing the place on my throat where her face was pressed against me.

"I know we haven't had a chance yet, but would you tell me what happened that night? When they took you," I said, trying to keep the growl out of my voice and failing.

"It doesn't matter, Asher. I'm safe now," she said, concern marring her pretty blue eyes, but I shook my head.

"I know, Baby. I know, but I need to hear it. Please," I begged, and that was a fucking first. I never begged.

Nova stirred against me, and I eased up on the grip I had on her body. But I couldn't bring myself to let her go. As if she understood, I felt her small hands against my chest, and listened to her inhale before she started speaking. I breathed in her peppermint rosemary scent, now permanently mixed with my own manly musk, and I thanked the gods she was safe.

"I was looking for my sisters when he grabbed me. He was human, but he must've seen my eyes glowing with my Fox after we talked. I was so emotional, I guess I wasn't guarding myself as closely as I normally would," she said, as if she needed to apologize for getting kidnapped.

"Nova, what happened wasn't your fault. Look at me. It. Was. Not. Your. Fault."

I had to see her when I said this, so I leaned back and lifted her face with a finger on her cute little chin. She blinked and nodded, and I replied with the same gesture, waiting for her to continue.

"He stuck me in the neck with some sort of paralytic, but it also had some of that formula to freeze a Shifter in one form. The thing is, I'm not just a Shifter," she said, and I nodded in understanding.

This could have been so much fucking worse if my little Vixen wasn't also half Witch. I managed to keep a lid on my rage, allowing it to simmer not burn, while she described her fear as she was thrown in the backseat of their car. She hadn't seen me, so no, she didn't know I was coming for her, and that broke my fucking heart.

"When they dragged me into that barn and laid me on the table, the careless assholes didn't even bother with straps. They were snickering about what a hot find I was, and how they hoped the boss would keep me in my human skin so they could play with me a little before he finished experimenting on me," she whispered, and I trembled.

"Fuck. Nova, I'm so sorry. Did they—"

"No! No, Asher, you got there in time," she said, trying to reassure me.

Fury filled me and I wished I could go back in time and kill those bastards all over again. Just the mention of what they were thinking of doing made my vision red. I felt Nova's hands on my face, and she lifted up, pressing my lips to hers.

"I'm safe, Asher. You saved me before they could do anything. It was just talk. By the time they brought their scientist in, and I saw who it was, you were almost there," she continued.

"Gabe almost shit himself when he saw me. He started cursing and yelling, and his distraction was exactly what I needed. I used my magic to push the paralytic out of my veins while he was chewing them out for taking me."

"Apparently, they were aware of our little under-cover operation thanks to Gabe, that piece of shit, but the fact we were at *The Thirsty Dog* and not *Quenched* messed them up. They were always focused on you, staying away from you, the big, badassed agent. So when they saw me, eyes glowing with my Fox, they thought I was fair game."

"Badassed?"

"Hell yes. Everyone at the DPCA thinks you're a superhero," she said.

I grunted, reminded of the moniker Gabe had called me. Ashman. That prick. I was glad he was dead. I didn't feel like a superhero. Yes, we got there in time, but I almost lost her. And *almost* was too close for comfort.

"Then you arrived, and you know everything else," she said, wrapping up the story. "Oh, but they were using an olfactometer at first in the other instances. Just thought you should know, you were right about that. My eyes gave me away, but they had the device on them when they took me. It's in my lab at the DPCA. Mother had me take it apart to see how it worked."

"Mmm," I made a noncommittal humming sound in the back of my throat.

I did not care about being right just then as I kissed her head, letting her feel my love and adoration in the caress. My heart squeezed inside my chest. I never thought this was possible. I figured I'd end up being another stud for my mother's Pride. But after meeting Nova, I knew that was not my fate.

This woman. This beautiful, brilliant, ballsy woman was my everything. She was my reason. And I would do anything to keep her safe and by my side.

"Fuck, I am so sorry. I know you have your Fox, and your magic, and your Clan, your family to protect you. You don't need me. But you have me, Nova. Do you know that? You. Have. Me."

"I know," she whispered, her beautiful eyes filled with tears as she nodded.

"For better or worse, Baby."

"Speaking of marital vows, um, this here?" she asked, holding up her ring finger. I grinned unashamedly and confirmed the truth.

"Yep. Tracking device. I was worried." I explained.

"And I'm glad you had the foresight to do that, but maybe tell a girl next time."

"Next time I'm putting a tracker underneath your skin," I warned before squeezing her again.

"Ha ha," she teased, but I didn't laugh.

It wasn't a joke. I was putting a tracker under her skin sooner or later. But I promised myself I would tell her about it this time. Whether it was before or after I did was another story.

"I'm so sorry I didn't stop them before they could get their filthy hands on you, Baby," I apologized once more, needing her to understand just how sorry I was.

"And I'm sorry I couldn't find the right formula to get you back sooner," she said.

"You got me back, alright," I reminded her, nuzzling her face with mine.

It was a sign of affection among felines, Shifter or not, and I couldn't stop once I started. Rolling her onto her back, I followed, pressing my face against her soft skin. I needed to stamp myself on every inch of her. It was possessive alphahole behavior, but I couldn't help it, and Nova didn't seem to mind. In fact, she seemed to relish it. She opened her thighs, cradling me with her body while I kissed, and petted, and worshipped her.

I didn't think I'd ever have my fill. And that was okay. Because we had until forever to sate our need for one another. This woman was mine in every way that counted, and I would not rest until the entire world knew it.

"I love you, Asher," she said, and my heart fucking melted on the spot.

This woman owned me. Body, heart, and soul. I was hers and hers alone. Did she know it? Could she understand the power she held?

My mouth salivated as her peppermint rosemary scent increased along with her arousal. I wanted to devour her. To lick her from head to toe. Stamp myself all over her. Make her come while screaming my name a thousand times.

Sexy, beautiful, genius of a woman. She meant so much to me. I wanted to kick my past self for ever making her doubt herself. And I vowed there and then to lift her up like the queen she was. To be her cheerleader. Her protector. Her lover. Her biggest fucking fan.

"I love you, too, Baby. So fucking much," I growled, claiming her lips once more.

"Show me," she said, licking her tongue into my mouth and sharing her sweet flavors with me.

Fuck. This woman was my everything. My all. And I was going to show her. Now. Right now.

And I did.

EPILOGUE NOVA

I SAT THERE STARING at the tiny band of gold stacked on top of the glittering sapphire on my finger. Mated and married in the same week. It was hard to believe, but I couldn't help the joy spreading through me. It might seem fast to most, but Asher and I were inevitable.

"Are you guys ready to eat?" Sybil asked excitedly.

She carried a tray loaded with finger sandwiches to join the other dozens of dishes spread out for folks to eat.

It was the first official day of spring, and the trees were covered in pink blossoms and green buds, promising new life, and the splendor of warmer days to come. The three children we rescued from the GHA were playing kickball with Mitchell and Tim in the field beside the playground they'd built next to the new and improved Harbor House.

Today was the grand opening picnic and Sybil had invited half the town to celebrate. My gaze traveled over the crowd, smiling as I saw Martina mingling with the Alpha of the Macconwood Pack and his human mate. My sister's relationship with the local Wolves had gotten much better the last few months, and I had no doubt that was due to her newfound confidence thanks to her mate.

Davian and Erryn were smiling at each other, swaying in the corner to music only they could hear. But that wasn't unusual. I'd grown up watching those two lovebirds and wondering if I would ever get that lucky. I didn't have to wonder anymore, though.

My own happy ever after ending was already striding towards me. Asher stood taller than most of the men there. With his head full of thick, glossy blond locks, he was easy to spot. The predatory gaze gleaming in his golden eyes had me pressing my thighs together tightly in the tight jeans I was wearing. Asher loved me in denim. And he loved me more when I wore nothing, which was probably why I was completely obsessed with the man.

"Hotshot," he growled, wrapping his arm around my waist, and pressing me tight to his hard body.

"I think I like it better when you call me Vixen. Or Baby," I said, teasing him.

"Do you, now? Well, I might be able to arrange that," he growled, nipping my lip between his teeth before soothing the minor ache with his tongue.

Sexy beast. My mate.

"Knock it off, you two, there are children here," Sybil mock scolded as she filled a plate with food and turned to hand it to one of the guests.

I rolled my eyes before turning to face her while still wrapped up in my mate's arms. If there was one thing you had to understand about Asher, the man was completely immovable unless he wanted to be moved.

"Better?" I asked, but she wasn't paying attention anymore and I felt put out for moving at all.

Oh well. I leaned back into Asher's powerful body, I smiled as I felt his purr vibrating through my body, and straight to my damn ovaries. Speaking of which, I had things to discuss with my gorgeous, sexy mate.

"What is it?" he asked, intuitively knowing when something was up.

"Um," I said, not really knowing where to start.

It was a touchy subject for me, and one we hadn't brought up since that night at *The Thirsty Dog*. In fact, we'd been so busy with the claiming and biting and reassuring one another that we were safe, whole, and together, we'd kinda been avoiding the things that broke us apart however briefly.

"Let's go over here," I said, pulling him towards my lab away from work.

I'd decided to keep the shed Mitchell had built for me with the help of a local White Witch, Sherry Morgan-McAllister, who'd used her magic to protect it and make it the kind of place I could work. It was the place where Asher and I had holed up until I managed to create the antidote that brought him back to me. The place where we'd both claimed each other so thoroughly, I'd had a tough time walking for days.

Worth it. Definitely worth it.

"Baby, tell me what's going on," Asher said, and I could feel his anxiety rise.

"Nothing bad," I said, and pushed him down on the sofa.

I needed him to sit and listen. I was a bundle of nerves, and I couldn't stand still. So, I paced in front of him, aware of his gold eyes racking my every move.

"Okay, this is kind of something we haven't talked about, but um, well, do you remember that night at The Thirsty Dog—"

"Of course, I remember.," he grumbled.

"But do you remember what we were talking about?" I asked, biting my lower lip.

Asher growled, reaching out to stop my pacing with

his big hands on my hips. He tugged me forwards and dragged me down onto his lap. Dropping one kiss on my head, he cupped my cheeks and looked me right in the eye.

"Baby, just tell me. You've got my Lion anxious as fuck."

"Well, your mother had barged into your house and that whole business about breeding, and I told you what SCAR did to me, but when you found me, you said it didn't matter. And that, that meant everything," I whispered, my vision blurring.

"Shhh. It's okay, Baby. I love you. I have everything I need as long as I have you, you know that, right? It's all okay," he said, kissing me before I even finished explaining.

I smiled and kissed him back for a second before shaking my head. Asher let me go reluctantly and I bit my lip.

"I'm not infertile. I mean, I don't think I am," I blurted. "You were right. I never tested myself after puberty, after adulthood. I always just took that report at face value. But it turns out, everything is in working order. So, someday, if you want, we can try," I whispered, not even aware I was holding my breath until Asher's eyes overflowed with tears and I gasped.

"Are you saying you wanna have my baby? Is that what you're saying, Vixen?" he asked.

"Yeah," I said, nodding my head. "I'm saying I want that. I want to try for a baby with you, Asher. I love you so much. And I know you love me. Even if it turns out we can't get pregnant, I know you will still love me. But I want to try. That is if you do," I said, realizing I was rambling.

"Geezus woman, I love you so fucking much."

He grabbed me them in a fierce hug, my big, beautiful mate completely undone by my whispered admission. Yes, I wanted his baby. And even more, I wanted him. He held me tightly to his chest, and I clung to him, reveling in his warmth and his strength.

I never thought I would have someone of my own. Being a foster kid, you grew up with all kinds of insecurities and abandonment issues. But I had my Clan, and my family, and now, I had him. Asher completed me in more ways than I'd ever expected. I knew most people thought my life was easy peasy and all because of my face. To some extent they were right, the world was one big beauty contest. But that wasn't the whole truth.

Nothing was ever that easy. The world was not just black and white. Pretty people had problems, too. I had a fuck ton. But I didn't have to shoulder them alone anymore. I had my Fox and my magic. I had people standing with me. I had my sisters. My brother. My Clan. And I had him. My mate. My one true love.

"Let's practice for that baby you want, Mrs. Donnelly," he growled, and I'd never heard such a sexy statement from my mate.

I stood up and turned around as Asher leaned forward, unbuttoning my jeans, and pulling them down my hips. I grinned, and he smacked my ass, making me gasp before he lifted me up and tossed me over his shoulder.

"Mine," he growled, and I had to amend my previous thought.

Hearing Asher call me *mine* in a voice thick with his Lion was the sexiest thing ever. I loved being his. And I loved that he was mine.

Whatever happened, we had each other, and knowing that made everything okay. It made taking chances and facing my fears worth the risk because he was worth it. He was everything.

"Eyes on me, Baby," he commanded, tossing me on the bed and for once in my life, my brain actually stopped functioning.

Just another thing Asher did for me. He brought me peace. He brought me quiet. And when his mouth came down on mine, I braced myself for the pleasure he was undoubtedly about to bring me.

My heart squeezed with love and my inner Fox yipped as our matebond pulsed around us. My magic danced along my fingertips, and I wrapped myself around him, welcoming, accepting, giving, and taking everything I could, everything I had.

"Love you so much," I moaned, needing him like I needed air to breathe, and hoping with everything inside me that he felt the same.

"Love you always, my sweet Vixen."

THE END.

Did you enjoy this installment of the Witch Shifter Clan? Be sure to check out River Dragon next!

C.D. GORRI

RIVER DRAGON

WITCH SHIFTER CLAN 3

RIVER DRAGON

Dreams can be beautiful, but they can also be deadly.

Sybil Harbor isn't like her sisters. True, they are hybrids like her, but Sybil is the only one of her kind. Now that Martina and Nova have found their mates, it's even lonelier for her. Well, it is until he walks into her life. Like a dream come true. Only her new man isn't what he appears, and the truth might kill her.

Perseus Calloway is on a mission. Living under an ancient curse, the Calloway Coven has been without its power for generations. But when a rumor of Dragons living just a few hours away reaches their ears, they send him to investigate. With Dragon blood, they can finally lift the curse. But what happens when the Dragon he finds isn't the Dragon he expected?

Sybil Harbor is more than just a beast. She's a flesh and blood woman who calls to his heart like no other. Percy has a choice to make. Save his family or save the River Dragon who captured his attention?

When she learns this daydream is more of a nightmare, Sybil's heart is on the verge of breaking. Will Sybil forgive Percy when his true intentions are revealed?

Find out in this installment of the Witch Shifter Clan series.

Trigger Warnings: The fictional characters in this book deal and discuss heavy issues such as kidnapping, and ancient curses. Violence, steamy scenes, and also some over the top obsession and possessiveness between the main characters. This is a paranormal romance where the focus is always on love and HEA, and everything inside these pages is pure fiction. It is not real or intended to harm. This book is written for entertainment. As always, please take care of your mental and emotional health.

THE CURSE OF THE CALLOWAY COVEN

"PERSEUS, you must find a way to end the curse," Father said as I leaned over his bed. "It is your duty, son. You must make things right for us all."

"I will, Father. I swear."

I left the room to the wails of my grandmother after my father's last breath rattled past his lips. The weight of my promise was crushing down on me as I entered my father's office. I needed to read it one more time. I needed to understand the mission I was about to enter.

There on the shelf, encased in glass, was a single piece of parchment. I took it down and sat it upon my father's desk. It was yellow with age, the ink barely visible, but I knew the words. Had memorized them over the course of my long life.

"For in the beginning, young Marian had loved the

monster Axelrod with all her being. But guilt and the wrongness of her actions motivated her to scorn the beast, and when he could not contain his fire, she cast him forth, spurning his advances and his vile ways.

A dutiful daughter of the Coven, she married her true mate, a worthy Dhampir of good blood, Tybalt Calloway. For many moons, Marian was loved by Tybalt, but alas the fruit of their marriage proved poisoned by the serpent, and Marian's hunger could not be sated by the mate she chose.

Having no other choice, her husband and true mate, Tybalt was forced to end her life in a merciful beheading on the same night the monster returned to take his vengeance.

Finding Marian dead, the beast, mindless and full of evil, cast a dark spell on the Calloway Coven.

'For your crimes against the heart, yours shall only know hunger until the Dragon's blood willing runneth once more through your veins!'

1765, Pennsylvania Colony, the New World, Calloway Coven."

Father was right. It was time for this madness to end. I needed to find a Dragon and bring it back to the coven where we would drain its blood and drink our fill. It was the only way to end this hateful curse.

The only question was where the fuck could I find a Dragon in the 21st Century?

PROLOGUE SYBIL

ABOUT THIRTEEN YEARS AGO...

"What do you think?" I asked, standing in front of my sisters.

"It's pink," Nova stated unhelpfully.

I rolled my eyes. I knew it was pink. Did she think I freaking forgot what color I'd used? I rolled my eyes at her. She was just so dang literal at times. My inner beastie purred softly. The Dragon understood Nova was who she was, and the creature inside me accepted that. It was my human side that took issue with my sister.

Sigh.

My hair was still damp, but I'd thoroughly toweled it dry so both Nova and Martina, my sisters, could see the bright color I'd used to dye it. Yes, it was pink. Just like Nova said. And, yeah, of course, I knew it was pink. I was the one who'd dyed it. To think, everyone called *her* a genius! Go figure.

"Wow, Sweet Syb! That is some color you got going on there," Martina said, eyeing my hair skeptically.

"What does that mean? You don't like it?" I asked, wanting to know.

I was being a little pushy, desperate maybe, but I always needed a little bit of extra reassurance. I wished I was more like Martina, all confidence and poise, or even more like Nova, who was a total brainiac and she knew it.

But I was just me. Just Sybil. The softer, quieter, less special of the three of us.

I knew in my heart that wasn't really true. Mama Ann, our foster mother, never treated us any differently. And Davian, our older brother and guardian, was awesome. He never failed to make us feel loved and cared for.

It was just, well, something in me that stirred up those harmful feelings. But I was working on it. Really, I was.

"No, not at all. I mean, I love it! It looks great, right Nov," Marti replied.

Her smile was too wide and her nodding too aggressive. And I saw her nudge Nova with her toe. But I appreciated her for both gestures. The Dragon did, too, choosing that moment to purr loudly.

"Yes. Sure. Um, it looks great, Syb, but why did you do it?" my smarty pants sister asked.

I shrugged and sat down crisscross applesauce on my bedspread, grabbing a wide-toothed comb from the side table. Parting my thick, newly dyed locks into sections, I slowly combed through each section before weaving them into six long braids. When they dried my hair would have that crimped look I liked so much. It was less than my natural curls, but more than the flat iron straight tresses most of the girls in our class preferred.

"Just wanted to do something different," I muttered, unable to explain it.

"Well, if you like it, we like it," Martina replied, nodding her head.

"Thanks, sis," I murmured and smiled over at her.

Nova shrugged one shoulder noncommittally, looking down to read whatever fancy new science book she'd borrowed from the library. She didn't understand, and I didn't expect her to. I mean, why would she?

Of the three of us, Nova was the most stunning. She looked like a freaking supermodel and her inner Fox was a real vixen, all white fur and glacier blue eyes.

Martina was no slacker. She was cute and curvy, and her Wolf was a total badass.

Truth was, I felt like an ugly duckling compared to the two of them. No one made me feel that way. I should probably explain myself better. I knew I wasn't hideous or anything. I mean, I wasn't exactly suffering in the self-esteem department. Typically, I was a happy-go-lucky version of myself.

I understood that everyone was unique, and we all had different things we brought to the table of life. Some people were beautiful. Some were smart. Some were generous and kind. Some were all those things at once. And some were all those things at different times.

Individuality made meeting people so interesting. Think how dull it would be if we were all the same! Ugh. I knew all that, and again, I did not believe I was gross looking or anything, but I made a promise when I was very young to always be honest with myself. And facts were facts. I was decidedly average when compared to my sisters.

Boring brown hair. Muddy hazel eyes. Pale skin. Sallow not creamy. My complexion was yellowish, sometimes green, as opposed to Nova's breathtaking ivory. I was short, even shorter than Martina. I had more on the bottom than the top, so where she was cute with an hourglass figure, I was pear-shaped with thunder thighs and a fat ass.

So, yeah, I needed to do something to separate myself from that mousy girl I saw in the mirror. Something to bring out the fire within. So, I did.

For all intents and purposes, it was a regular old Tuesday night. But for me, it was special. It was the night I decided to come into my own. To claim something for myself.

Our brother Davian was working late as usual. The three of us were tucked away in the bedroom we shared so as not to disturb him. Harbor House used to provide a haven for many children from tots to teens. They used to come to stay for short periods of time back when Mama Anne was alive.

But Davi and his mate Erryn were stretched thin as it was, raising the three of us. I didn't blame either of them for not having the resources or bandwidth to continue with Mama Anne's dream. We just never really had the chance to reopen our home as a sanctuary for those in need.

Mama Anne was the only mother I remembered. Kind, warm, stern when she had to be, but always welcoming and forgiving. She taught me to embrace both my Dragon and my Witch side. She even gave me lessons on how to control my magic, which seemed to have an affinity for water.

But she was gone now, and with her loss I felt the fading of her dream and it hurt. It really freaking hurt.

Like a physical ailment. And I knew it was something that would always haunt me.

So, even though I was only in high school, I started making plans. Big plans. Plans to do that someday. To finish what Mama Anne had started.

But before I could go about trying to save the world, I needed to focus on being the best me I could be. It really just came down to feeling good about myself.

How could I help anyone if I couldn't look in the mirror and feel pride, love, and happiness? I wanted those things. Heck, I needed them. And there was no reason for me not to feel them. My life was pretty great.

I loved my sisters, my brother, and his mate. We were a family. A good one. And I was a lucky girl. I knew that deep down in my heart of hearts. Just like I knew I was the only female Dragon Shifter in a thousand miles in any direction.

Heck, maybe more.

We'd just started our junior year at Maccon City High School, and I knew I needed something to lift my spirits. Something to be my signature. That was mine and mine alone.

So, I chose my hair. I claimed it as mine. Using dye was my outlet. It gave me confidence, bolstered my spirit, and made my Dragon purr happily inside my chest.

New hair. New me.

Wasn't that a commercial or something? Anyway, I decided it was gonna be my motto. Maybe not the new me bit. Maybe something else. I'd play with it for a bit. See what stuck. Either way, I was totally gonna rock that pink for a few months at least.

New hair. New attitude.

Now that seemed right.

CHAPTER ONE SYBIL

PRESENT DAY...

The smile on my face was laced with sadness, but there wasn't anything I could do about that. In order to do my job, I had to be strong. Working for the Division of Paranormal Creatures & Activity, or the DPCA as it was known, which was a secret government agency, under their new subdivision, Supernatural Child Protection Services, was not for the faint of heart.

All the same, it was my heart that was always left wrecked afterwards. I just got too involved with those under my care. It was a serious hazard, but one I was working on. I was a firm believer in the concept that each one of us was a work in progress. Some of us were just lucky enough to find our place, our purpose, and our people faster than others.

I wasn't lucky like that. But I had a purpose, and I had people, sort of. My sisters, their mates, and our brother and his mate were my people. They were my Clan. And my place was right there at the new Harbor House. After weeks of filling out paperwork and waiting for inspectors to give us the all clear, we were finally approved by the DPCA as the official South Jersey branch of the new SCPS.

The three young Shifter cubs who'd been staying at Harbor House over the past couple of weeks seemed uncertain as they gazed up at me, and I crouched down on the floor in front of them. Such brave kids. My heart squeezed inside my chest just thinking about everything they'd gone through.

They'd been rescued from the clutches of the evil Global Human Alliance, or GHA. They were a hate group that was trying to annihilate supernaturals through vile experimentation. My sister Nova and her mate Asher, who was also the newest member of the Witch Shifter Clan even though he was not a Witch, were responsible for delivering them to the safety of Harbor House after their terrible ordeal.

I'd been part of the team who'd rescued them, shifting into my Dragon to wage war on those horrible humans who held such hatred in their hearts, and all because we were different. My sisters and I knew all about that. Being Witches and Shifters, we'd each been abandoned by our birth parents after it was discovered we were more than just Shifters. There was magic in the world, and then there was *magic*.

Of course, Shifters believed in magic. How else could they explain changing one shape for another? But it was more complicated than that. Witches were able to use magic in a way Shifters could not. It was the combination of the two supernatural species that was hard to swallow. It was why we'd been left on mama Anne's doorstep some thirty years ago.

Knowing I was seconds away from crying my heart out, I tried for a smile, wanting to reassure the youngest of the three siblings. I was simply so moved by the circumstances, and not because I wanted to keep them or anything like that. There were so many supernaturals outside the human system who needed our help, the new dormitory Mitchell, Martina's mate, had just finished building at Harbor House was bound to be filled by the end of the summer.

So, no, I wasn't sad to see Johnny, Christabel, and Anthony go. I mean, I was, but not really. This was a good thing for them. A very good thing, and I was blessed to be a part of it. Sure, I could've tried for a stiff upper lip, but they did not call me Sweet Sybil for nothing. I was one of those over the top emotional people.

I was the laugh out loud type who never held in a giggle. Not even when it got me kicked out of Gym class at school. Of course, the opposite side of that particular coin of my personality was that I could cry at the drop of a hat. And I often did.

It was dumb. I knew it. But I couldn't help it. Everything made me cry. Songs, movies, TV shows. Hell, even commercials had been known to make me tear up. So it was not a surprise that I felt tears pricking my eyes at that particular moment.

Johnny, Christabel, and Anthony were going to be so happy now. My heart felt so full at that moment, I thought I might bust with it. Magic danced along my fingertips, and I knew if I didn't control it, something wonky would happen. Like I could maybe set off the sprinkler system or something like that. Water was my thing, and if I wasn't constantly monitoring my magic, strange things happened.

Once, when my mind started wandering during a class trip up in Paterson Great Falls for science class, I accidentally caused a disruption in the natural flow of the water. Of course, the normals didn't know I'd used magic, and it went down as some quirk of nature likely caused by the melting polar ice caps. Whatever. Davian tore me a new one when I'd gotten home that day.

Anyway, I made fists out of my hands, pushing my magic back inside of me. I turned my attention to my now former three young wards. They were the future of Shifter kind, and I felt really good about my life's choices. Dedicating myself to helping children like Johnny, who was the youngest of the three siblings, Christabel, who was the middle child, and Anthony, who was the oldest, was without a doubt the only thing I had ever felt one hundred percent certain about.

These kids were getting a real fairytale ending, and I helped get them there. No matter how minuscule my role, it still gave me a good feeling inside. A damn good feeling. I offered Anthony a smile, trying not to dwell on the fact my eyes were watery. I turned my thoughts to all the positives. They were safe now. Healthy. Whole. Together. And they were about to go live with the most wonderful couple.

I had the pleasure of working with their adoptive parents over the past few weeks. Tate and Cat Nighthawk ran the Macconwood-Nighthawk Teen Outreach Program, and they were both members of the Wolf Guard for the Macconwood Wolf Pack, which was going to be perfect for the three Wolf Shifter pups.

"Miss Sybil, what if we make a mess?" Johnny whispered to me, and I squeezed his hand in sympathy.

"What if they don't like us?" Christabel asked next.

"It'll be okay, guys. Miss Sybil wouldn't let us go if they were mean. Right, Miss Sybil?" Anthony said, nodding his head as he took his younger siblings' hands in his.

He looked at me and nodded solemnly, his expression far too grown for someone barely hitting double digits. I couldn't give them any guarantees, but I could give them the truth. Shifters had a way of hearing lies, so I wasn't gonna bother with that.

"That's right," I replied, feeling Anthony's trust in me like a balm to my soul.

It was a heady thing. To have a child's trust was such a responsibility, but in this instance, I knew I was right about the Werewolf couple who would be taking these three siblings into their home. They were good people, and they would do right by those pups.

"Cat and Tate are two of the nicest people I have ever met. Now, I don't think you have to worry about anything, but the basic rules apply, right? Like with making messes, Johnny, it is okay as long as you clean them. Just like you did here at Harbor House, right?"

I waited for him to nod before turning my attention to Christabel next. She was chewing on her lower lip, a habit she picked up while trying to stop sucking her thumb. I gave her a smile and a nod, letting her know I recognized her efforts and appreciated them.

"Now, Christabel, I don't know a single person who could not like you. The three of you are so special," I said, trying to show sincerity with every word I uttered.

"You mean it?" she asked shyly, tucking her blonde curls behind one ear.

"I really do. I'm positive Cat and Tate will tell you

themselves how much they like you if you give them a chance."

"But what if they don't want us after we get there?" she whispered.

"You will always have a place here if you need it, baby girl. But I know Cat and Tate are so very happy they get the chance to be your parents," I told her.

"They aren't our Mom and Dad," Anthony said stubbornly.

"Oh, I know, sweetheart. They do, too. But sometimes children are lucky enough to have more than one set of parents," I said, sharing a bit of my own history with them.

"We can have more than one Mom and Dad?" Christabel asked, and something in her big blue eyes just broke my heart.

"Yes, we can. I got to have two moms. You see, I'm like you. I came to live here at Harbor House when I was just a baby. I don't know what happened to my parents, but Mama Anne took me in and gave me sisters and a brother, and now I get to work with kids like me. Kids like you three. And, if you want, I'll tell you a secret," I said, biting back my grin as the three of them leaned in conspiratorially.

"You *all* feel like family to me. So you see, family isn't just who you're born to, but it's who you pick," I told them just as Cat and Tate walked into the meeting room.

I had it set up on the ground floor of the dormitory for prospective families to get to know the children. A safe, neutral place to get to know each other.

"Welcome," I said to our guests, and stood back while they greeted everyone.

I needed a breather. They gave me just the respite I needed, giving me a chance to pretend I was not so emotional. It always helped to do something mundane, like straightening the chairs. So I did.

"Hi there, Anthony, Johnny, Christabel. It's so nice to see you again," Cat said, automatically dropping to her knees to say hello to the kids.

She was joined by her mate, who held out a hand to shake Anthony's, automatically putting the older boy at ease while acknowledging his position as head of the tiny trio. My heart swelled with pride, and I bit my lip to stop the tears from flowing. They were going to make such a beautiful family. After a few minutes, the kids went to collect their things, and I was left with the two new parents.

It really was a splendid room. Real informal like. Mismatched couches, a giant throw rug, acres of bookshelves filled with everything from novels and picture books to board games and coloring books and crayons. There was a round table with six chairs around it that could be used to share a meal or play a game.

There was a television, but I had it so the sound could only go so high. I wanted to promote communication, so I had a video game system in there, but no movies.

The color palette was playful and soft, with warm yellows and pinks and calming blues and greens. It shouldn't have worked, but it did, and with the colorful rugs and throw pillows, it was really quite nice. A large toy chest filled with cars, dolls, trains, and action figures took up the space against the back wall, next to a Lego table and a giant tub of those colorful building blocks.

Christabel was clutching a stuffed bunny to her chest, and I gave her hand another squeeze before turning to face Cat and Tate. They were a striking couple. She was tall and beautiful with blue eyes and long golden hair, and he was bronzed and muscular with shoulder-length, pin-straight black hair.

"Well, Miss Harbor, I can't thank you enough," Cat began, offering her hand as tears filled her eyes.

"Please call me Sybil," I said, nodding my head and taking her hand before I was tugged into a super tight hug by the she-Wolf.

"We are going to take such good care of them," Cat promised.

"I know you are. They're brilliant kids. And I am here if you ever need me," I said, knowing she could hear the truth in my voice.

"Thank you. I can't thank you enough," Cat blubbered.

"Hey now, Baby. Easy now. No more tears. What will the children and Miss Sybil think?" Tate whispered, kissing his mate on her temple before turning to shake my hand.

"That I'm so damn happy to have them I sprung a leak?" Cat said, and we shared a laugh at her response.

Tate was still holding her close, and I averted my gaze to give the loving couple some privacy. But it wasn't like I could turn off my Shifter hearing or anything. Cat and Tate had that kind of fairytale romance someone like me had only ever read about.

Hell, I cut my teeth binge reading old romance novels that had belonged to Mama Anne when I was a kid. The words of praise and encouragement I could hear Tate whispering to his mate as he wiped the tears from her eyes, coupled with a look of pure adoration on his face was enough to make me swoon. Not because I had the hots for Tate, but because I craved that sort of love for myself.

If only.

"We're ready," Anthony said, re-entering the room with his siblings in tow.

He looked so grown up, but I supposed he had to be. He was technically the man of the house, but I hoped and prayed he'd lean on Tate. Something told me the Wolf Shifter would make a fine father. Each of the children carried a small backpack loaded with clothes and things they'd acquired while at Harbor House.

They stood there, uncertainty on their faces, and I recognized this as the part I'd been dreading all day. The part when we said our official goodbyes. I had to admit, even though this was difficult, I was glad to have the kids to focus on.

It was the perfect opportunity to walk away from Cat and Tate and their PDAs. I mean, they were PG, but I was wrestling with a green monster on my shoulder, and it was not a good feeling or look.

"Did you remember your toothbrushes?" I asked, and all three kids nodded.

Kneeling down, I opened my arms and welcomed their goodbye hugs, whispering my own words of well wishes and farewells.

"Will we see you again Miss Sybil?" Christabel asked, her eyes wide.

"Of course you will, sweet pup," Cat told the child, offering her a hand. "Miss Sybil will be here at Harbor House, and we live only a few minutes away."

I nodded my agreement, relief filling me at Cat's promise before I walked the new family out to their car.

Martina and Nova came to say goodbye as well, and the three of us stood in the driveway and waved them off. So many emotions filled me. I braced myself, knowing I was just seconds away from crying.

"Are you okay, Sweet Syb?" Martina asked, tightening her hold on my shoulders.

I nodded. I wasn't okay, though. Not even remotely. Always the emotional one, I offered my Alpha and sister a watery smile before she grabbed me in a tight hug. But only after the children were out of sight.

Sweet Sybil. They still called me that, among other things, and sometimes I hated it. To me sweet meant simple, but I wasn't either of those things. Not really. None of us were.

Nova reached out and rested her hand on my shoulder. Her too logical mind always had a hard time with understanding my emotional response to situations, but that was okay. She knew me well enough that I would not want to speak out loud until my sobs were under control.

I leaned on Martina, grateful for her strength, and squeezed out my last tears. Still, I remained silent. I knew if I talked, my wobbly voice would only display my feelings, and I was trying really hard to keep it together.

CHAPTER TWO SYBIL

A FEW MOMENTS and some hiccups later, Martina gave me one last squeeze before releasing me. I did not stumble, but it was a near miss.

"That's it. I'm calling it. We are going out tonight," Nova announced.

"Yeah! Good idea," Martina seconded.

"Guys, I just wanna stay home and—"

"No," they said at the same time, dragging me towards the main house.

"Sybil. We love you to bits, but if Nova and I don't drag you out of this place, you are just going to mope around," Martina said, and she wasn't wrong.

"And no one wants to see our Sweet Sybil mope," Nova added, her blue eyes twinkling at me.

I sighed, shuffling along with them. I didn't want to

go out, but maybe they had a point. The new residents weren't coming till Monday, and I had the entire weekend to myself. I knew Marti and Nova would be with their mates, and I shouldn't say no to hanging out with them.

Our Clan bonds were still new, and as Martina navigated her way through being our Alpha, I felt positive this was something she needed. Maybe even more than I did. Of course, I was always good at reading Marti and Nova.

The bonds of our sisterhood were stronger than ever, and I knew through those bonds how happy they both were. I should have been glad, and deep down I was. But I was feeling kind of sorry for myself, and well, a little jealous, truth be told.

Gods, I was such a bad sister.

I hated that I was envious of them for having found their fated mates. My magic pulsed beneath my skin, and I closed my eyes as my Dragon growled inside my chest. The creature was lonely, and I seconded that.

I didn't know how other Shifters felt about their animals. But for me, it was strange. I would not necessarily say I had two separate consciousnesses, but sometimes, I got the distinct impression my Dragon had her own opinions.

"Hey, are you okay?" Martina asked once we'd made it inside the main house.

The door was always open, but I supposed you would have to be nuts to try to break into Harbor House. Especially now that we were an official group registered with the Supernatural Council. The Witch Shifter Clan was as real as it got.

Martina and Nova had both moved out, sort of. They'd built single houses on our property to live in with their mates. Well, I should say Martina's mate, Mitchell, had built them. It had been quite a surprise when we'd learned the actual size of the land Mama Anne owned. After getting a few permits, and the local Macconwood Wolf Pack's okay—*since they were the most formidable Shifter group in the area, it behooved us to tell them our plans and get their nods of approval, which they gave without issue*—we started building.

There was always something going on outside, but I was used to the noise and to the new dynamic between my sisters and me. We had a bond nothing could break, but they were both mated, and I felt changes rippling through our relationship. Not that I disapproved of their choices in any way, shape, or form. I mean, I didn't. The guys were great. Better than great.

Not only had Mitchell and Asher contributed their time and expertise to making Harbor House fully functional, but both males left their former Pride and Pack and recently joined our Clan. That meant we had 7 members. Officially, speaking.

I still lived in the main house, sharing it with Davian and Erryn. though I had a room on the lower level of the dormitory for when new residents came in. I didn't feel right about leaving children in the dorms alone, but until we had more staff to help with them, I was it.

Martina and Nova both lived in new houses Mitchell's construction company had erected on our property.

As a social worker, I had a measly income. Davian and Erryn did way better, with their tech skills they both worked for Graves Enterprises. But they poured money into this place over the years, and into mine and my sisters' education, and I really wanted to be independent. They deserved to be able to enjoy themselves and their money without worrying about Harbor House or me.

Of course, I was the only one who still couldn't afford my own rent. Nova and Martina had saved a small fortune over the years, and they too helped fund repairs and most of the additions to our property themselves. Of course, it helped that both Asher and Mitchell had money, too.

Getting things up and running was costly. But my Clan mates were all too willing to give money to Harbor House and to offset construction costs. It was all my idea, and I felt horrible just taking and taking, but I had no choice. I couldn't afford it. I knew I could never repay them just like I knew they would never ask me to. Still, it was one more worry sitting heavily on my troubled mind.

"Come on, I know what you need," Martina said.

Her smile was gleeful as she pulled me into the bathroom and pushed me down to the vanity stool I still had from when we were teenagers.

"Alright, what color are we doing?" Nova asked.

She grabbed a few of my dye bottles from the acrylic display case I had sitting on the vanity. Exhaling softly, I didn't wince as Martina lifted my long hair and clipped it on top of my head. She grabbed one of the capes I kept beneath the sink and fastened it around my neck.

I had to admit this was a good idea. I'd allowed my hair dye to fade out over the last few weeks and they had a point. It was time for a redo.

"How about we go with the aqua?" I replied, my gaze flicking to the newest bottle in her left hand.

"Perfect." Nova smiled, placing the bottle on the vanity before slapping a pair of rubber gloves on.

Next, she started mixing. Nova had been working on a special additive to the dye to allow the color to last longer, and I was eager to try it. But I had to admit I was only half-listening as she explained how she used magic and chemistry to create the formula. It was cool and all, but I felt anxious and uneasy. My stomach was full of butterflies, and I laid a hand over the soft, squishy flesh there to try to calm the bothersome things.

"Okay, technically it is a sisters' night, but the guys will probably show up," Martina stated, sitting down next to me while I waited for the forty-five minute timer to be up.

I nodded and shrugged noncommittally. She wasn't wrong. Those fellas did not leave their women alone for long.

Lucky heifers.

She offered me the bag of chips she was snacking on, and I reached in and pulled a couple out. Snacks always helped. Martina had come to the wrong conclusion, but I appreciated her, anyway. I nodded and bumped her shoulder with mine while I chewed on the crispy jalapeno flavored chips, enjoying their company.

"Hey, I want some," Nova barked, grabbing the bag from Martina's hands.

"Don't eat them all, you skinny bitch," Marti whined and pinched Nova's butt in response.

"Ouch!"

It was just normal teasing, and I appreciated that. I laughed at their nonsense, wiping my cheeks.

"Hey, those kids are gonna be fine with Cat and Tate," Martina said, holding my gaze with her Alpha stare.

"I know. I'm fine, really. Anyway, thank you for this. A night out will be fun," I said, even though I really didn't want to go.

"Heck yeah! It will be awesome. The guys won't be there till after ten, so it will be girl time for a while and we can shoot some *slippery panties* and dance," Nova said, doing her best impression of the running man.

"Oh my gods. Nova, do not dance. And I mean that in the nicest way possible."

"*Shaddyap,*" she growled, swatting me with a pillow and exaggerating her Jersey accent.

"Don't get dye on my pillow! Wait. What the hell is a *slippery panty*?" I mumbled, shaking my head.

"First, if you haven't had slippery panties in a while, you been single too long," Nova said and snorted. "Second, I dance good."

"No, sister, I am afraid you really don't dance well at all," Martina clarified, and I nodded my head in agreement.

Nova looked hurt for a second before collapsing into a fit of giggles. She was beautiful and a genius, but she really had no skills on the dance floor. Like none whatsoever. Not that she shouldn't shake her ass and have fun anyway, but it helped to remind me she wasn't as perfect as she looked when she tried and failed to find the beat in the song that was playing through my wireless speakers.

"How is it she still can't recognize a bass?" Martina asked me and I just shrugged.

"Anyway, a slipper panty is a shot made with vanilla vodka, butterscotch schnapps, and hazelnut liqueur. It's so fucking good," Nova said, practically moaning.

"It does sound good," I had to agree.

"And since the guys are coming by later, we can scope out someone who can give you another kind of *slippery panty*, eh?" Nova added, wagging her perfectly sculpted eyebrows.

"No, no, I do not need you two trying to set me up," I replied, knowing that sort of thing had never worked out before.

I mean, why would it? Anytime Nova or Martina approached a man with the intention of setting me up all I had to do was watch his face go from interested to shocked when he realized they were not talking to him for themselves, but rather, for their pudgy little sister. And really, who wanted to deal with that mess? Not me.

"Um, actually, about the guys not being there early, Tim might beat us there," Martina said.

"Cool. Is he bringing Pete?" Nova asked.

Marti nodded, and I made a humming sound of approval. I liked their company, they were fun as fuck. Tim Truman was Mitchell's brother, but he was also Martina's schoolgirl crush. They had a good laugh over that when she reconnected with them. The man was also a hella good time. He was married to a local barber named Pete, who adored his husband like crazy. Tim was simply the most honest, fun loving, liveliest partier of anyone I knew.

This was starting to sound like a real party. I smiled at my sisters. Maybe they were right, and tonight would be exactly what I needed.

"You guys, this sounds awesome. Thank you both so much," I said, standing just as the timer went off.

It was time to rinse my hair and meet the next brand new me. I was seventeen when I started coloring my hair, ditching my mousy brown locks for something new and exciting, and I never looked back again.

After rinsing and conditioning my hair, I wrapped my head in a towel and got dressed. I chose tight black pants with a cropped shirt that showed more of my soft belly than I liked, but it had a low neckline and the bra I was wearing made my boobs look bigger than they were. The outfit definitely made me feel sexy, so I was willing to give it a try.

I applied extra makeup to my face, paying more attention to my eyes since I knew I'd be drinking, and lipstick was sort of a waste. Last, I unwrapped the towel and shook out my long aqua locks. I combed through the tangles, applied some hair product, and dried it with low heat. By the time I was done, my hair hung down my back in soft, shiny waves of aquamarine, looking like a waterfall. I smiled at my reflection.

"Holy shit," Nova stated, eyes wide as she looked me over.

"Wowza! Lookin' good, sister," Martina said, a Wolfish grin spread across her face.

"Thanks. You know, this might be my favorite color yet," I said.

And I meant it, too. My Dragon purred, and I felt my magic pulse deep within me. My Witchy powers were always the most settled when I felt confident, and nothing boosted my esteem like freshly dyed locks.

I grabbed my tiny wristlet that held my ID, my credit card, and my phone, and I repeated those four words I always said to myself whenever I dyed my hair, wondering if the me I found this time was the one I would keep. The one worth something. The one no one found lacking.

Yeah, maybe if I was lucky, I'd find someone else who thought I was worth keeping, too. My poor lonely heart squeezed inside my chest and my Dragon rumbled, echoing the statement. Loneliness was portable, and I didn't want to take it with me while I went to hang out with my sisters, so I forced myself to leave those negative thoughts behind.

New hair. New attitude.

CHAPTER THREE PERCY

THE BAR SMELLED of alcohol and perfumed bodies, all primped and posed for a night on the town. It looked like a typical upscale Jersey Shore bar with music blasting, dim lighting, dance floor, standing tables, and booths, and two main bars from what I could tell. There were a bunch of huge TVs and monitors where gaming systems were set up, and people playing and hanging out.

Drinks were being poured, food served. The staff seemed competent and moved about efficiently working the crowd. The throng of people made it damn near impossible to move. But there was one thing that made the place unique.

The Thirsty Dog was owned by a motherfucking Wolf Shifter. Had been for years. In fact, it was located smack dab in one of North America's most heavily populated Shifter towns, Maccon City. The bar was crawling with supernaturals. Though I'd picked up on the odd normal here and there.

How humans could stand being near so many powerful and predatory creatures was beyond me. Maybe their dull senses couldn't tell the difference between excitement and danger. I didn't really give a fuck either way.

"Pardon me, pal," some huge bastard muttered, hitting my shoulder with his big, beefy arm as he walked past.

Give me a fucking break already.

I tried not to react beyond a rough exhale that could only be described as a grunt as one after the other, a dozen massive fuckers bumped into my shoulder or chair, jostling me as they passed. It wasn't like the aisle was too small or I was too big. Sure, I had the stool pushed back, leaving a few inches of space between my knees and the bar, but no more so than the guy sitting next to me.

A man had the right to get comfortable, didn't he? But I understood. I was a stranger in these parts. A newcomer. My scent likely confused them and knowing Shifters the way I did, they didn't trust people they couldn't place.

But I wasn't there to start some shit with a couple of

meatheads. I knew they could tell I was different. Like them, but not. They didn't know what I was, and that gave me an edge. Just knowing I was an enigma to the burly bastards who kept throwing glowing glances in my direction gave me a sense of calm.

No, I wasn't there to fuck around or start fights. But I was no fucking pushover. Still, I bit my lip and kept my mouth shut. Ignoring them as one by one, those big fuckers knocked into me, trying to get a rise out of me.

Goddamn Shifters.

I stopped the snarl in my throat, but my annoyance must have showed. The fella next to me got up and moved away. Good. He was something smaller. Not a Wolf or Bear like many of the Shifters inside *The Thirsty Dog*. He seemed to understand he was lower on the totem pole of species, and I appreciated that.

The place was fucking full of goddamn Shifters, and my hackles were up. My natural instincts to fight or flee were riding me hard. But this was not the time or place for such things. My people were counting on me, but I could not afford to dwell on thoughts of my Coven. Not while so many enemies surrounded me.

My gums ached with the desire to bare my fangs, and I knew I should have sated my thirst before I left home. But our blood supplies were so low, and I would never take the vein from an unwilling donor. None of us would. It was what separated us from Vampires.

I needed blood to survive, provided by a live source, of course. Animals did not make the cut. They were okay in a pinch, but they did not sate my hunger for very long. And hunger was the only thing I really knew. It had been my constant companion since birth.

Modern technology was a marvel, enabling my people to set up numerous fake corporations over the past eighty years or so, allowing us to order from human blood banks. But nothing satisfied the hunger of a Dhampir like drinking from the source. And that was something we simply could not do.

Shame and fury warred within me whenever I thought about it. The curse on my people. The pain and torment of living with a thirst so strong, it ruled our every waking moment.

We were so far from what we once were. The Calloway Coven used to mean something. We used to be strong, powerful, and plentiful. But that was back before we'd been cursed. Now, with so few of us left we were hardly a blip on any radar. Those who were not bound to my line left decades ago, and those that remained had no choice.

As the last son of my line, it was my duty to make it right. My father, the former leader of our Coven, had been laid to rest after withering away to practically nothing under the ancient curse that had haunted us for so long.

Do you know how long it takes for a Dhampir, a half-Vampire, to die from something other than murder? A very long fucking time.

I was nearing my hundredth year myself, and this was the first time I'd ventured so far from my home deep in the woods of October Mountain, up in Massachusetts.

New Jersey wasn't much different climate wise, but Maccon City was part of that newly established cluster-fuck called the Jersey Shore, made popular by awful reality TV and TikTok influencers.

For fuck's sake, I'd rather be anywhere but there, but my people needed me. When rumors of a Dragon living in this hellhole of a summer town reached us, I had no choice. It was my sacred duty to bring back the blood of the Dragon, to restore our line, break the curse, and return our power.

My stomach turned with thoughts of what it was I had to do. But then I heard my grandmother's voice in my head, and I knew it was the only way.

"Your father is gone, Perseus. It is you who must avenge us."

She was right. As much as I cringed at the memory of her sharp features, the coldness in her pale blue eyes, Grandmother Calloway had a point. It was time for this to end. I had only one question for anyone who might frown upon what I was there to do.

Have you ever been hungry?

I didn't mean the kind of hunger you felt when you had a craving for popcorn or ice cream. I meant the kind that could break the will of even the strongest being. A soul crunching, marrow deep, heart wrenching, gut twisting hunger. The kind you knew would be your end.

That was what I was dealing with. It was what I had been tasked to fulfill. My name was Perseus Calloway, and I was the last hope for my people. I was at *The Thirsty Dog*, hunting for the one being who could end our curse and bring atonement to my people.

How many had been put down over the years since the curse had taken hold? Too many to count. And that was why I was there now. To put an end to the madness and the misery.

Regret had no place inside my cold, withered heart. I gritted my teeth and tossed back the shot I had ordered, frowning as I felt the burn of locally distilled whiskey heating my throat.

"Another?" the bartender asked, and I shook my head.

I needed a minute. He seemed to understand and nodded before moving on to the next customer. There were plenty to choose from, and I slid a hundred dollar bill out of my wallet and dropped it in his tip jar. I appreciated the fact he didn't ask me to leave my seat in favor of someone actively drinking.

I would order something else, eventually. I just needed a minute. Wrapping my head around my mission was essential to its success. Should have been easy, right?

Find the Dragon. Break the curse.

But things were never simple as that. It would have helped if I knew the details. If only someone knew what caused the last Dragon the Calloway Coven had gotten involved with to curse us, but no one could remember the reason. I only knew that somewhere in my ancestry, one of ours had crossed paths with a Dragon Shifter and it didn't end well. The magical beast cursed my line, and ever since we'd struggled to survive.

Oh, we still trained in the ways of our kind, skilled in combat and warfare. We still followed the path of our kind, chasing Hunter Vamps and protecting humanity. After all, Dhampirs were needed to rein in Vampire populations and to go after those bloodthirsty rogues. The problem was, the Calloway Coven could not be trusted not to give in to our own hunger.

Our half-Vampire nature meant we needed to drink blood from a living source to provide the necessary nourishment to our bodies. But my people needed more than that. You see, the curse meant our thirst was never truly sated.

So yes, we'd earned a reputation for being untrustworthy.

I wasn't saying we didn't deserve it, but it sucked. Soon, no one would work with us.

It was well known that joining with a Calloway Dhampir was dangerous. Nowadays, we were only tasked with what were essentially suicide missions. We were charged with chasing the Hunter Vamps no one else wanted to track to the ends of the earth.

Other Dhampir Clans and Covens steered clear of us. They did not want to put themselves in danger. Dhampirs normally fed off each other. Being half-Vamp meant we were also half-human, and technically our blood could sustain us. Managing our thirst was easiest when we did it among ourselves. But the nature of the curse meant we did not know when to stop.

Feeding was dangerous, and as such, we took more risks than most whenever we engaged with others of our ilk. Especially when side by side in battle where blood would most assuredly be spilled.

The curse the Dragon placed upon us caused our bloodlust to rival that of the most lethal Vampires. We'd done everything we could to keep normals, Dhampirs, and other supes safe from us, moving away from civilization and isolating ourselves. Feeding on animals and getting supplies from human blood banks, but things were getting harder.

Our power was dwindling, and we were so very low in numbers. Then suddenly, rumors reached us of real, live Dragons in Maccon City. It had been decades since there'd even been a sighting.

So, there I was, being a good little hunter, stalking my prey. It wasn't like I could just ask around and expect someone to point me in the direction of a Dragon.

Most supes were easily identifiable by scent or some other calling card, but not those beasts. They were too rare. Like me. Few knew what a Dhampir was, never mind how to deal with one. Which made killing us a little bit harder.

Thank fuck.

"Have you decided what you want?" the bartender asked.

"Can I see your selection of wine?"

"We got red or white, pal," he replied, one eyebrow quirked.

Fucker could only be a Wolf. I sighed and asked for red, trying to hold on to my temper. He poured my glass, and I had to admit the bouquet was actually very nice.

"Mm, what is this?" I asked.

"It's from a local winery, Devil's Blood," he replied with a wink, and I caught the glow of his inner beast behind that gesture.

Nodding, I dropped a twenty to pay for the wine and another to add to the tip I'd already given him on the bar. I continued to sip my wine, pretending for just a moment it was the other deep red liquid I craved.

It was a pity it wasn't really blood, but I'd trained myself to ignore that constant hunger. Just as I learned to compensate for my dull senses and magic as a result of the curse. They were only dull compared to other Dhampirs. Which meant they were still better than the average normal, and even some supes.

I took another sip, enjoying the way the fragrant liquid warmed my insides as it slid down my throat. I could feel the effects already and decided to slow my pace. Unfortunately, I was not immune to the effects of alcohol like most other supes were.

It would not do for me to drop my guard. I was in a strange place with strange people. Even if finding the Dragon proved easier than I thought, I wasn't foolish enough to think I would end the curse in one night.

But I was so close. For the first time in two hundred years, the Calloway Coven had a real shot at ending this goddamned curse and coming back to our full power. I sipped more slowly, ignoring the noise of the crowded bar, and reassessed the advantages I had over my quarry.

1. The Dragon had no idea he'd been outed and was currently being hunted.
2. I knew what to look for and what to expect from my prey. Someone of impeccable size, with brutish strength, a dim wit, and a propensity for charred food.
3. I was a trained professional. I knew how to wrestle with beasts and had been taught to slay monsters before I had my license to drive.
4. Last, there was the fact I wore beneath my shirt a medallion charmed to warm against my skin when in the presence of a Dragon.

So yeah, this shouldn't be hard at all.

Being cocky had caused my ancestor to bring this curse upon our heads to begin with. So, you would have thought I'd have known better. And yet, I didn't, which was why my jaw hit the fucking bar when *she* sat next to me.

"Hi! Can I have three lemon drop shots, please?" a strange female with turquoise colored hair and bright eyes asked the bartender.

The male leaned forward and gave her a slow look from head to toe, causing my entire being to vibrate with anger.

What the fuck?

"You can have anything you want, Sweet Sybil. Damn girl. You are looking fiiiiiine tonight," the bartender added, winking as he started mixing her drink order.

I wondered how much trouble I'd get into if I loosed one of the smaller blades I had tucked into my belt and took out his fucking eye.

Hmm. Too many witnesses.

Besides, when did I get fucking territorial over a woman? And a stranger at that.

I turned my gaze to the female and reluctantly agreed with the asshole Wolf Shifter. The woman did look fine as fuck. In fact, she looked hot. Sexy, curvy, and very, very hot.

Suddenly, I clutched at my shirt, lifting the sizzling medallion off my chest before it could singe my chest hair.

The fuck?

"Awww, thanks, Bobby," the woman replied.

Her sultry voice combined with a full-toothed grin just about knocked my fucking socks off. She flicked her hazel eyes to me and offered a small, tight-lipped smile. Nothing like the natural one she gave that asshole bartender, and I was incensed by the fact she offered him such a charming expression while giving me one that spoke of her discomfort.

Fuck. I was staring. I knew I was staring. And I needed to stop.

But it was impossible. She was stunning. Her hair was so damn pretty. The shimmery blue color made her eyes sparkle and glow. Maybe it was the ambiance of the bar with the dimmed lights and crowd of people that made her seem so damn special. But somehow, I doubted it.

It was just her. My gaze traveled, and I felt my cock harden as I took in the outfit she wore. Holy fucking curves. Her clothing emphasized her fuller figure, making my mouth water. She wasn't even trying to get my attention, but she had it.

All of it.

I wasn't sitting in that bar for pleasure, but suddenly it was all I could think about.

Pleasure. Hers. And mine.

No, they were not mutually exclusive. Then I realized, as I pressed my hand over my chest, that the medallion was still hot and growing hotter.

Fuck. It couldn't be. Could it?

The woman I was suddenly so taken with was my quarry. Sweet Sybil, as the bartender had called her, a fact that irritated the fuck out of me, was my prey. I'd been sent to find a Dragon to end the curse that had plagued the Calloway Coven for centuries, and she literally just sat down next to me in a bar.

This sexy, beautiful woman was the Dragon I'd been sent to find. The blood my people needed to restore their power pumped through her veins. My pulse raced and thunder roared in my ears as I was filled with a burning desire.

I had to have her. I had to have her blood. I just needed to figure out how.

CHAPTER FOUR SYBIL

MY DRAGON PERKED up the second I leaned across the bar and told Billy my order. But it wasn't the Werewolf hottie I'd known since grade school who was giving me butterflies. Nope. It was the stranger with the dark, spicy scent that made my beast take notice.

He wasn't a Shifter, but there was something about him. Something I couldn't place. I mean, I'd barely glanced at him, but I already had him memorized. He was tall and long, like the cover models for those cowboy romances I used to read. Even sitting, I could tell he'd have that same kind of build. All wiry strength, and lean, hard muscle.

His shoulders were wide, and when he moved, his shirt pulled tight, showcasing those muscles I had already noticed. But he wasn't like most of the guys from around town. He didn't look burly or too big like so many of the men I knew who spent every waking moment in a gym.

He looked elegant, drinking wine all alone at the bar. His posture oozed a sort of innate confidence, which was something I sorely lacked. I was surprised he wasn't surrounded by women, as good looking as the man was. One casual glance around told me I wasn't the only one wondering if he was single. There was a trio of young females a few seats down giggling and watching him in the mirror.

Figured.

I bit my lip, waiting for my order, wishing Billy would hurry up. I did not feel like sitting there, watching this guy flirt with other women. In fact, the very idea made my Dragon growl.

"Hi, you here alone?" a young blonde woman asked.

I pretended not to watch as the stranger sat with his elbows on the bar, fingers cradling his wineglass. He had his head angled away from the crowd as if in some kind of warning for everyone to back the fuck off. He clearly wanted to be alone, and I was fine simply admiring from the sidelines. Too bad the blonde hadn't noticed.

"Excuse me," he growled, turning away from the stranger without answering her question.

"Rude!" she snapped, turning away from him like he'd been the one who'd intruded on her privacy.

I bit my lip harder, trying not to laugh. He frowned, looking down, and as I watched him in the reflection of the mirror behind the bar, I realized he was looking at me.

Gulp.

I had to bite my lip to stop myself from groaning out loud. It was no small thing to be checked out by a hot guy. And he was hot. I just loved big, tall men. I'd always had a serious thing for them.

They just made me feel so small and petite, where I had no business feeling that way considering I carried an extra fifty pounds of chub spread out and around my five-foot two and half inch body.

Some guys liked to posture about their size, pretend they were all that when really, they weren't. I went on a blind date with a man once whose social media claimed he was six feet tall, but when I met him in person, he was five foot seven tops. And that would have been fine had he not lied.

But being less than truthful was not that guy's only problem. He'd been combative and bossy throughout the entirety of our date, which lasted twenty-seven minutes. That was only because it took that long for my rideshare to arrive outside the bar where I'd met him over in Barvale. Just another reason I was still single.

Nothing like a Napoleonic complex to make a short guy utterly unattractive. But this guy wouldn't be lying if he said he was tall. I could tell from the way his legs were opened, bent at the knees to give him more space, that this man was a fine size indeed.

He wore all black from his shoes to his pants and his button down. As if that wasn't enough to make him strikingly handsome, I took in his pale skin and deep burgundy locks with something akin to awe.

He looked like one of the heroes right out of the pages of the latest romantasy I couldn't stop reading. Like some Fae lord or Elvish King come to life.

Maybe he would whisk me off to his castle in some faraway world or steal me away to sate his carnal appetite for the night? I snorted at my stray thoughts, then gasped and put my hand over my mouth and nose.

Fuck. He didn't hear that, did he?

But, of course, he did. The gorgeous stranger was staring right at me. I cleared my throat and ignored Bobby's own snicker of amusement as he finished pouring my shots.

"Are you alright?" the man asked.

I handed Bobby my credit card and told him to run a tab before turning back to the ridiculously good looking man. His thick hair hung down his shoulders in fat glossy curls I was instantly jealous of. And if that wasn't bad enough, he had the greenest eyes I'd ever seen. Pure Kelly green and they were sparkling with some emotion, I wasn't sure what, as he asked his question.

"Oh, um, yeah. Sorry," I muttered.

"You have nothing to be sorry for," he said, turning his massive body to face me. "I'm Percy. What's your name?"

"Oh, um, hello, I'm Sybil."

"Sybil? Such a pretty name. You don't hear that very often, but it suits you," he said.

He had the most awesome voice. It was so damn deep it sent vibrations shivering through me.

Did he just call me pretty?

"Um, thanks. It's nice to meet you, Percy. Um, I have to bring this back there. I'm here with my sisters," I explained, just in case he thought I was with a man.

Not that he asked. Or would ask. Because why would he? Fuck. I was making it awkward. I cleared my throat again before turning to get the three shot glasses.

Uh oh.

I should have left my wristlet with the girls. But if I did that, I wouldn't have been able to pay. Shit. I needed to figure out how to carry all this back.

Why couldn't I be more suave like Nova, or able to multi-task like Martina?

It wouldn't do me any good to stand there like a

moron. I tried to just grab all three shot glasses that were filled to the brim with lemony vodka goodness, but my fingers were just too damn short.

"Shoot," I muttered.

Before I spilled any, two large hands gripped two of the shots, taking them from me with a muttered curse, at least that was what it sounded like.

"Allow me," Percy, the sexy, redheaded man said, staying my hand.

He wrapped his long fingers around the three shot glasses with no fuss and stood up to follow me. Fuck. Did I mention how big his hands were? I mean he looked like he could've been playing piano, or guitar, *or me*, with those things as masterfully as any expert. My body heated at the sudden turn of my thoughts, and I needed a fan or something to cool down.

"Oh, um, thank you," I replied.

I turned around before I did something stupid, like drooled on the man. Or worse, threw myself at him. I started walking, leaving him with no choice but to follow me. I mean, how would I even explain that kind of behavior to someone I just met?

Pardon the spittle and the tackle hug, but you see, my Dragon is feeling kind of feisty cause it's been a long, dry spell. Would you mind very much if I bounce around on your lap naked until I get us both off? There's a good fellow!

Oh yeah. That was a totally plausible scenario.

I rolled my eyes and almost walked right into some rowdy fucker who'd backed up a step, moving directly in my path. I squeaked, bracing myself for impact, but there was none. When I looked, I realized Percy had moved lightning fast to interrupt the man's progress. His left arm was wrapped around me, still holding one of the shot glasses in that hand. His forearm was pressing against my shoulder, and his elbow was pointed out, protecting me from impact.

"Watch out," he growled, and the guy looked over his shoulder, mumbling an apology as Percy glared.

"Are you okay?" he asked me, still keeping his arm around my shoulder.

Holy. Fuck.

"Yep. Yeah. Yes," I replied and cleared my throat.

Heat from his big body seeped into my skin, the warmth seeming to shoot straight to my core. I bit my lip, trying to dampen down my reaction to his posses-sive display. He was a stranger, but he'd put himself between me and some guy who'd stepped into my path like it was something he always did. Like Percy was responsible for my well-being.

Did I mention how fucking hot it was that he used his elbow to push the man away from me? Well, he did, with barely any effort. And it was hot. So fucking hot.

I squeezed my thighs together and sucked in a breath that held notes of his spicy, rich cologne. Geezus fuck, he even smelled good. Percy kept glaring at the man and his buddies as we passed, as if he was daring them to say anything. But the guy just raised his hands and muttered something that sounded like *my bad* as we moved past him.

Really, it was all over in seconds, but the significance of the interaction struck me as important. I mean, it wasn't every day a man went out of his way to ensure I was safe. Feminist pride be damned, I was completely turned on, which meant I was also bound to embarrass myself.

A Shifter and Witch hybrid, I might be, but smooth, I was not. Sure, I could take care of myself, but it was nice to not have to. It was even nicer that Percy kept that arm around me as we continued towards the tall table where Nova and Martina were standing, their wide eyes trained on me.

"Wow, Sweet Sybil, whatcha caught there? A stray?" Martina asked, her Wolf glowing behind her eyes.

"Hi, I'm Nova," my other sibling said.

Her bright blue gaze was unwavering as she undoubtedly memorized every one of Percy's features. I hated myself for the twinge of doubt that filled me as my beautiful sister introduced herself.

It wasn't her fault. Nova didn't do anything to attract men, but then again, she didn't have to. Still, I had no claim on Percy. He was a nice stranger who'd helped me carry drinks and made sure some drunk guy didn't bump into me as we pushed through the crowd.

That's all. Nothing doing here.

Feelings of inadequacy or even jealousy were ridiculous for me to even indulge in, so I pushed them away and watched as he nodded and introduced himself in return. I prepared myself for the usual reactions men had to my sisters. Especially Nova. It was gonna suck, but I was used to it. I just hoped he didn't drool.

"Sweet Sybil? That your nickname?" he asked, canting his head.

I just shrugged and nodded before he turned back to my sisters.

"Nice to meet you. I'm Percy Calloway. Sybil was kind enough to allow me to help her carry these over for you," he said and placed the shots on the tall table.

I noticed he managed to carry all three along with his glass of wine and had to admit I was impressed. Just how big were his hands? And what did that say about other parts of him?

Down girl. Do not stand here picturing his dick.

Of course, as soon as I thought that I was picturing his dick.

Was it long and lean like his fingers or thick and wide like his shoulders?

OMG. Was it both?

A growl rattled inside my chest, and Percy's eyes flicked to mine. I tried to cover it up with a cough, since I had no idea what he was or if he knew about Shifters. Keeping supernatural stuffs a secret was like the one major rule for our kind, and I could not believe I'd almost outed us just because I was daydreaming about Percy's cock.

"You okay, Trouble?" he asked me, and I squeaked.

"Um, I'm Martina," my sister said, interrupting Percy before I could react to him calling me Trouble.

"So, what are you doing in town, Percy? You're not from here," she said, staring rudely at him.

Shit. Alphas tended to be snappy when newcomers encroached on their territory, and I knew Percy was not a normal, but I had no idea what he was. Still, my own hackles were rising, and I didn't want my sister to scare him off just yet.

"Oh my God, Marti! Don't be rude," I scolded, and turned to face him, forcing myself to meet his eyes.

"Hi, I'm Tim and this is my husband Pete," Tim said, eyeing me like he was ready to grill me. I shook my head, knowing he would at least have the sense to not be a weirdo like my sisters.

"So, you like our girl?" he asked, and I sighed and closed my eyes.

"Ohmygawd, Tim! Okay, you guys are being fucking weird. Um, thank you for helping me," I said, wringing my hands and turning back to Percy.

"My pleasure," he replied, looking down at me with something akin to amusement on his handsome face.

"Um, yeah, yep, okay," I muttered, unsure of what else to say.

"Don't tell me you're sick of me already, Trouble," he added, his green eyes sparkling with something. Mischief maybe?

"Oh, uh, no. Of course not. I just figured you were here to meet someone," I said.

"I am."

"Oh," I replied, and winced at how sad that one syllable sounded escaping my lips.

"It's you," he said, and my gaze snapped back to his.

My heart thundered inside my chest as I watched a slow grin spread across Percy's sexy as fuck face. His crystalline gaze slid down my body in a way that damn near caused my ovaries to explode. I thought I heard Nova whistle, but I ignored her. I couldn't do anything else but breathe at that moment. I was just frozen under his rapt stare.

My sisters, both beautiful and sexy, were just two feet

away from me. Most other men readily dismissed me as *cute* and *sweet*, efficiently friend-zoning me after they'd set eyes on my sisters. I was pretty enough to garner attention from men, but they usually tucked me into *little sister* category before moving on to flirt with Marti and Nova.

I mean, I was *Sweet Sybil*. That was what everyone called me. I was the youngest of the three of us, even though we shared a birthday. I was the baby.

Cute. Nice. Sweet.

But for some reason, Percy was focused on little ol' me and not my admittedly hotter siblings. Wasn't that amazing? My body heated under his hungry gaze as it paused on my tits and lower before coming back to meet mine. He cleared his throat, one hand moving down to press against his fly, and I swayed slightly on my feet.

Did he really just adjust himself in public? Holy fucking hell.

No one should be that sexy. Then I thought about what he'd just said, what he'd been saying, and my mouth gaped open.

"Did you just call me Trouble like with a capital T?" I asked, surprised and admittedly even more turned on.

"I did," he said with a nod.

"Why?"

"Because, Little Girl, that is exactly what you are," he growled, raking me with his gaze once more. "The second I spotted you, I knew it. I bet everyone thinks you're an angel, but I see you, Trouble. I see you."

"Yeah? So, why are you still talking to me, then?" I asked cheekily, clearly enjoying myself.

"I never had the sense to run from *trouble* when I was a kid. Why would I start now?"

Percy grinned, putting special emphasis on the word trouble, and I swooned.

CHAPTER FIVE PERCY

THREE HOURS *and several rounds of drinks later...*

"Are you sure you'll get her home?" Martina asked for the umpteenth time.

"Yes. If she wants me to, then yes, I will take her home," I said and nodded my head.

Ultimately, we were all aware that Sybil was the one who held the cards. She'd refused her sister's invitation to leave early when her mate had arrived. The enormous Wolf did little more than nod his head in my direction, his rapt gaze on his woman. The other sister, Nova, and her big ass mate, Asher, had already left, along with Tim and Pete.

No one paid me much attention, probably because they were Shifters and did not recognize my scent or see me as a threat. Of course, that was good news for me, but I had to admit something inside me bristled with anger. They discredited me so easily. I was a stranger. And Sybil, well, she was just *her*.

Too trusting. Too sweet. Too naïve.

How the fuck could they justify leaving her with me? My gaze roamed back to where she was rocking out to whatever song was blasting through the bar. There'd been a live band for a while, but they were swapped out for a DJ some time ago. I had to admit, I wasn't really a music fan. But I was definitely starting to see the merit of it as I watched her ass swing from side to side in time with the heavy bass of the song.

Goddamn.

That ass was a fucking gift from God. *Sweet Sybil.* That was what everyone called her. Even the fucking bartender. But it just went to show how little they really knew her.

Sweet did not suit her at all for a moniker. Though I knew she would be. Sweet as cherry fucking pie warm from the oven. Still, I was much more fond of my own nickname for the female. Sybil Harbor might be sweet as pie, but that woman was Trouble, alright. Trouble with a capital T.

For some reason I could not be sure of, maybe it was just the Fates messing with me, or maybe this was a second phase of the curse my Coven was under, but over the course of the past few hours I'd become relatively certain of two things.

1. Sybil Harbor, youngest of the three Harbor sisters, was in fact a Dragon Shifter. A *female Dragon Shifter*, which was an even greater rarity.
2. Sybil Harbor, *aka Trouble*, was mine.

I was completely fucked.

Not yet, a naughty voice whispered in my head, and I felt my cock harden beneath my pants.

Not ever, I corrected that voice.

I had to figure out what the hell I was going to do. Could it be bloodlust that was confusing itself with actual lust and making me want her when I should have been plotting ways to get her back to my Coven? I had a duty. I was there for one reason, and one reason only. And that did not involve dipping my dick into her sweet, wet heat.

Fuck.

I swallowed my lust. Watching her sway and move on the dance floor with a hunger I could barely contain. She was so pretty. So damn pretty. I couldn't take my eyes off her. Blue hair, pink lips, bright eyes. And that body. Goddamn. Those tits I wanted to bury my face in, and an ass that would surely fill my hands—she was incredible. And yeah, I wanted her like fucking crazy.

Then visions of Trouble with puncture wounds on her wrists and ankles, and her long, pretty neck filled my head and rage unlike any I'd ever felt threatened to consume me.

Were the Fates completely fucked up? How could they have put me in the path of a woman so damn perfect and tempting only to taunt me with the fact she was the key to ending the suffering of my whole Coven?

This had to be a fucking joke., Maybe I could get out of it somehow. This was Maccon City. Maybe there were other Dragons here. Ones that were not so damn perfect and tempting.

Fuck. I wanted to scream and roar. I wanted to hit something. And of course, because the Fates were motherfuckers, they chose that moment to present me with the perfect opportunity.

"Alright, Percy. It was nice meeting you but we're gonna leave. I'm gonna tell Syb—uh oh," Martina said, finally moving to leave.

But her uh oh had my eyes flicking back to the dance floor where I saw two hulking males sandwiching Trouble between them. Now, I'd had plenty of time to realize something was different about the Harbor girls, and not just because they were Shifters.

Typically, liquor did nothing to affect supes because of high metabolism and whatever. But these three women did not have the same tolerance as other Shifters I'd met. It was kind of amazing to watch as they drank and became tipsy. No one in our unlikely group was drunk. At least, not *drunk* drunk. But they'd all gotten a pretty good buzz, and protective male that I was, I'd watched over them until their mates had arrived.

My eye twitched. My chest reverberated with a growl that seemed pulled from somewhere dark inside of me. Sybil was unaware of the two men, eyes closed as she bounced and wiggled. One of the two idiots licked his lips, staring at her tits as he moved so his hands hovered over her goodies.

"Fucking pricks," Marti snarled, and moved to intervene.

Her mate stilled her with his big hands on her hips, and he dipped his chin in my direction. I appreciated it. Really, I did. I knew once I started moving, I wouldn't stop until someone was bleeding. I just hoped the scent of blood didn't send me into a feeding frenzy. Unfortunately, I was too damn angry to care.

"Easy, Martina. I think our boy here has got it," Mitchell told his mate.

"He's right. I got it." I nodded, agreeing with the Wolf.

Two steps and I had one fucker by the wrists, twisting his arm in time to catch the first fist his partner threw at me.

"What the he—Percy?" Sybil shouted, eyes wide.

"Get back," I told her, but she was frozen, mouth open as I turned my attention back to the two angry Shifters.

"What's your problem, freak?" one of them yelled, trying a left hook.

I caught his sloppy punch and countered with a well-placed kick to the inside of his knee. Fucker fell with a loud thud. His buddy watched the move, so I didn't bother repeating it. Instead, I went right for his throat, punching him in his Adam's apple so hard, the asshole was stuck fighting for air. Sooner than later, a few bouncers closed in on us. But I already had my girl by the back of her neck and was moving us through the crowd outside.

"You alright?" I asked.

Concern marred my face as I looked down at her soft, ripe body, checking her over for any sign she'd been injured in the fracas. I was so damn mad, I was shaking with barely repressed violence. It felt good to hit those jerks, but not nearly as good as it would have felt had I been able to finish the job.

"W-why did you do that?" she asked, eyes wide and shocked.

"Why did I hit those guys? They were going to fucking touch you," I said, like the answer was clear.

She was going to say something else, but she was cut off by Martina and Mitchell. The couple must have followed us outside.

"Holy shit, Sybil! Your guy here is vicious. That was awesome," Martina shrieked. "Are you okay, Syb?"

"I guess I'm confused, I mean, what happened? Why would you even do that?" she asked.

Thinking about those two men being so damn close to her. And the one who'd actually had his hand hovering over her perfection made me want to go back in there to finish what I'd started.

"What happened was those two blockheads were crowding you on the floor and I was about to go get you, but then Mitchell noticed your guy here, chomping at the bit," Martina said.

"Is that true?" Sybil asked and turned her wide eyed stare at me.

I dipped my chin, not trusting myself to speak. But then again, I didn't have to. Martina gave us a play-by-play of my actions as we walked through the parking lot.

"So, did you want to go home with me and Mitch, or?" Martina asked, biting her lip.

I was completely fucking torn by that time. Part of me wanted to scream at the Wolf Shifter female. Martina should absolutely take her sister home and lock her up in a room, toss away the fucking key. She should never even consider leaving Trouble with a fucking stranger, especially not me. But there was another part of me that felt the opposite.

A darker, deeper part of my soul that I had worked so damn hard to hide. That version of me wanted to beat my chest like some warrior of old and roar to the world that this female was mine. I wanted to dare the whole fucking world to try to keep her from me, because that part of me was absolutely, frighteningly sure that Trouble was mine.

"Okay then. See you later, but Syb, make sure you text me and Nova when you're home."

Trouble nodded and hugged her sister goodbye, patting Mitchell's shoulder as he walked past. I understood that touch was important to Shifters, and the pat she'd given him was the kind of thing you would do to a brother or someone you viewed as your brother. That alone should have comforted me, but it still made me growl. I didn't want her hands on anyone else. Only me.

Mine.

Fuck.

"Um, so, do I thank you for beating those guys up?"

Trouble quirked her nose in an adorable expression that made me want to bend down and kiss her right on the tip. Of course, then I'd have to kiss those plump pink lips, and if I did that, there would be no stopping me. I shook my head, not trusting myself to speak.

Besides, I didn't want her gratitude. What I wanted was much more complicated than that.

"Okay, then, I guess I'll just call you Super Percy," she teased, and I growled.

"Super Percy? I don't think so. If you say it too fast, it sounds like something else," I deadpanned.

Couldn't she hear it? She was basically saying super pussy.

"*Ohmygod*! You're right, it sounds like I am saying super pussy! Ha! I am so sorry," she said before breaking out into giggles.

"Glad we can both agree that's a terrible nickname," I replied.

My stomach rumbled, and I closed my eyes for a fraction of a second, hoping to get my hunger under control.

"Fine, I'll just call you *my hero*. That better? Oh, are you hungry?" Trouble asked, stopping in her tracks.

I placed a hand against the small of her back, humming at the pleasure I received at touching her warm skin just there. There was a gap between where her shirt ended and those goddamn painted on pants began. The soft flesh revealed had been teasing me all damn night.

"Yes," I answered honestly.

I was hungry. But I couldn't decide what I was hungrier for. Food, blood, or her. One more look at her sweet, heart-shaped face and I had my answer.

Her. Definitely her.

CHAPTER SIX SYBIL

"GOOD?" I asked, watching Percy's brows furrow as he took a bite of the deep fried hot dog after staring at it for ten seconds with skepticism written all over his face.

"Mmm," he hummed in surprise approval, scarfing down half the dog with his second bite.

I smiled, taking my first bite with a sigh of absolute pleasure. *Dana's Dogs* was one of the oldest eating establishments in the area, and I had to admit it was still my favorite.

"My brother Davian used to take us here when we were kids," I explained, after taking a long pull from what had to be the best beverage on the planet, birch beer served in a frosted mug.

"These are amazing," Percy said after he polished off his first hot dog.

"I know. But try the relish next. It's homemade," I added, persuading him.

"I'd be an idiot not to listen to you, Trouble."

I grinned around my next bite. It had been over an hour since my last drink, and I was hungry. It was a good thing I heard Percy's stomach growling in the parking lot, giving me the perfect opportunity to ask him to join me for some midnight munchies.

"Give me your phone," he growled after ordering us another round of birch beer.

"Okayyy," I replied, unlocking it before handing it to him.

I bit my lip, curiously, trying to see what he was doing, but he'd turned it away from me. Huffing out a sigh, I waited impatiently while he grabbed his phone, and then I understood he was sending himself my number and inputting his own contact information. I couldn't stop smiling if I tried.

"Lemme see what you put me in as," I said, after he handed mine back.

"Hmm. Let's see, ah, *My Hero*. Nice," I said, biting my lip again.

Ooh this man. I just love the way he teases. Careful with the L word, Syb!

"What do you think I put you in as?" he asked, interrupting my inner hysterics.

"I don't know," I replied, my nose twitching anxiously.

He grinned and flashed me his phone, showing me his nickname for me. *Trouble with a capital T.* He'd entered the entire thing, and I was fucking delighted.

I was always sweet Syb, simple, kind, a little foolish to everyone else. But Percy saw something when he looked at me beyond the face, I showed the world. He saw mischief and cunning, maybe even daring, too, and I really liked that he did.

Liar. You love it.

After my third hotdog, and his sixth, we were both ready to tap out. Some people would say eating greasy food after drinking was not wise, but I was a real Jersey girl. Greasy spoons were a tradition, especially after pub crawling.

"So, where to next?" Percy asked as he turned the key.

I tapped my fingers on the dashboard of his truck. I had to admit I was surprised that he drove a big old Ford pickup. For some reason, I expected him to drive something low to the ground, like a Mustang or something.

"What's on your mind, Trouble?"

"Oh, nothing," I said, biting my lip. "I was just thinking about your truck."

"My truck?"

"Yeah. Do you work in construction or something?"

"Something like that. Truth is, where I'm from you can't really drive anything but a truck. The roads aren't great, and winter can be rough."

"You don't live around here?" I asked.

It was getting hard to breathe, like someone had wrapped a fist around my heart and was slowly squeezing as I waited for him to answer. Percy sighed, shaking his head and a mass of curls fell over one side of his face with the move.

Fuck, his hair was gorgeous, The rich auburn color so much better than anything I'd ever seen real or dyed. I wanted to run my fingers through it, but I stopped myself. I would never just touch someone uninvited, and the truth was I didn't think Percy liked me like that. He seemed to spend half the night either growling at me or focused on his food or drink.

It was strange, but maybe that was my fault. Maybe he wasn't really sending mixed signals. But what would you call it if a man was willing to beat up guys for getting too close to you, but pulled away when your knee bumped against his in a hot dog hut?

You're making this a big deal, Sybil, when it's not.

"No, Trouble. I live in Pennsylvania. My family has their own business, and we all have to do our part," he said, and it was more explanation than I'd expected.

"Oh, I see," I said. "So you're just here for work?"

"Something like that," he whispered, his green eyes on my face.

The air seemed fraught with anticipation, and I worried my lip with my teeth. We were still sitting in the parking lot of *Dana's Dogs*, and it was pretty empty. There was only one other car and for all I knew, it could have belonged to the employee who'd waited on us inside.

"When do you go back?" I asked.

"Soon."

"I see," I said, but I didn't. Not really.

My chest felt hot, and my breathing increased. There was something so oddly familiar about him it just put me at ease. I couldn't explain it. All my life, I felt like I never fit in. Being a Witch and a Shifter was not the easiest thing in the world. Being abandoned, regardless of what you were, also kind of sucked.

Davian, Martina, and Nova all understood because they lived through it, too. Our familial and Clan bonds were strong, but the connection I felt to them was different from what I was feeling between Percy and me in that truck in the middle of the night outside of Maccon City's only twenty-four-hour hot dog hut.

"Tell me what you're thinking, Trouble," he whispered, and I noticed he was leaning closer.

"I'm thinking you have to leave soon, and I might not get another chance to do this, Percy. But if you don't want to just say no," I whispered, lifting my face up to his, closing the space between us.

"Fuck," he groaned as I kissed him on the side of his mouth.

"Do you want me to stop?" I asked, my voice so low it was nearly drowned out by the sounds of our heavy breathing.

"No," he growled, cupping my face in his hands, and pulling me towards him. "Don't you ever stop."

Then he kissed me back, hard, and full on the lips. I moaned, giving him an opening, and he took it. I heard a seat belt coming undone, and before I realized it was mine, Percy was pulling me onto his lap. He must have moved his seat as far as it went because suddenly, I was sitting astride his lap.

Thank fuck for old Fords with bench seats. There was no center console to impede my movements, and I had enough room to press my core against the rock hard length of him as we tangled tongues. His arms were so tight around me, and he tasted so damn good, I couldn't stop myself from moaning and grinding.

"God, Trouble, you're so fucking hot," he murmured, tilting my head back and closing his lips over the place on my neck where my pulse was racing.

He groaned, scraping his teeth over my flesh, and sending lightning bolts of pleasure through my veins. His large hands ran down my sides, one closing over my breast and the other on my ass as he kissed and sucked, licking a trail to my chest.

"Will you let me kiss you here, Trouble?" he asked, squeezing my nipple through my shirt.

"Yes! Please, Percy," I begged, and nodded, needing him to do that and more.

"Tell me how it feels when I have my mouth on you," he instructed, pulling the bottom of my shirt up and over my tits.

"Fuck, Trouble. Lace? You've had lace on underneath this the whole night?" he asked.

Percy growled, the rolling sound reverberating through my body as he pressed his forehead against my chin. I moaned, sucking in a sharp breath when he squeezed and lifted my tits with both hands, pressing them together before pushing his face right into my soft flesh. Then I felt his lips and his tongue laving at my sensitive skin. Fuck, it felt so good. Like he was worshipping me with his mouth.

"Gonna do more than worship you, Trouble. Gonna make you feel good. Can you let go and feel good with me? Can you come just from me sucking on your tits?"

His voice was so deep and gravelly, so fucking sexy I felt each word like a tug on my core. Every syllable felt like fingers sliding over my clit, filling me with need and desire. My panties were gonna be ruined, I realized as he moved his hips, pressing the hard bar of his cock firmly against me.

"That's it. Feel me right there. Feels so fucking good, doesn't it?"

"Y-yes," I agreed.

"Good girl," he whispered praise, tugging on my nipples through their lace confines.

Then he pulled the material down, freeing my tits, and I whimpered, mouth open as I watched him staring at me.

"So fucking perfect," he growled, licking his fingers before tugging on my pointed tips and twisting them.

"Oh god," I moaned.

"My name, Trouble. Say my name when I make you come," he growled, closing his mouth over one aching nipple, his fingers tightening on the other one, then he sucked. Hard.

"Oh, g-Percy! Percy!" I groaned as I fell apart in his arms.

I never thought I could come from a man's mouth on my tit. But I guess you learned new things every day. And I knew he had to leave, but I really fucking hoped we would get to do more than this before he went. I just had to remember two things.

1. Percy did not belong to me.
2. I could not allow myself to fall in love with him.

Yep, should be easy peasy.

CHAPTER SEVEN PERCY

ONE OF THE wonders of modern living to creatures who lived as long as Dhampirs, Shifters, and the rest of the supernatural world was technology. Even if normals could not access magic, they had enough gadgets and gizmos to make up for it. That was for sure.

I stared at my cell phone, wondering what the fuck a man was supposed to text a woman after making her come on his lap without ever even touching her pussy, and I had to admit I was at a loss. The fact I also came inside my boxers like a goddamn teenager did nothing to inspire any confidence that I *should* text her.

Could I have embarrassed myself any fucking more? Shit!

But damn, she sure didn't seem to mind. Trouble just flashed those seductive hazel eyes at me afterwards, grinning like the cat that caught the canary. Then she hugged me. I mean the girl really hugged me.

She wrapped her arms around my waist and nuzzled her face against my neck, a satisfied hum sounding in her throat just before she pressed her lips right over my pulse.

Fuck.

It had been years since I'd been hugged, and never by someone I'd just, well, I didn't even know what to call what we did together in my truck in the parking lot of *Dana's Dogs*. I figured *not-fucked* was a close enough description.

Still, her clinging to me in the middle of the night, the scents of lust and passion heavy in the cab of my truck, was so fucking hot. Even though I'd just nutted in my shorts, my dick grew hard all over again just from her fucking hug.

Trouble had wiggled her sweet ass against my lap before turning her head. She blinked her eyes at me, the invitation in them clear, but I knew better.

I cannot fuck this woman no matter how badly I want her.

So, I took her home, pressed a kiss to her forehead, and watched her scoot out of my truck and move up the lighted path to her front door, not trusting myself to walk beside her. If I did that, I might follow her all the way to her bed, and there would be no stopping me then. So I forced myself to remain in my seat, waiting till she closed and locked the door before pulling away.

It was one of the hardest things I'd ever done in my entire life.

But sex and feeding were kind of a hand in hand thing with my kind, and if I thought I could control my hunger for even one second, I was fooling myself. It wouldn't be enough. Not right then. If I fucked Sybil Harbor, I would want to bite her. And if I bit her, I'd fucking drink her dry, and that was something I would never forgive myself for.

Maybe if I'd just fed, I could try it. But it had been a few days since I'd consumed my last blood bag, and I wasn't in control of my hunger the way I'd need to be if I was going to engage in sex with Trouble.

And that was about the time I'd decided I could not be alone with her like that again. She was too damn tempting. Too damn sexy for her own good. And mine.

Still, images of her coming apart in my arms just because of my lips on her sweet tits had me hard and achy for the last few hours. I'd dropped her off outside her home after the whole hot as hell *not-fucking* episode, and that was hours ago.

I couldn't fall asleep. I mean, how could I?

Hell, I was so riled up I wanted to pound on my chest and yell to the whole world that I made Sybil

Harbor come tonight. Like I was proud of my total lack of control and her headfirst response to me.

How fucked was that?

Of course, I didn't do it. I just paced back and forth across my shitty motel room, staring at my phone, and wondering what I could text the girl who was making me crazy. But Sybil wasn't just a girl, was she? No, she was the Dragon I was sent to find to kill to break the curse on my Coven.

Fuck. No.

Just like that, all the good happy thoughts I'd been having after my post noncoital orgasm up and vanished in a puff of fiery fucking smoke. My Coven was suffering. I had a job to do. But all I wanted was to lose myself in Trouble's sweet body.

Shit.

I tried to imagine the remaining members of my Coven. There were maybe two dozen of us left. My grandmother and I were the only ones of my line, and she'd taken over as leader after my father's, her son's, death. I was supposed to save us by bringing back the Dragon's blood for the Coven to consume as a whole, thereby breaking the curse.

I was supposed to take my place as head of the Calloway Coven of Dhampirs and return us to our former glory. But I had no interest in leading. Never did. And I had even less in mating the shallow female my grandmother had picked out for me. Susan Gentry was from an old family.

Good stock, my grandmother had said when she'd told me about the arrangement. But Susan Gentry, for all her poise and polish, did absolutely nothing to rouse my attention. Not like a certain blue-haired temptress who didn't even have to try.

All the longing in the world could not change one truth. Sybil Harbor was the Dragon I'd been searching for. But now that I'd found her, I couldn't just kill her. The thought was so fucking repulsive I fell to my knees and dry-heaved the second I had it.

Shit. My heart squeezed, and my stomach turned. Was I ready to betray my people, my family, for a woman I did not even know existed twelve hours ago? The answer appeared so fast and clear in my mind, it was obvious.

Yes. I would betray them for her. I would find another way to break the curse. I had to. It was the only acceptable plan.

My phone chirped, and I looked down, surprised to see she'd texted me.

TROUBLE WITH A CAPITAL T

Thanks for coming out with me after the bar. I had a really nice time tonight. Maybe we can do it again before you leave for home?

My heart was hammering inside my chest, but I forced myself to pause before answering. Yes, I wanted to see her again. Hell, I was definitely going to see her again. I just had to make sure we didn't spend too much time alone. At least, not until I broke the curse.

PERCY/MY HERO

I'd like that, too. Get some sleep, Trouble. I will text you in the morning.

TROUBLE WITH A CAPITAL T

Goodnight, Percy. You really were my hero tonight.

Damn. My chest ached, and my entire body quivered with longing and all for this woman. She was going to be the death of me.

But I really kind of hoped that was just a figure of speech.

CHAPTER EIGHT SYBIL

"ANOTHER DATE?" Nova asked, as I attempted to braid my hair for the third time.

"Yeah. We're going to the aquarium," I said, naming one of my favorite places in the world.

"The aquarium? I thought you were banned," Martina said, joining us from the kitchen.

"Only if I try to go during regular hours," I mumbled my reply.

I did not want to discuss that time my magic got a little frisky, and I ended up butt naked inside the shark tank during our tenth grade class trip. Technically, she was right. I was not allowed inside the small, but plenty awesome aquarium just a half hour away from Maccon City, during regular business hours. But I was friends with their head of security, a Bear Shifter named

Goliath whose teenage son, Jeremy, had run away after his first shift.

I'd worked the case a few years ago, and I'd been the one to find his boy in an abandoned hunting cabin close to his house. He'd been afraid his father would be mad when he discovered he'd accidentally shifted near the old man's Camaro and slashed his tires. Of course, Goliath only wanted his son safe and back home.

I'd worked with the two of them for weeks, establishing some basic ground rules and opening a healthy line of communication between father and son. It was one of the happier cases I'd ever worked on. Goliath was so grateful to me, he let me in anytime I wanted to visit as long as it was at night.

I checked my phone, Percy was due to pick me up in ten minutes. I bit my lip, opting for sheer lip gloss instead of color, and checked my outfit in the mirror. It was a sort of babydoll dress with a flattering v neck that brought attention to my boobs. I had about ten dresses cut similarly. In the spring and summer times, they were my go to for casual cuteness.

I loved the way they made my hips and ass appear a little less bulbous than usual. I was a fat-bottomed girl, what could I say? And while I was typically proud of that I wanted to look cute. I mean, I really liked this guy, and that style of dress bolstered my confidence.

"Well?" I asked my sisters, turning to face them.

"Nice dress," Marti said, smiling at me.

"Good color. Easy access. Perfect," Nova added.

"Oh my god, you are the worst! I am not wearing this for easy access," I muttered, rolling my eyes.

"Yeah? Then how come you ditched the chub rub shorts?" Nova asked, and I could feel my blush burning my cheeks as I swiped the shorts off my bed and stuffed them back in my drawer.

"Because *nunya*, Nova Harbor," I grunted.

"*Nunya?*"

"Yeah, nunya business!"

"Oh my gods, you two, just hush. Here, Sweet Sybil. Keep this in your purse," Martina said, handing me a small, zippered pouch.

"What is it?" I asked before opening it.

"It's an emergency date kit. Marti and I got the idea from Cat. You see, she does a version of this for the teenagers she works with, but we made it a little more fun for you. At least, I think we did," she said and shrugged.

My cheeks burned as I took in the little emergency date kit my sisters had prepared for me. Inside were at least half a dozen wrapped condoms in different sizes and, *gulp*, flavors.

"Really?" I gasped, but I was still looking, and my eyes bulged when I saw a tiny clitoral vibrator, a mini tube of lube, a pamphlet that when I unfolded it turned out to be a printed how-to guide for sexual positions as illustrated in the Kama Sutra, and a business card with a QR code for an ebook titled *The Female Orgasm and How to Make it Last.*

"The card is for you to give him in case he doesn't, *er,* close the deal with flourish," Martina said, grimacing as she wrung her hands together.

"Ohmygod! You guys! No, like really *no,*" I said, shaking my head, caught somewhere between exasperation and outright hysteria.

"Sweet Syb, it is nothing to be ashamed about. Not all men know how to make a woman come, and since he isn't a Shifter—*I mean,* he isn't, right? I couldn't really tell—"

"You know what," I said, stopping them both with one raised hand. "I will keep the condoms, and, okay, I will keep the lube. But you can have the card and the pamphlet back. Besides," I said, dropping the unwanted items on the vanity just as I heard his truck pull up.

"Besides," I said, grinning widely. "He has already proven he can close the deal with all the flourish I need."

Nova and Martina were still shrieking when I raced out the front door and ran down the path to meet Percy's pickup truck. He jumped out of his seat and moved quickly to the passenger door, holding it open before I got there.

Fuck. He was hot.

Tall and wide, his handsome face turned to me as I floated to him. Well, obviously I wasn't floating, but it sure felt like it those last few feet of space. Without stopping, I placed a palm on his shoulder and stepped onto the runner, turning my head to kiss him hello before vaulting into the seat.

"Hi! Come on, let's go," I said, hurrying him along.

"What are you running from, Trouble?" he asked, narrowing those shocking green eyes as he looked at me.

"Them!" I said, not bothering to lie.

I pointed to my sisters who were just then coming out of the house, giggles and hands waving as they shouted something that sounded suspiciously like *congrats on your flourish*. But I had no desire to stick around to find out.

"Ah, I see," Percy replied.

The corner of his lips tilted upwards in a humor filled smirk as he blurred to his side of the truck. Damn. He moved fast. Shifter? I still wasn't sure. I sniffed casually, but his smell was all spice and cologne and man.

I couldn't get anything else from it. But he had an aura of power, and he was inhumanly fast. I didn't want to be a jerk about it, but I was definitely going to ask him about his species or classification or whatever the fuck. I mean, hey, a girl had to know who she was hopefully shimmying out of her panties for, right? And boy, did I want to shimmy.

An hour and a half later, we were slowly wandering through the darkened halls of the aquarium hand in hand, like teenagers, and I had to admit, it was the best date I had ever been on. Percy seemed to enjoy the exhibits as much as I did, especially the shark tunnel.

"This is amazing," he murmured, looking up as a black tip reef shark passed overhead.

"It's my favorite spot," I told him.

"Do they really allow people to scuba dive inside there?" he asked.

We'd read one of the many posters displayed on the back of one of the benches outside the tunnel before walking in. Silly as it sounded, they really did allow normals to swim with the apex predators, after they'd already been fed of course.

"Yeah."

"I mean, why would humans want to do that? Seems dangerous," he mumbled, watching as a pair of sting rays raced across the top of the clear acrylic tunnel.

"I guess it's the rush they get being close to something dangerous," I replied, suddenly wanting to know. "Some people just can't help it. They go looking for *trouble*."

"Mm," he replied, turning to face me with a mischievous grin on his face. "Is that right?"

Damn. He was so big and handsome. His thick auburn hair was pulled back from his chiseled face in a loose, low ponytail. A hint of shadow covered his cheeks and fuck if that didn't make him look hotter. The black jeans and t-shirt he wore should have made him appear casual, approachable, but the way they clung to his muscular frame had me thinking thoughts entirely unsuitable for an aquarium.

Well, maybe, if it was during regular hours, I conceded.

"Actually, funny story, I, um, did that once."

"You went scuba diving in a shark tank?"

"Sorta," I mumbled. "Except, I was naked without scuba gear, and I didn't mean to go diving, but well, you see I—"

"No, no, I need you to explain this clearly, Trouble. You ended up in a tank full of sharks with no clothes? How? Why? And who do I have to kill?"

"Oh my god, no one you nut job," I said, shaking my head.

Percy stalked over to me, stopping only when he had me pressed up against the side of the enormous acrylic tank surrounding us. Because it was after hours, the main lights were off, and only the glow from some of the ambient lights inside the tank were lit. The soft blues and pale whites were pretty, casting shadows on the floor and making everything seem magical.

"Trouble, who pushed you in a tank?"

"No one. I mean, it was me," I confessed.

"You?"

"So, you know how we're both supernaturals?"

"Yeah," he replied slowly.

"Well, I'm a Shifter," I said, not revealing my animal because it was weird.

I mean most people assumed Wolf or Bear or Cheetah. Even Bunny. But no one ever guessed Dragon. Maybe it was because females were so rare, they were practically unheard of. After I revealed my animal, folks usually got so caught up in it they either treated me like an experiment or begged me to show them. I wasn't in the mood for either, so I left it like that, and Percy didn't push. Just another thing for me to like about him.

"You're a Shifter. Are you a water Shifter or something? A goldfish? A guppy?" he teased.

"No. I'm not a goldfish or a guppy, but, um, I am a water Witch," I explained.

I bit my lip, watching as his brow furrowed and his hands dropped to my sides.

"Witch? You're a Shifter, though," he murmured, and I heard the question mark at the end.

"Hybrid, actually. My sisters and my brother, too.

We recently formed our own group, approved by the Supernatural and Shifter Councils and everything. Martina is our Alpha. We're the Witch Shifter Clan."

I stopped, holding my breath as Percy stood there. He seemed to be trying to understand what I'd just told him, and I got it. I mean, not everyone approved of or even knew that hybrids existed. I still did not know what he was, but I needed him to know that about me.

Secrets were dangerous all around, and I really liked Percy. I wanted there to be honesty between us, but I was smart enough to know it wouldn't come from nowhere. If I wanted to build a relationship based on truth and trust, then I was okay being the one to go first.

"Are you sure?"

"Yes, I'm sure," I said, looking down.

Maybe I'd been wrong. My stomach squeezed, threatening to tie itself in a knot. Shit. I should have kept my mouth shut.

"Hey, thank you for telling me," Percy said, rubbing the back of his neck and I shrugged.

Oh well, in for a penny, I mused, turning to face him again.

"Yeah. My kind are rare and there're plenty of supernaturals who are prejudiced against hybrids. They think we're nothing but trouble," I said, allowing my Dragon to peek out through my eyes.

"Sybil, I don't think that," he started, but I cut him off.

"But I also heard some people get turned on looking for trouble," I said, opting for bold. "What I want to know, Percy Calloway, is *do you?*"

"Do I what?" he asked, swallowing a big gulp of air as I bit my lip and batted my lashes at him.

He raised one perfectly sculpted eyebrow, his gaze zeroed in on me as I moved closer. Stepping right into his space I ran my hands up his chest and smoothed them over his wide shoulders.

I tilted my head back, lifting my face close as I could get to kissing him without lifting on tip toe.

"Do you get turned on *looking for trouble?* I'm asking what gets you hot, Percy," I whispered, the spicy scent of his cologne filling my lungs.

"Thought that was obvious, *Trouble*. Guess I better show you," he growled, grabbing my hips.

My heart hammered inside my chest. I mean, holy fuck, that was a lot of hot guy standing there in his tight cotton tee. It was clinging to his sculpted chest and abs, his jeans riding low on his hips.

Hot dayummm.

He looked like a dream come true. Like the song said, a vision of love, and it was everything I ever wanted in a man. A sweet fantasy that came to life just for me. Me. I really meant that. He was looking at me like I was the only woman who existed in the whole universe.

I had all of Percy's attention, and it was riveting. Talk about some serious *swoon*. I mean look, I tried to be a self-assured modern woman, but it wasn't always easy having a genius who looked like a supermodel for one sister and a sexy Alpha for the other.

For a woman harboring a Dragon inside her, I could be sort of a mouse. Especially with men. I was always getting friend-zoned by guys I'd crushed on, and I was so damn afraid it was going to happen again. But Percy was looking at me like he wanted to eat me, and I had only one thing to say about that.

Yes, please.

Too damn lust-filled to be embarrassed by my thoughts, my eyes widened, panties grew damp, and my heart kept up a rapid tattoo as I wondered what I should do next. I didn't have to wait very long to find out. Thank fuck. Percy took over, wresting the decision from my trembling hands.

He captured my lips and pulled me into his big, hard body. My Dragon purred inside my chest, and I swooned. Honest to god, I literally swooned. Were it not for his iron firm grip on me, I'd have melted into a puddle at his feet. As it was, Percy held me upright, taking control of our kiss as he cupped one hand behind my head. The other slid up my skirt, grabbing onto my ass.

Holy hell. I shivered. My core clenched on air as he gripped one entire cheek in his enormous hand. I moaned when he squeezed, moving his hand to get a better grip. His index finger slid into my crack as he pressed me more firmly against him and I thanked the gods I chose to wear a cute pair of cheeksters and not the hideous thigh saver shorts I often went with when I wore a dress.

"If we don't stop, I'm going to fuck you in front of the sharks," he growled, nipping my lip between his teeth.

"I'd let you," I replied, meaning it.

"Fuck, Trouble," he growled, shoving his tongue deep down my throat and making me moan with the ferocity of his passion. "There're cameras in here, and friend or not, I'd have to kill that Bear for seeing or hearing any fucking part of you."

I was still trying to recover after that last toe curling kiss, but his whispered words sounded so sincere the bloodthirsty beast inside of me was roused. In fact, my Dragon was practically fucking panting with need.

For someone who was a proud pacifist, my inner creature was somewhat fond of violence and violent displays. Even the mere promise of one. So much so, I was pretty damn sure I was going to need a new pair of underwear before the end of the date.

"Maybe it's time to leave?" I said, but I could hear the question at the end of my sentence and if I could, that meant he could.

"You don't know what you're asking for, Trouble. Fuck, you taste so good," he whispered, his lips clinging to mine.

It was a chaste kiss. Well, chaste-ish. His lips were so soft and warm, and they felt so right pressed against me. I felt hot and needy, drunk with desire for him.

"Percy?"

"Shh. Just give it a second. It will pass," he said, pressing his lips to my temple.

Damn. Why was that hot? It shouldn't have been. But it was, and I squeezed my thighs together, trying to relieve the ache. It was obvious he was not going to do anything inside the aquarium. But then why didn't he want to leave?

Confusion warred with embarrassment, and I froze. Shit. I just threw myself at this man and he was saying no. That seemed to get through the fog of need I was currently lost in, and I straightened in his arms, trying to move back. But Percy didn't drop his hands.

"Hey, it's not what you think," he said, green eyes zeroed in on mine.

"No? Well, sorry if there's any confusion. I just

threw myself at you and you politely declined," I said, pushing against his hold, calling on my Dragon's strength.

Percy frowned, and for one minute I felt him hold on to me, despite my strength. Surprise had me pulling back, but then he dropped his hands, and I stepped away. Immediately, I was aware of how cold it felt without him.

The aquarium's HVAC system ran twenty-four seven to ensure quality environmental control for their inhabitants. I knew enough about the place to acknowledge that, but it still wasn't the reason I was shivering.

"What are you?" I asked, not caring if it was rude.

Suddenly, I just needed to know. Was what I felt between us only one sided? I didn't think he was a Shifter, but he was definitely something. And most supernaturals had their own version of fated mates lore. Not that I thought that's what we were. We weren't that. I mean, we hardly knew each other.

We are. Mine. Mate.

Shut up, I scolded my Dragon.

It had been a really long time since I'd had a guy, any guy, in bed, and well, maybe I was just horny. Plenty of people mistook sex for love, and that was all this was.

Well, no. It was not even that. After all, I had just offered myself to him on a silver platter and he turned me down. Percy and I weren't having sex of any kind.

Why it hurt so much to even think was not something I was willing to answer.

Fuck. You are not in love with this stranger, Sybil. Do you hear me?

But he's like everything I ever wanted. A dream come true.

I closed my eyes and counted to five before opening them again. What the hell was wrong with me? Did dream lovers often refuse their intended? No. They didn't. I was being foolish, naïve, just plain silly. I hated that about myself. Hated that I wished for the moon and got served a slice of cheese instead. Hated even more that I would accept that pitiful substitution with a fucking smile because I was so damn weak.

My Dragon purred sadly, knowing it was true. But there was still one last chance. If Percy was some sort of species of supernatural that did not believe in fated mates, maybe he just didn't know.

Maybe he simply couldn't see the connection I knew we had.

My heart pounded. I was risking everything by going into this with him. After all, it was only recently that supes had started to accept the fact there were hybrids out there, and we were real people who deserved respect and kindness and love. Our entire Clan was based on that belief. I wasn't hiding who I was from anyone. Especially not from him.

Sure, I was rushing it, but he was leaving soon, going back home. When else was I going to get the chance to ask?

"What are you, Percy?"

"Why? Why do you want to know?" Percy asked, answering my question with a question.

I really fucking hated when people did that. Sweet Sybil would have just smiled politely. But I wasn't Sweet Sybil right then. I was Trouble with a capital T.

"Because," I growled.

"That's not an answer, Trouble. And it didn't seem to concern you last night or five seconds ago."

"What's the big deal, Percy? I know you're not staying, and you've made it very clear that a little fooling around was as far as you want to take this thing. But I want more. I feel like you mean more," I whispered, baring my soul to this man. "So, tell me, what are you? Maybe then I can understand why you're pushing me away and shutting us down before we even begin. Maybe then I can figure out why I feel like you are so important to me."

"Fuck, Trouble, no that's not what I was trying to do—"

"Tell me, Percy, please. I just admitted a lot more than I meant to, so I don't think it's too personal a question anymore. Do you?"

"What about you? Will you tell me what you are?" he asked.

"If you asked me, I would tell you anything. Everything. I was just ready to tear off my clothes for you a second ago, in public, so yeah. I'll answer your questions, Percy. You just have to ask."

CHAPTER NINE PERCY

"I'M A DHAMPIR."

"A what now?"

"A half-Vampire."

I watched as Sybil tried to make sense of my words. Most Shifters ignored the Vampiric world. I couldn't necessarily blame them. Vampires were notoriously secretive and preferred to live on the periphery of the supernatural world, policing their own, and only interacting with Shifters, and Witches, and other supes when absolutely necessary.

"Dahmp-peer," she said, repeating the word phonetically.

"That's right."

"And you are a half-Vampire? Like your mom was

one, but not your dad?" she asked, her face scrunching up adorably.

"No. Um, here, let's sit down, and I will try to explain. Dhampirs are not Vampires. We are a sort of subspecies. Half-Vampire beings who require blood to survive, have access to some magic, and enjoy a certain longevity of life."

"How old are you?" she asked, catching on immediately.

"Older than you, Trouble," I replied, not wanting to freak her out entirely.

Yeah. Then you better not tell her you were sent to hunt her down and drain her fucking blood to feed your Coven and end an ancient curse then, huh?

I scrubbed a hand over my face and ignored my inner sarcastic asshole. Trouble had a few very key things wrong about what was going on between us, and I owed it to her and to myself to try to figure it out. First things first.

"How much older?" she asked.

"Old enough to know better, but like I told you when we first met, I never had the sense to run from *trouble* when I was a kid. Why would I start now?"

"Okay, so you are a Dhampir. Does your kind believe in fated mates?" she whispered so softly I barely heard her.

"Yesss," I replied, dragging out the last sound as I

gripped her chin between my thumb and forefinger. "We have legends of fated mates among our kind, though they are rare. There is something you should know, Sybil. My Coven was cursed, and I am not free to choose."

"Not free? A-are you mated already?"

"What? No," I said, shaking my head.

Revulsion filled me at the idea of touching another woman, and even though I knew I couldn't tell her everything I could tell her some of it. Fuck, she deserved so much better than me, but I wasn't a good enough man to walk away from her. The second I touched her, I was done for. She was mine. Whether or not I could keep her, well, that was another question.

"It's true, my grandmother arranged for me to be betrothed to a female of our kind. But I have not signed any agreement and I have never touched her, Trouble."

She closed her eyes, brows furrowing, and I hated the pain I saw etched across her face. Sybil's breath hitched, and I gave her a small shake, needing her to look at me. But when she opened her eyes, a stream of tears flowed down her cheeks, and I was shocked. Fucking shit that I was, I made her cry. And I never hated myself more.

"So, you have a woman waiting for you back home?" she asked.

I heard despair and guilt in her voice, and it filled

me with equal parts shame and rage. I did not want anyone else but her. Didn't she know that? Couldn't she tell? Maybe not. Trouble was feisty, but she also had a measure of vulnerability I hadn't counted on.

"No. It's not like that. I've never touched her. Not ever. And I have not agreed to the betrothal contract. There is no one else I want. Just you."

She tried to pull away, shaking her head. But I held her firm, refusing to give up my claim. She was mine. I needed her to listen.

"Do you hear me? I only want you," I repeated.

"B-but you pushed me away?"

Her lips quivered. Fuck. I could not deal with her tears. Anger? Yes. But crying? No way. I hated that I caused her to doubt herself. She had to know no one compared to her as far as I was concerned.

"I have not been with a woman for years, but I recall the sounds of lovemaking. I have no desire to share any part of you with cameras on walls or even sharks behind their plastic tanks."

"What—" she started, but I shook my head, not allowing her to finish.

"I won't stand for it, Trouble. No one else gets to hear you. No one else gets to see you. When I have you, and I will fucking have you, it will be the two of us alone," I growled.

I knew I sounded ridiculous. Like a fucking cave-man. But I didn't care. Not one bit.

"*When* you have me? And what do you mean years since you've been with a woman?"

"I am old, remember?" I replied, and she laughed through her tears. "And yes, it is *when* I have you. Not *if*. You are mine, Trouble with a capital T and I intend to be buried between your delicious thighs sometime in the near future."

"Yeah?"

"Yeah. I don't say things I don't mean. You'll just have to trust me on that," I said.

"You mean, you feel this too?" she asked, sounding so vulnerable I felt all my barriers give way.

"I feel it, too," I confirmed, holding her gaze, and seeing the moment her Dragon flashed across her eyes with the lengthening of her pupil and sudden flare of pink.

My stomach twisted, and my gums ached. Fuck. I needed to feed. I could not risk taking her vein, not then. She must have seen my struggle, felt the danger, because her nostrils flared and that time, I allowed her to pull back.

"You smell different," she whispered, sniffing delicately.

"It is the curse."

"Will you tell me about it?"

"Soon. For now, it is easier if you understand that typically a Dhampir will feed once a month and be fine, but not us. The Calloway Coven has suffered under a curse that means we must feed much more frequently or else we lose ourselves to the bloodlust and have for many generations," I explained.

"That must be awful. Can I help?" she asked, and I had to brace myself for the wave of hunger I felt that hit me harder than before.

She was so caring. Thoughtful. Wanting to give when she had no idea what she was offering. She was precious, and suddenly I understood why the Fates had chosen her for me. So I could protect her. My sweet, sexy Trouble was too damn soft for this hard, cruel world. She needed me.

I would have to find another way to break the curse. I had no idea how, but I would. Because if there was one thing I knew for sure, I wouldn't give her up. Not now. Not ever.

Mine.

"Tell you what. Let's go visit the dolphin exhibit, then we can grab another round at *Dana's Dogs,* sound good?"

"That sounds good," she replied, her hazel gaze focused on my lips.

"Trouble," I warned.

"But, if you feel this way, why don't you want me—"

I couldn't let her finish that sentence, so I crushed my lips to hers, taking her mouth in the kind of kiss I'd never shared with another being. I poured everything I had into it. My yearning, my thirst, my need for her. It wasn't enough. I grabbed Sybil by the waist and yanked her on top of my lap.

Somehow, we wound up seated on one of the many benches that seemed to pop up around every corner of this maze-like aquarium. Sybil moaned into my mouth, opening sweetly for me, offering me the world. And I took. Fuck, did I take.

I swallowed down her sweetness in great gulps, my cock so fucking hard I was liable to make an ass of myself for the second time with this woman if I didn't stop. I slid my lips to her neck, allowing myself one lick of her tender skin before I pulled her up to a standing position with me.

"Do you understand yet? Do you realize how much I want you?" I asked, pressing my hardness against her one more time before moving back.

"Yes, Percy," she said, swaying slightly on her feet.

Her gasp when I grinned was enough to make me frown. My gums ached, and I caught my reflection in one of the tanks, seeing my fangs had descended.

"Next time, I will feed right before I see you. Then it won't be so dangerous," I said, cupping her cheek before I moved away.

I knew I looked scary as fuck, and I wanted to shield her from it. From me. I couldn't deal with her fear. But Sybil's eyes never left mine. She watched in silence for a moment before straightening her clothes and patting her pretty blue hair.

Then, as if I needed another shock to my system, she held out her hand, turning her attention to the fish we passed. Her chatter was quite pleasant. It helped calm my hunger and my lust.

I sniffed. *Hmm.* She didn't smell like fear. She smelled fucking delicious. And that was only one more thing for me to worry about.

Trouble. Sweet, sweet Trouble.

The rest of our date went well. Better than well. It was amazing. So good, the next night, we went out again. And the next night again. The days and nights blurred together, and I had to admit I had never had so much fun.

Sybil worked as a social worker, and she was damn good at her job. It seemed to fit her personality, and of course, she did something that involved helping people. The darling woman couldn't help herself.

Every hour in her company I wanted her more and more, but I wasn't able to get to the blood bank, and I managed to stave off our more carnal desires with some heavy petting and a ton of cold fucking showers. But I'd succeeded in my mission tonight and after gorging myself on a bag of O positive, I stuck another in a cooler in the backseat of my truck for later. Just in case.

It wasn't that I was planning to fuck her. But yeah, I was planning to fuck her.

Sybil gave every indication she was more than ready, and I had enough of waiting. Kissing her was heaven. Touching her, fucking divine. But I needed to feel her slick pussy wrapped around my cock. And I meant needed. Not wanted. By then, it was a primal urge. A biological imperative.

Sybil Harbor was made for me, and I could not wait another second to stake my claim on the sexy as hell woman. My phone buzzed, and I answered it without looking, thinking it was her calling me.

My Sybil. Mate. Trouble with a capital T.

But I was wrong.

"Perseus? Where the hell have you been? It's been a week since your last report. Have you found it yet?"

Grandmother's voice sounded shrill over the phone, and I closed my eyes against the way it grated on my nerves. Maybe it was that or maybe it was the way she'd said *it* when referring to the Dragon.

"Not yet."

"Have you lost sight of your mission, boy? It is up to you to right these wrongs and bring that monster here to die!"

"I said. Not. Yet. I will call when there is something

to report," I growled, hanging up before I said something I would regret.

"Fuck."

I rubbed a hand over my face, exiting my motel room. I knew she was right to be angry, but I just couldn't follow through with the mission anymore. I could not do that to her. Not my Trouble.

I looked at the time on my cell phone before tossing it on the seat next to me. I was half an hour early for a five-minute drive, but I was willing to risk it.

Today we were meeting at a local bookstore, something Trouble was looking forward to. She could hardly contain her excitement yesterday when she told me about a local children's author who was holding a reading in town. She explained that the woman had grown up in Maccon City, like her, and they'd attended the same schools.

I had to admit I was surprised when Sybil offered that she was a social worker of sorts for a secret branch of the government. We'd skated around what species of supernatural I belonged to up until our date at the aquarium. I loved how her cheeks had turned pink when she brought up not wanting to ask me because she knew it was rude.

"Percy, I don't want you to tell me anything unless you want to. I mean, I know these things are rude to ask. But you are a supe too, so you know that much," she'd whispered,

and it had sounded like a question rather than a statement.

"Yes, Trouble. That I am."

I felt I needed to confirm what she was saying, giving her something for whatever she was giving me next. It felt right. Important somehow that I reciprocated her trust.

"Okay, good. It's fair then. You don't know what I am, and I don't know what you are, but someday we can maybe tell each other," she'd said, biting her lip in that way she had that drove me wild.

The second I understood she meant more to me than anyone else, I had to tell her what I was. Of course, I hadn't revealed that I knew what she was. All of what she was, or that I'd come to Maccon City looking for a way to end the curse.

How the fuck was that conversation supposed to go, anyway?

Hey Trouble,

So you know how my family was cursed? Well, I don't want you to get mad or worried, but I was sent here to find a Dragon Shifter to bring back to my Coven. Yeah, see, we need Dragon blood to end the curse that causes our bloodlust thereby restoring us to prestige and power in the Dhampir community.

Kind of lucky I ran into you, you see, we haven't heard of Dragons in these parts for centuries, and even then, they were all supposed to be male. So, imagine my surprise when I ran into you. Don't worry. I'm not gonna kill you, though. I wanna fuck you instead.

Maybe keep you. I know holidays might be weird with my family wanting to drain you and all, but what do you think?

Yeah. That didn't sound plausible to me either. So, I bit my fucking lip and just enjoyed my time with her. She was nothing like I'd expected. Trouble was full of surprises.

She started talking more about reading and books, and how she wanted to see this author on Saturday because the kids she worked with loved these stories best. She'd seemed apologetic, like she felt bad for missing a chance to be with me. I just grinned.

I was a sucker for Trouble's smiles, and this writer made her smile, so I'd asked to come along. She blew me away with the grin she gave me after I'd asked, and I wanted to high five myself.

Shit. I'd never felt anything like this. I mean attraction, sure, but not like this. It was like I wanted to consume her. And not in a Count Dracula *I vant to suck your blood* kind of way. I just needed to be with her as much as possible.

We'd seen each other every day since that first night. Memories of the way Sybil fell apart in my arms with my mouth and hands on her tight little nipples made my cock throb every fucking time I got in my truck. I wanted her so fucking badly.

But I wasn't sure I could handle it. So far, I'd managed to snag a bag of platelets from the high school gym where they'd been holding a blood drive. It was fucked up, but I needed to do something to sate my hunger. Between my cock and my gums, I wasn't sure which would burst first whenever I was near the sexy as sin woman. All I knew was that my entire being ached with wanting her. And I was done waiting.

My search for a Dragon Shifter to replace her was still on and I'd come close a few times. Their scent was almost untraceable, but now that I knew what she was, I looked for any scent with similar notes. Plus, I had my medallion to confirm my suspicions.

I pulled into a spot outside Crescent Moon Books and scanned the windows for confirmation I was in the right place, though I knew I was. Maccon City wasn't exactly overflowing with bookstores, and this one had a pretty unique name. Plus, there was a huge sign outside welcoming local children's book author Jozette Falk to the store to do a reading that started in about twenty-five minutes.

Yeah, I was early. But that was okay. I could scope out the store, do some recon at the same time. Who knew? Maybe I'd find the Dragon I was looking for.

Once inside the store, I was surprised at how vast

the selection was. I'd expected the usual sort of romances, thrillers, and kids' books that would likely attract the sort of foot traffic they likely saw. But I was pleasantly surprised to find Crescent Moon Books had rows upon rows of biographies, histories, yes, the usual pulp fiction, but so much more than that. They had an enormous section featuring local writers. And another was set up just for indie authors whose books were not typically available in the larger stores.

"Can I help you?" a pretty woman with a slight limp who smelled of Wolf asked, and I smiled politely at her.

She was wearing a wedding band and cradling a small bundle in her arms which, after it gave a shrill squall, I realized was not books. The woman shushed her bundle sweetly, bouncing her babe up and down in soothing motions. Then she turned her attention back to me.

"Sorry, this one is giving me fits with bedtime," she explained.

"No worries. It must be nice to have the baby here with you," I commented unable to help myself.

It had been so long since we had a baby in our Coven, I wondered for a brief moment if such a thing was even possible anymore. A strong sense of hope surged inside me, and I blinked against the moisture that suddenly filled my eyes.

"It is, thank you. Hey, do you need a minute?"

"Oh, um no. Pardon me. Must have gotten dust in my eye," I said, embarrassed by my emotional display.

"I see. Well, here is a map to help you navigate our shop. If it is the occult section you're looking for," she added with a whisper, "just let me know."

I nodded and took the map, noting they had a second floor with even more books. Holy crap. This place was huge. I kind of loved the fact that my sweet and naughty little Trouble was also a nerd girl at heart. Reading was one of my favorite past times, and I was not embarrassed to admit I was a hardcore romantasy fan.

I wonder if Trouble would be down for a little roleplay.

Just picturing her curvy as sin body dressed up in a sheer confection with fairy wings and glittery cream smoothed over her pale skin had my eyes rolling in the back of my head. Fuck. I cursed under my breath and hissed behind my teeth. The last thing I needed was a fucking tent in my pants at a book reading for kids.

Thank fuck that was all it took for me to settle down. There were way too many Shifters in there for me to walk around with a boner. Speaking of which, my entire body froze as the medallion beneath my shirt heated my skin. I looked up, expecting to see Trouble, but instead I was greeted by a very strange sight indeed.

Almost a dozen children, ranging in age from tween to toddler came scrambling inside the small bookstore.

"Well, well, well! If it isn't my honored guests," the proprietor who'd helped me earlier said as she came around to greet them all.

"Aunt Clara! Aunt Clara!"

"Can I hold Junior?" the oldest blonde haired girl asked.

"Sure you can, Calla, my sweetheart," the woman, Clara, replied. "Where's your Aunt Jozette?"

"She's coming. Uncle Castor, Uncle Edric, and Uncle Nik are helping carry her stuff. Dad and Uncle Sander are with them too," the same little girl answered.

I stood there frozen as the gang of Dragonlings raced by. My heart thundered inside my chest so damn hard I thought I might fracture a rib. If there were Dragon young present, that meant there were adults nearby, which in turn, meant I did not have to betray Sybil.

I mean, I would never harm children. That was not where I was going with my line of thought. But I had never even considered the possibility that there was an entire fucking Clan of the creatures living just hours away from my tortured Coven.

Holy fuck. So many. How could there be so many? How did none of us know?

"You're early!"

Sybil entered the bookshop with a cheerful grin, and my heart constricted all over again. Her sweet voice reached my ears before I even realized she was there. Then I looked down at her outfit, and my pulse raced.

Fuck. Was it hot in there?

She had on another of those short, flirty dresses. The material looked soft and silky as it swirled around her creamy thighs. A zillion tiny yellow flowers danced across the fabric. It dipped down into a deep v in the front, giving me a tantalizing view of her cleavage and the tops of her ripe breasts before fluttering against her arms in short cap sleeves.

It wasn't meant to be provocative, I was almost sure. But Sybil had a gorgeous body on her, full of soft curves and secrets, and I wanted to uncover every single one. She made the innocent confection into something naughty without even trying, and I wanted to put her over my knee and spank her ass for giving everyone else a glimpse of what was mine. I refrained barely. Especially when a group of big motherfuckers followed her inside the store.

I was too focused on my soon to be mate to even realize my medallion was going crazy at their approach. They nodded as they passed, seeming to know Trouble, and I stopped myself growling only barely.

It wasn't until we were seated behind all the kids, near to where those giants copped a squat on the huge story time rug that it finally hit me. I was sitting in a bookstore in Maccon City, New Jersey—home of the largest group of Wolf Shifters in the world. A town I'd come to hoping to find a monster who could end the curse my family, my Coven, had been under for centuries.

I succeeded in finding one mythical creature, only to have the Fates throw a curveball at me. The sweet, sexy Dragon Shifter I discovered was actually my fated mate. I had yet to claim her, but I knew what she was to me, and with every second that passed, I knew I loved her.

So, I'd resigned myself to the fact I was betraying my people by choosing her. But I was fine with that. I could not bear the thought of a hurt Sybil, much less an exsanguinated one. In fact, I was pretty sure I would kill anyone who tried to hurt a single blue hair on her pretty little head.

I needed a new plan. I needed to find another Dragon. I'd just decided that before she came waltzing into the store in that fucking dress, sending every brain cell I had below my belt. No, I was not paying attention to my surroundings. Not when all that skin was on display. How the fuck was I supposed to do that?

But it didn't matter. Because against all odds, I was sitting in a bookstore, listening to a children's story being read by its author who was a local, and I was surrounded by motherfucking Dragon Shifters.

I glanced down at her, noting her smiling face as she

sat straight, just like the kids, and listened to the story being told. It didn't seem to surprise or bother her that she was surrounded by fucking Dragons. But I guessed it wouldn't. She was one, after all. Not that she'd told me that part yet. But she would. I knew she would.

This female was changing everything. I still didn't know how I was going to do my duty to my Coven and keep Sybil for my own, but I was damn well going to try. My heart slammed against my ribs as I imagined a world without her in it, and I *knew*, I just fucking knew I could never allow that to happen.

She was too big. Too important. Her hazel eyes flashed up at me, concern on her face, and I smiled reassuringly, tipping my chin, encouraging her to listen to the story. She gave me a look that I interpreted to mean *are you sure?* I nodded again, pressing my lips to her temple, and wrapped an arm around her shoulders. Sybil sunk into my side, and fuck, she felt good there.

What the fuck was happening to me?

I didn't hear a single word the sweet-looking author said as she read from her fairytale book. I was too busy trying to get my own damn emotions under control. That's when it really hit me.

I was a Dhampir. Trained to fight and protect. Always on edge. Cursed with a hunger that had been the end of too many of my Coven. And yet, the whole time I sat there in the midst of monsters there was only one thing I was concerned with. One person whose well-being mattered more than anything else. It was her. All her.

I didn't have to struggle to control my hunger while I was acting as Sybil's protector. Buffering her from the enormous, powerful Dragon males who, I had to admit, did not seem like much of a threat at that moment, was taking all my concentration.

I wasn't delusional. I did not have a hope in hell of beating so many of the mythological creatures, but I wouldn't need to. I would just have to get her to safety if anything happened. So while the author read, I plotted. Counting escape routes, taking note of all the exits, and calculating how many I could reach while Sybil made it outside.

But all my imagining was for naught. These males seemed nothing like the monsters I'd been taught Dragon Shifters were. Nothing like the one who'd cursed my ancestor. These were family men. I swallowed down on the bitterness that rose in my throat.

How could I contemplate hurting any of these strangers? They sat on the crowded area rug with their mates at their sides and their young scattered between them. Dragon Shifters shouldn't be bouncing babies in their arms while their toddlers climbed up on their shoulders. At least, not in my mind.

Then again, I had never expected to meet a female

Dragon either. The world was a lot different from the one I'd been taught in the Pennsylvania mountains. Maybe my Coven had it wrong. Horrible dread and fragile hope rose inside of me, warring with each other for dominance.

I did not know how to handle my feelings or any of these revelations, as they became clear one by one. Especially not the one that seemed most important. I was going to fail my Coven. For her.

I had a new master. A new mission. Sybil was everything to me now. My focus. My purpose. My reason. The hell I was going to catch from this change in objectives was going to be brutal. But I'd deal with it. I would do anything for her.

"You alright?" Sybil asked.

"Yes."

I nodded. And I meant it. I'd swear on a stack of bibles that right then, in that moment, with her small hand on my chest, I was more than alright. I was fucking perfect.

She really is Trouble. With a capital fucking T.

CHAPTER TEN SYBIL

"DID YOU LIKE THE STORY?" I asked Percy, wondering why he'd gone so quiet.

I was clutching my copy of *The Maiden Saves Her Dragon* to my chest. We'd waited in line when the reading was over, and Jozette signed my copy for me to add to the library I'd been building at Harbor House. After the reading, Callius invited us to join him and his Clan for lunch down at the beach by his castle.

Yes, it was a real castle. I was already in college when they'd started building it, but I would never forget my reaction the first time I saw Castle Falk. It was like a fairytale. A strange noise brought my head up, and I realized Percy was clenching his jaw. Shit. Maybe I should have said no?

"Hey, we don't have to go to lunch if you don't want to. I'm sorry it was thoughtless of me not to ask first—"

"What? Why would you say that, Trouble?" he asked and looked perplexed.

"Well, you seem uncomfortable or anxious, or something," I replied, shrugging helplessly.

"I do? I'm sorry, I just have a lot on my mind, but I want to spend time with you," he said, reassuring me with his words.

If that didn't make me feel better, the enormous hand he placed on my thigh sure did. His fingers were so long he had half of my pretty sizeable leg in his grip and when he squeezed, pure pleasure had me soaking my panties. We'd been taking things pretty slow because of the whole Dhampir thing, and I had yet to tell him all of my truth. He knew I was a hybrid Shifter and Witch, but not that I was a Dragon.

It was a lot to take, and I'd wanted to ease him into it. But I knew one thing for sure as he brushed his fingertips closer and closer to my core almost absently as he navigated towards our destination. And that was this, if this man didn't give me some dick soon, he was going to find out all about my Dragon when I roasted his fine ass for being such a *pussytease*. Was that even a thing? I'd have to ask my sisters later.

"Holy shit. Is that a castle?"

I grinned.

"Yep. Castle Falk."

"You been here before?"

"Yeah, I have. They hold great Christmas parties here. The Castle is occupied by five brothers, we met them at the store, and their families. That big house further down the beach is owned by two more of their Clan."

"Clan?"

"Yeah, Clan. Look, Percy, I didn't want to tell you this way, but I—"

Just then, something ran past the car, and I let out a surprised giggle. It was a young Wolf chasing a couple of kids who'd gotten too close to the parking lot.

"Was that a Wolf Shifter? In broad daylight?" Percy asked, and I heard the shock in his tone.

"Yeah. This is all private property. There are wards placed around that gated entrance to discourage normals from coming too close," I explained.

"Shifters who live here come to hang out and shift and just be themselves. There are lots of spots in Maccon City like this," I said, letting my love of my home shine through.

"I've never heard of anything like it. Wait for me," he said.

"Well, it's our little slice of heaven even if I didn't always think so," I replied, waiting for Percy to come around the truck and open my door as he'd asked me to.

I didn't mind. It was kind of chivalrous, the way he was always opening doors for me and holding my hand. It reminded me there was a side of Percy I knew so little about. His family. His upbringing. I knew we only had so much time together before he had to go back to his home, but I really hoped he was going to come back.

He has to.

It was just another thing we hadn't really talked about yet. But it was a conversation we needed to have. I was pretty sure I was eighty percent in love with the man.

"Just look at those waves," he said, grinning as a huge swell crashed against the sand.

"It's still too cold to swim, but I never miss an opportunity to hang out by the water. It's just another reason I love it here," I said, smiling as Callius and his Clan waved us over.

"Come on," I said, taking Percy's hand in mine and pulling him along.

"Glad you could come," Callius shouted over the roar of the wind.

"Thanks for having us," I replied.

"You know you are always welcome, daughter of my heart," he replied with a serene smile and slight bow.

"Stop it, Cal, you're going to embarrass her in front

of her date. Hey, Sybil, how are you?" Fred, his mate, said, turning to me with open arms.

I hugged the beautiful blonde Werewolf hello, and smiled as their firstborn, Calla joined in the introductions. Percy stood beside me, not awkward at all as he returned greetings. There was an enormous table set up with trays of food. Piles of sandwiches, salads, and fruit, along with mouthwatering treats, filled every inch of space.

That was what happened when Shifters had a picnic. We tended to eat a lot. Like a lot a lot. After we made our selections, I sat down on a blanket with Percy and we ate our lunch, watching the waves and chattering as the kids set up corn hole and other games.

"Percy! Sybil! Come play!" Edric Junior shouted.

The beautiful child's smile was so infectious, I couldn't resist. Percy grinned, and we joined a few of the other kids in a game of volleyball that ended with me on my ass, and Percy whispering his promise to kiss it better when we left.

"I'm going to hold you to that," I said, loving the way his eyes heated as he looked at me.

A shriek from the waves tore my attention away from Percy, and I frowned as I saw a flash of pink being knocked down by the waves.

"No! Bianca!" shouted Devine, one of the newer members of the Falk Clan.

I didn't know the Dragon well, but he'd always been polite. With no hesitation, I reached out with my magic, reveling in the pulsating power that blasted from my fingertips as I manipulated the waves to lift the Wolf pup who'd gotten away from her father. The gasp I heard came from Percy, but I couldn't break my concentration until I knew the man had his daughter in hand.

"I told you, it is not a day for swimming," growled Devine, but he was clutching his daughter tightly and I knew he was just worked up.

"Is she okay?" I asked, wincing at the tiny Wolf pup's soaked bow.

"Thank you so much, Sybil. I think this one will finally learn to respect the Atlantic now," he said, frowning at his whimpering pup. "Now, I want you to shift back, my darling, and we will talk about this inside when you are warm."

"Oh gosh, thanks Syb!" Sunny said, clapping a hand on my shoulder before running after her mate and husband.

The she-Wolf was one of the happiest people I'd ever met, and she didn't seem worried at all by her husband's gruffness. If she wasn't worried, then neither was I, I decided. No one else seemed upset by the shenanigans, and I knew from experience that this kind of thing happened all the time. But Percy apparently didn't.

"You just—*was that—how?*" he sputtered.

"Hey, it's okay. Just breathe," I said, and he frowned, taking my hand, and pulling me away off to the side.

I thought for sure he was going to lay into me. After all, it was one thing to tell someone you were a Witch with a proclivity for water magic and quite another to lift a small Wolf pup out of the water with nothing more than a jolt of magic. But he didn't yell or scold. He just pulled me into his arms and squeezed me tight.

"You're so fucking amazing," he growled, crushing me in his arms.

"Percy?" I whimpered, needing more from him.

I felt anxious and achy. My entire being seemed to bristle with awareness. Desire had never been a sure thing for me, and certainly not mutual in the way it felt with him. Maybe I was kidding myself, but the fire in his eyes was more than enough to have me pushing my body against his.

"So fucking good. So perfect. Mine," he growled and pressed his mouth to my neck.

I felt his teeth scrape over my flesh and every inch of me went on high alert. My panties were soaked and there was no way I was going to walk back over to everyone at the picnic and give those overbearing males something to frown about.

"Sybil, I know we have a lot to discuss, but I really want you to come home with me. Right now," he growled against my ear.

"Yes, I want that too," I replied. "Let's go."

"Shouldn't you say goodbye?" he asked.

"I'll text them. Come on," I said, tugging his hand even as I raised mine in a wave to where Callius and Fred were watching us.

Percy nodded, and I fucking loved that he took me at my word. He didn't second guess me or question if I was sure, like I was a child who needed someone else to make my decisions for me. He trusted me to know my own mind, and that was so fucking hot.

I didn't need to wait or think about it anymore. I just needed him.

Like now.

CHAPTER ELEVEN PERCY

I SLAMMED the door to the motel room I'd rented when I first arrived in Maccon City, my breath coming in great big heaps. Sybil turned to face me, a wicked glint in her eye, and suddenly I forgot all about our accommodations, or lack thereof. We drove in silence, the sexual tension so fucking heavy I could have sliced it with one of my blades.

I cupped the back of her neck with my hand and dragged her to me. Her ready submission had me harder than a fucking cinder block and I growled as she swept her tongue into my mouth with long, hard licks. Trouble was one helluva kisser, and I knew if I thought about how she got so good it would make me want to punch things, so I pushed the thought from my head and focused on how good she felt in my arms.

"Fewer clothes," I grunted, stepping back from her sweet, soft, heat and pulling my shirt over my head.

Doubt crept in as I watched her standing there, looking like a fucking angel in the dingy ass motel room. Shit. I knew this wasn't a fairytale. We had more fucking obstacles between us than she knew. But my body was on fire.

Even though I was very aware she was way too good for that room, too good for me, I was still a selfish asshole. There was no way I would turn her away. Not unless she said no.

"You deserve better than this fucking place," I told her truthfully. "I'm not a good enough man to walk away from you, Trouble, so if you don't want this, this is your shot to tell me to fuck off."

"Stop talking," she said, her hands moving to the buttons on the front of her dress.

She peeled away the fabric, revealing her glorious tits and acres of soft, creamy skin, and my tongue was hanging out of my fucking mouth. My gut clenched, hunger rising, but I pushed it back. I wouldn't be able to choke down the plastic bag of platelets in my fridge just then. If I tried, I'd likely puke.

No. I can control it. I have to.

Sybil pushed the dress all the way off, taking her cheeky little panties with her and I swear to fucking god I drooled. Actually drooled. Her tits were pushed up in another of those goddamn demi-cup bras, and before she could do away with it, I was there.

"Percy," she moaned my name, tossing her head back as I cupped her mounds and pressed them together, dipping my head to get a taste.

She was so damn delicious. The perfect combination of smoky spice and sweetness. I wanted to fucking devour her.

"On the bed," I growled, pushing my pants and briefs down.

Sybil stared at my cock as I fisted my shaft, giving myself one hard tug before raising my eyebrows and jutting my chin behind her.

"On. The. Bed. Trouble. Now," I commanded.

She swallowed hard but finally moved, scuttling back until she sat down hard on the bed, causing her delicious body to jiggle with the move.

Holy fuck.

Thank god she listened so well. Truth was, if Trouble kept staring at me like that, like I was something she wanted to nibble, I was liable to come all over my hand, and I was not doing that tonight. No fucking way.

"There are so many things I wanna do to you," I groaned, falling on top of her.

Sybil's lips were parted the second our bodies touched, so when I crushed my mouth to hers, she was open and ready for the rough swipe of my tongue. I licked into her, needing to taste her, wanting to devour every inch of my sweet little Trouble. And I intended to.

"I need to be inside this hot little pussy right now. I'll do the rest later. Are you ready for it, Trouble? Can you take all of me right now?" I groaned, sliding the blunt head of my cock between her soaked folds.

She scratched at my shoulders, spreading her legs wide for me as I notched myself against her entrance. She was so fucking hot and wet, and I knew she was gonna be tight. I should have maybe prepared her better to take me. I was big, and she was so damn small, but the baser side of me, the needy primal side wanted to leave a mark.

Possessive instincts I never felt before had me gripping her hips and rearing back so I could watch. My head was already inside her slippery little hole and the sight was so fucking hot, I squeezed her hips even harder. Sybil didn't seem to mind, not one bit, if the juices dripping all over my dick were any indication.

I heard her groan and gasp, and I flicked my eyes to her face. Caught up in her rapturous expression, I switched my focus from where my cock sat poised at her entrance to her wide eyes, which were trained on our bodies.

Holy fucking hell.

This woman was full of surprises. My naughty little Trouble was watching our bodies as they came together, her eyes glued to my dick. Fuck, I couldn't wait anymore. I thrust my hips hard, impaling her on my cock for the first time. And it was everything I thought it would be and more.

"Fuccckkk," I groaned, pleasure searing my soul as I felt her pulse and squeeze around me.

"Percy!" she screamed at my rough invasion, clinging to me like a vise.

Being inside her was almost too much. But at the same time, it wasn't enough. I needed more. I needed to touch every inch of her. So, I did. I pressed my body into hers, crushing her into the mattress, rubbing my legs against hers, wrapping my arms around her. I kissed her mouth, forcing hers open as I thrust my tongue down her throat, moving in time with my hips. She felt so good.

So hot. So soft. So warm. So fucking mine.

Trouble must have liked it, too. Must have felt the same fire in her bones because the hot little minx clung to me. She wrapped around me like a vine, taking everything I gave her and demanding more with her sexy little moans and those hot as fuck scratches down my back. She was everywhere. Sybil surrounded me, filled my senses with her sultry sighs and tantalizing scent.

She'd systematically torn down every preconceived notion I had about mates, love, and Shifters in general. She changed everything. And now, with her body so warm, wet, and welcoming, she was marking me from the inside out. Staking her claim on my body, heart, and soul. And nothing had ever felt so right.

"Tell me how you feel, Trouble," I gritted between clenched teeth as her pussy spasmed around my length, squeezing me so damn tight.

"So good. You fill me so good, Percy," she moaned, her wet heat spasming.

She was close. But I needed her to come. My balls tightened, her sweet slick slit pulling the come from my cock. But I wasn't going alone. Not this time.

"That's right, Baby. I'm the one filling your pretty little pussy, I'm the one hitting you so fucking good. Now come for me like a good girl," I grunted, reaching between us so I could slide my fingers over her slippery clit.

"Percy!" she shouted my name, and I started moving in earnest.

"Goddamn," I grunted. "I need you to come, Trouble. NOW!"

Her pussy tightened, her channel quivering as she exploded into oblivion. And I followed her, chasing my own orgasm while pushing hers to new heights. My fangs descended and before I knew what I was doing, I'd pierced the flesh at the base of her neck.

Fuck. Oh fuck.

Moaning around the mouthful of Sybil's blood coursing down my throat, I fought for control, demanding I stop. But her hips tilted, allowing me to slide deeper, and I groaned, swallowing her down as her still spasming pussy pulled me under one more time.

"Fuck, Trouble, I'm sorry. I didn't mean to bite you—"

I tried to stop, but her body tightened, her channel squeezing me as another, more powerful orgasm rocketed through her. She tugged my head, bringing my lips to the still open wound on her neck, and unable to resist, I took another pull of her life's force, swallowing it down, and damning myself. My name fell from her lips almost reverently, like a prayer. Then I felt it, Trouble's mouth on my shoulder, her fangs piercing my skin.

Oh fuck!

Fire burned through me as she struck, sucking down one swallow of my blood. The realization of what she'd done pounded into my brain, and still I was stunned. She'd claimed me with her bite. Bestowed the honor of being her mate upon me.

Me.

This woman was going to be my undoing. Sexy little minx. Powerful hybrid badass.

Sweet Sybil could not have been a worse nickname for this feisty as fuck female. Didn't they know her at all? Those people she'd claimed as family. That was alright, though. She had me now. Sybil could be sweet to them, but for me she was Trouble. And I fucking loved it.

She'd chosen me and marked me as her own, and now she had my fealty even more so than before. Any oaths I'd made or loyalties I had were second to her. Fuck yes, she was my life. She filled me everywhere.

I rolled my hips, drawing out our pleasure until neither one of us could take anymore. Then I pushed us even farther, spilling my seed deep inside her, possession and pride filling me as she took it all. Sybil's eyes were still closed when I finally rolled off her, hating the loss of her body pressed against mine, but I imagined she needed to breathe, so I moved.

Seeing our combined cum dripping out of her puffy pink lips should not have turned me on, but it did. I got up and went to the bathroom to wet a cloth to clean up some of our stickiness from her thighs. After doing that, I rolled to my side, cradling her against me.

Mine.

"Percy?"

"Mmm?"

"How do you feel?" she asked, and I heard the smile in her voice.

"Amazing. Why?"

"Because you bit me, and then you stopped. I thought you said that wasn't possible."

Holy shit.

She was right. I grinned and sat up, looking down at her.

"Will you tell me about it now?" she asked, her soft hand stroking my thigh.

It was time, I figured. Past time, really. But she deserved to hear the truth from me. The whole truth.

"I told you about my people, my Coven, and that we were cursed. But I didn't tell you how—"

I opened my mouth to explain it. I wanted to tell her everything. But first, I needed her to know how much she meant to me. That I loved her. And just how fucking special she was before I confessed all my many sins to her.

But before I could utter a word, a blast sounded from somewhere close by, something hit me in the chest, pushing me backwards and I fell. I tried to speak, to tell her to get down, to get safe, nothing came out. The world seemed to slow, and smoke and dust motes filled my vision. I tried to breathe, but nothing happened. Panic gripped me.

I saw Trouble, following me on all fours, scrambling

across the bed as she tried to reach me. Her mouth was open like she was screaming, and tears poured from her eyes, but I couldn't hear a word. I looked down to see what she was staring at and was stunned.

Sticking out of my chest was a three foot long stake. The sharp end would have been wrought in cast iron and dipped in silver, which turned out to be more symbolic than necessary. It was one of the many training weapons we had back at the Coven. In fact, it was the same one I'd used myself on Hunters and enemies dozens of times.

I tried to move, but my body failed me. All I could do was watch in horror as Trouble was ripped from our bed. The hands clutching her flesh belonged to people I knew well. People who would die as soon as I could move. She struggled valiantly, but I knew the second a syringe came into view she'd be knocked out for the trip back to the Coven.

"Perseus, what a disappointment you turned out to be," Grandmother said, standing over me.

"Should we remove the stake, Ma'am?" a familiar voice said, and I frowned as I tried to place the young male.

Daniel Gentry. The brother of Susan, the female my grandmother wanted me to take as my mate. I knew I'd pushed the line between what my Coven would tolerate and what they would see as betrayal.

But I was working it out. And Grandmother should have trusted me to do what was right. No, I would never hurt Sybil. But I was starting to doubt if the Coven's interpretation of events all those centuries ago were true.

Rage filled me, only matched by the level of my despair. They had Trouble. They were taking my mate. They couldn't fucking have her. Draining her was not the answer. I had to tell them. I had to, but I couldn't get the words out. The hit to my chest was taking all my air, zapping all my energy.

I gripped it with my hands, determined to pull it out, but that motherfucker Gentry saw me and used his foot to push it in further, pinning me to the floor.

Oh, I am going to kill you slowly, I promised with my eyes.

"Put the bitch in the car and leave him to lie in his own filth. He will bleed out on his own," Grandmother told that piece of shit Gentry.

Her voice was cold and unfeeling as ever. Why hadn't I noticed that before? Next, she turned her hawklike face to mine.

"Yours will be a slow and painful death, Perseus, but that is what you deserve for your betrayal. I've left the future of the Calloway Coven in the hands of a man for the last time. I will end this curse by bleeding that filthy animal dry. We will be powerful once again and you will be dead. Another worthless male too weak to survive, just like your father and grandfather."

Grandmother sneered and looked down her long nose at me one more time, then she was gone.

They were all gone.

And they had my mate with them.

Noooooo!

I'm coming for you, Trouble. Don't you fucking give up. You fight. You fight for me.

CHAPTER TWELVE SYBIL

TENDRILS OF FEAR crept up my spine as I felt whatever drug they'd injected me with fill my veins. It had some sort of paralytic effect, and I searched deep down for my Dragon, calling on my creature to help me fight it off.

Fuck. Where was she?

I wanted to scream, to roar, to roast these fuckers to ash, but my Dragon was sleeping, and I couldn't move. Then it hit me. These people knew Percy. I replayed the things they'd said in my head, and I wanted to weep. This was his Coven, and they'd hurt him, possibly killed him—*fuck, no, don't go there.*

But why? Why hurt one of their own? Why kidnap me?

It could have been some sort of jealousy thing. Percy had told me he was kind of promised to someone else.

Some supernaturals had iron clad betrothal agreements, but Percy made it a point to tell me he'd never signed a contract.

But some would feel his attention on me to be a slight to them. So maybe this was an angry relative or something? Maybe I could talk my way out of whatever this was.

"P-please, look I don't know why you took me," I started only to shriek as a strong backhand hit me right in the face.

"Shut up, filthy whore!" the male growled.

He was the same guy who'd fucking grabbed me. I blinked, trying to clear my eyes of the tears that sprung up there. But I couldn't move any other part of my body and my head was now painfully turned to the side. His cold, grubby hands gripped my chin as he righted my head. He lifted his fist this time, but before he could connect it with my face, someone stopped him.

I blinked again, grateful for the interruption. I didn't really want to get hit again. A pinched face stared down at me, and I wondered if maybe getting punched wasn't better than being forced to look into those cold, hard eyes.

"That is enough, Daniel. So, you're awake," the older woman said, frowning at me.

"Well, I guess I should be grateful my weak grandson found you at all," she said.

"Grandson?"

"Perseus Calloway. Such a disappointment, but that is your fault, isn't it? That is what your kind does. Seductive serpent. Heartless harlot. Tearing up families. Did you think I would sit and watch you destroy the rest of our line?"

"Please," I tried. "I don't know what you're talking about. I would never hurt Percy. I l-love him," I whispered.

But that was clearly the wrong thing to say. The old bitch slapped me hard, and I felt warmth spill from my nose. Three pairs of eyes turned to me, theirs red with lust. Percy's grandmother snarled, shoving a cloth over my face.

"No! Remember yourselves," she growled at the others.

My adrenaline spiked, and fear filled me. I understood what was happening. My nosebleed was rousing their hunger. These Dhampirs were cursed with bloodlust, and if I didn't stop bleeding, they were going to suck me dry.

"Fight it! Do you hear me? You will fight it. We must be at the altar when the moon rises, then we will feast on this whore's blood and end the curse! Now, give me another vial," she said, reaching out for another syringe filled with god knew what.

I wanted to pull away so badly, but I still couldn't

move. I watched in horror as she stuck the needle in my neck. One precious second was all I had until darkness took me, and in that time, I had only one thought.

Percy!

———

IT WAS pitch black outside when I woke. I blinked my eyes slowly, searching for any hint of light. When I tried to move, I found my fingers and toes wiggled. That was good. Whatever drug they'd given me was wearing off. I tried to reach my Dragon, but the beast was still out cold.

I was strapped down to something cold and hard by my wrists and ankles. Lifting my neck, I bit back my panic, momentarily gratified to see I'd at least been covered with something. Someone had dressed me in a pale nightgown of sorts, and I wanted to cry, realizing I looked like what I was. A sacrifice.

A whoosh of air sounded through the room I was stuck in and suddenly flames licked the walls. It was a neat trick. Dramatic lighting worthy of an *Indiana Jones* movie. I blinked as robed figures filled the space, about two dozen all together.

"What are you doing? Let me go!" I shouted.

Freaked out beyond compare, I struggled against my bindings, but the people, the Dhampirs, ignored me completely. Their red-tinted eyes were glued to their leader. It was the old woman from the car. Her robes were ornately decorated with gold thread, and she held a huge dagger in her hand. This was Percy's grandmother. The one who had her grandson impaled by a wooden stake who wanted to kill me, too.

"You can't do this! Percy is my mate. He loves me! He doesn't want you to do this!"

"He never loved you! Percy is dead because he chose lust over loyalty. He was supposed to bring you back here to do what I am doing, foolish monster. He was hunting you to lull you into a false sense of security. He had every intention of bringing you back here to drain you dry, Dragon—"

"He didn't know I was a Dragon," I mumbled caught somewhere between anger, fear, and despair.

Percy was my dream come true. But something bothered me about what she was saying. There was an inkling of truth to her words. She truly believed every word. And I had to wonder, had Percy stalked me? Had he hunted me because he knew what I was? Had he been planning to bring me back here, to drain me?

"Of course he did. You aren't that stupid, are you? A chubby thing like you could not have hoped to catch the eye of a male like him. But you bewitched him, just like your ancestor did to ours! Tricky beasts tainted with unnatural magic," she said, spitting at me.

Devastation caused me to sob. My dreams quickly turned into nightmares. I was about to die, and all because I was stupid enough to believe Percy could have loved me.

"Tonight we end the curse placed upon us by this monster's ancestor! We will feast on the Dragon's blood, gorging ourselves until our veins are full and our bloodlust sated!"

A great cheer went up, and I started shaking. Percy's grandmother turned to face me, a maniacal look in her eyes as she lifted the dagger high and positioned it over my heart. I took a deep breath, not wanting to die, I pulled on my magic to search for anything I could use to help, but I found fire and air, and no water. None but my tears.

Maybe they would be enough.

CHAPTER THIRTEEN MARTINA

A FEW HOURS EARLIER...

"She isn't answering her cell," I said, pacing across the kitchen.

"Wasn't she with her new man?" Erryn asked, rolling her purple eyes and shaking her head.

"Yeah, but Cat Maccon texted, saying she'd been trying to get in touch with Sybil all afternoon. Johnny wasn't feeling well today, and he wanted to talk to her to feel better. I know she wouldn't blow those kids off," I said.

"Well, are you texting her or calling?" Davian asked.

"Both. She isn't answering either!"

"Hey everyone," Nova called out a greeting as she waltzed into the kitchen with a couple of grocery bags. Asher followed close behind her.

"What's going on?" the big Lion male asked.

"Sybil is missing," I replied.

Anger and worry had my magic in a tizzy. My voice was deep with my Wolf and flames danced across my fingertips.

"Um, okay," Nova replied cautiously watching my fire.

"I'm fine," I growled. "Look, I want to run a trace on her phone. Can you do that, Asher?"

"I can, but it's not exactly ethical," he replied.

"Have you tried our Clan bonds?" Nova asked.

"Of course I have, but it's like, it's like she's not even there," I whispered, hating the real fear that gripped my heart.

"One second," Asher replied and grabbed his cell phone.

I knew he had contacts at the DPCA who could easily get me the info I was looking for, and I was right. My new favorite brother-in-law had it in a matter of minutes. After some discussion and a call to my mate, we were all sitting in one of Mitchell's big work trucks when Davian broke the silence.

"Are you sure this is a good idea? I mean, she's at a motel. With a guy. And I, for one do not need the visual to fuck up my brain," our older brother said with a sigh.

"If I thought she was just fooling around with her

guy, I would leave them alone, Davi. But something is wrong," I said, feeling it in my gut.

If I was the Alpha of the Witch Shifter Clan, that made Davi the moral compass, Erryn the blade, and Nova the brains, with Mitchell and Asher acting as Enforcers But Sybil, well, our Sweet Syb was the heart.

It was my job to make sure every member of our Clan was safe and secure. As Alpha, I had a duty, and it was Sybil who'd believed in my abilities more than anyone else. She was the reason I was there. And I would protect her till my dying breath, like I would any member of my Clan.

I hoped I was wrong. I hoped Davi was right, and we would pull up outside the rinky-dink motel to find Sybil with her panties down. But as Mitchell slowed the truck behind an ambulance, my chest heaved.

"Sybil!" I screamed, jumping out of the truck, everyone close on my heels.

But it wasn't Sybil I saw. It was Percy. He was struggling against two huge paramedics, both Bear Shifters, but that wasn't what worried me. It was the fact he had a really big fucking stick coming out of his chest.

"Fucking stop! I have to go," he growled, sitting up.

"Dude, you are gonna die if you pull that out here," one of the Bear Shifters said.

"No, I fucking won't. Just give me a bag of blood," he growled.

"You motherfucker! Where's Sybil?" I roared, jumping on the foot of the gurney.

The Bear Shifters startled, but Asher was there, showing his badge and telling them to back up. Percy met my gaze, anger, fear, and pain lacing his eyes.

"They took her, and I am going to get her back."

"Who? And Why?"

"My Coven. They think bleeding her will end the curse, but it won't! Get me out of here, Martina. I'll get her back. I'll end this tonight."

"Not without us, you're not," I argued. "And I am going to need more of an explanation from you."

"Fine. I'll explain on the way. I need blood, though."

"Blood? Why?"

"Because I'm a Dhampir and I need it to heal. I need to be at full strength. There will be two dozen of them, and they will be in a blood frenzy," he explained.

"Fine. You want this out?" I asked, pointing to the stick. He nodded.

"Nova! Grab a blood bag for Percy. He's going to lead us to Sybil. And if he doesn't, we're going to rip him to shreds," I promised, right before I pulled.

CHAPTER FOURTEEN PERCY

I'D NEVER KNOWN anything like the fury raging in my veins as I pushed open the door to the ceremonial chamber on my Coven's lands. I knew what I would find, but even knowing didn't prepare me for the flood of emotions threatening to rip me apart at the scene before me.

Men and women I had called family, my Coven, stood in robes, their eyes tinted red with bloodlust as they gazed at *my mate* with hunger. My grandmother stood before them, her gilded dagger lifted high, right over Sybil's precious heart.

A roar unlike anything I ever heard ripped from my lips and faster than lightning I blurred across the room, my fist knocking the blade from my grandmother's hand and pushing the old woman across the altar.

The rest of the Witch Shifter Clan filtered through the door and that was when the real fighting began. Using only brute strength, I grabbed the iron manacles on Sybil's wrists and ankles, breaking them apart with only my rage to fuel me.

"Are you okay? Trouble? Are you hurt?"

She moaned, her hands pushing against my chest as I cupped her face and tried to hold her. She wouldn't look at me. Why wouldn't she look at me? Great, heaving sobs wracked her chest, and I released her. My heart wrenched painfully as it became abundantly clear she did not want my hands, my touch, me anywhere near her at that moment.

I forced myself to step back, just in time to catch that prick, Gentry. He'd snuck up behind me with a knife in hand, attempting to finish what he'd tried earlier. But this time, I was ready.

"Stay back," I shouted, pointing at Sybil.

She might be pissed at me, but I was still going to protect her. She was my mate, and keeping her safe was my goddamn prerogative. Dhampirs were trained for battle, and Gentry knew the same moves as I did. In a whirl of motion, he attacked, and I blocked. With every blade he pulled from hidden pockets in his attire, I deflected, disarming him one at a time.

The fight raged on behind us, but I could not afford to pay it any mind. Daniel Gentry was a formidable opponent. But I had something he did not. I had the rage of a man whose mate had been threatened burning inside of me. His eyes widened as I relieved him of his last weapon.

"You betrayed us for some monster," he spat at me, falling back when I punched him in the diaphragm.

"You can't kill me for being loyal to the Coven!" he shouted.

"That isn't why I'm killing you," I grunted, wrapping my hand around his throat, and lifting him off the ground.

Gentry gasped, clawing at my hand as I squeezed the life slowly out of him.

"Then w-why?" he rasped.

"You. Touched. My. Mate." I growled each word, squeezing harder with every syllable uttered.

One hard shake was all it took to snap his worthless neck. I opened my hand and dropped him to the ground, turning around when I heard an unholy hiss fill the room.

"Stop!! Everyone, stop! Or she dies anyway!" My grandmother yelled, holding her blade to Sybil's throat.

I looked around, counted the bodies, those dead and the ones in cuffs courtesy of Asher and Nova. Fuck. This was a mess. I never considered ending the Coven. It wasn't how I imagined things would go. But after tonight, I was completely fucking fine with it.

What I could not stand was Trouble being afraid of me, or hating me, or whatever that was before. I needed to talk to her. To ask her about it. But first, it looked like I needed to kill the cold bitch who was my paternal grandmother.

"Stop. Look, you don't need her anymore. I drank from her. I have the blood of the Dragon inside my veins. Just take me," I said, trying to reason with the old woman.

"You were supposed to save us! Your father died. Your grandfather. Then I had to kill you because you let your lust rule you just like them—"

"What are you talking about?"

"The curse you fool. It was never the way it was written. I was there! You think Marian wanted Axelrod? Ha! Never. She never wanted him. He stole her, raped her, took her against her will. There was only one who held her heart—a monster!"

"She loved the Dragon?" I repeated, bewildered.

"I never understood why Axelrod fought for her so. She was unworthy! Loving a Dragon instead of a man. A monster? And then she cursed us, not him."

"What are you saying?" I asked.

"Marian's parting curse. We need to gorge ourselves on the beast to willingly fill our veins with Dragon blood, don't you see, Percy?"

"You're delusional. You all are. Did you think this

would work? That you could kill an innocent and somehow redeem yourselves. She is worth more than this whole fucking Coven, do you understand? But if it is her blood you want, you can have that which runs in my veins and no other! I swear, grandmother or not, if you touch her again, I will end you," I roared, angry beyond belief.

"You're going to want to releasssssse meeeeee. Now," Sybil said, hissing her words and cutting off myself and my grandmother.

My gaze moved to her. Grandmother dropped her knife, backing away. Nova grabbed and cuffed her. She and Martina both crept closer when I'd been distracting her. But Sybil, she'd been doing something else. She'd been calling on her Dragon.

Holy. Fuck.

Her dress was torn, and there were patches of dirt and bruises on her skin. Anger pulsed through me, and I wanted to hurt Gentry all over again, that fucker. But she was alive. And she had never looked more beautiful. Her skin glowed, and her pupils had shifted, the slits turning vertical, her blue hair floated around her shoulders. I was completely captivated.

A pulse of magic blasted from her body and one moment Trouble was all creamy skin and blue hair, and the next, she was shimmery pink scales and flashing eyes. She opened her maw and screeched, the sound so loud the windows shattered, and the walls quaked.

I knew I would never forget that mournful cry as long as I lived. It was burned into my soul, just like everything else about her. Trouble turned her Draconian stare on me, anger, sorrow, and pain hit me in waves, flowing from her, through our matebond and I fell to my knees.

I had fucked up so epically. I watched her take flight, powerless to do anything about it. I couldn't make her stay. I couldn't chase her. She was a motherfucking Dragon, and she deserved so much better than me.

But knowing that didn't make me want her any less. It didn't make my love for her dissolve. If anything, I loved her more. I was going to fix this. I was going to prove to her that she belonged with me.

First, I had to deal with the repercussions of my grandmother's actions and a Coven to set to rights. Then, she better watch out because I wasn't quitting.

"I'm coming for you, Trouble. You can fucking count on it."

CHAPTER FIFTEEN SYBIL

"WELL?" I asked, turning around slowly.

"It's, I mean, is that really your color?" Nova asked.

And I had to say even stunned my sister was a knockout. The beyotch. I snorted and rolled my eyes.

"Yes. This is it. Six weeks with no dye, just using your conditioning treatments, and counting on my Shifter restorative abilities and voilá. This is me. Au natural."

Martina got up from her seat on Mitchell's lap. Davi grinned, and Erryn nodded. Asher tilted his head. Tim gasped, and Pete asked Nova something about whether or not she'd be willing to share her formula. It felt weird, just standing, and waiting for someone to say something.

"Fucking hell, Trouble. I didn't think you could look more beautiful."

I froze. That voice. It was him. There. In my house. How? Why?

"Um, we're gonna go, uh, there is something Mitchell has to show us outside," Martina said, standing.

"I do?" her mate asked, before hissing and rubbing the new burn spot on his t-shirt. "Shit, yes, Um, I mean, I do. Come on everyone. Except you two. You guys stay here."

"Really subtle, bro." Asher snorted.

"You know, you have split ends. Maybe ask your girl to help with that," Mitchell said, grinning as the Lion male grabbed at his hair.

"I do not! Nova, tell him I do not!"

"Oh my god, I am going to separate you two, I swear," Davi growled, as they all shuffled outside.

I bit my lip. Six weeks had passed since everything went down. Six long weeks without a word from Percy. I thought maybe he'd forgotten about me. Or maybe he finally got his head clear and realized I never meant anything to him.

Just thinking it hurt me more than I cared to admit. I watched in shock as he pressed his fist against his chest, his eyes trained on me. Fuck, were they filling with tears?

God, he looked so good. And so bad. I meant he looked like he felt bad, not that he was unattractive. I sniffed and wiped my cheeks. Shit. I was crying, too.

"W-what are you doing here?"

"It took longer than I thought to wade through the mess my people had made. Um, you should know, it's over."

"The curse?"

"Yeah. That, and well, the Coven. As the last member of the Calloway line, not currently in jail, I dissolved the Coven and released the remaining Dhampirs to go live with other Clans and groups."

"I see. H-how did you end the curse without my, um, without my blood," I whispered, hating the way my voice shook.

"I didn't. Your blood runs in my veins, Trouble. The actual curse read *For your crimes against the heart, yours shall only know hunger until the Dragon's blood willing runneth once more through your veins.*' It didn't mean a Dhampir of my line had to drink a Dragon's blood. That was a mistake."

"So, what did it mean?"

"It meant a Dragon had to willingly give their blood to their Dhampir mate. For your blood to flow in my veins was a result of our choosing one another, my sweet Trouble. You claimed me and I claimed you. And

I know I fucked up, but I'm here now, and I want to make it up to you—"

"How? Are you gonna change the past? Are you gonna tell me you didn't stalk me because you wanted my blood? You gonna say you didn't try to trick me so you could take me to that horrible place to bleed me?"

"It started out that way, but the second I saw you, I couldn't. Do you understand? The moment I breathed your scent and laid eyes on you, I knew I could never hurt you," he whispered. "Please listen to me."

"No. I don't want to listen. You did hurt me, Percy. You lied to me and that hurt!"

"I didn't lie. I just didn't tell you everything."

"That's still a lie," I said, turning my back on him so I could compose myself.

But that was a mistake. I heard his steps echo in the kitchen as he crossed the tiled floor. His big hands grabbed onto my arms, and he pulled me until my back was flush against his chest. His hold was crushing, it was so tight, but at the same time, it wasn't enough. I cried harder, and he wrapped his arms around me, his face pressed against the hair covering the back of my neck.

"How I feel about you is not a lie. I love you. So fucking much. You're my heart. My soul. I need you, Trouble, and even if I didn't need you, I want you," he growled, kissing my head, my neck and squeezing me tighter. "I want you so fucking much. I'll do anything you say. Anything, but for fuck's sake, don't send me away. I love you, Baby. Do you understand? I love you so much. Please," he whispered.

I shook my head. I couldn't handle this. His confession of love was tearing me apart. What was I supposed to do with that? My heart hurt. My Dragon chirped pitifully inside of me, the beast hadn't been the same since we flew out of that horrible place.

"Shhh. I got you," he whispered, holding me still. "Tell me you don't feel the same. Tell me you don't love me too. You can't because that's a lie. You're it for me, Trouble. Everything I ever wanted. Everything I will ever want. And I'm it for you. I'm yours."

I closed my eyes, slumping against his hard body, counting on him to hold me in the shelter of his arms until I stopped trembling. It was all too much. He was too close. Too far. Too everything. The words coming out of his mouth were everything I ever wanted to hear him say. Confessions of love. Promises. Testaments.

Lies?

A dark part of me whispered, but my Dragon roared, and I knew that wasn't true. Closing my eyes, I looked inside myself and found that tiny pulsating ethereal rope tying me to the man wrapped around my body. It was our matebond. Weak, but there, and it held so much promise and potential.

My heart squeezed, and my breath hitched. I never had anything like this, anyone of my own, and I really wanted someone. No, not someone. I wanted him. I wanted Percy. But did I dare trust myself again? I mean, I picked him the first time, and it was lies.

"I feel you, Trouble. I see you. I swear to you, I mean every word. I love you, Baby. We can do this. Me and you can do this together."

I wanted to believe him so badly. I wiggled against his embrace. Percy tightened his arms for a second before he loosened his iron grip, allowing me to face him. His breath hitched, and he reached up tentatively, cupping my cheeks and wiping my tears with his thumbs.

God, he looked so good. His auburn hair was loose and messy, and his Kelly green eyes were full of emotion. I whimpered, pressing my lips together before opening them. I had so much I wanted to tell him.

How mad I was.

How relieved.

How much he hurt me when I found out the truth.

How much I hurt me when I left him.

But looking into his eyes, I discovered I didn't need to say any of it. Everything I'd felt, Percy had gone through, too. I saw it written all over his face.

"My brave, badass Trouble. You have to believe me when I say I love you. I love you so fucking much. I need you. Don't send me away. Please give me another chance," he pleaded.

I closed my eyes, needing to believe him more than ever. He was the only one who didn't think of me as sweet and simple. He was the only one who saw my spice, not just my sweetness. He was the only person who ever believed in me like that.

You could call me foolish. Call me stupid. Call me anything you wanted to. But the truth was I loved him. I wanted him. And I needed him. I needed him so much.

"Okay." I gasped, trying not to sob all over the place. Percy sucked in a breath, eyes wide like he wasn't sure he heard me.

"Okay?"

"Yeah," I repeated, nodding my head. "Okay. I believe you. But if you hurt me again, I'll eat you."

His eyebrows disappeared into his hair as Percy wrapped his arms around my waist, and I grinned, allowing my Dragon to peek through my eyes at the man I loved.

My mate. My Dhampir. My Percy.

"Percy," I whimpered, reaching up on tiptoe at the same time he leaned down.

"Trouble, Trouble, Trouble," he groaned, crushing my lips with his. "Fuck, I love you."

His hands roamed down my body, cupping the

globes of my ass as he lifted me up. I wrapped my legs around his waist.

"I ever tell you how much I love these fucking dresses?" he asked, groaning as he lifted my skirts, walking me backwards to the next room.

"My dresses?"

"Yes, these fucking dresses. Flirty, sexy, teasing me with all those glimpses of your perfect little body, making my mouth water for you."

"That door," I panted against his lips, urging him to take me to my bedroom.

"Mmm," he groaned. "Is this your childhood bedroom, Trouble?" Percy grinned, dropping me on my bed.

I nodded, biting my lip.

"You want me to fuck you on that bed?"

I nodded because yeah. Yes. I did. I really did.

"Clothes off. Now."

I hurried to do as he said, desperate for him. It wasn't graceful or sexy, but naked was the goal, and I achieved that in record time. I sucked in a breath, holding it as Percy crawled onto my bed, his thick cock jutting from between his thick, juicy thighs.

God, I loved his body. He was long and built, ropes of muscle cording him, covered in skin pale as moonlight and dusted with freckles the same color as his hair.

"You ever have a boy in this room?" he asked, one eyebrow raised.

I couldn't lie. But I also did not want to tell him. So, I shrugged.

"I never fucked anyone on this bed," I said, biting my lip.

"Well, that's about to change," he growled, wrapping his big hands around my thighs, and spreading me wide open.

I thought it was going to be like last time. Hard and fast and so damn good, but Percy was just full of surprises. Instead of lining up his cock with my sex, he dipped his head and licked a trail from my asshole to my clit, making me gasp and lift off the bed.

"Stay still, Trouble, or I won't let you come."

I growled, threading my fingers through his hair, my magic pulsating through me, caressing the space between our skin, linking him to me with every move. I moaned and pulled on his auburn tresses as he devoured my pussy.

My god, the man could feast. He licked and sucked, and then by unspoken permission he bit me right on the inside of my thigh at the same time he pushed three thick digits into my sheath, pulling an orgasm straight from my body.

"Good girl," he growled.

His sultry words words went straight to my clit, stroking against my sensitive flesh like hands.

Percy laved at my tits next, taking time to suck each nipple and twirl them between his teeth. Then he nudged my thighs wider, sliding his thick cock through my slippery folds.

Up and down, he coated himself in my juices, but he didn't fill me, and goddamn it, that was what I wanted.

"Are you ready for me, Trouble?"

"Yes! Yes, I am so ready."

"Take my cock and put it where you want me."

I grabbed his cock, positioning him right at my needy hole. Then I wrapped my legs around his waist, trying to pull him closer. I felt the fucker's smile against my mouth as he kissed me.

"Bossy little thing, aren't you?" he whispered, nuzzling my mouth, and kissing me deeply.

"Percy, I need you inside me," I growled, and his eyes flared.

"I got what my Trouble needs," he grunted and shoved his thick cock inside me with one hard thrust.

Sensation after sensation threatened to drown me, and I sobbed and clutched at Percy, marveling at each new level we reached. We moaned in turn, grunting and groaning, the slapping of our bodies reached a crescendo, like some sort of lewd symphony, and I loved it. I loved everything about it. Like I loved him.

Mate. Mine.

Percy kissed my neck, scraping his fangs against my skin, and I nodded. I wanted him to feed from me. To give him nourishment to share my essence and be that for him meant the world to me. It was just the edge I needed to tip over into bliss.

"Drink from me, mate. Only me. Forever me."

"Only you. My love. My mate," he growled before striking.

His moves grew erratic, and as his first orgasm began my next one flowed over me. Wave after wave of pleasure rippled through me like the surf crashing against the shore. Even as he drank, taking from my body, I felt Percy filling me up with his seed, with his love. The exchange was beautiful, climactic, and perfect.

He was everything I ever wanted and more. My dream. My love.

Mine.

EPILOGUE PERCY

"SO, why do they call you a *River Dragon?*" I asked.

I followed my beautiful mate through the woods behind Harbor House with the picnic basket she filled with fresh baked cookies just a little while ago. Watching her hips sway in front of me in that flirty little pink dress she had on had me adjusting my cock inside my shorts.

Fuck, but she was hot. Sweet, sexy Trouble. She'd changed her hair to her natural color a few days ago, but was already experimenting with streaks in a variety of blues and aquas just underneath her thick ponytail. It peeked out from under the glossy tresses with every bouncy step, and I fucking loved the way it looked hanging down her back. But she wasn't changing her hair color to stand out anymore because she thought her sisters outshone her.

Silly Trouble.

Nothing could outshine her as far as I was concerned. But I didn't care if her hair was pink, purple, or shaved off. I loved her whatever colors she came in.

I simply loved her. But if my Trouble wanted to dye her hair, then I was one hundred percent behind that decision. As long as she did it because she wanted to, and she'd already assured me that was the only reason.

It was the first official day of the season, and Trouble explained it was something she and her siblings used to do every year after Memorial Day. They started every summer with some water sports at the river that ran through the woods.

Apparently, they'd invited some locals from the Macconwood Pack and the Falk Clan. There were about twenty-nine kids coming, which explained the nine dozen cookies my fine as hell mate had baked. Not to mention our new arrivals, who brought the residents of Harbor House to a half dozen between the ages of five and thirteen.

After a somewhat rushed application process, I was officially on the staff at Harbor House, pouring in a hefty chunk of my assets into the foundation in my mate's name. It would go towards medical, schooling, whatever was needed for the residents we took in. That was a good and worthy cause. After all the misery my people were responsible for, I figured using the family money in the name of something good was a way to cleanse the past. Plus, it made Sybil happy, and I would do just about anything to see that woman smile.

"Well, you see, the Falk Clan arrived in Maccon City a little too late to really help me with my Dragon. I'd been changing since I was a child, but when Callius discovered what I was, he took me on as a kind of mentor. And when he realized I had some elemental magic, water magic, as you well know, he asked me if I'd ever tried swimming in my scales."

"And?" I asked, slightly jealous but really just glad someone had been around to help guide young Sybil.

"See, the others can't really swim when they shift."

"But you can?" I asked, grinning.

"I can," she replied with a smile. "And if you're a real good boy, I'll show you."

The idea of seeing my sexy fine mate in her element filled me with pride and joy, and I slung an arm around her and squeezed her to my side. This woman was everything to me and every day by her side brought with it something new and wondrous.

Life didn't have to be so boring or cut and dried. I

was learning something new every single day. And it was all thanks to her.

"What're you thinking about?" she asked, narrowing her eyes at me.

"I was just thinking I'm really happy I went looking for you, Trouble. Really happy."

"Hmm," she hummed. "Me too."

EPILOGUE 2 SYBIL

A FEW YEARS LATER…

"Percy? Percy!"

"What?" my big sexy mate came running into the meeting room.

He was juggling our twins, Marion and Robyn, in his hands while Teddy, our four year old foster son, had his entire body wrapped around his calf. He looked so damn hot covered in our babies, and I was gonna tell him so later that night when I had him alone. But right then, I had big news.

"What is it, Trouble?" Percy asked, placing the babies in the playpen, and setting Teddy up with some age appropriate building blocks.

"Remember when we said we were going to branch

out and try to help other groups of supernaturals, not just Shifters and Witches?"

"Yeah, of course. You know, you're smiling but it's full of mischief, Trouble. Last time you looked like that you were telling me you and your sisters voted me in the Clan."

"Mmm hmm."

I bit my lip. He wasn't wrong. Percy, like my sisters' mates, was a part of the Witch Shifter Clan even though he was neither. It didn't matter. He was mine, and that made him Clan. It also made him family. Sometimes family was someone you chose. And I picked Percy. I always would.

"Well?" he asked. "Did something happen?"

"Um, yeah. You just became the first agent in DPCA history to be certified in *Supernatural Childcare of Beings with Blood Related Dietary Needs*."

"That's a mouthful," he said with a grin.

"I know. But isn't it amazing? Harbor House can officially take in Vampires and Dhampirs now."

"Wow. Trouble, that's great, really. Thank you," he said, pulling me towards him and giving me a chaste-ish kiss.

"Ew," Teddy said, giggling as he covered his eyes.

Marion and Robyn were too young to care what their Mom and Dad did, and the other kids were busy with story time. Calla Falk started volunteering when she turned sixteen, and she was as good at making up fairytales as her Aunt Jozi.

I motioned to one of the other permanent staff members to keep an eye on the kids and I pulled my mate out of the room. He let me, of course, otherwise I wouldn't have been able to move the big sexy lug.

"Have another surprise for me?" he asked, pulling me flush against him as we ducked into the supply closet.

"It's not a surprise, but I did want to tell you how much I love you mate of mine."

I batted my eyelashes at him, taking in his handsome features and loving the way his gaze heated and his body hardened pressed against me. Nothing felt better than being in Percy's arms, except maybe when I was in his arms, and he was kissing me. As if he read my mind, he proceeded to do just that.

"Goddamn, you taste so good," he growled, cupping my ass beneath the skirt of my dress, and hoisting me off the floor as he deepened our kiss.

"Percy," I whimpered.

"I got you, Trouble. I always got you," he said, locking the door before pressing me back against it.

"Now, keep those moans locked down, Baby. Remember, nobody gets to hear you, but me."

I nodded my head, biting my lip as my mate tugged my panties aside. I felt him move between us, freeing his thick, hard length from its confines before stuffing me full of his cock. Goddamn was right. He felt so good. Every time with Percy, it just got better and better.

"Tell me how you feel, Baby," he demanded, whispering in my ear.

"So good. You make me feel so good."

"That's right. I make you feel good, and you feel fucking perfect squeezing me with your pretty pussy."

His naughty words heated my blood, tipping me over the edge, and he slammed his hips harder into mine, stuffing his shoulder against my mouth to quiet my moans. I bit him, hard. But he just groaned, loving the blend of pleasure and pain. His cock pulsed inside me, and I reveled in the feel of him filling me with his seed.

"Love you, Trouble. Love you so much."

I smiled, feeling cherished and loved like I had every day since he came to Harbor House looking for me. Looking for Trouble.

THE END.

ALSO BY C.D. GORRI

<u>Contemporary Romance Books:</u>

<u>Cherry On Top Tales</u>

Her Yule His Log

His Carrot Her Muffin

Her Chocolate His Bar

His Pickle Her Jam

Her Trick His Treat

His Wood Her Fire

Her Birthday His Package

<u>Wild Billionaire Romance</u>

His Wild Obsession

His Wild Temptation

His Wild Seduction

His Wild Attraction

Bonus Scene His Wild Halloween Night

<u>Jersey Bad Boys</u>

Merciful Lies

Devious Lies

Pitiful Lies

Mergers & Acquisitions

Desperate Measures

Desperate Needs

Desperate Desires

Desperate Actions

Carolina Rugby Romance

A Reason To Try

The Break Down

***

Wyvern Protection Unit:

Jersey Sure Shifters/EveL Worlds:

The Guardians of Chaos:

Twice Mated Tales

Hearts of Stone Series

Moongate Island Tales

Mated in Hope Falls

Speed Dating with the Denizens of the Underworld

Hungry Fur Love

Island Stripe Pride

Motley Crewd Shifters

NYC Shifter Tales

A Howlin' Good Fairytale Retelling

Witch Shifter Clan

Lords of Nightfall

When Worlds Collide

Young Adult/Urban Fantasy Books

The Grazi Kelly Novel Series

The Angela Tanner Files

G'Witches Magical Mysteries Series

Co-written with P. Mattern

Witches of Westwood Academy

with Gina Kincade

Blackthorn Academy For Supernaturals

Be sure to check out my BUY DIRECT BUNDLES and get 30% off when you buy available only my website.

Click here for The Official C.D. Gorri Reading List - free download

CHECK OUT MOTLEY CREWD SHIFTERS TODAY!

Once upon a time…
Nah, scratch that.
These aren't those kinds of stories.
Yeah, there are supernatural creatures, magic, and love inside these tales. But there's also crude behavior, foul language, and steamy sex scenes, involving boorish alpha males with bad attitudes and over the top possessive behavior.
Still wanna stick around?
Excellent!
Now, we have all heard there are more things in this universe than you or I *or anyone* truly knows.
Well, this group of supernatural misfits is testing the limits of what they know in order to chase the one

thing they never thought they'd have a shot at controlling...*their destinies*.

But only the Fates can determine true love, and in Barren County, New Jersey, these Urban Cowboy Shifters are going to find out the hard way.

Sometimes it's not about the family you were born into.

Sometimes it's about the family you choose.

Or in this case, *the Crew*.

Meet our Cowboys:
Maximillian Leeds
Emmet Quinn
Dante Bianco
Kian O'Malley
Zeke Gordon

**This is a series of interconnected paranormal romance standalones with steamy scenes, foul language, crude behavior, plus size heroines, mating rituals, claiming bites, possessive book boyfriends, HEA endings, raunchy humor and more.*

VISIT WWW.CDGORRI.COM/SERIES/MOTLEY-CREWD-SHIFTERS for more.

ABOUT THE AUTHOR

USA Today Bestselling author C.D. Gorri writes paranormal and contemporary romance and urban fantasy books with plenty of steam and humor.

Join her mailing list here: https://www.cdgorri.com/newsletter

An avid reader with a profound love for books and literature, she is usually found with a book in hand. C.D. lives in her home state, New Jersey, where many of her characters and stories are based. Her tales are fast-paced yet detailed with satisfying conclusions. If you enjoy powerful heroines and loyal heroes who face relatable problems in supernatural settings, journey into the Grazi Kelly Universe today.

You will find sassy, curvy heroines and sexy, love-driven heroes who find their HEAs between the pages.

Wolves, Bears, Dragons, Tigers, Witches, Vampires, and tons more Shifters and supernatural creatures dwell within her paranormal works. The most important thing is every mate in this universe is fated, loyal, and true lovers always get their happily-ever-afters.

In her contemporary works, you will find fiercely possessive men and the smart, confident, curvy women they are crazy about. As always, the HEA is between the pages.

Thank you and happy reading!
del mare alla stella,
C.D. Gorri

http://www.cdgorri.com
https://www.facebook.com/Cdgorribooks
https://www.bookbub.com/authors/c-d-gorri
https://twitter.com/cgor22
https://instagram.com/cdgorri/
https://www.goodreads.com/cdgorri
https://www.tiktok.com/@cdgorriauthor